A CAST OF THOUSANDS

Novels by Steve Shagan

Save the Tiger
City of Angels
The Formula
The Circle
The Discovery
Vendetta
Pillars of Fire

A CAST OF THOUSANDS

STEVE SHAGAN

POCKET BOOKS

New York   London   Toronto   Sydney   Tokyo   Singapore

POCKET BOOKS, a division of Simon & Schuster Inc.
1230 Avenue of the Americas, New York, NY 10020

Shagan, Steve.
        A cast of thousands / Steve Shagan.
                p.   cm.
        ISBN: 0-671-74132-2
        I. Title.
        PS3569.H313C37   1993
        813'.54—dc20   92-32118
                                                                      CIP

First Pocket Books hardcover printing February 1993

10   9   8   7   6   5   4   3   2   1

For
my wife, Betty, and my friend Edward Anhalt

No put money in show business . . .

—**Chief Sitting Bull**
*(From an interview while touring
with Annie Oakley)*

The
Scam

1

THE ARCTIC BLIZZARD HOWLED THROUGH MANHATTAN'S GLASS-AND-steel canyons, reducing the morning rush hour to a slippery crawl. High above Sixth Avenue the huge tinted windows of the Gemstone Pictures building rattled ominously. The storm's eerie wail seeped through the cork-lined walls of the executive screening room where Frank Solish shifted uncomfortably in his cushioned chair. Gemstone's chief of worldwide sales considered the moaning wind a fitting underscore to the grim picture he'd been watching for the past ninety-eight minutes.

Seated a few rows behind Solish, the film's writer and its director whispered nervously. The youthful team had flown in from the coast on the red-eye, dropped their bags at the hotel, and left immediately for the screening. The two filmmakers had produced a highly successful TV series, but this was their first effort for the big screen.

For them the picture represented three grueling years of outrageous story conferences, devious managers, vengeful ex-wives, and the star's unquenchable thirst for Stolichnaya.

Against all prevailing wisdom they had brought the picture in on time and on budget. And now, in less than three minutes, their professional futures would be decided. All their aspirations were riding on Solish's approval. The diminutive sales chief had coughed sporadically, sneezed at dramatic moments, and shifted in obvious discomfort. The apprehensive duo had no way of knowing that the disconcerting sounds and motions had little to do with the quality of their picture.

Solish was grappling with the first signs of flu and a chronic case of hemorrhoids. His head throbbed and he felt chilled—goddamn New York winters, he thought, it was eighty-three out on the coast. Eighty-three degrees in February! No wonder everyone out there was whacked out of their skulls, and it wasn't coke. That was too simplistic. You couldn't blame it on schmeck. It was that year-round smoggy sunshine and those choked freeways that snaked through a crazy-quilt grid of disparate communities. The Valley was Guatemala with green cards. Beverly Hills had been sold to the Iranians. Downtown L.A. was Ellis Island with AK-47's— an ethnic combat zone patrolled by a police force that would have made Heinrich Himmler blush with pride.

And Hollywood was an illusion, a dreamland in which one's day centered on "taking" meetings and eating lunch in overpriced, mediocre restaurants. Still, there was something to be said for eighty-three fucking degrees in February.

Solish blew his nose and sighed in relief as the picture ended on a freeze-frame of Jack Wheeler's soulful eyes. A muted trumpet played a haunting melodic refrain. End credits supered over the freeze-frame. The music swelled and Solish felt goose bumps pimpling his arms. He had to admit the picture touched a nerve. It was a brilliant portrait of a fallen CIA agent. The writing was dazzling. The direction subtle yet dynamic. And despite his legendary juicing, Wheeler had performed magnificently. The film would receive rave reviews, Academy attention, and foreign festival awards—but it was a stiff. A loser. It would play to empty seats. The public didn't want to see their own problems up there on the screen. They wanted cops and Wops and multi-orgasmic blondes and kiddies who outwitted wiseguys, and boyfriends who rose from the dead and returned to their grieving lovers. They wanted comic strip heroes and happy endings. This picture was too real. Too honest. It was strictly Third Avenue and maybe Westwood. It wouldn't sell any popcorn in Kansas City and without K.C. you were dead.

And what the hell was the Jig doing in the movie? Christ, the only Black in the picture a hooker. The feminists and civil rights hustlers would raise hell. He didn't remember a black hooker being in the script.

She must have been added in a rewrite. Well, at least she wasn't a dyke, that would have stoked a fire storm; but Harry Walters had approved the project—so be it. Harry didn't tell him how to sell them and he didn't tell Harry how to make them. They were a good team, and in an industry not famous for executive longevity they had enjoyed a long run. And now they were closing in on the greatest scam in the history of the business.

The screen slowly faded to black, holding Wheeler's melancholy eyes to the last frame. The recessed ceiling lights came up full. Solish rose and, ignoring the writer, addressed the bearded director.

"We gotta talk."

"You mean all three of us," the director said.

"You want to bring him"—Solish indicated the writer—"bring him."

The sales chief suffered a profound aversion to writers. He had never known a screenwriter who didn't consider himself the noble warrior taking on the barbarians. In reality, writers were largely an avaricious collection of mediocre talents who busied themselves revising each other's work. The feeding frenzy of rewriting produced a literary gang bang in which the sole screenwriting credit had become as rare as a virgin's ass in Nicky Blair's Sunset Strip trattoria. Fortunately, he had little to do with the screenwriting fraternity. This picture was a special situation because the writer was also the producer.

"Okay, both of you upstairs wit me," Solish said.

As they made their way to the elevator he silently cursed himself. He had said "wit." He had failed to enunciate the *th* ending. He'd been taking a crash course at Berlitz, trying desperately to lose his Brownsville-Brooklyn accent. He recalled his teacher's admonition to enunciate the *th* endings and roll the *r*'s.

The moaning wind accented the deathly silence as they rode up in Solish's private elevator to the twenty-eighth floor. The gleaming brass doors opened to a seemingly endless corridor decorated with framed posters of Gemstone's past and present pictures.

Following Solish, the two partners felt like Mickey Rooney in *The Last Mile*. "He hasn't got an office," the writer whispered, "it's a gas chamber."

"Careful," the director cautioned, "they say the whole place is bugged."

Solish held the door open and they entered his outer office. A pleasant-looking middle-aged woman sat at one desk, and an attractive young English girl was stationed opposite her.

"Anything?" Solish asked the older woman.

"Mr. Parnelli phoned from his limo. The flight was on time despite the storm."

"What else?"

"There's a list on your desk but nothing important. Your wife called."

He nodded and turned to the director. "Coffee?"

"Black, no sugar, thank you."

The English secretary rose and smiled at the writer. "And what can I get for you?"

"Black coffee, please."

"Tea for me," Solish added.

Solish's inner sanctum was wrapped in glass on three sides. The furniture was Italian modern mixed with French antiques. A glass case displayed a row of gleaming Oscars. They stood like silent sentinels, reminding visitors of Gemstone's past triumphs.

"Sit down, fellas," Solish said, and walked up four steps to a raised platform upon which rested an imposing verde-jade marble desk.

He peered out of the window at the gusting snow flurries and again thought, Eighty-three degrees in dreamland. Seated below the platform, the writer whispered to the director, "If you were on stilts you'd still be below this prick."

Solish turned. "You say something?"

"Just admiring those Oscars," the writer said.

The door opened and the English secretary entered and served them.

"Did you get the booth at Twenty-One?" asked Solish.

"Yes, one-fifteen."

"Let me know when Parnelli arrives but hold the calls."

She nodded and closed the door quietly. Solish sipped his tea and stared out at the raging storm. The writer and director toyed nervously with their coffee as they waited for the verdict. Solish sighed heavily, placed his teacup on the desk, and jabbed his forefinger at the director.

"What's the black broad doing in the movie?"

The question ricocheted around the room like a bullet seeking a target. The writer started to respond, but the director squeezed his colleague's arm and smiled hopefully at Solish. "I assume that's a joke."

"You think it's a fucking joke? The only Black in the film and she's on her knees? Is that an appropriate image for this studio to convey to the public?"

The director measured his words. "I understand your concern, but there is a white girl alongside the black girl. The white girl actually does the number."

"White hookers don't count," Solish argued. "White hookers don't have committees."

"Maybe I can explain," the writer offered.

"I don't want to hear it!" Solish snapped. "You shouldn't even be in this meeting. Writers have nothing to do with what's on the screen, that's the director's province! The director is the one we trust with our money. If he makes a mistake we're in fiscal jeopardy—if you make a mistake, we put another piece of paper in the typewriter."

Solish turned to the director. "There's a compound felony here, bad enough you used a black hooker, but why does she speak French?"

"It seemed different." The director shrugged. "I don't know . . . artistic."

The sales chief grabbed his stomach as if he'd been knifed. "Did you say 'artistic'?" He groaned.

"Yes I did," the director replied with authority, thinking the game was already lost.

Solish's voice was dead calm. "I've been in this business a long time. I started selling pictures in Paramount's Buffalo exchange when I was nineteen. I've sold them all: horror movies, slapstick comedy, action-adventure, epics—in the old days we made a few epics. I've sold shit and I've sold diamonds. You never know where the hits are coming from. No one is that smart. But I've learned one unassailable truth." His voice rose. *"Art is a line at the box office."*

The windows rattled, punctuating Solish's diatribe. After a moment he sneezed, blew his nose, and said, "You made more picture than we had any right to expect." The tone of his voice had mellowed dramatically. "I don't know how you did it on the budget we gave you. I'm proud of the picture. Everyone at the studio is proud of it. We're going to handle it very carefully."

The sudden switch in attitude rendered the filmmakers speechless.

"See Lew Freeman down the hall," Solish said. "He'll fix you up with first-class tickets to Rome. Jack Wheeler's shooting a piece of crap over there, some biblical long-form TV thing. He worked in your picture for scale. He deserves to see this cut before it's finalized. Meeting's over. Call me from Rome after Wheeler's seen it. And if you want any pussy tonight ask Freeman."

The bewildered duo rose and started for the door. Solish shouted after them, "Trim the spook! Play everything off the white broad!"

The writer stopped and turned as if to reply but the director propelled his partner out the door. "Let it go. He loved it!"

Solish pressed a button on his phone console.

"Yes?" the English secretary asked.

"Get Red for me."

"Whom would that be, sir?"

"Lucille Ball—who the hell do you think I mean? Aurora Flint!"

"It's only eight o'clock out there. She's probably en route to the studio. Shall I try her car phone?"

"No. Forget it."

"Mr. Walters called."

"Why didn't you buzz me?"

"You asked me to hold the calls. He said he'd phone you at the Waldorf at four-thirty P.M. our time." She paused. "Shall I try your wife?"

"Tell her I'm staying over tonight because of this frigging blizzard and I'll call her from the hotel."

He descended the platform and walked to the tinted window. Far below, pedestrians scattered like frightened ants seeking shelter from the driving storm. Traffic crawled and the snow was beginning to stick like a mantle of white purity covering the grime, garbage, and the homeless shivering in their cardboard shelters.

If they could pull it off, Solish thought, it would mean $50 million after taxes. He would buy that villa in Arles and the flat in Belgravia. They'd keep an apartment on Fifth Avenue. They'd travel. He'd be able to pay attention to Doris and the kid. He was only fifty-five. He had time. Christ, if they could just pull it off. The Old Man had laid it out and God knows you had to love him.

8

Leo Resnick. The ageless, indestructible genius emeritus of the Unione Siciliano. A pioneer in his field, not unlike the Mayers, Cohns, and Warners. Solish could see Resnick's tanned, thin body sitting in his bubbling Jacuzzi. The sprawling, walled desert estate was an appropriate environment for the aged mastermind of organized crime.

Resnick's fiscal genius had made millions for the Italian Combination. The Old Man had also been the guiding light behind Gemstone's founders. Resnick was a great man and this would be his greatest score. He had designed an ingenious plot that would provide himself and Gemstone's top executives with a colossal windfall.

Solish sighed, and shook his head in disbelief; he, the impoverished Brownsville street kid, would be rich and famous—Jesus Christ. A gust of wind rattled the window and a sudden wave of depression overwhelmed him. Ignoring his shrink's warnings about the dangers of wallowing in the past, he let himself tumble down the dark tunnel of time.

He was a kid on a trolley after school. It was winter and he had a heavy cold. He took the BMT subway, then a trolley to the foot of Atlantic Avenue past the docks to that two-story tenement, to the dentist who owed Solish's father a favor. It must have been forty years ago, but he remembered the mustached, portly dentist who had reluctantly worked on his teeth. Dr. Jacob Graff didn't charge the Solishes for his services and spitefully didn't use novocaine while working on young Frank's teeth; but it wasn't the physical pain that haunted Solish. It was the innocent question he had asked Graff. *"Does it hoit more wit a cold?"*

And Graff, himself a Jew, had mocked the youngster's Brooklyn Yiddish singsong intonation. "It hoits more wit a cold? You're in America. Stop talking like a mockie."

He never forgot that ridicule. The memory was indelible. Neither success, nor time, nor therapy had diminished the humiliation of that distant moment.

The buzzer sounded, severing his connection to the past. He went up the carpeted steps and pressed the intercom button.

"Yeah?"

"Mr. Parnelli is here," the older secretary said.

"I'll be a minute."

He entered his private bathroom, dropped his pants and shorts, and proceeded to apply salve to the fiery boils on his buttocks. Salvatore "Boom Boom" Parnelli, he thought, the fascist film distributor Resnick had chosen to front the scam. Solish despised Parnelli's anti-Semitism but Boom Boom was essential to the score.

He washed his hands and sighed. Fuck it, he'd do business with Khaddafi if it would help achieve the score; besides, at the appropriate time, Parnelli would be made to understand that in business there was no room for anything but business. Solish dabbed a few drops of expensive cologne on his face, straightened his tie, and left the bathroom.

He opened his office door and saw the dark wiry man with the ace-of-spades eyes. He forced himself to smile broadly and exclaimed, "Salvatore!"

Parnelli returned the smile and they shook hands.

Solish shook his head in feigned admiration. "The islands must agree with you, Sal, you look terrific."

"I'm good, Frank," Parnelli said flatly, "like always."

AURORA FLINT CAREFULLY EDGED HER XJ-S JAG CONVERTIBLE INTO the fast lane. Her bright red hair streamed in the sea breeze and her oversized shades filtered the sun's glare. Off to her right the sea glittered into infinity, and to her left, soaring red clay palisades and royal palms shadowed the Pacific Coast Highway. The southbound traffic was unusually heavy for a February morning but managed to move at a fast clip.

She dreaded the summer commute from her Malibu home to Gemstone's Culver City studios. From July 4th through Labor Day the coastal highway from Santa Monica to Zuma was jammed with Isuzu pickups and the beaches were invaded by hordes of shrieking kids who joyously kicked sand over sun-worshipping Valley girls. Transistors blared. Frito chips decorated the surf. Lifeguards' whistles pierced the eardrums. It was a scene to be avoided at all costs.

Aurora had resigned herself to circumventing the coastal highway in the summer months by taking a long serpentine detour through the mountain passes. But for the rest of the year Malibu was heaven: tranquil, clean air, long walks on the beach, and magnificent sunsets. The distance from town also provided her with an excuse to avoid week-night social events. She had long ago paid her after-hour dues. Dinner parties were right up there with weddings, Bar Mitzvahs, overproduced movie premieres, and charity gigs. She had never attended any of those events without being pitched a story idea. The parameters of the pitch extended to funerals and fucking. Once you achieved a position of power, nothing protected you from the pitch.

She braked gently as the traffic slowed. The car phone's static cleared and Jack Kramer's whiny voice came on in mid-sentence as if the connection had never been disrupted.

"The Steadicam guys are puking. They can't get a shot. We've been out here since six A.M. Everyone's seasick. The waves are over the mainsail. The crew is sprawled on the deck vomiting green bile."

"What does Trummel say?"

"That slimy queen won't come out of his cabin."

"You're the producer, Jack. What do you expect me to do, turn into a pillar of Dramamine?"

"You're the project officer."

"Put Trummel on."

"I told you, Stanley is sulking. He won't come up on deck. He's in his stateroom smoking those filterless Camels and playing backgammon with his valet."

"Well, I'm in my Jag on PCH. You want me to make the shot?"

There was a burst of static punctuated by Kramer's frantic voice, "I'm losing you, Aurora, don't hang up!"

A mustachioed Iranian driving a Mercedes 500SEL pulled up alongside and smiled. Aurora ignored him, thinking what an incredibly homely race they were. No. No. Don't entertain that racist bullshit. Bad karma. You know better. There are very few beautiful people in the world.

She pressed the accelerator as the traffic picked up speed. She glanced at the sparkling, blue-green Pacific and smiled, thinking that somewhere off Catalina, Jack Kramer, and his star, Tracey Warren, and that slimeball director Stanley Trummel were rocking and rolling in heavy seas. Nature had rendered justice where man had failed.

It was delicious. There was a God.

The picture in question was aptly titled *Backwash*. She hated the story, disdained its producer, and despised its director, but Harry Walters had considered the project to be box office. "There's a certain moronic purity to this script," Walters had said. "Japan

12

and Europe will suck it up. They can't resist American action thrillers laced with sex, violence, and spectacular effects."

She had to admit the plot of *Backwash* met each of those prerequisites. A vacationing widowed stockbroker falls off a fishing boat in Cuban waters and is rescued by a drug smuggler and his sister, who struts around the cabin cruiser wearing what could only be described as anal floss. She slowly drives the stockbroker mad with lust and agrees to relieve him on one condition—he must assist in killing her brother, with whom she has enjoyed an incestuous relationship. The story hurtles toward a gory climax of hammerhead sharks enjoying the brother's body parts while sister and stockbroker sail happily off into a sequel.

"Aurora! Aurora! Do you hear me?" Kramer's desperate voice came through the speaker.

"I hear you, Jack," she replied. "Bring everyone in. Call me when you get to the studio."

"You're a prince, Aurora."

"A *princess*, you *putz!*"

She pushed the disconnect button and glanced at the digital dash clock: 9:27 A.M.—12:27 P.M. in New York.

The Jag sped under the dark overpass and swung around the sharp curve before bursting into the bright sunlight flooding the Santa Monica Freeway. Crossing to the center lane, she pressed the automatic phone button connecting her to Gemstone's New York office.

Almost instantly, the sexy, husky English voice announced, "Mr. Solish's office." Aurora knew the attractive girl was gay and had been personally selected by Doris Solish.

"This is Aurora Flint. I'm calling from my car."

"I know Mr. Solish wanted to speak to you, Miss Flint, but I'm afraid he's at lunch."

"I see . . . what's your name?"

"Corinthia."

"Pretty name. How's the weather?"

"We're having a full-blown blizzard."

"Must be fun."

"Will there be anything else?"

"No. Nothing else. I'll buy you a lunch next time I'm in New York. I've never met anyone named Corinthia."

Aurora hung up angry at herself. Why the honey-on-the-razor-blade stuff? What is it with you? I wish I knew. I miss New York. That's part of it. Blizzard or no blizzard I miss the Apple. Not Brooklyn. Not roots. Certainly not family.

Her mother was still upset with her for changing her name from Fivush to Flint. She tried to explain that Flint played better and seemed to go with her steely gray eyes and fiery red hair. Her mother still lived in a drab apartment building on Eastern Parkway. During Aurora's infrequent visits she marveled at the enduring consistency of the foul odor permeating her mother's hallway—a sickening blend of chicken soup and braised beef.

Her mother bragged to the neighbors about her beautiful daughter who had attended NYU film school, made a connection, left for California as a production assistant to a TV producer, "and in no time at all she's running a studio."

It had not been that simple. It had taken her almost ten years and a pair of bruised kneecaps before she graduated from television to features. Her rise from a production assistant on TV sitcoms to a power player at Gemstone Pictures had not been without sacrifice. Two marriages had been lost to her career obsessiveness and she had turned a few tricks she wished she could forget. Ironically, her position of power had left her with a sense of almost total aloneness. She had little success with men and her experiments with women were interesting but meaningless. She dreaded growing old and witnessing the death of romance. She desperately wanted a satisfying relationship with a man, but the men she knew were not interested in romance or sex, and certainly not marriage. The men she dated wanted to make movies.

She swung the Jag into the exit lane and remembered what her brain doctor had said, *"You must be enjoying your life to some degree or you wouldn't be any good at your work."* There was some truth to that. She was damn good at what she did and almost never made any enemies. She always let the emperor have his clothes and never left her fingerprints on the murder weapon. In a town that buried its dead alive she was considered to be a straight shooter. And she was not unattractive. Her figure was firm and curvy. She jogged, lifted weights, and avoided meat, tobacco, and drugs. Her boss, Harry Walters, was one of the few men who truly impressed her.

Walters was a class act. His reputation as a savant was rooted in his theatrical background. He had produced six smash Broadway musicals and won three Tony awards. He had also produced a series of classical plays at Lincoln Center. He was polished, well read, and happily married. It was an Industry syndrome: the interesting men were spoken for.

She stopped for a light at Pico and Motor and noticed a billboard at the entrance of 20th Century-Fox. The poster advertised a clinker produced by Perkins and Swackhammer. Arrogant assholes. They had come over to Gemstone with an imbecilic script and complained to Walters that she had stalled their project. "Project," for Chrissakes; $48 million on a bullshit fantasy: a teenage boy is struck by lightning and becomes a god.

The traffic light changed and she turned into Motor Avenue. She didn't mind junk movies. There was nothing wrong with good junk movies, they were like Big Macs—tasty, fast, and cheap. But you didn't spend $48 million on junk food. Walters had backed her up. Loyalty was one of the qualities she admired most about him. Harry would never undercut a member of The Team. For better or worse, Gemstone's operating officers were a family: Solish, Walters, Flint, Smalley, and Wexler. But lately Walters's weekend activities had stirred the demon of suspicion—for the past two months he had been spending his weekends in Palm Springs. He was neither a sun worshipper, a golfer, nor a tennis player. *Why the desert?* And to compound her suspicion, Solish had been flying out from New York to meet Walters in the Springs. Solish detested everything within a two-hundred-mile radius of L.A. *Why the desert?* It was mystifying and troubling.

Turning off Jefferson, she rolled to a stop at the studio gates. The gray-haired security guard with the pleasant Irish face smiled. "Good morning, Miss Flint."

"Morning, Tommy. Has Mr. Walters come in?"

"About ten minutes ago."

She drove slowly down LeRoy Street, named after the late director. TV extras were lined up at the coffee truck sipping watery coffee, munching greasy doughnuts, and smoking themselves into the pink room at Cedars-Sinai.

Gemstone's TV division was a highly successful operation producing four long-running prime-time series and three syndicated game shows. Aurora was intrigued by that invisible line separating television from theatrical films. The big bucks were actually in television and yet almost everyone—writers, directors, actors, producers—wanted to cross over to the Big Screen.

She pulled into the parking space that bore her name. She'd been at Gemstone for almost five years but still thrilled at seeing her name on the slot alongside Harry Walters's. She got out of the Jag and shook her head in admiration as she glanced at Walters's Volkswagen Jetta. Cool. Understated. Theater.

She got off the elevator on the fourth floor of the administration building and walked down the bare wooden floors past the framed faces of dead actors. Walters insisted the building be maintained as it was at its inception in 1927. Tradition. Theater.

She opened the door of her outer office and her secretary, a lanky blonde with sad eyes, handed her a cup of coffee.

"Thanks. You look tired, Maggie."

"I had one of those toss-and-turn nights. I need some sex."

"Amen. What's happening?"

Maggie read from a typed sheet.

"Michael Heller."

"No."

"Jerry Blake."

"Yes."

"Sonni Strong."

"I'm in Damascus."

"Nails Grant."

"No."

"Stanley Trummel from last night."

"He's at sea. What else?"

"Story meeting at eleven forty-five. Dailies have been pushed back to six-fifteen. Smalley needs to talk to you, and your mother called. It seems there's a blizzard in New York and the landlord has cut off the heat."

"Terrific," Aurora sighed.

"THIS IS THE MOST TERRIFYING, BIZARRE VILLAIN I'VE EVER COME across," Charlie Morton began his pitch. "This is gold. Pure fucking gold."

Leaning forward in his Italian leather chair, Harry Walters gave Morton his rapt attention.

The plump producer with the two prominent buck teeth was affectionately nicknamed "the Chipmunk." Sitting in front of Walters's desk, listening to the pitch, Aurora marveled at the appropriateness of the nickname—the producer did indeed bear a striking resemblance to that busy rodent.

Morton was one of a select group of independent producers with whom Gemstone had exclusive "first-refusal" deals. The studio paid his company a fixed fee for development of screen material. Once a producer had successfully nursed a screenplay from the page to the stage, his fees escalated dramatically. But the odds were not good; only one out of forty screenplays made it to the screen. It was therefore critical for an independent producer to have as many scripts in development as possible.

Aurora sipped her diet Coke, half listening to Morton's pitch. Her attention was tuned to Walters. The handsome studio chief held a certain fascination for her. She thought he looked like his office. Neat. Spare. Understated. There were only two decorative objects on display: three Tony awards softly illuminated in a glass case and a framed poster of Ava Gardner as she appeared in *The Barefoot Contessa.*

Walters's light blue eyes, fine, chiseled features, and high cheekbones lent him an aristocratic air. He dressed with casual elegance and looked altogether refined. Aurora could not recall a single moment during the past four years when he had lost his composure. No matter how tense the situation, Walters conveyed a cool authority. She'd seen him charm distraught, egomaniacal stars, imperious demanding directors, acerbic agents, and through it all, retain his mythic affection for the bizarre process of filmmaking. He knew when, how, and on what to spend Gemstone's annual production budget of $300 million. He enjoyed the respect of his counterparts at other major studios and more than once had helped a competitor out of a tight spot.

Harry Walters was Hollywood aristocracy.

But Aurora didn't trust him.

She couldn't define her misgivings. He had never betrayed her and yet there was something about him that troubled her. He was pleasant and charming but emotionless. She suspected that underneath his benevolent mask there was ice-cold calculation.

Morton concluded his pitch and Walters said, "I would agree that you've described a unique heavy, but you haven't got a protagonist or a girl. I'm sorry, Charlie, I just don't see it." He paused and asked Aurora, "What's your feeling?"

"It's thin and familiar. You have a heavy who moves through supermarkets squeezing women's nipples until they faint. Finally, nipple squeezing isn't enough and he's forced to stalk and butcher his female victims. So we're back to serial killers. There are at least five takeoffs on *Silence of the Lambs* in various stages of production. It's three years too late. Besides which, it's tasteless."

The Chipmunk rose and his upper lip drew back over his buck teeth. "Taste? Taste? What the hell has *taste* got to do with anything? Look at the grosses. What did business last year? You call that shit tasteful?"

"What Aurora is suggesting," Walters calmly interjected, "is that from a woman's point of view the idea is offensive. Remember, women constitute fifty-three percent of the audience."

"I'm not demeaning women. We'll create a terrific role for a woman. She can be the female cop who finally nails the nipple squeezer. This is a movie about basic desires. Hey!'' Morton snapped his fingers. *''Basic Desires.* That's a hell of a title. We should register it.''

''For some future project,'' Walters replied with finality. ''I'm sorry, Charlie—it's a pass.''

Aurora suddenly felt sorry for the Chipmunk. His contract with Gemstone was expiring and he needed a development deal. ''Wait a minute,'' she said, rising. ''What if the nipple squeezer was a woman?''

She saw a flicker of interest in Walters's eyes.

''Remember the villainess in *Fatal Attraction?* Audiences loved her.'' She crossed the room, thinking God forgive me that I do this for a living. She turned to them, cleared her throat, and said, ''Suppose we have a woman who crushes testicles until her victims' eyes roll up and they faint, crumpling at her feet.'' Aurora walked slowly, menacingly, toward Walters's Louis Quatorze desk. ''She's a beauty, someone like Julia Castle. She seduces men but at the critical moment her hand flashes out like a striking cobra, grabbing their balls and squeezing until there's nothing left but mush. Until he—''

''Enough!'' Morton exclaimed. ''You're giving me cramps.''

''See what I mean?'' Aurora smiled triumphantly. ''By making the nipple squeezer a woman we also give the writer a chance for a strong back story. She's deranged because her father molested her in the bassinet. She's seeking vengeance on the male species for her father's sins. We can flashback in frame cuts to the psychic pain inflicted on her as a child.

''And while she seeks out random victims, her CIA husband remains unaware of his wife's ball-crushing activities until—''

''Hold it,'' the Chipmunk said, ''I'm sold.'' Sensing a deal, he indicated Aurora and nodded at Walters, ''She's dynamite. It's okay with me, Harry. Let's go with the ball squeezer.''

''Good.'' Walters nodded. ''I'll have Wexler draw up a deal memo for a treatment with an option for screenplay.''

''Why not go straight to screenplay?'' Morton asked hopefully.

''Too premature. All we have is an idea. I don't want to spend screenplay money until I see a treatment.''

''Okay,'' Morton readily agreed. ''I'll try and get Jerry Dicola.''

''Not him,'' Walters cautioned. ''He uses three names on the screen: Jerry Francis Dicola. I find that offensive and egocentric.

19

Out of ten thousand members in the Writers Guild there may be twenty-five who can write a simple declarative sentence, and five who have anything original to say. Where do they come off using three names?

"Think of Monet, Pissarro, Mahler, Michelangelo, Shakespeare, Joyce—geniuses who used two names and sometimes one. Only in the movies do we break the boundary of good manners and allow these hacks to fill the screen with three names."

"Maybe Dicola would agree to omit his middle name," Aurora suggested.

"I'll talk to his agent," Morton said. "Terrific meeting. Just terrific."

The Chipmunk turned abruptly and left. A seasoned producer knew when to take yes for an answer.

Walters came around his desk and smiled at Aurora.

"The things we do, eh, kid . . ."

"Yeah, the things we do. By the way, I told Kramer to bring the cast and crew of *Backwash* in. They were in heavy seas and couldn't get a shot."

"Smalley warned us about trying to double the Pacific for the Caribbean in February," Walters said. "Sometimes you pay the five cents and go to the Caribbean. I told Kramer that I'd authorize the expense."

"We'll be all right. We'll shoot miniatures in the tank and dispatch a second unit to the Carib while Trummel is cutting."

"Makes sense. Anything else?"

"Yes," she said coyly, "where'd you get that tan?"

"The Springs. Why?"

"Just wondered."

"I go to the desert for the waters."

"I'll bet—like Bogey in *Casablanca.*"

"I mean it. I take the natural sulfuric underground wells at the Spa. Marvelous. Rejuvenating. You ought to try it."

"I hear it's great for the ovaries." She smiled. "See you at dailies."

The door closed and Walters checked his watch: 1:15—4:15 in New York. He pressed the intercom button on his desk. "I'll be in screening room C."

"What about lunch?"

"Tuna salad."

"The Frank Sinatra or the Kevin Costner?"

"What's the difference."

"Sinatra is oil and vinegar, Costner is mayonnaise."

"Sinatra and an Amstel Light, and, Gloria, please call my wife and tell her I'll meet her at The Grill about eight."

Outside, Walters slipped on a pair of sunglasses and cut through a narrow alley to Harlow Street. He strolled past several colonial-style bungalows occupied by various stars working on current pictures. He greeted art directors, production managers, and two TV producers, one of whom reminded him to talk to Steve Saunders, the recalcitrant star of a long-running Gemstone TV series. Walters nodded. "I haven't forgotten." The producer thanked him and wished him well with the opening of a new picture.

He continued walking toward a huge stage, thinking he'd soon be rid of trivial problems. Once the scam went down, he'd have sufficient capital to float a public stock issue and form his own company using the old United Artists concept: the filmmakers would be partners in the pictures they made. The studio would recover its negative cost and charge a distribution fee, after which the artists would share in the gross film rental income. He would create an artistic oasis in a desert of conformity—a nirvana where artists could share a free exchange of ideas.

He'd clear the minefield of the "advisers" who now came between writer, director, and star. His studio would be a fountainhead of creativity from which a great renaissance of filmmaking would emerge—a golden age of American cinema.

He entered a charming Spanish-style plaza and noticed Herb Stoner on the opposite side of an ornate fountain. The director of West Coast publicity was engaged in a heated discussion with a well-known Hollywood madam—a handsome woman whose stable of girls was clean, reliable, and discreet. The madam was listed on the studio payroll as an outside casting director. Stoner charged her services to various pictures in production, but for special circumstances there was Magda von Stellhoff. The blond Nordic goddess was Gemstone's Patriot Missile, an instrument of perfection used only on select targets. It was fair to say that Magda was the Stradivarius of fellatio. While Walters had not sampled her favors, he was gratefully aware of the results of her awesome gift.

A few summers ago, Gemstone had been filming a romantic

comedy on the island of Ischia off the coast of Italy when Walters received a frantic call from the film's producer, who proceeded to explain the problem. The star, Richard Bryan, suffered from acute satyriasis and had screwed his pretty English co-star into a semi-comatose state. Although younger than Bryan, the actress could no longer continue working, her concentration having been drained by endless orgasms.

Walters flew out to the location on the corporate jet, stopping in London to pick up Magda von Stellhoff. The Aryan wunderkind spent one weekend with the amorous star and by Monday morning a subdued, pale-faced Bryan shuffled onto the set. Magda returned to London five thousand dollars richer, and Bryan finished the film without making any further sexual demands on his English co-star.

Smiling at the memory, Walters came out of the sun-drenched plaza, turned the corner, and entered screening room C. He waited a moment for his eyes to adjust to the dimly lit lobby before crossing to the public phone booth.

The Waldorf lobby was alive with tourists, shoppers, and frantic groups of Japanese businessmen who found themselves grounded by the raging blizzard.

Frank Solish was seated in the center booth of a bank of public phones just off the lobby. He kept the door open for air. A long scarf hung loosely around the shoulders of his cashmere overcoat and his Soviet-style fur hat rested in his lap. He sucked on a Tums tablet to relieve the heartburn that had resulted from his lunch with Salvatore "Boom Boom" Parnelli. He had laid down the ground rules exactly as prescribed by Leo Resnick. Parnelli had grunted his agreement between mouthfuls of linguine and gulps of Chianti. The luncheon had gone well enough until Parnelli's parting comment: "You tell that Jew-prick Wexler to do his job. I'll take care of my end. It's my ass out there."

Solish sneezed and shook his head. Fucking weather. He glanced at his watch—4:32 P.M. Where the hell was Harry? His fingertips began drumming nervously on the booth's metallic ledge. The lingering image of Jack Wheeler's eyes at the conclusion of *Midnight* had haunted him throughout the day. He identified with the character's aloneness and emptiness.

A sudden jolt of pain radiated under his upper right bridge.

Fucking dentists—that bridge cost more than the Golden Gate. The dentist had said, "You need periodontal work. The gum line is receding." They had some act going, but what can you do? You're trapped. Well, if nothing else, success had assured him the benefit of novocaine.

His thoughts were interrupted by the sharp ring of the phone. He closed the door, swiveled around, and grabbed the receiver.

"Hello."

"It's me, Frank."

His partner's voice was instantly reassuring.

"How are you?" Walters asked.

"Fighting a flu. Fucking blizzard here. It's twenty degrees and blowing. I'm staying overnight."

"Makes sense."

"I had lunch with Boom Boom. He's a scumbag but he'll stay in line. I spoke to Resnick. We're on for Friday night. Tell Wexler and Smalley."

"What about including Aurora?"

"The Old Man doesn't trust her. Too young. Too principled. Unreliable. You'll have to play it straight in dealing with her. We've got to be goddamn careful. We don't want to wind up making little ones out of big ones. Those federal dungeons are not the Waldorf."

"That's paranoia, Frank. No one ever did time for being unethical. Just be calm. It'll all work out. Think of it, almost fifty million apiece after taxes."

"I can't think of anything else, I can't eat. I get heartburn on skim milk. I can't sleep. All I think about is the score."

"Good. By the way, how did you like *Midnight?*"

"Brilliant but a tough sell, although I think Wheeler's a lock for Best Actor nomination."

"I agree. It's an extraordinary performance."

"I sent those two kids to Rome. I thought Wheeler should see the picture before we locked it off."

"Classy, Frank."

"I must tell you, that black hooker worries me. The activists will be all over us."

"Let's hope so," Walters replied with surprising equanimity. "That's why she's in the picture; protests generate box office. If

23

the civil rights people ignore the picture, I'll have Herb Stoner hire pickets. The same gag we used on the Jesus movie. See you in the desert—take care of yourself, Frank.''

Solish hung up and blew his nose. He and Walters had been a team for almost ten years, but his partner's casual ruthlessness never failed to surprise him.

Walking back to her office from the commissary, Aurora wondered whether she should have mentioned Palm Springs to Walters. If something shady was going on, he certainly hadn't reacted with any nervousness or hesitation. She was probably imagining things.

She entered the administration building and took the creaky elevator to the fourth floor. As she walked down the corridor past the actors' portraits, she glanced for a moment at the photograph of John Garfield, né Julie Garfinkle. What a trip, she thought, from Brownsville to Broadway to Hollywood to the blacklist and *crash*. God, he was handsome. Not pretty but sexy. *Body and Soul* . . . yeah—'bye, Julie.

Maggie looked up from her typewriter. "Stanley Trummel is on his way."

"Any luck with Jerry Blake?"

"Not yet. What did you have for lunch?"

"A Lana Turner—not bad if you like egg salad. Anything else?"

"Swackhammer called."

Aurora nodded and went into her office.

She sat at her desk, shuffled some notes, and glanced at the French poster of *Moonrise*. It was the first film she had supervised for Gemstone and it had won Best Picture at the Cannes Festival.

That had been a memorable week. Besides winning the top award, Aurora witnessed an incident that had become an enduring Hollywood legend. The star of *Moonrise*, Julia Castle, and her director, Paul Scott, had invited Aurora for a drink at dusk on the busy terrace of the Carlton Hotel. They were joined by a pretty French actress and an infamous Italian count. During the course of cocaine and champagne, the count placed two ten-thousand-dollar casino chips on the table. His proposition was simple. The French actress would go down on the breathtakingly beautiful Ms. Castle right there under the table. If the American actress did not crack in five minutes, she would be deemed the winner, but if she succumbed, the French girl would pick up the chips. The principals agreed and the French actress disappeared under the table. Julie Castle continued to sip her Cristal champagne and appeared impervious to the French girl's action. Afterward, Aurora thought it had taken less than three minutes before Julia screamed, knocked the table over, and with paparazzi flashbulbs popping, draped her pretty legs over the French girl's shoulders and leaned back across a Saudi prince's table, her eyes closed in ecstasy.

The count and Paul Scott pulled the frenzied French actress from between Julia's magnificent thighs. A jet-set crowd circled the scene as Julia got to her feet and drew herself up. She shook her long pale hair and turned, her wrists flashing her diamond bracelets. Her yellow eyes glittered as she faced the riveted spectators and delivered her immortal line, "I can't help it if people find me irresistible." She tilted her chin, squared her shoulders, and strode across the terrace to cries of *"Brava!"* It was, Aurora thought, Julia Castle's finest moment.

Maggie's voice interrupted Aurora's reverie.

"Jerry Blake on one."

"How you doing, baby?" the boyish voice inquired.

"I'm fine. Listen carefully, I'm making a firm offer for Alex Carlino to direct *Snowblind.*"

"Not without Brian Kelly starring," Blake said.

"We're talking to Steve Edwards's agent."

"I've got to level with you, Aurora. I need a job for Brian Kelly." He paused. *"Snowblind* is a male buddy picture in the Swiss Alps. Why not have Kelly play Edwards's sidekick? I need this favor, sweetheart. I'm talking to you as if we're in a booth for two. What do you say?"

"You're taking advantage of my affection for you, but okay. I'll make Kelly firm for the supporting role."

"Second position billing?"

"I can't promise that. We're trying to get Julia Castle to play Melissa. I can guarantee you no worse than third, but it depends on you delivering Carlino."

"It's done, baby."

"What am I looking at?"

"How much is Edwards getting?"

"Fuck off, Jerry."

"Okay, let's say Edwards is getting four. I want two for Carlino and one for Kelly. You have the above-the-line for seven mil."

"You're not counting Julie Castle."

"You'll never get her to do this potboiler. She's in rehearsal for a Broadway play. I can sell you Jennifer Andrews for half a mil. You probably have fifteen below-the-line, so you got the whole enchilada for twenty-two five."

"I'm not sure about Andrews but let's close on the others."

"Terrific. By the way, I ran into Harry Walters last week at Le Vallauris in the Springs. Solish was with him, and guess who else was in the restaurant?"

"Surprise me."

"Leo Resnick."

It took a second for Aurora to put it together. "I thought he was dead."

"A lot of people that crossed swords with him are dead but he's very much alive. There's a colony of retired mobsters down there."

"I know," Aurora said. "They take the waters."

"The waters? What waters?"

"Fax the deal to me, Jerry."

"You're a prince, baby."

She hung up slowly, reflecting . . . Walters, Solish, and Resnick. Coincidence? Of course, it had to be. She rose, walked to the window, and looked down at the extras milling around the coffee van. Leo Resnick . . . a legend. The sole survivor of the original combination of Luciano, Dalitz, and Lansky. The kingpin behind the Teamster locals servicing Vegas and Hollywood.

Seated alone in the darkness of screening room C, Harry Walters watched Ava Gardner in *Pandora and the Flying Dutchman*. The picture had been made when the raven-haired actress was at the height of her beauty. Walters toyed with his Frank Sinatra tuna salad and swallowed some Amstel Light, but his eyes were fixed on that magical beauty up there on the screen. He worshiped beauty. There was an unqualified fidelity to classic beauty—a preciseness that had caused the ancient Greeks to eternalize it in marble. Ava Gardner had had it for most of her life. But it was rare. The only one around now with that mythic beauty was Julia Castle.

A CAST OF THOUSANDS

He wished they could come up with a suitable property for her. Julia reminded him of a girl who danced in the chorus of his first musical. He'd use the stage door off Shubert Alley and enter that surreal backstage universe: dancers, actors, musicians, singers, stagehands, glittering sets, and the smell of danger and anticipation. You could hear the buzz of the audience as the musicians tuned up. He'd find her at the stretch bar limbering up those racehorse legs. She would turn her luminous eyes on him and smile. A hurried kiss, a whispered something, a trace of perfume, and then the stage manager's ready-light would blink and everything went dark.

The overture began.

Places.

Stagehands ready at the pinrail and follow spots.

Curtain time.

He would climb into the far reaches of the second balcony and still be able to pick her out of the line. How special she was. How perfect that time. But he'd let her go. Lost her to ambition. He was young. Successful. Admired. She was the girl of the moment and he never realized how much he . . . ah, hell, it was a long time ago.

He drained the Amstel and lit one of the five cigarettes he allowed himself each day. The smoke drifted up into the projection light and his spirits rose with the rush of nicotine. Can't drift into sentimentality, he thought—sangfroid . . . sangfroid.

4

LEO RESNICK'S PALM SPRINGS VILLA WAS SITUATED ATOP A GRANITE plateau high above the desert floor and sheltered from the winds by Mount San Jacinto. A marble terrace circled the main house and afforded a panoramic view of the valley.

The heavily guarded compound included four red-tiled Spanish-style casitas, two swimming pools, and a clay tennis court. A purple splash of ten-foot-tall bougainvillea cascaded over the thick white walls enclosing the villa. Strands of barbed wire were laced between the thorny bougainvillea vines, and strategically placed TV cameras constantly monitored the grounds.

From their terrace table the conspirators admired the sunset and exchanged small talk while waiting for Resnick to address the matter at hand. The Old Man nodded occasionally at a comment but seemed distant. In point of fact he was computing the strengths and weaknesses of his confederates: Frank Solish, the supersalesman—the Brownsville street kid still fighting his grim Orthodox upbringing; Harry Walters, the charming but enigmatic studio chief; Ray Smalley, the avaricious mick who policed every dime spent on Gemstone's pictures; and Irving Wexler, the crafty chief of Gemstone's business affairs. They were an odd lot, but they shared two qualities that made the score viable: position and greed.

As the sun dropped behind the mountain, the villa's lights came on, dramatically illuminating the tennis court, swimming pools, olive trees, and palm-lined access road.

"Quite a vista," Walters remarked.

"I've grown to love the desert," Resnick said. "I wish my son had lived to see it." His bruised gray eyes stared pensively off at the twinkling lights. "David died the death of an idealist—a lost life in a lost cause."

He waved his hand as if to set aside the memory, "But, I have his child. I thank God for my granddaughter." The Old Man sighed. "Everyone else is gone. My son. My daughter-in-law. My wife. My friends. But David was . . . ah . . ." He shook his head sadly and fell silent.

The men on the terrace knew all about David Resnick. He'd been a Navy fighter pilot and served with distinction in the Korean War, after which he settled in Israel and was killed in the Six-Day War. Two years later his widow took her life. Their child was raised by Leo and his wife. The little girl grew up to be an attractive young woman, but the anguish caused by his son's untimely death had never left Leo. The pain remained a constant just beneath the surface.

Resnick drained his glass and signaled the butler to open another bottle of champagne.

"You fellows," he said to the men, "you fellows are young so you don't know." He sighed. "If you live as long as I have you'll find yourselves alone, clinging to bits and pieces of memories, wondering if you could have acted differently, changed things."

The cork popped and the white-jacketed butler refilled their glasses. Resnick swallowed some champagne and said, "I find that action is the only remedy for soothing old wounds. That's why I designed the scam. That's why we're here. Once we achieve our goal, I'll donate my end to the John Wayne Cancer Clinic at St. John's. They took good care of my wife—rest her soul. For me money is not the issue. It never was. It was action." He paused and nodded at Wexler. "Go ahead, Irv."

"Without boring you with SEC statutes," Wexler began, "the end result of our efforts will not be illegal but the means are fraudulent. We have entered into a conspiracy to defraud Gemstone stockholders."

"How are the stockholders being defrauded?" Walters asked.

"Gemstone common closed today at forty-two. We're going to

offer the stockholders a chance to sell at seventy-five. How does that constitute fraud?"

"Come on, Harry," Wexler complained. "The offer will be made through Parnelli's Sirocco Films. It's a bogus proposal that will never be concluded."

"The takeover offer will be on the table long enough for any astute investor to cash in," Ray Smalley countered.

"Absolutely," Solish agreed. "Who's getting hurt?"

"Seventy-five is cheap," Wexler explained. "Just two years ago Hikoru Yosuta offered a buyout price of a hundred and forty dollars a share. Our esteemed chairman of the board shot him down—got Congress up in arms with all that self-serving crap about how Gemstone will not mortgage its heritage and its art to the Japanese. Yosuta got scissored in a political fire storm and withdrew; but he offered a hundred forty. That's a far cry from seventy-five. Even Gemstone stockholders have memories and it only takes one disgruntled stockholder to trigger a class action suit. Once that happens we're all under a federal magnifying glass."

Smalley said, "If the stock is worth a hundred forty a share, why is it currently selling below forty-five?"

Wexler shrugged. "The whole range of entertainment stocks are depressed. And in my judgment, undervalued. Remember, boys, we have a tradition, no matter how big the grosses we almost never show a profit.

"Our accounting procedures are mystical. The last thing we need is an army of IRS forensic accountants poring over our personal expense accounts and selective items charged off to various pictures. And no one will ever confuse 'Boom Boom' Parnelli with Mother Cabrini. His company, Sirocco Films, is under indictment in France for laundering narcodollars."

"Enough!" Resnick said indignantly. "Charges of money-laundering have never been proven. The French thing is political. Sal stepped on the wrong toes. Sirocco has financed and distributed some major hits.

"Parnelli made a run at Magnum Pictures and came up with close to two billion dollars. The takeover didn't fly but he raised the money; so his bid for Gemstone is not without precedent. Besides, when the offer is made, Harry and Frank will hold simultaneous press conferences on both coasts and issue statements to the effect that Gemstone management intends to resist Parnelli's bid. You'll take out ads urging our stockholders not to be tempted by the immediate cash windfall; that their stock is worth far more than seventy-five dollars a share.

"Once we publicly urge and advise Gemstone stockholders not to be seduced, our skirts are clean. We'll have already unloaded at seventy-five. We'll walk away with fifty million apiece—give or take a nickel. Those stockholders who sell will do fine." Resnick shrugged. "All we're trying to do is what others have done in the past. By using the device of a bogus takeover we're inflating the price of our stock."

"Can we get Boom Boom off the Jews?" Solish asked. "At lunch last week he grumbled about how the Hollywood Jews have prevented him from expanding his film operations. One of these days he's gonna say that in print."

"Let him talk," Leo said with a wave of his hand. "The fact that he's despised makes him the perfect shill. When his offer falls apart, people will applaud."

"We've got to make this look good," Wexler cautioned. "If anyone cracks, spills, leaks, or does something stupid we may be spending the next ten years making license plates."

"Don't exaggerate, Irv," Walters replied. "We saw an opportunity and took it. Is there any law against an officer of a corporation unloading his stock?"

"No. But that isn't the case here. We are conspiring to pump up Gemstone's stock using the cover of a phony takeover by Parnelli, who receives ten percent of our collective profits for his participation. Once the stock hits seventy-five dollars or thereabouts we sell—Parnelli withdraws and the public is fucked. Let's face it, this is a criminal conspiracy."

"I don't see how we can be held responsible for Parnelli's fiscal misadventures," Solish said. "At the eleventh hour his financing fell apart. There's nothing new or illegal about failed takeover bids."

"Hey, fellas, I'm not the government," Wexler protested. "I'm a co-conspirator. I'm simply warning you that we have to walk on water."

"Irv's right," Resnick agreed. "We've got to play the game carefully and cleverly—always publicly defending Gemstone against Parnelli's offer. In my view the risks are minor when measured against the gain, but if anyone has second thoughts, now's the time to voice them."

No one spoke. The men sipped their champagne and watched the distant lights of the valley grow brighter as the night sky slowly enveloped the desert.

Walters lit his third cigarette of the day. "There is one problem—our CEO, Max Schuller."

"What do we have on that Nazi bastard?" Resnick asked.

Wexler shuffled some documents and read from a blue sheet. "He migrated from Hannover in '46. We know about his activities in the S.S. intelligence unit at Bergen-Belsen death camp. In those days America was a haven for Nazis with backgrounds in political espionage. At any rate, he took advantage of his mentors in the State Department. He graduated Dartmouth business school and made a fortune in platinum futures. He sits on six corporate boards and serves as Republican Party co-chairman in New York State. His name appears on a host of philanthropic activities. There is, however, a chink in his armor. Schuller is a frequent customer of a bordello on East Sixty-fifth Street."

"How do we know this?" Resnick asked.

"Lew Freeman in my office is Schuller's pimp," Solish said.

"There's something else," Wexler added. "According to the corporate insurance policy, Schuller suffers from an irregular heartbeat and takes a drug called Inderal to regulate the problem."

The wind ruffled Resnick's silver hair and his eyes were the color of lead. "Leave the Schuller problem with me," he said with finality.

The butler entered and whispered to Resnick, who nodded and announced, "Dinner is served."

They filed into a white-walled dining room supported by soaring Moorish arches. The table was set with silver platters of thinly sliced Scotch salmon garnished with chopped onions, capers, and slices of lemon. A uniformed butler poured a cold Gavi di Gavi.

Solish raised his wineglass. "To the score."

They echoed the toast and sipped the fine white wine.

"One thing Irv mentioned bothers me," Smalley said, disturbing the momentary euphoria. "It's that goddamn hundred-forty-dollar-a-share offer Yosuta made and Schuller torpedoed."

"What bothers you?" Resnick asked.

"Suppose I'm a Gemstone stockholder and Parnelli's buyout offer of seventy-five dollars a share is on the table but only two years ago the Japanese offered a hundred forty bucks a share and Gemstone's CEO shot it down. Why would I now accept seventy-five?"

"Because," Resnick replied, "Gemstone stock is currently selling at forty-two. You'll double your money overnight."

"Maybe so, but I'm still suspicious and I'm thinking of starting a class action suit."

"It's a problem," Walters acknowledged.

"Fuck it!" Solish exclaimed, "MCA sold out. MGM sold out. Columbia sold out. Fox sold out. What's the problem?"

"Their hands were clean," Wexler calmly replied. "They weren't conspiring to defraud their stockholders. Everything was up front."

A morose silence fell across the candlelit table.

"Wait a minute," Walters said in a hushed voice. His eyes were wide and intense as if they had caught a glimpse of an elusive truth. "Wait a minute," he repeated almost to himself. "Irv, let's say you're this suspicious Gemstone stockholder. Parnelli has filed a takeover bid at seventy-five dollars a share, almost double current market value. But—and this is a major 'but'—only two years ago Gemstone's management rejected a Japanese offer at a hundred forty a share, so why would you accept the current bid of seventy-five. Right?"

"Exactly." Wexler nodded.

"Okay," Walters said and unbuttoned his shirt at the neck and loosened his tie. "Parnelli's offer is on the table but you're not buying—even though you can double your money, you're not buying—you're suspicious."

"Right," Wexler said.

Walters rose and moved slowly around the table. His eyes were hypnotic. He commanded their attention the way a great actor held his audience. "Okay, Parnelli's filed his offer with the SEC. Everything's in place. The bets are down. But we have suspicious stockholders. Now, let's say that at this same time Gemstone has a picture in production." He circled the table, playing to each man as he moved. "Not just a movie. I'm talking about an epic, a colossus, *Cleopatra, Quo Vadis, The Longest Day* all rolled into one. A monumental period piece. A celluloid mural. A great canvas. A cast of thousands." He paused dramatically. "And it's out of control. It's a disaster. Gemstone is the joke of the industry. Money pumping day and night, week after week, month after month.

"Nothing cuts. The dailies are a mess. Nothing matches. There are fistfights on the set. Accidents. Cast and crew members arrested for snorting schmeck. All of this is happening on a distant location with an international cast of stars. Everyone's getting top dollar along with their entourages: wardrobe, makeup, butlers, chauffeurs, nurses, nannies, and it's all out of fucking control.''

Smalley studied the handsome studio chief, wondering if he had taken one story meeting too many.

Walters turned to Wexler. "So there you are, Mr. Stockholder. Gemstone is being drained, sucked dry by this monumental catastrophe. The very existence of the studio hangs in the balance. Now, Mr. Stockholder, you can either double your money and get out at seventy-five dollars or risk going into the toilet. Are you going to be thinking about Yosuta's two-year-old offer? Are you going to file a class action suit? Are you going to turn down Parnelli's offer? Answer me, Mr. Stockholder—what are you going to do?"

"Cash in," Wexler said without hesitation.

"You bet your ass!" Walters exclaimed triumphantly.

"Are you suggesting that we actually make this epic?" Smalley asked with a trace of fear.

"Absolutely."

"What about our normal slate of films?" Solish said.

"Status quo. And you, Ray"—Walters pointed to Smalley—"you have to play it straight in front of Aurora and the staff. You're opposed to making this monster. You too, Irv. It's strictly my decision. I'm going against the collective wisdom of my colleagues."

"Suppose—just suppose," Wexler said, "a funny thing happens on the way to oblivion and the monster gets up and walks—the picture works. What then?"

"The ultimate fate of the picture is irrelevant. It's strictly a red flag waving at our stockholders. Once Parnelli's offer is filed with the SEC we cash in—we're out."

"Suppose the picture finishes before Parnelli files?" Wexler said.

"That's extremely unlikely, Irv. But even if the impossible happens we control the negative."

"There's one major problem," Smalley cautioned. "How do we find an epic screenplay that's ready to go?"

"Not to worry." Walters smiled. "We'll be shooting by July."

ADRIAN SUMMERS SIPPED THE CHILLED VODKA AND PRESSED THE
Play button on the Sony.

Silvi's voice trembled with controlled fury.

*"You're thinking I won't write off all the years—well, you're wrong,
I'm leaving you for good!"*

Her voice was followed by a door slamming. Adrian knew it
was a momentary pause. Some months ago he'd been taping a
story idea when she burst into his study and he inadvertently
recorded what would prove to be her curtain speech.

He listened to the tape with increasing frequency, seeking atone-
ment in the pain. It seemed a more appropriate method of absolution than reciting Hail Marys.

The sound of the door flying open and banging against the wall
preceded Silvi's continuing assault.

*"You despise me, don't you? You despise me because I remind you
of how it was before you died.*

*"You and your long-lost success, and long-lost war and long-dead
father. It was him, wasn't it? You never knew him but he pulled the
strings. You envied him his heroic death and chased his medals."*

There was a slight pause as she caught her breath.

"What was it you wanted?"

Here it comes—the heavy artillery.

"Was it other women?"

It wasn't a question. It was an accusation.

"Nothing very creative about that. Most women found you to be attractive. You were young. You were a star. Broadway. Hollywood. Writing awards. Medals of valor. You were just terrific. Well, it's over.

"I'm tired. Tired of betrayals. Tired of nightmares. Tired of heroin needles, of nursing you through withdrawals, and your handwringing and your maddening silence."

Another short pause before the shell-burst.

"Get angry, Adrian! Lose your temper. Make believe I've hidden your stash!"

He swallowed some vodka, computing the seconds before she resumed the barrage.

"My anger pleases you, doesn't it? It reinforces your sense of doom. You wear failure as if it was a Medal of Honor."

A loud crash of a glass breaking.

"You can have the house. It's all yours! I wouldn't dignify the years by taking anything from you.

"And you'd better get used to handling life's little details; like maintaining Timmy's grave."

Sobs followed by a scream.

"It's really over, Adrian!"

Door slam. Loud. Sharp. Final.

He pressed the Stop button on the recorder and drained the vodka, thinking the door slam was an appropriate sound effect. During the course of their marriage there had been many door slams, in many rooms, in many cities.

He walked to the portable bar, fixed a fresh drink, and slipped a cassette into the stereo. The Goodman Sextet played "Here's That Rainy Day," filling the room with the lilting sound of failed romance. The bluesy clarinet stirred the ashes of the past; Goodman took no prisoners but the sound belonged to another time. It was part of something dead—like himself. Like the kids at Firebase Kelly, like the Tony award, like the Academy nominations, and the rush of celebrity, and the Monkey, and Silvi's slender volume of poems, and Timmy's dead eyes staring. It was all amorphous now. Ectoplasmic. People, places, and time had melted into a formless mass of memories. He and Silvi were history. Maybe they deserved to be over, but they had managed to put up a noble struggle. How many marriages survive a child's death? How many survive the Monkey?

He had lost control for a while, but almost everyone he knew was touched by madness. Insanity was the principal legacy of a fucked-up century. A century whose accomplishments were measured by constant wars, Auschwitz, Hiroshima, penicillin, pollution, and the filtered cigarette. Well, a few more years and the century itself would be history—*fin de siècle.* A thousand years from now some enterprising alien would comb through the radioactive ruins and discover a framed junk bond and fly back to his universe thinking he had found Earth's holy grail—and maybe he had.

Adrian walked to the bookcase, studied the titles, and selected a volume of Irwin Shaw's short stories. On his best day, Shaw wrote with the precision of a diamond cutter, and to Adrian's thinking, "The Girls in Their Summer Dresses" had been written with an almost transcendent awareness of man-woman relationships. He held the book in his hand, wondering why Silvi had mentioned other women. He wasn't a saint but neither was he a player. Other women had nothing to do with needles and a dead child . . .

Carrying the book and his drink, he entered the bedroom with its stifling, unrelenting memories. He placed the book on the night table and glanced at his own handwriting on the notepad.

Harry Walters's office—11:30 A.M.

He sat on the edge of the bed, sipped his drink, and shook his head in wonderment. Was it true or had he dreamed it? For sanity's sake he played back his conversation with Walters's secretary.

"Mr. Summers?"

"Speaking."

"This is Harry Walters's secretary at Gemstone Studios. Mr. Walters is out of town but asked if it would be convenient for you to meet with him here, at the studio, eleven-thirty Tuesday morning."

"Did he say what this is about?" Adrian had somehow managed to ask.

"Is there a problem?" she replied imperiously.

Couldn't she have said, "I'm sorry but Mr. Walters didn't say."

She had to knife the walking dead. *"Is there a problem?"* She knew fucking well there was no problem. It was like asking Lugosi if he left the crypt at sundown . . . Jesus. Hold it. Why are you making an opera out of this? She's a secretary doing her job.

"Are you there, Mr. Summers?"

"Yes . . . I'm just checking my schedule."

"If there's a problem with the time, we can—"

"No," he interrupted. "The time is fine. I'll move something around."

"Good. I'll leave a drive-on at the gate. See you then."

Harry Walters . . . He hadn't seen him in years. Walters was Mr. Broadway, Mr. CBS, Mr. Gemstone—the ace of hearts—the genuine article. What did he want?

Adrian rose, went into the bathroom, and swallowed a Dalmane and a Valium. He brushed his teeth, stripped, got into bed, and opened the Shaw collection to "A Sailor Off the Bremen." He started to read, then stopped and glanced up at a portrait of Silvi.

You're really alone, he thought. They're all gone. He craved the warm wet suit of heroin. A solid jolt and the demons disappeared. No, goddamnit. That was over. He was alive and well in Dreamland where anything was possible.

AURORA SIPPED HER THIRD CUP OF BITTER COFFEE AND READ THE LAT-
est script changes on *Backwash*. The pink pages had been rewritten
by Stanley Trummel. The director fancied himself a screenwriter
but ego was a lousy substitute for talent. His writing was dreadful,
although at this point it didn't matter. The film's producer, Jack
Kramer, had relinquished his authority to Trummel. The object of
the exercise was simply to finish.

She initialed the script changes and thumbed through the production stills of the past weeks' work. Despite her misgivings she
had to admit the film had a kitschy hard edge and could possibly
be a hit. Tracey Warren, the actress portraying the drug smuggler's
sister, played up her sexuality and wisely threw her lines away.
Strutting around the cabin cruiser sweaty and half-naked, she was
like a sensual time bomb ticking her way toward catastrophe.

Trummel had shot enormous close-ups of her tanned skin
beaded with drops of perspiration and intercut those shots with
close-ups of the mesmerized stockbroker. The dope-smuggling
brother and rescued stockbroker had been underplayed to perfection by competent actors, but Tracey Warren was the engine of
the piece. You knew that, sooner or later, she would drive the
stockbroker to the breaking point and whisper, "Get rid of my
brother and I'm yours." The plot was a ripoff of Billy Wilder's

classic *Double Indemnity*. It was a formula that had been borrowed more than once and almost always worked.

Aurora sighed heavily at the thought of facing Trummel. The reptilian director had refused to utilize miniatures or authorize photo doubles and a second-unit team in the Bahamas to shoot the seagoing action they had failed to get off Catalina. She would have to placate the sexually repressed queen. She drained her coffee and thought if Trummel would come out and put on a dress his venal nature might take a turn for the better. Everything about him was a sham, including the role he played of a bleeding-heart liberal—the champion of the downtrodden masses.

The intercom buzzed, interrupting her thoughts.

"Yes?"

"The Chipmunk on one."

"Good morning, Charlie," Aurora said with a smile. She never quite understood the soft spot she had for the hustling producer.

"I got great news, sweetheart. Jerry Dicola is willing to drop his middle name. Why? Because he loves the story."

"What story?"

"*Basic Desires*—the ball squeezer, for Chrissake."

"What about it?"

"Like I said, Dicola is willing to confine his screen credit to his first and last name."

"Good."

"There's a quid pro quo here. He wants to go directly to screen-play—no treatment."

"Fuck him."

"What?"

"You heard me," she replied, angry at herself for using the exple-tive. It was a lifelong habit; anger triggered the four-letter words.

"Dicola is the best thriller writer in town," Morton said sooth-ingly. "I got him to break precedent against his agent's advice. He'll drop his middle name and you say 'fuck him'?"

"You heard Walters. He wants to see a treatment before commit-ting to a screenplay."

"Suppose I sweeten Dicola's screenplay price in return for drop-ping his middle name and having to write a treatment?"

"Work it out, Charlie."

"You're a prince, sweetheart."

*   *   *

She slammed the phone down. The next time anyone called her a prince she would have them thrown off the lot. She picked up her coffee cup just as Maggie buzzed.

"Stanley Trummel is here."

The door opened and the dwarfish director with the large head and no shoulders burst into the room. He wore his usual costume of skintight faded jeans, black T-shirt, black beret, denim jacket, and dirty sneakers.

"Baby!" he exclaimed. His arms went around her and she got a strong whiff of stale tobacco.

"Can I get you anything, Stanley?"

"Not a thing. My stomach's still in my mouth from that goddamn day at sea." There was an unmistakable feminine lilt to his speech.

"*Quelle* day!" he said, waving his arms. "The fucking waves were twenty feet high."

He sat on the leather couch and curled his legs under his ass. Using an exaggerated wrist move he lit an unfiltered Camel and blew the smoke up toward the recessed ceiling lights.

Aurora walked to her desk and pressed the intercom.

"Hold the calls, Maggie."

She sat down opposite the director and studied him. He reminded her of the Babylonian devil god in *The Exorcist*—half rodent, half reptile. A closet pagan queen. Trummel's virtues were speed and bullshit. He shot fast, spoke fast, and lied easily. He had a dead-on, no-surprise style of composition that worked only if he was shooting a simplistic screenplay.

"I expected you this evening after dailies," she said.

"We're moving over to stage ten so I thought we'd get it out of the way."

"I understand you're not going to use miniatures or a second-unit director and crew to get the pickup shots with photodoubles."

Thin streams of smoke shot out of his wide, flaring nostrils. "I'm not making shrunken kiddie movies. I won't use trick shots."

For a brief, thrilling moment she thought he would walk. "We're not budgeted for first unit in the Caribbean and we can't go back to Catalina," she said. "Unfortunately the text of that sequence is essential to the story."

He drew on the Camel and his words came through the smoke. "I was thinking of writing a new scene."

She wanted to celebrate. He would write something to replace the water scene. They would finish on time.

"You mean a scene to replace the seagoing action?"

"Exactly. I'll retain the essence of the original but take it off the water and rewrite it using a visually interesting setting—something we can shoot on the stage." He waved the cigarette. "You know, of course, Fellini shoots everything on the stage."

"Stanley, let me be frank. Nothing would make me happier than to have you do the rewrite. Almost anything you write transcends the crap we buy from those hacks." She paused, thinking she had laid it on too heavy. But her fears were unwarranted. He was basking in her compliments. "You're a late comer to the craft," she continued, "but your screenwriting is superb. In my opinion *Pell Street* should have been nominated."

"Thank you, sweetheart. You know these West Coast writers, they take umbrage whenever a director writes his own script. *Pell Street* didn't have much of an audience in America, but, honey, the grosses in Europe . . ." His wrist flared as he brushed a few strands of his pony-tailed hair, "and the reviews. I'm not talking about minor cable critics, I'm talking about Simon, Canby, Ansen, *The New Yorker, Rolling Stone,* and all of Kael's disciples, even that putz Andrew Kaplan on that Yiddish paper." He grimaced and his lips drew back over large square capped teeth. "I won't kid you. I did expect a larger audience."

My God, she suddenly thought, the Chipmunk and the Pagan Queen back to back—this could be one of those days.

"Great writing, Stanley, like great painting, has historically defied public acceptance in the lifetime of the creator. Only after the artist dies is his work acknowledged."

"You're a breath of fresh air, sweetheart, an antidote to the venom in this town. I make no secret of my disdain for Hollywood. I become physically ill when the wheels touch down at LAX. I agreed to do this picture for you, Aurora. Only for you." He paused. "Let me tell you about the new scene." He uncoiled and rose.

"Don't tell me, Stanley. Write it. Surprise me."

Two streams of smoke shot out of his nostrils. "I'll have the scene on your desk by Friday." His voice turned cold and charmless. "Tell Smalley to check with me about the set." He started for the door, stopped, and as an afterthought said, "By the way, my chauffeur is too goddamned chatty. The man doesn't know his place. I want a new driver."

Stanley Trummel, the Scotch-and-soda liberal, the champion of the proletariat, had spoken.

She walked to the window and threw it open, hoping to rid the room of tobacco fumes. The phone console buzzed and, after taking a few rapid breaths of fresh air, she returned to her desk.

"Yes, Maggie?"

"Walters's secretary just called. He wants to see you—it's urgent."

"It's a dumb idea," Aurora said. "I'm sorry, I didn't mean to imply that—well, you know."

Walters smiled benevolently. "Since when do you have to pull punches with me. Tell me exactly what you think."

She rose and walked over to the glass case and stared at the illuminated Tonys. She had to compose herself. She had to find the right words. Ray Smalley patted his bald head and exchanged secretive, knowing glances with Walters.

"Let's discuss the property first, okay?" she suggested.

"Fine," Walters said.

"The script's been around forever. Columbia bought it from that imperious Limey, Ian Ramsey. The project wound up in the courts. It was litigated to death. The property is jinxed; besides, how can you do business with that English slimeball?"

"Ramsey is out. The screenplay has reverted to Adrian Summers."

"You mean Summers would produce it?" she asked incredulously.

"Why not?"

"Well . . . you know . . ." She chewed nervously on her lower lip. "Oh, hell . . ." She tossed her thick red hair. "Let's forget Adrian for a minute." She was angry at herself. She shouldn't have called him Adrian. It was too familiar—too revealing. "The story has no audience," she said.

"No one knows what an audience will buy," Walters countered.

"Ask yourself, Harry," she persisted, "who the hell wants to see those bleeding hearts running through Spanish trenches in 1937?"

"I agree," Smalley concurred, winking at Walters. "You're talking about a budget of, hell, I don't know—maybe sixty million."

"Have you read the script, Ray?" Walters asked.

"Years ago. But I remember those battle scenes: massed infantry assaults, aerial dogfights, armor, artillery, thousands of extras, a mix of nationalities, and it's a period piece. Every prop, every costume, has to be researched for authenticity. It's a monster, Harry."

Aurora felt relieved. She wasn't alone.

"Forgetting the material," she said, "I think we have to discuss Adrian Summers."

Walters knew that Aurora had had a fling with Summers when she worked at CBS.

"I hate doing this." She chewed her lip. "But he's an integral part of the project."

"I understand," Walters said.

Aurora glanced at Smalley.

The hawklike chief of production said, "Nothing you say will leave this room. You have my word."

Aurora sighed. "Summers kicked the Monkey years ago, but when his son drowned he fell apart. After he returned from Mexico his office became a shooting gallery. I was at CBS at the time."

"So was I," Walters reminded her.

"But you ran the network from New York. I was at the studio. I saw the Monkey."

"Adrian was hooked in Vietnam," Walters said coolly. "He was badly wounded and underwent years of reconstructive surgery. He was heavily doped up for months. He became an addict not by choice but by circumstance. His son's death was a setback, but he's been clean for years."

"How do you know that?" Smalley asked.

"I had Wexler do some checking."

"Silvi left him," Aurora said. "She's taken a house at Malibu not far from my place. I've seen her walking alone on the beach." Almost to herself she added, "I thought she was . . ."

"She was what?" Walters pressed.

"Very attractive."

"What does their divorce have to do with anything?" Walters asked.

"It's not a good sign. Silvi stuck by him through the worst of it."

Aurora rose and rubbed her wrist nervously. "I know there

were stories about me and Adrian. Nothing very profound ever happened. We had a moment, nothing more. I care about this studio and what I have to say is totally objective.

"Placing a project of this size in the hands of an emotional cripple is courting disaster. We all know Adrian was a major talent. His early work was very special . . . that play he wrote . . . when was it?"

"In '75," said Walters.

"Terrific piece," Smalley added.

"I know that . . . I know that," Aurora said, "but he hasn't done anything in years. He's shlepped that Spanish script around forever." She sighed heavily. "This sounds heartless but how can you send a reformed junkie off to Spain to produce an epic like *The Volunteers?*"

"That's my problem, isn't it?" Walters's voice assumed a hard edge.

"I agree with Aurora," Smalley chimed in. "We'll be the joke of the town. And what about our Kraut CEO in New York? What's Schuller and the board going to say?"

"Fuck Schuller and the board!" Aurora snapped, and turned to Walters. "I'm thinking of you, Harry. You've got the best track record in the business. Why run the risk?"

Walters and Smalley exchanged quick glances. Everything she said was true. Her comments reflected the fire storm on the horizon. This was the scam's first challenge—it was "in house" but it had to be faced.

Walters rose. "It's risky, I grant you that. But I've been around long enough to know that now and then you take the risk and you remember a man's best day. *The Volunteers* is a great screenplay about a unique moment in modern world history. I've always been intrigued by it."

Trailing wisps of smoke, he crossed the spacious office and studied the Ava Gardner poster. After a moment he turned to them. His pale blue eyes radiated authority and intelligence. You would follow him into hell itself, Aurora thought.

He spoke to them as a teacher lecturing his pupils.

"Your objections are well founded. *The Volunteers* is epical, an immense canvas not easily captured on film; and Adrian's stability and stamina are unknown factors. But I can make the same case for any producer, star, or director working on our cheapest pot-

45

boiler. We depend on men and women we hardly know. We do business with people that we would not invite into our homes.

"Every time that camera rolls, our fate hangs in the balance and yet we remain anonymous. We win no awards. We sign no autographs. The locusts don't surround us at industry functions. We're ridiculed because we finance films that are without any artistic merit. We do it because movies don't hang in museums. They depend on mass, worldwide audience acceptance. Yet every so often we manage to underwrite a picture we're proud of.

"We're modern-day Medicis, trying to keep an American art form alive and vibrant. But in order for any art form to survive it must challenge the boundaries of its form. We either meet that challenge or dry up and atrophy.

"*The Volunteers* represents the most challenging property we've ever considered. From 1936 to 1939 Madrid was the frontier that separated liberty and slavery. It was in Spain that the two incompatible forces of freedom and fascism first collided.

"It was a pivotal moment in modern world history and it marked the last time that men and women from all over the world volunteered their lives to preserve someone else's freedom. Those volunteers fought against the same forces that overran Europe only months after Madrid fell. Spain was the proving ground for Hitler and Mussolini. The democracies turned their backs on Republican Spain but the will of those volunteers and the Spanish Loyalists was never broken. It was the last great lost cause. Adrian's screenplay captures all this and more.

"The era of compulsively moronic and sadistic films with little or no story value is not going to last forever. The audience is getting older and they may want to escape from the trivia we give them. *The Volunteers* is a film in the grand manner about a war that was fought on moral grounds and deeply felt, and if we're lucky, it just might take the audience back to a time when there were such things as moral choices."

He sat down and with finality said, "I want to make this picture."

There was a palpable silence. Smalley thought Walters's performance was worthy of an Academy nomination.

"Does anyone else know about this?" Aurora finally asked.

"Frank Solish."

"What did he say?"

"Depending on the cast, he can get significant advances from the key foreign markets."

"What about the young audience?" Smalley asked.

"As I said, Ray, the Spanish Civil War was perhaps the only one in which young men and women from all over the world volunteered to fight for freedom. It's the greatest underdog story of all time. This is a *movie* movie. The kids have never seen anything like it."

"Suppose you're wrong," Aurora said.

Walters sighed. "I'll resign and go back to Broadway and have some fun for a change."

"Will you take me with you?" she asked coyly.

"What would I do without you? But we're not going to fail. Adrian is due here in an hour. Have him met at the gate and escort him to my office; but don't reveal anything. Just be nice."

"I'm always nice," she said.

"Good—because he'll need all the support we can give him. And, Ray, that goes for everyone in production."

"It's your money," Smalley said.

"No. It's the stockholders' money."

"When did you get this idea, Harry?" Aurora asked.

"Ten years ago when I first read the script. I've been hoping the property would come out of litigation at a time when we were cash rich. Well, it's happened." He paused. "I'll see you back here at eleven-thirty."

As Aurora left, she failed to see Smalley give Walters a surreptitious thumbs up.

A BRIGHT WINTER SUN SLICED THROUGH THE TALL, STATELY BUILDINGS, painting Park Avenue in abstract patterns of light and shadow. Surreal clumps of black ice, the last vestiges of the blizzard, clung to curbsides. The breath of pedestrians and the exhaust of vehicles vaporized in the frigid air.

Salvatore Parnelli and Frank Solish relaxed in the rear of the sumptuous corporate limousine; a glass divider sealed them off from the chauffeur. The stereo played Sinatra and the TV was tuned to the business channel.

Parnelli poured some cognac and handed the glass to Solish, who nodded his appreciation and sneezed onto Parnelli's hand.

"Jesus Christ, Frank," Parnelli said, wiping his hand on his cashmere chesterfield, "what the hell is it with you?"

"Sorry. I can't shake this cold."

"No wonder. You fly from here to the Springs almost every week. That's a fifty-degree swing in temperature."

"Can't be helped. Resnick is too old to travel."

"That old man knocked down a lot of people in his heyday," Parnelli mused. "Hell of a career. He started with Moey Dalitz and the Purple Gang in Cleveland. He got control of the West Coast Teamsters and made a lot of money for a lot of people."

"He still does," Solish said. "This scam may be his biggest score."

Parnelli stared pensively out of the tinted windows. "That was a hell of an idea Walters came up with—a runaway picture. That locks in the score—even the wiseguys will go for the seventy-five-dollar buyout."

"Harry's smart and lucky," Solish said. "He's got that magical touch."

"Has he hired this junkie? What's his name?"

"Adrian Summers. They should be meeting right about now."

"Who else is in on this?"

"You, me, Walters, Wexler, Smalley, and the Old Man in the desert."

"You sure that redheaded broad isn't involved?"

"Absolutely."

"What about all the studio help?"

Solish wiped his nose and stared off at an attractive woman who had just gotten out of a cab. "The staff people won't know anything. We're maintaining our normal production schedule."

"Well, I have to trust you fellas to handle your part. My end is off and running."

"What time is your flight?"

"Seven-fifteen P.M. Qantas to Auckland and then Squillante's private jet to Rarotonga."

"Funny, I never heard of Rarotonga."

"It's in the Cook Islands."

"Near Australia?"

"It's two thousand miles north of New Zealand."

"Who does it belong to?"

"It belongs to itself. It's the capital of the Cook Islands."

"How does Squillante fit in?"

"Count Aldo Squillante is an honored Knight of Malta. He's my connection to the bank in Palermo—Santa Maria della Croce. They launder hot money for Pakistani opium dealers, the Emir of Abu Dhabi, PFLP terrorists, and Colombian *coqueros*. They got wires to Panama, London, Paris, Luxembourg, and that BCCI-controlled branch in Atlanta."

The phone console buzzed and up front the chauffeur held the receiver to his ear. Solish pressed an intercom button.

"What is it, Ronnie?"

"The Waldorf?"

"Yeah. Circle the hotel until I tell you to park."

"Right, sir."

They stopped at a light on Forty-fourth Street.

"Tell me, Sal, how do you arrange collateral for three billion dollars?"

"You'd never understand. Besides, it's none of your business. I got my end. You got yours."

"I know that," Solish said amicably, "but it interests me."

"You really want to hear this?"

"Yes. I do."

Parnelli sighed. "There aren't fifty people in the world who understand this, but it goes something like this. Squillante transfers two billion from Banco della Croce to Banco Nacional de Bolivia—from there we pick up another eight hundred million in Colombian narcodollars. Now the two point eight billion is wired to a dummy corporation at Credite Hollandia in Amsterdam—it sits there for three, four weeks. Then it goes to another dummy account at Crown Security Bank, Cayman Islands.

"From there it's wired to Banque Belgique in Brussels and it sits for a few weeks before being transferred to Europa's branch in Luxembourg. Upon receipt the Europa-Luxembourg laundry wires the money to Sirocco's account at City National, Chicago."

"Christ . . ." Solish shook his head in amazement. "Who puts up collateral for the initial transfers?"

"The whole transaction is bonded by Centurion Insurance Limited in Rarotonga."

"What's in it for them?"

"Twenty-five million shares of Gemstone at the buyout price."

"But that buyout offer is going to collapse."

"So what? We're gonna sell out at the top. Centurion winds up with a twenty-five-million-dollar profit for bonding the three billion. The beauty of this scam is no one gets fucked except the public."

"But how does the three billion filter back to the Palermo bank?"

"The principal is withdrawn when my offer caves in and it goes back down the line the same way it went up the line."

"You're right, Sal. It's too much for me."

"Don't worry about it. Wexler will get it. He's a smart Jew."

There it was again. After the scam, Solish vowed to himself, he'd do his best to have Parnelli straightened out.

"How are you guys gonna deal with Schuller?" Boom Boom asked.

"Resnick is handling that."

"That Kraut bastard has strong connections in D.C. and Wall Street. He blocked the Jap takeover two years ago, and he could stop us cold."

"It's being taken care of, Sal."

They were approaching the line of gleaming limousines parked in front of the Waldorf.

"Who you got in the suite?" Parnelli asked.

"One of Lew Freeman's specials. You won't be disappointed."

"You know something, Frank," Parnelli said. "You're losing that Brooklyn Yid accent. Lately I notice you're rolling those fucking r's."

FROM HER OFFICE WINDOW AURORA WATCHED THE VINTAGE BENTLEY park in front of the administration building. Her secretary, Maggie, got out of the passenger side and waited as Adrian Summers stared off at LeRoy Street where an enormous head of Fidel Castro seemed to be floating in midair. The prop was suspended by a crane cable and held upright by a team of grips.

From her vantage point Aurora noticed the sunlight framing Adrian's fine, aesthetic features. His face had been reconstructed by army surgeons but his eyes were haunted by savage secrets. God, how she had loved him—at least she thought so at the time. It was the summer of '78. That was the season they were all at the network.

Walters was then head of programming, she worked in program development, and Adrian produced a Tarzan ripoff series called *Trader Jim*. The TV series was after his Broadway play and before he had written his acclaimed screenplay, the one that made Julia Castle a star. So they were all connected in that unique incestuousness peculiar to Hollywood.

She turned from the window and shivered slightly as she remembered their ill-fated affair. She had been devastated when it ended. But Adrian had warned her: Whatever it was they shared was transient. Meaningless. There was the boy. And Silvi. The dark-haired beauty. The keeper of secrets. The gardener in Needle Park. The custodian of nightmares.

Still, Aurora had no regrets. It was one of those deeply felt affairs that never leaves you.

She walked to the oval mirror on the far wall and studied her reflected image. Her eyes were clear and alive. Her bright red hair was thick and glowing. Her broad nose complemented her wide mouth and Slavic cheekbones. In any other business she would have been desirable and sought after, but she had made it behind the camera. She was a power player. She could approve the start of a picture. She was one of the boys—"a prince." It hadn't been that way with Adrian, but that was ancient history—Hollywood mythology. In the last analysis everything in Dreamland was mythic. They were all surreal figures in a Daliesque landscape. They weren't real. They made movies.

There was a polite knock at the door and Maggie ushered Adrian into the office. For a moment they stared at one another before Aurora went to him, hugged him, and kissed him lightly on the mouth.

His breath was sweet and the fragrance of his aftershave lotion triggered a flood of memories. The scar line running from the corner of his right eye down to his jaw had discolored since she had last seen him.

"You look marvelous," he said. "I've been thrilled for you. No one deserved success more or worked harder for it."

"I've been fortunate. Working for Harry Walters is a dream come true."

"He was always a straight shooter. A good soldier."

"He still is," she said.

Adrian glanced at the French poster of *Moonrise* with its Palme d'Or seal and hoped his tone of voice was nonchalant. "Do you have any idea what this sudden summons is about?"

"I'll let Harry tell you."

Walters came around his desk smiling, his hand extended to Adrian.

"By God, it's good to see you, Adrian," he said, shaking hands. "It's been what? Twelve years?"

"Fifteen."

"Right—*Trader Jim*. Christ, what thin ice we skated on in those days."

"In retrospect it seems like fun."

"Maybe so, but at the time it was hell. Always up against an air date. No scripts—ah, well—ancient history."

Walters introduced Adrian to Wexler and Smalley. The two men nodded and stared at Adrian as if studying an artifact.

Walters indicated a chair. "Have a seat, Adrian."

The recessed ceiling lights had been dimmed except for a solitary pencil beam shining down directly over Walters's desk.

"Anyone care for coffee, Coke, something stronger?"

"I'll have a black coffee," Aurora said.

"The same," Adrian added.

Walters glanced at Wexler and Smalley. "How about you fellows?"

"Nothing, thanks," Wexler said.

"Me neither," said Smalley, "I'm coffeed out."

Walters pressed the intercom button.

"Gloria, two black coffees, please."

"I'll have a Sweet'n Low," Adrian said.

"Did you get that, Gloria?"

"Yes, sir."

Walters sat in his high-backed leather chair and leaned back. "You look remarkably well, Adrian."

"For an ex-junkie." The second the words left his lips he wanted them back.

An embarrassed silence enveloped the office but Walters relaxed the tension with casual ease. "We're all 'ex-somethings,' but we haven't got drawers full of medals. You do. You paid a terrible price for serving in that godforsaken conflict. The trauma of that nightmare was brilliantly dramatized in your play. You have nothing to apologize for. You kicked heroin. Most of us can't kick nicotine."

The door opened and the secretary swept in, served the coffee, and handed Walters a fax.

"Just came in."

While Walters read the fax, Adrian felt his pulse quicken and his cheeks flush. The presence of Wexler and Smalley testified to the fact that this was a meeting of some importance and the antici-pation was taking its toll. What did he have that they could possibly want? He wished he hadn't mentioned the heroin addiction. The remark had been triggered by nerves and overwhelming insecurity. He couldn't handle the fact that he was an invited guest in a Dream City throne room.

Walters tossed the fax into an Out box and addressed Wexler, "Marco's been released from the hospital. He'll resume shooting tonight."

Wexler nodded. "I'll notify Fireman's Insurance."

"Imagine the luck, Adrian," Walters said. "We're shooting a remake of Hemingway's 'Macomber Affair' in Kenya and out of the entire crew, this viper chose to bite the director. They had to fly the snake and the director back to Mombasa for venom tests. During the flight the snake died; but the director survived."

"Served the snake right," Smalley said. "Never bite a director."

"That snake should be given an award posthumously," Aurora grumbled.

"I don't disagree," Walters said amiably. "Marco is a superb director but a disaster as a human being."

Walters lit his third Sherman of the day. The smoke rose above his head and drifted up into the strong light beam. Aurora knew the suspense was killing Adrian, but Walters was playing it out with his unerring sense of timing and drama.

"I may be a lone voice in the wilderness," Walters finally began, "but I believe we've abandoned our historic traditions. We've lost touch with our heritage. We've forgotten the Magic Lantern." He rose and stood in the shadowy area just behind his desk. "Since the silents our technological advances have been extraordinary but our product has been pedestrian."

He moved closer to his desk so that the hot light chiseled his face in a silvery light. Walters could find a key light in a cave, Aurora thought.

"We make fast food, Adrian," he continued, "safe, tasty fatburgers. We spend a fortune on junk movies. And more often than not the audience show up because they have no choice. They have nowhere to go. We all make the same pictures.

"Some work is better than others but it's almost impossible for any movie, no matter how dreadful, not to get a rave review *somewhere*. Cable systems have spawned self-proclaimed film critics, vaudevillians, performers, some of whom have become showbiz icons, and almost without exception, they'll give a junk film a better break than a serious film. After all, what can they say about a car crash? A homosexual ghost? A burning building? A drug bust? A killer dyke?

"We've lost our way. And any art form that abandons its vision to perceived commerciality is doomed. Where are the dice rollers? Where are those old-time robber barons—those pioneers who perceived that movies were destined to become the universal language of mankind . . .

"Think of the silents, Adrian. No zoom lenses. No Steadicams. No Chapman crane. No Sun Guns. No rear projection. No front projection. No Panavision lenses.

"Hand-cranked cameras and slow, grainy film. And what did they turn out? Magnificent works. Murals. Motion pictures in the grand manner. Think of it. *Ben-Hur, Greed, Potemkin, Birth of a Nation, Four Horsemen of the Apocalypse, Quo Vadis, Ten Days That Shook the World.*

"And the directors—Eisenstein, Von Stroheim, D. W. Griffith, De Mille—geniuses. Muralists. Visionaries. They gave the world enduring masterworks and illuminated history for the masses. They dared to dream. Those uneducated pioneers instinctively knew that any art form is only as healthy as the breadth of its vision."

Walters crushed the cigarette out and sat down in the hot light.

"We're a cash-rich studio, Adrian," he said matter-of-factly. "Our fatburgers have done well. But it's time to resurrect the historic grandeur of our past. It's time to undertake a great canvas." He paused dramatically before saying, "I want to make *The Volunteers* and I want you to produce it."

Adrian thought his thumping heart would burst from its cavity.

"You do have the rights to the script?" Walters asked.

"Yes. They reverted to me after the litigation." He heard himself speak but his voice seemed detached.

"You may as well know," Walters said, "that excepting myself, everyone else in this room is opposed to making the picture, but having said that, I can assure you of their absolute support."

"I've got something else to add," Aurora said. "My reader, Bradovich, wrote a scathing synopsis of the last draft of *Volunteers*. Unfortunately it's been circulated."

"No one gives a damn about Bradovich's opinion!" Walters

snapped. "Almost without exception readers are failed writers with an ax to grind."

"Well," Adrian said, "the last draft was written in '83. It could use some cutting and polishing."

"You'll be too busy to rewrite," said Walters. "I want to start principal photography no later than mid-July."

"July . . ." Adrian murmured, "that's only five months of preparation, of casting, of setting locations. Not to mention signing a director who's available and capable of handling a picture of this size."

"We can do it," Walters said confidently. "Isn't that right, Ray?"

Smalley nodded. "We'll have to marshal the troops here and abroad but, yes, it's possible."

"A lot depends on how we manage the casting," Aurora said. "The picture's loaded with international star cameos."

"We'll cast it," Walters said resolutely. "I want to open this picture Christmas '94 for Academy consideration. I want it shot in seventy millimeter. We're going to roadshow this one, Adrian. Reserved seats. This picture is either an event or it's nothing. Frank Solish is certain that he can presell Europe before we expose a frame of negative. If there ever was a picture of particular interest to Europeans, *The Volunteers* has to be it.

"The screenplay may require polishing, but I don't want to lose its scope. I want all the battle scenes. The siege of Madrid. The bombing of Guernica, the Ebro, Brunete, Jarama, the University front, and, of course, the personal stories."

"You're talking about a lot of money," Adrian said.

"Don't worry about the money. Once we have a director we'll work out a schedule and a tentative budget. The rewrite should not reflect cuts for the sake of economy."

Aurora uncrossed her legs and turned to Adrian.

"Who do you want for the rewrite?"

"Eddie Beaumont."

A pall of silence fell across the room, and eyes rolled up to the ceiling.

Aurora finally said, "Eddie Beaumont is dead."

"Not unless he died this morning," Adrian replied.

He felt heady, stoned, but his voice was firm. "I spoke to him yesterday. He's alive and well and living in Brentwood. He's about to sign off on his sixth marriage."

"I think you're mistaken," Wexler said. "Seems to me I attended Beaumont's funeral several years ago."

"Absolutely," Aurora chimed in, "his agent—that fat prick, excuse the language—I lose it when I think of that monumental hypocrite. He delivered the eulogy and made it sound as though Beaumont overdosed on social significance."

"Adrian is right," Smalley interjected, "Eddie Beaumont is alive. I saw him at The Grill with a dark-haired pussy cat. The old bastard was all over this lollipop. You're confusing Eddie with Larry Beaumont, the character actor."

Adrian said, "Eddie just finished the final draft of a ten-hour miniseries based on the life of Leon Trotsky."

"I apologize," said Aurora. "You're absolutely right. I told Bradovich to try and get CBS to co-produce it with our TV division. I hear it's a fantastic script."

"All right." Walters smiled. "Now that we've resurrected the late Eddie Beaumont, I have to say he's perfect for the project. He may be old but his credits are unmatched and his range is remarkable. From that classic spoof about airline hostesses, to the exotic tapestry of *The Life and Times of Burton,* and in between: dazzling thrillers, sensitive romances, two Oscars, four nominations, three Emmys, and a Peabody."

"There's no question that Beaumont's a distinguished writer," Aurora agreed. "The problem is, he's not current."

"Who is?" Walters asked. "We drape the mantle of genius on almost any film school graduate who happens to come up with a derivative comedy. The Spanish Civil War requires a writer with a profound sense of history. Eddie Beaumont's career spans fifty years. He's the embodiment of what the old Screen Writers Guild stood for: integrity and artistry. You want him, Adrian—you've got him." Walters paused. "By the way, is Jerry Blake still your agent?"

Adrian nodded. "But he stopped taking my calls."

"He'll take them from now on," Walters stated. "Aurora will work out a deal with Blake for the screenplay and your services as producer."

Wexler rose. "You mean an option for Adrian's services if the picture goes."

"No, Irv. I mean pay or play. No options. Now who's Beaumont's agent?"

"That fat pr——" Aurora caught herself. "That pretentious ass-hole Fred Axelrod."

"Call him."

"No," Adrian interrupted, "I'll see Eddie myself. I want him to go the distance. We'll need rewrites for location problems. Besides, I think he may be leaving the Axelrod Agency. Let me handle it."

"Fine." Walters pressed the intercom button. "Gloria?"

"Yes?"

"Call administration—I want a bungalow office on Harlow Street for Adrian Summers and three parking spaces for his production company. I want a table assigned to him in the executive dining room. And starting Monday have some experienced secretaries for Mr. Summers to interview."

Adrian felt a lightning bolt of heat scorch its way through his chest.

"And Gloria," Walters added, "be certain that the gate people are alerted. I don't want Mr. Summers being asked for credentials every day."

"They're automatically notified," she replied curtly.

"Maybe, but they even question me occasionally. Just do it."

"What shall I charge this to?"

"Use 1936—the year the Spanish Civil War began."

"One-nine-three-six?"

"Yes, now get Herb Stoner for me."

He released the intercom and addressed Smalley. "Make that number official."

"Right."

"Well, we've taken care of the producer, and hopefully the writer, now let's turn our attention to the director."

"Shouldn't we discuss the director at a separate meeting?" said Wexler, fearful that Walters was moving too fast.

"Let's discuss it now," Walters insisted. "I want this meeting to end with the key elements agreed upon. Besides, I don't need a list. I know who should direct this picture."

The console buzzed. "Herb Stoner."

Walters picked up the receiver. "Herb, I want you to plant in the trades and those cable lollipops that Gemstone Pictures has signed Adrian Summers to produce the most expensive and challenging motion picture in the studio's history." He paused. "Yes, I'll wait."

Aurora wondered what had triggered the frenzy in the otherwise laid-back Walters. What strange virus had infected him? Why the rush to production? Maybe *The Volunteers* had suddenly received some attention. The international rise of multinational financing companies might have fueled a burst of offers for the script.

Smalley and Wexler exchanged a quick glance, wondering about Walters's choice of director. Whoever it was had to have a certain panache, and top-drawer credentials. If not, the scam would be too obvious. The director was the ball game. Summers had been out of it for years, but he was no novice. He'd smell a rat if they weren't careful. It was a critical decision; the director had to be gifted but unstable, someone who would crack under stress.

Adrian touched a handkerchief to his forehead, dabbing at the beads of sweat oozing out of his pores. Something was definitely lurking under Walters's rush of euphoria for the project, but it didn't matter. He was back. The office. The trades. Phones ringing. He couldn't wait to tell Silvi. It was happening. The "why" was irrelevant. He was back in action. Once his executioners read the trades they'd be on the phone congratulating him with cries of "Let's do lunch, sweetheart!" It was part of the Dream City follies—when the dead rose, you took them to lunch.

"Yes, Herb. A buzz. No title," Walters instructed the publicity director. "We'll wait for casting and organize an opulent, old-fashioned press dinner at Chasen's. No . . . no. Spago is too trendy. This is a distinguished project. It requires a traditional restaurant. But that's for later. Right now, just get a buzz going. Adrian Summers will be on the lot as of Monday and I want every courtesy extended to him. Thanks, Herb."

"You were about to tell us your top choice for director," Aurora said.

As Walters lit another cigarette, Adrian asked, "Can you spare one of those?"

"Of course—forgive me. I thought I was the only one who used these things."

Adrian's fingers trembled as he lit the Sherman.

"In my view," Walters spoke in a low, confidential tone, "the only man capable of doing justice to this picture is Paul Scott."

Aurora was speechless.

Smalley glanced at Wexler and rolled his eyes. Walters had gone too far. The scam was in jeopardy.

"He's a great director." Adrian's words came through the smoke. "Trouble is he's disappeared."

"That's right," Smalley said, "he went off the edge: coke, pussy, horses—Christ knows what else."

"He made two disasters before he fell off the world," Wexler said, "one for Universal and one for Columbia."

"Julia Castle broke his heart," said Aurora, then paused and added, "You all know that I'm opposed to this project but I have to admit that a healthy, stable Paul Scott is a superb idea. The man has crafted three of the greatest films I've ever seen."

"You're prejudiced because he directed *Moonrise,*" Smalley said. "You got yourself a trip to Cannes and won a prize."

"I don't consider *Moonrise* to be a great film. I'm talking about *The Christopher Connection, Prophet,* and *Discovery.*"

Walters addressed Adrian. "Assuming we can locate Scott and he's got his act together, would he be acceptable to you?"

"Absolutely. I worked on *The Discovery* with Paul. I've never seen anyone pour more dedication and creativity into a film."

"Irv, who's Scott's agent of record?" Walters asked Wexler.

"I believe it's Marcus Kirgo."

"Start with him, then check with Scott's business manager."

"Right."

"Ray, call the Directors' Guild. They must have a forwarding address for Scott's residuals." Walters turned to Aurora. "Are you still friendly with Julia Castle?"

"Yes."

"Phone her. See if she knows anything."

"She's in rehearsal for a Broadway play. I don't know if she'll talk about Paul, but I'll try."

"Good. If we have to hire a professional investigator we will."

Walters rose, signaling the meeting was over. "I respect everyone's concern, but I'm going forward and I expect your total support. This is a dangerous undertaking, but the great producers understood the need to risk everything—to roll the dice on something they believed in. In this business the effort almost always exceeds the achievement, but there is no virtue in playing it safe. Safety is mediocrity. I learned how to take risks on Broadway. There is no greater gamble in show business than producing a Broadway musical. One critic, one self-proclaimed savant, can close you. But not the movies. Today, almost any picture can fill a double truck ad with critical raves from cable personalities. We also have the benefit of ancillary markets: commercial TV, cable, cassettes, and syndication.

"This project may not be as risky as it would appear to be. Who knows? Every movie is a delusion seeking an illusion. I'll see all of you at dailies. Adrian and I are going to have lunch."

Aurora walked slowly along Chaplin Street. She questioned herself as if undergoing an imaginary cross-examination. Why the urgency to acquire and produce *The Volunteers?* Why would Walters ignore the collective advice of his staff? Why would he gamble on Adrian's mental stability? Why compound the risk by selecting Paul Scott to direct?

And underscoring those questions was Jerry Blake's mention of Solish and Walters being present in the same desert restaurant frequented by Leo Resnick. Coincidence? Probably. Le Vallauris was the only classy restaurant in Palm Springs; but still they hadn't been visiting the desert for the waters—something very strange was brewing.

She sighed, shook her head, and proceeded to play devil's advocate to her own fears. Number one: Adrian had been clean for the past two years. A friend at the Betty Ford Clinic had confirmed that Adrian not only was clean, he was also off methadone. And despite his fall from grace, Adrian was no willow. He had survived the war, and almost endless surgery, the loss of his son, and the dissolution of his marriage. He had kicked heroin and managed to hold on to his sanity. He was tough. Very tough. Maybe he *could* muscle this thing through. As to Paul Scott—if he could be found and if he was sane—there wasn't a director in town who could hold his viewfinder. And God knows Scott had every right to fall off the wheel; Julia Castle could drive a saint to snort schmeck.

As to the size and cost of *The Volunteers*, if Walters stood for anything it was showmanship. He was a gambler in the grand manner, and although highly successful, he had to be frustrated with the imbecilic commercial films they turned out year after year. What better time to underwrite an epic film? Gemstone was a wealthy studio, and Harry had been right about the general creative atrophy of the industry. They had abandoned their birthright. And despite Bradovich's bitchy critique of the script, *The Volunteers* had all the fundamental qualities that made for box office: life-and-death conflict, moral choices, doomed romance, and, in the end, undaunted men and women risking everything in the face of overwhelming odds.

She left the bright sun and entered the cool shade of a sound-stage. The sign on the stage door read: *"Backwash*—a closed set. No visitors."* The security guard saluted her. The red flasher whirled. They were shooting. She waited and the terrible doubts returned. Why did Harry Walters appoint himself to be the deus ex machina for Adrian Summers? The question hung in the air. Ominous. Unanswerable.

THE TAXI SLOWED AS IT APPROACHED THE WALDORF, WHERE A LINE of limousines inched forward, waiting to discharge their formally attired passengers. Max Schuller ordered the Pakistani taxi driver to double-park at the entrance.

"Must be a big event tonight," the driver commented as he threw the flag.

"It's a fund raiser for the governor," Schuller replied and handed the dark-skinned man a ten-dollar bill. "Keep it."

Anticipating the bitterly cold night air, he pulled on his gloves, adjusted his homburg, and turned his coat collar up. He got out of the taxi and sidestepped between limousine bumpers to the sidewalk. Excusing himself, he moved quickly through the milling crowd and entered the lobby.

The few seconds of exposure to the frigid air accentuated the warmth of the hotel's imposing lobby. Schuller removed his gloves and walked deliberately to the Tower elevator. The gleaming brass doors opened and a tall, jeweled, ball-gowned, fur-wrapped woman came out of the elevator with her tuxedoed escort.

"I'm not kidding, Jason," she snarled, "fifteen fucking minutes and we're out!"

"Fine with me," the man replied meekly.

Schuller entered the elevator, pressed the button, and shook his head. How fortunate he was. The divorce had been expensive but worth every cent. He was free. No wife. No children. No avaricious relatives. He was truly liberated and he enjoyed it. His bizarre sexual appetites were tabloid material but what did it matter?

He exercised absolute control over Gemstone's aging board of directors and had the unqualified support of Ira Kosstrin, the ninety-eight-year-old surviving founder of Gemstone. Having successfully fought off Yosuta's takeover bid, Schuller was now immune to inside or outside predators. Wisely, he had given Solish and Walters a free hand, and they had produced consistent profits for Gemstone. The studio enjoyed the major share of the box office receipts for the past five years—a record unmatched in recent film history.

The elevator lurched to a halt; the doors opened and as he proceeded down the thickly carpeted corridor, he felt a sense of satisfaction and anticipation. His Nazi past remained sealed in the State Department archives. America had been good to him. He had succeeded beyond his own ambitious dreams. He served on the board of directors of half a dozen corporations. He owned a majority interest in an undervalued Oklahoma-based oil company and had recently acquired a Thoroughbred breeding farm in Lexington. His mansion on the Hudson was the weekly playground of the rich and famous. Women were attracted to him not for his solid Prussian looks, but for his power. There was something theological about power; one only had to know how to use it.

The single cloud in his otherwise silver-lined life was his medical problem; but the Inderal had stabilized his irregular heartbeat and Dr. Martens had assured him, "Neither work nor sex will kill you, only stress kills."

He turned right at the far end of the corridor, thinking he had managed to dump stressful problems on that anxiety-ridden Jew; but Solish never complained. The monkey-faced little man was a climber who groveled for favors. Walters was another matter. The handsome, reserved studio chief was secure unto himself.

Life couldn't be better, Schuller thought as he slipped the key into the lock and opened the door to the corporate suite.

She was standing behind the bar sipping champagne and smoking a long pink cigarette. A splash of blond hair fell across her shoulders as if it just happened that way. She had a strong, wide nose and high cheekbones. She wore a classic black dress that made a case for simplicity.

She smiled. "Good evening. I'm Magda von Stellhoff."

"Good evening," Schuller replied as he removed his overcoat. My God, he thought, she's stunning. Lew Freeman had described her specialty but hadn't touched upon her beauty.

"Come have some champagne," she said softly.

There was something cunning and untamed in her dark blue eyes. She was like him—*Herrenvolk.* German aristocracy. The S.S. poster girl. Himmler's pure Aryan. A Valkyrian goddess of fire and ice. They would get along fine.

He picked up his glass, raised it, and toasted. "To you, my dear."

"Good health," she replied and stared at him over the rim of her glass.

She came around the bar and curved herself into him, fondled him and felt him grow hard. She put her lips to his ear and whispered, "Go into the bedroom, take off your clothes."

He felt his heartbeat accelerate. "Are you in a rush?"

"On the contrary. We can begin. Then have a leisurely dinner and"—she smiled sexily—"continue."

"As you wish." He bowed slightly, placed his glass on the zinc-topped bar, and strode out.

She waited a moment, then removed a premeasured vial of propranolol hydrochloride from her handbag and poured the contents into Schuller's champagne glass.

Resnick had explained to her that propranolol hydrochloride was a chemical blocking agent used to treat abnormal heart rhythms. It was sold by prescription under the name Inderal—a drug that Schuller used regularly. It was tasteless, colorless, and difficult to trace. Anything exceeding three hundred milligrams would produce classic angina symptoms—shortening of breath, chest pains, and finally massive coronary occlusion.

On two previous occasions she had set someone up to be hit but had never acted as an assassin herself. Tonight's assignment unnerved her, but she was in no position to deny Leo Resnick anything. The old man had been her mentor and made her a small fortune and, more importantly, offered her the mantle of his protection. Her fee for this evening's work was two hundred thousand dollars in Swiss francs. The money had already been wired to her numbered account in Bern.

She picked up both glasses of champagne, which were easily distinguished—the one with Inderal was full, while her glass was less than half full. She tossed her hair, straightened her wide shoulders, and walked through an alcove leading to the master bedroom.

Schuller was in the bathroom. His suit, shirt, and tie hung neatly in the mirrored closet. She placed the champagne glasses on a night table and pulled the bedspread down.

She slipped off her dress, removed her bra and pantyhose.

"Leave your shoes on, please," the German-accented voice instructed.

He was standing naked at the bathroom door. His soft, pink body was almost hairless. He reminded her of a pink-bellied porpoise. She smiled and, wearing only her high-heeled shoes, crossed to the night table, picked up the champagne glasses, and handed him the full one.

"We must finish our champagne," she said. "Champagne loosens all my inhibitions."

She touched her glass to his, tilted her head back, and swallowed the golden bubbles, but her eyes never left his. She watched him drain his glass.

"Good. Now, please lie down."

She knelt over him and began to tease him: tasting, nibbling, her hands moving at the same time—touching, squeezing. She moved down and he felt her hot breath and darting tongue light a fire in his belly. She saw his eyes close and his fist clench.

She stopped. Then started. Bringing him to the edge, then moving away. He pleaded for her to grant him release but she toyed with him. After a moment she felt him suddenly quiver and saw his face contort. For a second, she thought, he would reach orgasm—that she had miscalculated—but she hadn't. His face was blue. He gasped for breath and clutched his chest. His eyes rolled up so that only the whites showed. A few words escaped his purple lips. "Call for help . . . I . . . I'm having an attack. I'm . . ."

She rose from the bed, picked up her pantyhose, and pulled them on. She walked over to a full-length mirror and slipped her dress on, adjusting it carefully. She crossed to the night table and dropped both champagne glasses into her large handbag.

She glanced down at Schuller. His lips were drawn back over

his teeth. His eyes had rolled up into his head and his feet quivered. She lit a cigarette and waited until all his movements ceased.

She crushed the cigarette out and flushed it down the bathroom toilet, then re-entered the bedroom and covered his body with a blanket.

"Auf Wiedersehen." She smiled and doused the lights.

10

HARRY WALTERS SIPPED THE STEAMING JAMAICAN COFFEE AND glanced nervously at the kitchen clock. The digital numbers read 7:10 A.M.—10:10 in New York. What the hell had happened? Where was Frank? Had something gone wrong?

Uncharacteristically, he lit an early morning cigarette. Inhaling deeply, he felt the rush of nicotine calm his jangled nerves. It was still early, he told himself. Everything's in place. Resnick didn't miss—not in this kind of thing.

He forced himself to think about the previous evening. His dinner with Carla had been pleasant. He had switched off his own problems and managed to pay attention to her abiding concerns about their daughter's failed marriage. He had assured Carla that Lisa was strong, bright, and capable of dealing with a divorce; in any case she was still young, attractive, and well out of a bad situation.

Buoyed by the excellent food and fine wine, they had come home in good spirits, and once in bed, Harry found himself admiring his wife's still-firm, youthful figure and graceful beauty. Uninhibited, they made love easily, and he found her to be every bit as passionate as the day they married. What distressed Carla about their marriage was the nature of his business. He was the king of dreams and she had no role to play in the royal court. She was a wife, and in Dreamland wives were less important than their maids. Everyone wanted a reliable maid; hardly anyone wanted a wife.

The phone rang sharply and Walters grabbed the receiver. "Hello."

"This is Charles Carlson calling from Circle Promotions in Miami," the recorded male voice intoned. "We can offer you a hundred phone calls to sell your product for the price of only one call. If you're interested, press one."

Out of sheer anger Walters pressed "one." The voice continued, "Please leave your name and the product you have to sell—an agent will phone."

"My name is Carmen Miranda and I sell kiddie-porn."

He hung up and shook his head in disgust. The whole universe was wired. The computers were in charge. He stubbed out the cigarette and dropped a slice of rye bread in the toaster. The phone rang again and for a fleeting second he wondered if it was a call back from the Miami computer.

"Hello?" he said tentatively.

"You alone?" Solish asked.

"Yes, Frank."

"I'm afraid I've got bad news. A little over an hour ago, a maid at the Waldorf discovered Max Schuller's body. He apparently stayed overnight in the corporate suite and died in his sleep."

"My God. I talked to him Tuesday. What was it?"

They were speaking in a prearranged code as a precaution against a tap.

"Dr. Greene's preliminary finding is death caused by massive coronary occlusion. As you know, Schuller had a long history of heart problems."

"I'm sorry to hear this. Max was bright, supportive, and, above all, a gentleman. I'll miss him."

"We'll all miss him. The press has been calling for a statement. I'd like to read this to you before Lew Freeman sends it out."

"Go ahead," Walters said, thinking that once again Magda had performed magnificently.

" 'The board of directors of Gemstone Pictures deeply regrets the passing of its chairman and chief operating officer, Max Schuller. Mr. Schuller's selfless dedication and devotion not only to Gemstone Pictures but to the entire motion picture industry will be missed. Paragraph. Frank Solish, vice president in charge of world-wide distribution and sales, has been named interim chairman of Gemstone Pictures.' The rest of it has to do with his bio and funeral arrangements. Can I release this statement?"

"Sure. It's fine."

"When can we talk?"

"You tell me."

"Say six-thirty P.M. my time."

"Okay . . . where's the Patriot Missile?"

"On the Concorde."

"I'll call Aurora."

"Right. And Harry, don't forget to have the studio flag lowered to half-mast."

"Yeah . . . Be nice if we could find a swastika—take care, Frank."

Aurora hung up the phone feeling light-headed but wide awake. Events were spinning out of synch. She felt trapped in a silent movie—people, places, and things blurred past her in a surreal rush, and yet there was a curious common thread to the seemingly disjointed, disparate happenings.

She swung her legs over the side of the bed, stepped into her panties, and pulled on a Mickey Mouse T-shirt. She walked to the terrace window with its expansive view of the ocean and watched the angry waves explode against the breakwater. She bit her lip and replayed the recent events: the swift "pay or play" deal for *The Volunteers,* including Adrian as producer. Walters almost never made anyone pay or play until he was certain the film would go. And there was the unusual instant approval of the ancient Eddie Beaumont and the suggestion of the eclectic and elusive Paul Scott as director—and now Schuller checking out and Solish assuming control. And underscoring everything was the lingering shadow of Leo Resnick.

The bathroom door opened and Lamont Ferris appeared with a towel wrapped around his midriff. A thick growth of matted black hair covered his belly, chest, and shoulders; it reminded Aurora of climbing ivy. Ferris was a television director who had achieved a certain renown for having directed TV movies concerned with medical problems. It was said that Ferris gave great disease. Aurora tolerated him because he was harmless and safe.

"Anything wrong?" he asked.

"No. Want some coffee?"

"Sure."

"That call sounded like trouble."

"Max Schuller died last night."

She picked up the phone and buzzed the kitchen.

"No sugar," Ferris said as he slipped his jeans on.

"Carmela . . . *Sí* . . . *dos cafés sin azucar y dos jugos de naranja en seguida, gracias.*"

"Schuller was always sick, wasn't he?" Ferris asked.

"Yes. He had a congenital heart problem."

She went into the bathroom. Ferris checked his watch and pulled his turtleneck sweater on. He had a ten o'clock meeting at Fox to discuss a teleplay about an alcoholic cop who shoots his AA instructor. The story was typical night-time soap thinly wrapped in social significance.

Aurora returned to the bedroom wearing a velour jogging suit.

"Don't wait for me," she said. "Have some juice and coffee."

"What about you?"

"I'm taking Red for a run."

"You want to go to Lochman's party Sunday?"

"I don't think so."

"Listen, uh . . . you have a script at the studio—I think it's a Perkins–Swackhammer project about a kid who's struck by lightning, becomes a god, and changes the world. I wonder if you would——"

"I wouldn't," she interrupted. "Remember one salient fact, Lamont: Fucking is fucking and business is business. Besides, we're not interested in that piece of crap."

She jogged along the foaming surf line. The surging sea was topped by whitecaps palette-knifed into the cresting waves. Way out on the horizon a single beam of brilliant sunlight illuminated a patch of sea.

"Come on, Red!" she shouted. An Irish setter with a glowing coat bounded along beside her.

She passed an aged muscular man who suddenly veered off and

plunged into the sea. The Irish setter barked at the wizened man and took a few tentative steps into the freezing surf.

"Come here, Red!" Aurora shouted. "Right now!" The dog responded and raced back to join his puffing master.

She jogged thinking about the Spanish picture. Fuck it, why worry? If it went over budget, so be it. Gemstone was a rich studio. And who knew, maybe it would work. Stranger things had happened. Walters might be right—one could never dismiss those three Tonys. Harry was an astute showman, and a great epic film was overdue. Yes . . . why not? As for Paul Scott, he was capable of excellence—*if* he could be found and *if* he was together. One could certainly empathize with the missing director. Being married to Julia Castle was asking for trouble. She was just too damn beautiful, too talented, too wild—but then Cannes was a long time ago. Julia had matured. She had studied. She took her craft seriously. There probably was no room for any lasting romance. With luck they would find Scott and he would be reasonably sane.

The whole thing might work. Just contemplating a film of that magnitude was stimulating.

She slowed down as she noticed her dog trying to reach a large sea creature tossed up onto the surf line. She trotted over and saw, at the very edge of the surf, the bloody remains of a seal. The animal had been sliced almost in half by the propellers of a cabin cruiser.

At the sight of the dead seal's open trusting eyes, her heart broke and she burst into tears, sobbing uncontrollably. It seemed like an omen.

ADRIAN PARKED THE BENTLEY IN AN EMPTY STALL BETWEEN A FERRARI and an Edsel. Eddie Beaumont's Spanish-style house was perched atop a flat bluff on an expensive street in Pacific Palisades.

He walked up the flagstone path and rang the bell.

"Is that you, Adrian?" Beaumont's voice came through a speaker.

"Yes."

"Door's open. Come down the hallway, take the first left; I'm in the study."

It was almost one o'clock but Beaumont was still in his pajamas and bathrobe. He was seated behind a cluttered desk, holding a cordless phone to his ear. He waved his free hand and indicated he'd only be a moment.

The study was a small book-lined room dominated by a large cork board with rows of five-by-seven index cards pinned to it. Adrian thought the veteran writer looked twenty years younger than his seventy-three years. Beaumont was an eagle-faced man with a shaved head that lent him the look of a Prussian nobleman. His face was almost unlined, his eyes alert and intelligent. His knowledge of world history was encyclopedic. He was a grand master of screenwriting—a survivor of six marriages, countless outrageous story conferences, and several parachute drops into

Occupied France during World War II. He had conducted a torrid affair with a tempestuous Italian actress that reached its climax when both were arrested by the Carabinieri for tangoing naked in the Fontana di Trevi. He had rewritten screenplays for Samuel Brontson in the producer's heyday when he was using Dupont's frozen pesetas in Spain.

In the early sixties Beaumont seized a Nazi war criminal in a pricey Madrid restaurant and succeeded in bringing the mass murderer's presence to the attention of Mossad agents. Some weeks later the man was found shot to death in the elephant moat at the Barcelona zoo. He had once choked a famous director in the middle of a take in order to make a point. He was totally unafraid of the prevailing power structure and had, some years before, blown the whistle on the film critics of *Time* and *Newsweek*, both of whom were peddling their own scripts to the studios while criticizing the work of men and women with whom they were competing.

"Yes, I'm still here," Eddie said, then cupped the receiver and whispered to Adrian, "It's my so-called agent."

He uncupped the receiver, and said, "You finished? Good. Now listen carefully. You're sitting in that goddamn office eating Milk Duds and telling me I should be cognizant of CBS's internal problems. Fuck CBS's problems! I can bottle my problems and ship them to CBS! I delivered the script and I want to get paid."

He listened for a moment. "Absolutely not. No meetings on *Trotsky* rewrites until I get paid."

Beaumont hung up, rubbed his eyes, and leaned back.

"The fat asshole is sitting in an empty building at a dead agency eating candy and dumping on his few remaining clients."

"Why are you still with him?"

"I'm not. My papers ran out six months ago but Axelrod's the agent of record on *Trotsky*. There are only a handful of great agents left and none of them want to represent an old warhorse like me. My lawyer, Arty Falk, handles my negotiations."

A beautiful blue-coated cat with yellow eyes jumped up on the desk and Beaumont petted her.

"She's a beauty, Eddie."

"And bright—good taste. She always hissed at my last wife." He paused. "You look well, Adrian."

"I'm okay . . . you know, Silvi and I are divorced."

"No . . . I didn't know. I'm sorry. Come on. We'll have a drink before lunch. The maid is making tuna salad. It's a gourmet dish based on my fifth wife's recipe. She was a major ball breaker but a great cook."

Adrian followed Beaumont into the sunken living room. A large picture window afforded a splendid view of the Pacific shimmering in the distance.

Beaumont went behind the bar and mixed vodka martinis. On a shelf above the bar, two gleaming Oscars were perched side by side.

"Cheers," Beaumont said.

"Cheers, Eddie."

A Swedish maid wheeled in a serving cart with the salad and an open bottle of white wine.

"Do you wish to eat on the terrace?" she asked.

"Please," Beaumont replied.

Adrian noticed three men grouped around a cluttered table in the dining room, making notes and running tapes on mini-computers.

"Forensic accountants," Beaumont said, indicating the men.

"What's a forensic accountant?"

"Accountants that get more money than ordinary accountants."

"What are they doing?"

"Working for my sixth wife. I'm in the midst of a divorce. They're going over all my receipts, bills, check stubs, residuals, charge slips, pension checks, stock dividends—the works."

"I don't know how you do it, Eddie—six times . . ."

"I thought this one would work, but I didn't bargain on her addiction."

"Drugs?"

"No. Neiman-Marcus. Come on, let's eat."

They went out onto the terrace. The air was fresh and smelled faintly of the sea. Far out on the horizon a dark smudge marked the track of an aircraft carrier steaming south to the naval base at San Diego.

"Spectacular view," Adrian said.

Beaumont smiled. "On a clear day you can see the Honolulu Hilton."

Adrian filled their wineglasses while Beaumont spooned the salad onto their plates. The blue-furred cat meowed in protest.

Beaumont placed a small amount of tuna on a dish. "It's not that she's hungry. She feels left out."

He put the dish down. "Here, Jellico." The cat sniffed the salad but decided against it.

"This is a lovely spot, Eddie."

"Fought like an S.S. Panzer to hold on to it. Six determined women and a small army of divorce lawyers failed to take it."

"Why don't you just live with a woman? Why marry?"

"I like marriage. I'll be seventy-six in June. People think I'm seventy-three. All the ladies I knew are gone. I need a woman in the house."

"But what price glory?"

"Right . . . Maybe it's time I settled for a live-in maid." He sipped his wine. "What brings you out here?"

"The Volunteers."

"What about it?"

"I'm producing it at Gemstone."

Beaumont's fork was suspended in midair.

"You're kidding."

"No. I'm not. They're drawing up the papers."

"My God . . . *The Volunteers* . . . it's been twenty years since we first . . ." His voice trailed off in disbelief.

"It's Harry Walters's project. Everyone else at Gemstone is opposed to it but he's the boss—so we're on."

"He's quite a guy. I've never worked for Walters but I've heard only good things about him."

"He wants to shoot by July and suggested Paul Scott to direct."

Beaumont put his fork down and refilled his wineglass. "Scott's a sensational director but wasn't he committed?"

"I don't think so. He just dropped out. It's rumored that Julia Castle destroyed him, but my guess is he folded after the failure of his last two pictures."

"With good reason—they were unintelligible. He seemed to be mixing styles—Impressionism and Expressionism. Whatever he had in mind missed. But on his best day, Paul Scott is as good as it gets."

"The studio's running him down," Adrian explained. "Once they find him I'll go see him. We had a solid relationship on *The Discovery*. He whipped that company together like a classical conductor—you could see the synergy and harmony up there on the screen."

"What do you want me to do, kiddo?"

"The rewrites, and stay with it all the way through. You were in Madrid during the Fascist siege. You'll remember things I've forgotten."

"Where are you going to make it?"

"In Spain."

"What about the old scars? A lot of people fought on the Fascist side. You'll have trouble."

"Maybe, but it'll be worth it. We'll have to construct the Gran Via and the University front but the battlefields are still there: Jarama, Brunete, Guadalajara, Belchite, the Ebro."

"You mean to tell me Walters wants all those battle scenes?"

"Absolutely."

"I can't believe it. It's like a dream. I wonder what motivated him to take it on?"

"He says it's the kind of epic film that the industry has neglected. He believes in it, Eddie."

"This is a very great thing for you, but—"

"But what?"

"History tells me there's more to it than meets the eye." Beaumont paused. "Maybe it's just an old man's battle scars but when miracles happen, I look for secret agendas."

"All that matters is we're making the picture. I have to know if you're with me."

"Are you kidding?" Beaumont smiled and raised his glass. "*Viva España*, baby."

They toasted, clicked glasses, and the two old friends felt the rush of old dreams, old times, and the romance of lost causes.

THE POLO LOUNGE'S NARCISSISTIC LUNCHTIME DIN HAD SUBSIDED. Lonely wives, early afternoon call girls, and eastern fashion models had supplanted the earlier crowd of agents, producers, writers, and studio executives. The preferred booths were opposite the bar and dimly lit. The semidarkness provided a cloak of anonymity which was absent in the brightly lit interior dining room or sunlit patio.

Harry Walters and Mickey Dutton were seated in the number one booth toying with their espressos. Dutton was a handsome middle-aged man with Brillo-like salt-and-pepper hair. His dark pin-striped suit was hand-tailored but the cut was circa 1952. His shirt collars were winged and the pattern of his tie was reminiscent of the Union Jack. Everything about Dutton was permanently arrested in the Eisenhower years—except his canny instinct for a morsel of gossip, rumor, or legitimate show-biz news that made for a surefire press release.

His open-faced innocence, superb press contacts, and unmarried status made him a major player—his stable of wannabees rivaled those of film stars. Dutton considered most women to be recreational distractions. Business was where it was at. His publicity firm had a small but select clientele that was the envy of much larger bicoastal ad-pub companies.

Mickey Dutton was the man to see if you had a particularly

difficult film to sell, a new actor to publicize, a novel that required special handling, and conversely, he was adept at keeping the lid on bad news. The print, TV, and national magazine reporters regarded him as a man who could be relied upon for an interesting column lead. He was ruthless but discreet. His motto was simple: *"It's not who you know; it's what you know about them."*

Dutton lit a cigarillo and said, "I hear that picture those kids made is pretty good."

"You mean *Midnight?*" Walters said.

Dutton nodded. "The word is Jack Wheeler's a lock for a Best Actor nomination."

"He delivered a remarkable performance."

"Still juicing?"

"Unfortunately. But we only lost three days. Jack Bennett and Steve Mandel took a rough cut of *Midnight* over to Rome to show Wheeler. The boys said he loved it."

"Why shouldn't he? That picture might revive his film career. The juicing has made him damn near unemployable."

"How do you know that?"

"I handle his press. He threw the producer of this biblical epic through a plate-glass window at the Hassler—cost me a fortune to kill the story." Dutton sipped his espresso, added a few drops of sambuca, and said, "Too bad about Max Schuller but Solish's taking over has to be very comfortable for you."

Walters shrugged. "I just make movies, Mickey."

Dutton waved to two women sitting at a table diagonally across the room.

"Isn't that dark-haired woman the one who wrote the novel about sex and drugs in Hollywood?" Walters asked.

"That's her."

"She's got a face like a used razor blade."

"With a snatch to match," Dutton said.

"How would you know?"

"I promoted her book."

"Nice." Walters smiled. "Who's the pretty blonde with her?"

"Her lover. A wannabee." Dutton blew some smoke up toward the ceiling. "What can I do for you, Harry?"

"I want you to handle a very fragile situation. I say 'fragile' because if it breaks the wrong way a lot of people are going to bleed.

I want you to know the facts up front. There is a very connected individual involved in this. There can't be any mistakes, Mickey."

"How's the money?"

"You tell me."

"You mean I write my ticket."

"That's exactly what I mean."

"Who do I have to kill?"

"You just plant a certain item—it'll be the kickoff of a continuing story, but your involvement has to be off the record."

"Are you my sole contact?"

"Absolutely. Eventually you'll have to talk to Herb Stoner but only routine pub stuff—a cover." Walters swallowed some water. "Interested?"

"Tell me what you want."

"Give *The Wall Street Journal* an exclusive—Salvatore Parnelli's Sirocco Film Distribution Company will be making a takeover offer for Gemstone Pictures."

Dutton's brain whirled. Schuller dead. The sudden emergence of Adrian Summers's Spanish project. Solish acting CEO. Rumors of Walters and Solish having made numerous trips to the desert. Connected individual involved . . . Leo Resnick's villa is in the Springs. This was a big-time shuffle.

"Who else knows about this?"

"I can't tell you that."

"Well, the *Journal*'s going to check it out. The Hollywood stringer is a friend of mine but his editor will check with Parnelli, with you, and Solish."

"No problem."

"How much space do you want on this?"

"Just a prominent plant to start with. The story will take care of itself."

"Is Herb Stoner in on this?"

"No."

"How do I get paid?"

"You'll be hired by Stoner to publicize a new actress who's starring in a film we're winding up. She's got something, Mickey. You'll have no trouble selling her."

"What's her name?"

"Tracey Warren."

"Oh yeah—*Backwash.*"

"Right."

"Publicizing her and the movie will be my cover for being around the studio."

Walters nodded. "Right. Ask Stoner for enough money to include the Tracey Warren situation and this special assignment. If you'd normally ask twenty-five hundred a week to publicize an actor, tell Herb you want five."

"He'll scream."

"Probably . . . but he'll have to come to me."

Dutton drained his brandy snifter. "You think I'd be doing the right thing if I were to buy a few thousand shares of Gemstone?"

"My feeling is that Gemstone stock is undervalued; but playing the market is always a risky enterprise."

"I got it," Dutton said, and his eyes narrowed. "Shit . . . look who's coming over, Freddie Manduke—the lounge lizard himself."

A tall man with large ears, a long sloping nose, and mournful eyes was heading their way. He reminded Walters of an exhausted elephant.

"Harry." Manduke smiled, offering his hand.

Walters grasped the clammy hand and indicated Dutton. "You know Mickey."

"Sure. How you doing, Mickey?"

He didn't offer his hand to Dutton.

"I'm fine, Freddie."

"Listen, Harry," Manduke said, "I just got in from New York. I've got a terrific project for you."

Manduke was a pub-crawling, name-dropping street hustler who had access to narcodollars.

"I'd suggest you call Aurora Flint," Walters said.

"She won't take my calls."

"Well, I don't run the story department."

"I'm talking about a Robert Hamlet original."

"Call Aurora," Walters said, dismissing Manduke.

"Sure, Harry. I'll call Flint. Nice seeing you, Mickey."

Dutton nodded and the elephant disappeared into the semidarkness.

"I've got to get going," Walters said. "Go with the story, Mickey."

"Done."

Walters scribbled a number on the inside cover of a matchbook. "Private line."

The tanned, silver-haired studio chief walked toward the exit and deftly palmed a tip to the maître d'.

After a moment the hatchet-faced writer and her blond companion came over to Dutton's booth.

"Hi, Mickey."

"Hi, Selma."

"This is Donna." The writer indicated the blonde. "I'd appreciate you spending a few minutes with her. Donna wants to be an actress."

"I would never have guessed."

"Talk to you later. Anything you can do to help would be appreciated." She turned to the blonde. "Mickey's the best—see you later, sweetie."

"Take care, Selma," the blonde said and turned to Dutton. "She's a doll."

"Yeah—a prince. Sit down, honey."

She sidled up to the publicist so that her thigh pressed against his.

"Wasn't that Harry Walters, the head of Gemstone?" she asked.

"That's right."

"Gee, I'd fuck him even if he didn't give me a job." She licked her lips. "He's some cutie pie."

"You have no idea, baby."

"THIS IS A FRIGGING DIAMOND!" STEVE SWACKHAMMER EXCLAIMED.

"Pure gold," his partner Tony Perkins added.

The high-handed, high-priced, self-proclaimed producing wizards were still pitching the same project Aurora had rejected months ago.

"You may be right, but I don't see it," she said. "It's a dumb, charmless script."

"Is a kid getting struck by a lightning bolt and becoming a god not original?" Perkins said.

"It's the magic genie," she replied. "It's a rip-off of that TV sitcom. Come up with something fresh."

"Don't you understand science fiction?" Swackhammer persisted, flexing his muscles so that his skintight black leather jacket rippled. The swarthy producer fancied himself a macho tough guy. His partner was the low-key salesman. They played good cop–bad cop.

"I understand science fiction," she replied indignantly. "I admire Ray Bradbury's inventiveness and his unique ability to bring credibility to what's incredible. But this"—she indicated the red script on her desk—"this is a witless notion dressed up like a movie."

"How the fuck would you know?" Swackhammer's jaw muscles

tightened. "You put *Basic Desires* into development with Charlie Morton. We grossed more money in Pittsburgh with *Ace High* than the fucking Chipmunk's made in twenty-two starts."

"What Steve means is," Perkins said, trying to be conciliatory, *"The Child God* has terrific potential as opposed to *Basic Desires.* We read Bradovich's coverage; it's pretty rank."

"You're missing the point, Tony," Swackhammer corrected his partner. *"Basic Desires* is autobiographical!" He pointed at Aurora. "A cunt that crushes balls is her life story. Well, fuck you, sweetheart. We're going over to Columbia."

She felt a rush of joy. She could have climbed up on her desk and tap-danced.

"I'll notify Irv Wexler that you're in breach of contract and that you'll be leaving the lot. Anything else?"

"Walters will have your ass, baby!" Swackhammer growled.

"Harry Walters can have my ass any time he wants it."

Swackhammer's face flushed with rage. "If you were a man I'd rap you right in the head!"

"If you were a man you'd grow a head." Aurora got to her feet. "Now get out of my office before I call security!"

Swackhammer stood stock still, glaring at her. Perkins took his partner's arm and moved him to the door.

"We're taking *Cheerleaders* with us," Swackhammer said. "Even that faggot reader of yours Bradovich liked that one. You just made Mike Britton's day at Columbia."

"I certainly hope so."

The door slammed. Aurora sank back down into her chair. She felt clammy and tense. Swackhammer had a reputation for pushing around people who couldn't defend themselves. She flashed on the bloody seal tumbling in the surf. God damn these bastards. God damn these hustlers. They make one hit picture then piss millions away on the next three and strut around like toy Napoleons.

Maggie's voice came over the intercom, "Bennett and Mandel on one."

Aurora shook out her bright red hair and took a deep breath before saying, "Hi, fellas."

"We finish the mix on Tuesday," Bennett said, "and wondered when you and Harry would like to screen it."

"I'll check with him," she said and added, "We're all very proud of the picture."

Mandel said, "Solish gave us a scare before sending us to Rome."

"I heard about it. Next picture make the black girl a nun." She paused. "How was Rome?"

"Wild," Bennett said. "Wheeler's driving the TV people crazy. He complained to us about the Moses character having a lack of motivation. But he loved *Midnight* and was grateful for having had a chance to see it before we locked it off."

"It's a pity," she said. "I mean Wheeler's drinking. He's such a great talent."

"Well," Bennett said, "I'd use him again. He's got more presence drunk than most actors have sober. We brought you a little gift in Rome—nothing spectacular but you've been terrific and totally supportive. We haven't had the opportunity to—well, you know."

"I appreciate the thought and I'll let you know about the screening."

The moment she hung up, Maggie's voice came on, "Sonni Strong on two."

"Christ!" Aurora hissed in disgust.

"This is her third call."

"Okay, I'll take it."

Aurora pressed the flashing Lucite button and picked up the receiver.

"Hello, Sonni."

"Hello yourself! I was promised a toilet six weeks ago. I've got to go down the hall to a common crapper. Unless I get a private toilet I'm taking my project to Disney."

"I'm sorry, Sonni, we don't have private bathrooms. Harry Walters maintains the studio as it was in 1927. I don't have a private toilet."

"Your old flame Adrian Summers has one. He just came on the lot and he's got a bungalow on Harlow Street. All the bungalows have private bathrooms."

"What can I say? You'll just have to make doo-doo down the hall. Your contract does not specify a private toilet."

"You have my notice! I'm going to Disney and I'm taking *Flying Surfers* with me!"

"You'll have to come up with the development money we've advanced," Aurora cautioned the irate producer.

"Wexler can talk to my agent. I'm out of here."

"You'll be missed, Sonni—but when you gotta go you gotta go."

Aurora hung up, rose, and walked to the window in time to see Adrian Summers and Eddie Beaumont entering the main gate in Beaumont's cherry-red Ferrari.

The top was down and in the hazy sunlight Beaumont appeared to be a lot younger than she would have thought—it might have been the Ferrari or the angle of his black beret.

The phone console buzzed. She pressed the speaker button. "Yes, Maggie."

"Walters would like to see you in his office."

Walters was on the phone with the missing director's attorney. "I tried that, Burt," Walters said, "but Aurora thought it would be an inopportune time to ask Julia Castle about her former husband's whereabouts. You're Paul Scott's legal representative. You're the only one who can turn this thing around. You must know where he is."

Cradling the receiver, his feet up on the desk, Burton Klein gazed out of his Century City office window at the remnants of the old 20th Century-Fox lot. Anything concerning Paul Scott was dicey, but Walters was a true gentleman, a man one could trust.

"What's the nature of your interest in Paul?" Klein inquired.

"I'm prepared to make him a pay-or-play offer to direct *The Volunteers.*"

There was a polite knock at Walters's door, and Aurora entered. Walters cupped the receiver and said, "Paul Scott's attorney."

She nodded and sat down in front of the desk.

"*The Volunteers,*" Klein said. "Isn't that the Adrian Summers project? The Spanish Civil War script?"

"That's right."

"I saw something in the trades about it."

"This isn't for publication, Burt." Walters winked at Aurora. "But we've made Summers pay or play as the producer. Gemstone is going into production on *The Volunteers.* The screenplay is being polished by Eddie Beaumont, but we need the director's input. In my view, Paul Scott is uniquely qualified to direct this picture. I consider him to be one of perhaps five great living directors. If for some reason he doesn't want to undertake a film of this magnitude—fine. But I would appreciate an opportunity for Adrian to meet with him. They worked together on *Discovery* and have great regard for one another."

Klein glanced at his framed law degrees on the wall and sighed heavily. There was a rich deal to be made but he had to proceed carefully. "Can we have breakfast at the Beverly Wilshire coffee shop at say eight-thirty?" he asked.

"When?"

"Tomorrow."

"Done."

"I look forward to seeing you, Harry."

Walters hung up, lit his third Sherman of the day, and leaned back.

"We may be in business," he said to Aurora, then paused and stared thoughtfully at her for a moment. "Something wrong?"

She shrugged. "One of those days. Perkins and Swackhammer are going to Columbia."

"What precipitated that?"

"*The Child God.* I just stuck to my guns."

"Have they officially notified Wexler?"

"I have and they confirmed."

"Good. I'm delighted they're leaving. I made a mistake signing them."

"There's more. Sonni Strong's going to Disney."

"The missing toilet?"

Aurora nodded.

"Well, I hope Disney has a toilet seat that suits her," Walters said.

Aurora rose and glanced at the Ava Gardner poster. "I'm glad that Frank has been appointed acting CEO."

"So am I. Makes life a lot easier."

"How old was Schuller?"

"According to the obituary, seventy-one."

"I never really knew him." She sighed and said, "The boys asked when you'd like to see *Midnight.*"

"Have them bring it to the house next Thursday. Let's invite Adrian, Eddie Beaumont, Charlie Gordon, and anyone you like."

She nodded and suddenly burst into tears. Her shoulders shook and she covered her face with her hands. Walters sprang to his feet and moved quickly to her. His arms went around her and she buried her face in his chest.

"Easy does it . . . Easy does it . . ."

She slowly regained control and stopped sobbing. He handed her his monogrammed handkerchief.

"I'm sorry," she said, dabbing the tears.

"Sit down."

He poured a snifter of brandy and handed it to her.

She took a sip and felt its instant warmth.

"You don't have to say a thing," Walters said gently. "No explanations required. Finish that brandy and go home. You're exhausted, baby."

"It isn't work. This morning the tide tossed a dead young seal up onto the beach. His eyes were open—wondering. Innocent. I . . . I . . ." She stopped, unable to go on.

Walters understood. Her strength of character, he realized, made everyone forget how vulnerable she was. She was a sensitive young woman playing hardball in a treacherous masculine game.

As she swallowed the brandy a slight flush appeared on her tear-stained cheeks. Watching her, Walters thought how astute it was of Leo Resnick to have left her out of the loop. She was, God help her, a romantic.

"You've had a difficult time," he said soothingly, "what with seeing Adrian after all these years and having to deal with hustlers and egomaniacs. That kind of thing takes its toll. Go home. Get some rest. Forget the studio for ten minutes."

"Thanks, Harry." She rose to leave.

A gleaming brass nameplate was affixed to the stucco wall beside the bungalow's door. The engraved letters read ADRIAN SUMMERS, and just below, THE VOLUNTEERS.

"Not bad," Beaumont said admiringly as he followed Adrian up the steps and inside.

Adrian's secretary was a pleasant middle-aged woman with playful eyes. Ray Smalley had recommended her highly. "Millicent," Adrian said, "say hello to the infamous Eddie Beaumont."

Beaumont removed his beret and kissed the surprised woman's hand.

Taken aback by the writer's courtly gesture, she stammered, "Your . . . your secretary is at lunch, Mr. Beaumont. I'll show you to your office."

She led them into a wide low-ceilinged room just off the reception area and snapped on the overhead fluorescents. The office was dominated by a battered wooden desk that bore the burn scars of countless writers' cigarettes.

Slowly scanning the worn furniture, Beaumont's eyes came to rest on a cracked leather sofa. He shook his head in wonderment and murmured, "I've been here before."

"You're kidding," Adrian said.

"No. This is the office. I had an affair with Roberta Webster on that sofa almost thirty years ago—'63 or '64. She was co-starring in a B-movie, something to do with Turks . . . wait a minute . . . wait a minute . . ." He snapped his fingers and smiled with satisfaction. *"Istanbul Express."*

"I collaborated on the script with a genuine weirdo—long dead. The story was based on a paperback by a German writer. It was one of those hot, dry L.A. summers. We had no air-conditioning. I would pace and this fellow would type.

"He'd sit at that desk naked, except for a pair of silk panties— for some reason he wore his girlfriend's panties. We had a lot of laughs in this room."

"Well," Millicent said, "the bathroom's still in the same place. There's a small fridge, three phones, and, as you can see, an IBM word processor. Is it satisfactory?"

"Lose the overhead fluorescents. I'll need a desk lamp with one of those low-wattage easy-on-the-eyes bulbs. Lose the IBM machine. I don't type. I'll need a few dozen Flair pens, a dozen yellow legal tablets, a hundred five-by-seven index cards, a pegboard, a box of pins, and a water carafe."

"I'll advise your secretary. Her name is Stacey Wilcox. Frankly, Mr. Beaumont, I'm surprised. Almost every writer I've worked for uses a word processor. It's fast and efficient."

Beaumont nodded. "And the plane is faster than the horse, but has the quality of life improved?"

Adrian smiled. "Come on, Ed. Let me show you the master suite."

A CAST OF THOUSANDS

Adrian's office was dressed with modern furniture, a wet bar, and, for some unknown reason, a piano. The windows faced out to a huge permanent Hawaiian sun-and-surf cyclorama. The illusion was striking. It was as if one could open the window, jump out, and land on Waikiki beach.

The walls were decorated with framed sketches of Venice used in a silent Gemstone classic called *Grand Canal*. Adrian's desk was made of highly polished cherrywood and featured a sophisticated interoffice communication console.

Millicent placed a stack of pink message slips on the desktop along with a *Daily Variety* and *Hollywood Reporter*.

"The calls keep coming ever since that item ran in the trades."

"What item?" Beaumont asked.

"That Gemstone had signed Mr. Summers to produce an epic film."

"You're a star, Adrian," Beaumont said.

"A fallen star."

"Not anymore. It only takes one green light. You're hot, kiddo."

"You sound like fat Axelrod. How about some lunch?"

"I could have a salad."

"Millicent, will you have the commissary send over two tuna salads."

"You want Sinatra or Costner dressing?"

"Surprise us."

Beaumont walked to the bar, opened the cabinet doors, and removed several bottles.

"I'm going to make you one of my world-famous martinis."

"A little early for me."

"Nonsense. Luis Buñuel drank one martini at lunch and one at supper—every day. He lived to be eighty-eight, enjoyed excellent health, and managed to direct six great films."

He stirred the drinks and said wistfully, "Imagine after all these years a return to Eden. I performed magnificently in this bungalow."

"Writing or screwing?"

"Is there a difference?" He shrugged and shook his head. "I can see my collaborator sitting there at that old Remington wearing his panties and typing with two fingers. We managed to write a pretty good potboiler."

Beaumont poured the drinks and handed a glass to Adrian.

"To *The Volunteers*," he toasted. "*Suerte!*"

"*Suerte!*" Adrian replied.

They sipped the martinis and Beaumont said, "Well, Adrian my boy, how do you want me to handle the rewrite?"

"Walters doesn't want to lose size but the dialogue needs polishing and the structure has to be tightened."

"Why don't I reread the last draft over the weekend," Beaumont suggested. "Then break it down into scene cards, put them on the wall, and see what we have."

"Makes sense. This is a damned good martini, Eddie."

"Thanks. Tell me. What's Aurora had to say about this project?"

"Why do you ask?"

"I just wondered."

"She's against making the picture."

Beaumont walked to the window and peered out at Waikiki beach.

After a moment, he turned, stared at Adrian, and said, "It's none of my business but this whole thing has happened suspiciously fast."

"Certain projects take years," Adrian said. "*Cuckoo's Nest* took thirteen years. *Gandhi* took twenty years. It's always a crapshoot. You break your heart trying to get something made, then suddenly the nickel drops and you have a deal. It's movies."

"You can also make the case that some of the best films were made for all the wrong reasons," Beaumont said. "It took me eight years to get *The Last Season* made. Everyone admired the writing but the prevailing wisdom said that no one cared about doomed lovers—until *Love Story* broke out."

"Mr. Beaumont?"

A shapely baby-faced young woman appeared in the open doorway.

"I'm Stacey Wilcox. I'll be typing the script changes and, in general, managing your office. I'd like to make a list of whatever it is you require."

"Only God can make that list, my dear, but"—he drained the martini—"let's get at it before the Sinatra salad arrives."

He followed the curvy secretary out.

A CAST OF THOUSANDS

Adrian picked up the pink message slips and examined them one by one as if they were priceless artifacts.

He felt a curious exhilaration as he sat at the gleaming desk holding a fistful of phone messages. After years of exile and silence the pile of pink message slips held a kind of extraordinary significance.

This wasn't a heroin-induced dream. They were actually going to make the picture.

14

FRANK SOLISH WAS SEATED IN A PUBLIC PHONE BOOTH JUST OFF THE Waldorf lobby. He suffered a heavy, persistent cold and an intermittent toothache. The dentist had served ample warning, periodontal work had to be done and soon.

He touched a handkerchief to the beads of cold sweat oozing out of his forehead. Christ, how he hated winter, and summer was no bargain either. Well, he'd soon be immune to the brutal New York weather. The scam was on track. Adrian Summers had been signed. Parnelli was en route to New Zealand. Schuller's ashes were on their way back to Germany. The former CEO's will had contained a proviso that his urn be placed in an S.S. war memorial cemetery outside Hannover.

His own situation was solid. The board of directors was pliant and agreeable; and "the Mummy," Ira Kosstrin, was not a factor. The surviving founder's advanced age was beginning to take its toll. This morning Kosstrin requested box office receipts on a Gemstone picture that had premiered July 4, 1930.

Solish cracked the booth's door and spit a thick glob of phlegm onto the Oriental carpet. He shivered slightly and wondered why they hadn't called. It was 6:35 P.M.

The Buick stopped for the long red light at Ramon Drive and Leo Resnick glanced off at snow-capped Mount San Jacinto—a thick white doughnut-shaped cloud wreathed the mountain's

94

peak. The strange formation had been stationary for a week and none of the weather experts had offered a reasonable explanation for its presence. Some local Mexican supplicants saw the Virgin in the creamy cloud. The Agua Caliente Indians believed it was a sign from their mountain god, Campeche. Whatever its source, its presence had been a boon for tourism—people were flocking to the desert resort just to see the mysterious cloud.

Resnick's chauffeur drove slowly, cautiously threading his way through the heavy traffic moving east on Palm Canyon Drive. They turned right at the corner of Tahquitz and pulled into the parking lot at the rear of the shopping mall.

The Old Man got out of the Buick and walked toward a public phone booth occupied by Resnick's house woman; as he approached she hung up, got to her feet, and left. He entered the booth, sat down, and watched the woman walk nonchalantly to the Buick and get into the rear seat. He checked his watch and decided to give it another two minutes.

Harry Walters was seated in the public phone booth in screening room C. While waiting for the call, he thought about Aurora's tearful breakdown. She was burning out. He would send her to St. Moritz on the location search with Alex Carlino, the director of *Snowblind*.

Shifting nervously in the booth, Solish felt cold drops of sweat snaking down his rib cage, causing him to shiver. The phone rang suddenly, sharply. He pulled the door closed and grabbed the receiver.

"Frank?" Resnick inquired.

"I'm here."

"Harry?"

"I'm on."

"When does the takeover item run?"

"Friday's *Wall Street Journal.*"

"Anything on Paul Scott?"

"I'm working on it."

"Go ahead, Frank," said Resnick.

"Parnelli's en route to Rarotonga via New Zealand. The boardroom is quiet. Kosstrin still shows up but he's losing it. I think Schuller's death pushed him over. We opened *The Late Great* in fifteen hundred theaters to solid business. My salesmen are happy. Everything's normal."

"Good," Resnick said. "Once the *Wall Street Journal* story breaks both of you must issue statements to the effect that Gemstone Pictures will actively resist any and all takeover attempts. Max Schuller's legacy will not be handed over to Salvatore Parnelli or anyone else—that kind of denial is essential. And, boys, if I were you, I would exercise my stock options at tomorrow's opening bell. We meet at the villa two weeks from today."

The line clicked off in Solish's hand. He left the booth and walked across the lobby toward the bar. He needed a brandy— something to swish around his throbbing upper bridge.

Walters hung up and entered the screening room and pressed the intercom connection to the projectionist. "Okay, Pete—let's start with the *Backwash* dailies."

Resnick strolled across the parking lot toward the Buick. A bag lady sitting on a wooden box held her gnarled hand out to him.

"Mister . . . Mister . . ." she pleaded.

He dropped three twenty-dollar bills into her lap.

She stared at the money in awe and her sour breath hissed through her gapped and broken teeth. "Christ . . . Jesus Christ . . ."

15

ADRIAN HEARD THE TIRES CRUNCH AGAINST THE GRAVEL AS THE BENT-
ley rolled to a stop. He studied the two-story white clapboard
house and listened to the rhythmic pounding of the surf.

There were memories in this place—joyous and tragic. The
beach house had been left to Silvi by her father, who had a large
stake in the old Signal Oil Company. Although she was a successful model when they first met, Silvi had been born to money and
didn't have to work. She supported them in the lean years of their
marriage and used her own money to buy their Mulholland Drive
house.

She opened the door almost immediately and stared at his angu-
lar face, seeing once again its fragile handsomeness.

"I'd almost given up on you," she said.

"Sorry. I couldn't get out of the studio."

He followed her down the long corridor, thinking she could still
handle a runway.

She wore beige slacks and a blue silk blouse. Her shiny dark hair
was parted in the center, framing her oval face. Her straight nose,
full mouth, and dark Florentine eyes lent her a mysterious beauty.

The living room was spacious and rustic. A crackling fire burned
in the fireplace. Sliding glass doors opened to a sundeck overlooking the beach and sea. A Chopin interlude played on the stereo.

"Sit down," she said, indicating a beige sofa.

"I've been sitting all day going over script changes and returning phone calls. It's amazing, the same people who had me buried read the item in *Variety* and were on the phone—'Hey, sweetheart, gotta have lunch. Gotta see you. Always loved that script.' These are the same people who avoided me like the plague."

"It's movies." She shrugged and lit one of her infrequent cigarettes. "I'm thrilled for you, Adrian. This picture becoming a reality after all this time is nothing short of miraculous, and for you a long overdue validation." She paused. "How about a drink?"

"Stoli on the rocks would be nice."

As she started for the bar he asked, "Would you mind if I changed the music?"

"What have you got against Chopin?"

"He's not Sinatra." Adrian smiled.

"The cassettes are all there in that rack, help yourself."

He shuffled some cassettes before feeding one into the stereo. Sinatra sang "Street of Dreams."

She returned, carrying two glasses, and handed him his drink. They toasted the picture and he said, "It's good to see you, Silvi. You look swell."

"You're the only one I know who still says 'swell.' Something Noel Cowardish about that."

"Why?"

"Everyone says 'terrific.' My wife lost the baby—'terrific.' My son flew to the moon—'terrific.' They dropped the atom bomb on the school yesterday—'terrific.' Everyone and everything is terrific."

"Hollywood," he said.

"I suppose." Then, after a long pause, she said, "What did you want to see me about?"

"Oh, I don't know, I thought we might have a quiet dinner up the road at Le Blanc. Used to be pretty good."

"It's in Chapter Eleven. Besides, I have a dinner date."

"Anyone I know?"

"I don't think so." She sat on the bar stool with her back against the bar and sipped her white wine. "Tell me about the picture."

"So far it's just an announcement although they have signed me and Eddie Beaumont—'pay or play' as they say."

He walked over to the mantelpiece and studied a framed photograph of himself, Silvi, and the five-year-old Timmy. They were posed in front of Gaudí's Sagrada Familia church in Barcelona.

"That summer in Spain—we were okay that summer. You, me, and Timmy. We were a family." He sighed. "Whatever happened to families? Almost everyone I know is alone. I wonder if they still have families in New York?"

She smiled. "Probably in Queens."

"Probably." He nodded. "The closest thing to family out here is a smile from the maître d' at Chasen's."

Sinatra sang "I Want to Be Around."

Adrian opened the terrace doors and stepped out on the wooden decking. The distant lights along the sweeping curve of Santa Monica glittered like an endless necklace of emeralds, rubies, and diamonds. He was transfixed, staring at the gentle Pacific swells. Silvi came out and stood beside him.

"Looks tranquil but underneath all hell is breaking loose." He paused and his voice trembled. "Timmy looked as though he was sleeping—not a mark, just colorless, motionless." Adrian shook his head in disbelief. "When the tide grabbed him I was drying out at the V.A. Hospital."

Silvi sighed. "We've been over it a thousand times. It wasn't your fault, or my fault, or even Timmy's fault. He was swept away by a sudden undertow. That's all there is. You're not responsible."

The wind played with the ends of her hair, and for a moment their eyes locked before she said, "You better go."

He followed her back inside and handed her a sealed envelope. "I want you to have this."

"What is it?"

"A check—a sizable check." He smiled. "This one won't bounce."

"I don't need it."

"I know that. I just want to share it with you."

She accompanied him to the door.

He traced the arc of her cheekbone with his forefinger. "We ran a better race than we finished."

"No we didn't. It just seems that way. Take care of yourself."

She stood at the open door until the Bentley's taillights had disappeared.

16

WITH THE ADVENT OF JAPANESE OWNERSHIP THE COFFEE SHOP IN THE Beverly Wilshire Hotel had surrendered its historic Mexican décor to Romanesque marble pillars, vaulted ceilings, and immense picture windows. There were few customers. The heavy winter rain had reduced the breakfast trade to hotel guests, most of whom were Japanese. It was a good place for movie people to breakfast without being noticed.

Seated at a rear table on the Wilshire Boulevard side, Harry Walters noted an item on page A6 of *The Wall Street Journal.*

The story was bannered but brief:

Salvatore Parnelli's Sirocco Film Distribution Co. filed notice with the SEC of intent to purchase five percent of outstanding Gemstone Pictures stock. The notice was filed without comment, but Mr. Parnelli had previously made an unsuccessful bid for Magnum Pictures. Gemstone's longtime CEO, Max Schuller, recently succumbed to a heart attack and sales chief Frank Solish was appointed as chairman pro tem. Mr. Solish stated that Gemstone would use its considerable financial assets to defeat any possible takeover attempt by Mr. Parnelli, who was out of the country and unavailable for comment. Gemstone's stock rose 1¾ points at the close of yesterday's market.

Walters folded the paper, sipped his coffee, and smiled as he saw Burton Klein following the maître d' toward the table. He rose and shook hands with the wiry, studious-looking attorney. Klein was only thirty-eight but his client list was one of the most formidable in the business. The law office with which he was associated represented a Who's Who of directors, actors, and writers.

"Good to see you, Burt."

"Sorry I'm late."

"No problem. I just got here."

The maître d' seated them and asked, "Would you care to see a menu?"

"Not for me," Klein said, "I know what I want. I'll have a white omelet with mushrooms and a side order of bacon."

"I'll have the same," Walters said.

The maître d' snapped his fingers at the waiter and motioned for fresh coffee and juice.

"Traffic was bumper to bumper all the way from Brentwood to Beverly Glen," Klein said.

"Happens every time it rains. This city can't accommodate anything but sunshine."

The waiter poured some fresh coffee and filled their glasses with orange juice.

"This is the best OJ in town," Klein said. "Japs did a hell of a job on the hotel."

"Spared no expense," Walters agreed.

Klein nodded. "They took a run at Gemstone a few years ago. Yosuta made what I thought was a generous offer—somewhere around a hundred and forty-five a share."

"Max Schuller shot it down. Called in all his political muscle. Mortgaging an American art form to the Japanese was sacrilegious, if not treasonable."

"I doubt that patriotic crap had anything to do with the outcome," Klein said. "Schuller beat Yosuta in the Delaware courts. He was a smart Kraut."

"Isn't it remarkable," Walters said reflectively. "There's Ira Kosstrin almost a hundred years old and still active. He shows up every day. He doesn't do anything but he's at his desk."

"It's all in the genes, Harry. No matter what the medicine men say about tobacco, exercise, and cholesterol, it's all in the genes."

A waiter served their white omelets, bacon, and toast.

Klein ate quickly, washing the eggs down with gulps of coffee. He wiped his lips with a napkin and asked innocently, "Anything to this story about Parnelli's accumulation of Gemstone stock?"

"I doubt it's a takeover attempt. I think Parnelli's simply making a wise investment. His interest was probably triggered by Schuller's death."

"Five percent of Gemstone stock is a lot of interest," Klein said.

Walters sipped some coffee. "He'll need a hell of a lot more than five percent to take Gemstone over. We're a very rich company, Burt."

Klein said, "According to the trades, Gemstone's *Late Great* opened big and I hear good things about *Midnight.*"

"We've been very fortunate."

"You're to be congratulated for resurrecting Adrian Summers and *The Volunteers*. I always thought it was one of the finest pieces of screen literature I'd ever read."

"It's certainly one of the most expensive." Walters said. "But Adrian's obsession has become my own. I'm determined to make the picture. It's a propitious time and we have the resources to undertake a motion picture of epic proportions."

Walters chewed the last of his bacon, swallowed some coffee, and glanced around surreptitiously before saying, "I want Paul Scott to direct *The Volunteers.*"

"Is that a firm offer?"

" 'Pay or play'—you name the price."

"You're kidding."

"No. I mean it. I don't want to haggle. We can make Scott's deal in five minutes."

"And Adrian agrees?"

"Of course. He and Paul worked together years ago and tried to peddle *The Volunteers* as a writer–director team."

Klein stared off at the Wilshire Boulevard traffic crawling eastward in the driving rain.

"Harry . . ." Klein's voice was low and conspiratorial. "I'd only discuss a client's personal problems with a man I absolutely trusted. I'm leveling with you and I don't mean to be disingenuous, but Paul Scott has suffered severe psychic pain." The wily attorney paused. "He's an extremely troubled man."

"I know that he had a hellish time with Julia Castle," Walters said.

"That's not entirely true. I've represented Julia in legal matters for the past six years. She and Paul had a brief, stormy marriage but she's not solely responsible for his problem."

"I didn't mean Julia consciously hurt Paul, it's just that her remarkable beauty seems to invite trouble."

"Her beauty is irrelevant," Klein said. "Julia has had her wild, zany days but she's matured into a fine actress. She's doing this new play for Equity scale. It's a difficult role and the critics will be gunning for her—but she's unafraid."

"You don't have to convince me, Burt. I'm hoping she'll consider the role of Rebecca in *Volunteers*, but first we've got to set the director."

The star attorney leaned forward, glanced around, and in a hushed voice said, "Paul Scott is suffering from agoraphobia. He won't leave his villa. He won't go into the streets. He won't visit a public place. He will not mingle with humans. He mistrusts anything with human hair on it. He's reclusive. His withdrawal has little to do with Julia. She tried her best to help him. They were not at odds with one another.

"What crippled Paul was the fact that his work defied public acceptance. And with few exceptions he was damned by the critics. Even those blond lollipops on the cable channels hurt him. He feels the industry's need for moronic pictures precludes any further pursuit of his craft.

"Having said that, nothing would please me more than to see Paul on his feet, directing an important picture."

"How do we achieve that?"

"I'll phone him and tell him that his former colleague, Adrian Summers, is going to produce *The Volunteers* for Gemstone and would consider it a great favor if Paul would see him. Now, Harry, this is critical, if I get Paul to agree to a meeting, Adrian must refrain from asking him to direct. Adrian will have to tap-dance, feel his way, but the idea of directing must come from Paul. We have to play this one astutely."

Walters nodded. "I understand. When will I hear from you?"

"Before lunch."

* * *

They crossed the cobblestoned parking alley separating the original hotel from the newly built annex.

"Harry?"

"Yes?"

"Confidentially, would you recommend me picking up a few thousand shares of Gemstone?"

"I never play the market but Gemstone's stock is undervalued."

They reached the overhang of the annex and Klein said, "I'm parked down the block at a meter. Thanks for breakfast. I'll be back to you shortly."

They shook hands and Klein dashed out into the driving rain.

Walters stared after Klein in amazement that a top attorney who made no less than half a million a year was too cheap to spring for a parking attendant's tip.

After presenting his ticket to the attendant, Walters noticed an attractive Japanese woman staring at him with undisguised interest. He nodded politely and glanced off at the multicolored array of foreign flags whipping in the wind.

After a moment, he felt a light tug at the sleeve of his Burberry. It was the pretty Japanese tourist. "Pardon me, sir." She spoke English without the usual Japanese inflection.

"Yes?" he said.

"Forgive me, but I must ask you—aren't you the famous actor, Peter Lawford?"

He thought, why not? She obviously was unaware that Peter Lawford had died. It'll make her trip. "As a matter of fact I am," he said.

"Would you autograph this for me?"

She presented him with a Gucci gold pen and a Neiman-Marcus notepad. He signed the page "Peter Lawford" and handed the pen and pad back to her.

"Thank you so much."

"My pleasure."

His Volkswagen Jetta came up the ramp and he gave the attendant a five-dollar tip and slipped behind the wheel. As he drove past the Japanese woman he noticed a look of consternation in her eyes; an actor of Peter Lawford's stature would not be driving a Volkswagen.

Dr. Price stared thoughtfully at Aurora. "How did you feel about seeing him again?"

"I'm not certain. Tense. Mixed emotions."

"When you had this brief affair, what did Adrian represent?"

"A man with whom I felt alive and desirable."

"Were you in love with him?"

"I tried to protect myself against that."

"Why?"

"He was married and made it very clear that he loved Silvi and would never leave her."

"But that didn't stop him from sleeping with you."

"We were both younger. Both lost." She shrugged. "We needed each other."

"And now you're uncertain about your feelings."

"I feel a need to protect him."

"Against what?"

She shifted in the deep leather chair and peered out the window at the forlorn ficus trees on the patio, wondering if Dr. Price watered them.

She sighed. "I have a feeling that there's some secret motive behind Walters's approval of the picture. My suspicion is based on nothing more than intuition, and Harry may actually mean what he says about our industry dying of creative atrophy."

"But you don't believe that?"

"No . . ."

"Why?"

"It's happening too fast. *The Volunteers* is a monster to prepare and produce."

"Meaning Adrian is over his head?"

"In view of all his problems—absolutely."

"You told me that he kicked his heroin habit."

"But what happens when the pressure starts? And then there's the suggestion of Paul Scott to direct. I mean to even think of putting a sixty-million-dollar picture in the hands of a man who's fallen off the world is madness."

"Let's put the director aside for a moment. What else makes you suspect?"

"Again, it's speculation: Schuller's death almost coinciding with the *Volunteers* project and the rumors of a takeover bid by Sal Parnelli. I don't know. Maybe it's just me. Maybe it's my own insecurity."

"What triggered this suspicion?"

"When Jerry Blake told me that he'd seen Solish and Walters dining in a Palm Springs restaurant with Leo Resnick."

"Were they at the same table?"

"No."

"Why would you connect Solish and Walters to a gangster, or for that matter to anyone else in the restaurant?"

"I don't know."

"It's paranoia. You know that, don't you?"

"I only know what I feel."

"Tell me about the seal."

"I can't talk about that."

"Why not?"

"It makes me cry. I can't handle that."

"Your tears over that dead animal is classic transference of your aloneness. It's all there. The animal's eyes represent your own feelings of inevitable betrayal by everyone around you."

"Please, it's too early for that Freudian crap."

Ignoring her remark he went on: "Let me ask you this—suppose your suspicions turn out to be well founded. Suppose this sudden production of *The Volunteers* is indeed a ploy, a setup for something else. And let us further suppose that Adrian Summers is being used and you're aware of it, and if you step forward you'd be risking everything—would you still tell him the truth?"

She glanced up at the ceiling, closed her eyes, and thought, I must be truthful here. I must not fantasize. "I don't think so," she almost whispered. "I've worked too hard too long. My career is all I have."

"So you would let the seal die to save yourself."

"No—not the seal."

"Aurora . . ." Dr. Price said, "Adrian Summers *is* the seal."

18

WALTERS PUNCHED A SERIES OF NUMBERS ON HIS PRIVATE LINE AND waited. His fingertips drummed on the desktop and the driving rain beat steadily against the window.

"Mr. Dutton's office," the secretary announced.

"Harry Walters for Mickey."

"One moment, please."

"How you doing, Harry?" said Dutton.

"I called to give you my compliments. Solish tells me that the takeover story is the talk of Wall Street."

"Stock's up two and a half points," Dutton said.

"It's only the beginning," Walters said. "I'm meeting with Herb Stoner and Tracey Warren late today. You'll be signed as her outside publicist so just send the bills. You'll have to make it look good, of course."

"If she cooperates, no problem. I'll get her national space. How does she come off in the picture?"

"Low-down and erotic."

"Terrific. I'll have her in for a photo session. I'll shoot for a *Vanity Fair* feature—if not, *Esquire* or *Playboy*. We'll see." Dutton paused. "I could use a follow-up to today's item."

"I can give you this much. Parnelli is en route to Rarotonga to obtain an insurance bond on a three-billion-dollar loan."

"Where the hell is Rarotonga?"

"Cook Islands. Just say that Parnelli is lining up a consortium of international banks to arrange financing for a possible takeover bid of Gemstone Pictures. Mr. Parnelli could not be reached at his Rarotonga hotel."

"Got it. I think I'll feed it to CNN. The print media will pick it up from the tube."

"You're the doctor, Mickey. I'll call you later."

Walters hung up and pressed the intercom button.

"Get me Herb Stoner, please."

He released the button, rose, poured himself a fresh cup of coffee, and thought for a fleeting moment about Max Schuller's demise but shook it off quickly.

"Stoner on one," his secretary announced.

Walters pressed the speaker button on the console.

"Good morning, Herb."

"Good morning, Harry."

"Listen, I'm very distressed about the Parnelli takeover item in this morning's *Wall Street Journal.*"

"My sources in New York think it was a West Coast plant."

"By whom? And to what purpose?"

"Probably Sirocco's publicist."

"Who's that?"

"Ziggy Mendelson."

"Do you know him?"

"Sure."

"Can you check it out?"

"I already have. Ziggy denies it."

"What else would he say?"

"He might be telling the truth. He despises Parnelli."

"But he works for him."

"A gig's a gig. Everyone's got bills."

"I suppose so. On another matter, we have to start a national build on Tracey Warren. She's terrific in *Backwash* and Wexler is negotiating with her agent for two more pictures. I want to hire Mickey Dutton to promote Tracey and the movie."

"Good idea. Mickey's terrific."

"Why don't you set up a meeting."

"What should I offer him?"

"Five a week."

"Pretty rich."

"It's one break in a national mag."

"True. I'll take care of it."

Walters clicked off and punched an automatic connection to Ray Smalley.

"Production," Smalley's secretary answered.

"Harry Walters—is Ray there?"

"Yes—just one moment."

Walters lit his fourth Sherman of the day and glanced at the Ava Gardner poster. Beauty. Rare. Elusive. Julie Castle was the only true beauty around and he had finally found a role for her.

"Morning, Harry."

"Morning, Ray. A couple of things. I've got Herb Stoner trying to determine where that Parnelli item came from."

"Hell of a shock," Smalley said.

They were talking in prearranged code in case of a tap or a bug.

"In any event, Frank issued a strong denial," Walters said. "I'll be goddamned if that fascist is going to take control of this company. Gemstone is not for sale at *any* price."

"I think everyone knows that, Harry."

"When does Alex Carlino report for pre-production location reccy on *Snowblind.*"

"The fifteenth."

"I'm going to send Aurora with him."

"Good idea."

"I'd like you to stand by for a possible meeting concerning Paul Scott."

"Any luck?"

"We'll see."

He released the intercom and scanned both trade papers. There was a blind item alluding to friction on the set of *Testaments,* the TV miniseries shooting in Rome, starring Jack Wheeler. How could he have missed Wheeler? He pressed the intercom.

"Gloria, add Jack Wheeler's name to those actor availability inquiries."

"Yes, sir." She paused. "I have Burt Klein on one."

Aurora stood in the darkness behind the crew members. High up on the Chapman crane, Stanley Trummel was seated alongside the camera operator checking the scene below.

A CAST OF THOUSANDS

The sequence about to be shot took place in the bar of a seaside hotel carved out of the jungle. It was the scene Trummel had written in which the character played by Tracey Warren seduces the stockbroker and convinces him to murder her drug-dealing brother. It was the pivotal scene of the picture and the set had been meticulously lit to convey a sinister sense of tropical heat. The light was fractured by a slowly revolving ceiling fan casting shadows over the faces of the patrons.

A marmoset monkey clung to the bartender's shoulder. The customers were white-suited cocaine dealers, bush pilots, smugglers, and secret police on the take. Slinky, dark-skinned women were seated at rattan tables, their cigarette smoke drifting up into the light.

Trummel peered through the camera lens for a moment, then whispered a last-minute instruction to the operator and focus puller, both of whom nodded in agreement.

"Makeup!" Trummel shouted down.

"Yes sir," the makeup man said, shielding his eyes from the overhead lights.

"Let's have a few beads of sweat on Tracey's forehead and throat."

The makeup man walked the length of the bar to the pretty yellow-haired actress and, using an eyedropper, placed several drops of glycerine on her forehead and neck. Satisfied, he quickly cleared the set.

"Quiet please!" the assistant director shouted.

The stage was as silent as a crypt. No one moved. No one spoke.

"Pay attention, everyone," Trummel said from his lofty perch. "Remember, it's two A.M., there's a sense of weariness and danger. We can hear the rolling thunder of an approaching storm. This is a scene about greed, murder, and sex. Tracey?"

The actress glanced up at Trummel and saw his wide nostrils and beady eyes in the flare of a match as he lit a cigarette.

"Remember, sweetie," he said, "the shot ends on a choker. You'll be full screen so don't lean on the lines."

"Let's shoot it, Stanley. It's hot as a motherfucker."

"Right, sweetie."

Aurora smiled, thinking the dishy blonde hit the queen right in the bonzo—hooray for Tracey.

"Okay, let's make it!" Trummel shouted.

A second assistant appeared out of the darkness, touched Aurora's arm, and whispered, "Miss Flint?"

"Yes?"

"Harry Walters would like to see you in his office."

"His cat?" Aurora said incredulously.

"His cat." Walters nodded. "Paul Scott ran off to Jamaica with his cat. He leased a villa in the jungle above Ocho Rios."

"His cat . . ." Adrian murmured in disbelief.

Walters leaned forward; his light blue eyes twinkled mischievously as if privy to a delicious private joke. "To be specific," he said, "the cat's name is Honeybear. Paul found her wandering along Third Avenue. She was a lost kitten and he adopted her. Apparently, the cat is the only living creature with whom he shares a loving relationship. Don't look so surprised. In this business people worship stranger things than cats."

Smalley felt he had to play devil's advocate before the game was lost. "Forgive me, Harry, but are you suggesting that we hire Paul Scott to direct a picture of this magnitude? That we get into bed with a man who's vanished into the Caribbean jungles with his cat?"

Walters shook his head sadly, rose, and walked to the window. He turned his back on the room, parted the drapes, and studied the action on LeRoy Street.

Smalley wondered how Walters would get Paul Scott past seasoned players like Summers and Flint. Irv Wexler had absolute faith in Walters's unique ability to sell anything to anyone. Harry Walters was the finest actor Wexler had ever seen.

It was a wild idea, Aurora thought, but not out of character. Walters had a long history of hiring writers, directors, and actors who'd been written off, and more often than not they had performed brilliantly. But still, if Scott had truly lost it and was nevertheless hired to direct *The Volunteers,* they would all be hiding out in the jungle.

Adrian was torn. Paul Scott's behavior was, to be generous, bizarre and his professional capabilities suspect, but given a certain set of circumstances any man could be driven to that terrifying place where reality and fantasy could no longer be separated.

Walters turned from the window and sighed. "Sometimes I feel as though I'm pulling the sled by myself. If I paid attention to backstage gossip none of you would be here. So let's keep a little charity in our hearts. And let's not forget that Paul Scott is a two-time Oscar winner and a world-class director." He moved to his desk and stood directly under the dramatic spill of the overhead ceiling spotlight.

Deciding to play against Walters for the sake of legitimacy, Wexler said, "Call it what you like—I agree with the critics. Scott's last two films were the work of a madman."

"You're wrong, Irv. Those pictures represented an attempt to break out of the tight structure of traditional film form. They failed but they were magnificent failures. Those films demonstrate the work of a rebellious artist. And when the audience rejected him and the critics ridiculed him, Scott reacted like a true artist. He turned his back on the industry, took his cat, and went off to Ocho Rios."

"What about Scott's mental health?" Smalley said.

"What about anybody's mental health?" Walters countered.

Adrian sighed. "It's one hell of a gamble."

"I don't agree," Walters said. "What's troubling all of you is the fact that Paul ran off with his cat. You wouldn't be concerned if he had squirreled himself away in the jungle with a teenage lollipop—one of those busty blond kids who grow out of the sand at Santa Monica. That sort of thing is socially acceptable, even admired. But Paul Scott is not predictable or conventional and that, kiddies, is what makes his work special." He paused. "It's up to you, Adrian. It's your picture."

"You know how I feel. We worked together years ago and got along famously. I think Paul's an extraordinarily gifted director; if you're willing to gamble, so am I."

Walters nodded and tore a slip of paper from a notepad and slid it across the desk to Adrian. "That's Scott's phone number in Ocho Rios. He's expecting your call."

"How much does he know about the project?" asked Adrian.

"Only that you've received a green light on *The Volunteers* and as a colleague and friend you'd appreciate his advice on casting, production, et cetera. Don't ask him if he'd consider directing unless and until he indicates some interest—should that happen, go for it. Tell him he's the only one you've ever considered to direct what is essentially a lifelong dream of yours. He can have anything he wants. He can take his cat to Madrid with the veterinarian of his choice. I'll put them both on the payroll.

"Whatever he asks for, no matter how outlandish, go with it. I want him, Adrian."

"Suppose he turns me down? Or the subject never comes up?"

"We'll go to the next best candidate, but let's think positively. Let's think in terms of Paul Scott."

"I'll do my best," Adrian said.

"However it turns out with him, I'd like you to fly from Kingston to Madrid. Have Eddie Beaumont meet you there. It's been ten years since you saw those Spanish locations. Things change. Have Eddie with you so that he can write to existing locations. Aurora will be in St. Moritz with Alex Carlino on a similar reccy. I'd like her to meet you in Madrid so that she's aware of physical production problems."

"I'm glad someone told me." Aurora smiled. "It's fine with me if it's okay with Adrian."

"Of course—it's a damn good idea," Adrian said.

"I've got a list of possible candidates for principal roles," Walters said. "These are just suggestions but I took the liberty to check with Jack Wheeler's agent. Wheeler will be available in twelve weeks. In my view, he'd be perfect for the role of Kopek."

"What about his drinking?" Adrian asked.

"We had no problems," Wexler said. "He was a good boy on *Midnight.*"

"According to the trades," Aurora said, "there's trouble on the set of *Testament.*"

"Gossip," Walters said. "There are creative differences but Wheeler is off the sauce. If we eliminated every actor who takes a belt we'd all be selling shoes."

"I take it this means I go from Kingston to Madrid to Rome," Adrian said.

Walters nodded. "I meant it when I said I'd like to be shooting in July."

Smalley and Wexler exchanged knowing glances. Walters had turned a snowball into an avalanche. The monster had risen from the table.

"And now," Walters intoned ruefully, "the *pièce de résistance.* Adrian, I'd like you to come back from Rome via New York and see Julia Castle."

A sudden palpable silence pervaded the office.

"Julia Castle . . ." Adrian murmured as if mesmerized.

"When you first wrote this script, Julia was in high school. She

114

didn't exist—so to speak. She's not only a beauty, she's a fine actress. The role of Rebecca, the American nurse, could have been written for her."

Adrian was amazed at Walters's retention of the screenplay.

"Don't you agree?" Walters asked.

Adrian nodded. "I love the idea, but it's dangerous. Julia and Paul working together means trouble. Important trouble—big-time trouble."

"There may be some problems," Walters acknowledged, "but they won't be major. I think Scott and Castle will jump at the chance to work together, especially in a classic film."

"I agree," Smalley said.

"It's a slow fuse," Adrian persisted.

Walters sighed. "Every picture has a built-in fuse. Just remember, a failed marriage doesn't constitute sufficient cause for a great actress to turn down a great role. Julia and Paul may be many things but first and last they're artists."

Walters rose. "Ray will arrange tickets, expenses, hotels, everything. Aurora, you'll have a copy of Adrian's itinerary so after your Swiss reccy you can meet him in Madrid."

"Fine."

"And, Adrian, if you want to invite Silvi along, it's on the house."

"Thanks. But I don't think so. She might come over once we start shooting."

"Well, give her my best. Hopefully this picture will restore more than one meaningful relationship."

They filed out and Walters pressed the intercom button on his phone console.

"Get Mickey Dutton for me, please. And find out what Gemstone closed at."

"I have that for you. The closing price was forty and a half."

He sat down and leaned back. Gemstone common had slipped two points since rising briefly on the *Wall Street Journal* item. Why? Takeover rumors almost always drove a stock price up. It had to be Parnelli. His Sirocco Films had lost credibility after the botched takeover of Magnum Pictures. On the other hand, maybe he was expecting too much too soon. The stock would fluctuate but it wouldn't soar until Parnelli actually filed a takeover notice with the SEC. Not to worry, by the time *Volunteers* started principal photography Parnelli would have the $3 billion necessary to file.

"Dutton on one," his secretary said.

"Hi, Mickey."

"What's up, Harry?"

"Let's have a drink at The Grill at, say, seven-thirty."

"Anything pressing?"

"We found Paul Scott."

19

SALVATORE "BOOM BOOM" PARNELLI HANDED THE CREAM-COLORED bar girl a three-dollar bill. The Rarotonga currency was unique both in its odd denomination and its fanciful engraving of a beautiful Maori girl riding atop a shark. The waitress tucked the bill into her sarong and removed a white flower from behind her ear and placed it on the table alongside a bottle of Cook's extra-strength lager.

She held up the bill and said, "For ten more I show you Tangorora."

"Maybe later," said Parnelli.

He knew exactly what she meant. Tangorora was the god of fertility. He sipped the beer and shook his head thinking you can be in the asshole of creation and someone's on the hustle. He glanced at the jabbering Japanese tourists and felt satisfied with his choice of The Mango.

The bar/restaurant was a thatched-roof tourist trap surrounded by a bamboo veranda strewn with bright red hibiscus and vines of tangerine-colored bougainvillea. The only drawback was The Mango's proximity to Elizabeth Street with its constant roar of Yamaha motorbikes.

He lit a thin Sicilian stogie and stared at the distant green-carpeted volcanic mountain; a fiery sun had just dipped behind its peak, casting brilliant prismatic beams against the darkening tropical sky. Off to his left, Maori fishermen cast their nets in the palm-fringed lagoon. The strong beer and tobacco caused him to feel slightly light-headed. He was still woozy from jet lag although he had slept the night through and gone for an early morning swim.

Boom Boom was at peace with the world. The score of a lifetime was within his grasp—and it was overdue. He would be fifty-eight next time he blew out the candles. It had been a hellish trip from the Sicilian mountain village of Lercara Friddi to this tropical bar. He'd shot every trick in the book and understood very early never to trust anyone. Everyone wanted to kick your brains out. He'd had some luck along the way but this was a big-time score. This was the kind of score that beat the real enemy—time. Time was a killer. Bottle it. Einstein it. Analyze it. Add. Subtract. Nothing stopped it. It kept moving. A silent thief. Even death didn't stop it. Time fucked with you in the coffin.

He drew hard on the stogie and swallowed the smoke with the beer. He still had time and a real shot at important money. And why not? He deserved it. He'd been scuffling all his life.

He checked his watch, looked out at the busy street, and saw the green Mercedes roll to a stop near the corner. The fucking limey was right on time. Squillante had done his job. He watched them get out of the Mercedes and dodge their way past pigs, chickens, dilapidated taxis, and roaring motorbikes.

Count Aldo Squillante wore a white suit, with solid gold family crest buttons, a Panama snap-brim hat, and designer sunglasses. Squillante had inherited a title and a decaying, drafty apartment building in a pricey Roman piazza. He had never worked a day in his life. He collected rents and busied himself widening his connections to old Italian money. He moved through an arcane world of nobility, drug dealers, laundrymen, and gun runners.

Walking beside Squillante was Charles Glenn. The tall, gaunt Englishman was president of Centurion Insurance Limited. He carried a briefcase and an umbrella and resembled the archetypal nineteenth-century British colonial. The cut of his black pin-striped suit had gone out of fashion shortly after the Boer War. The vanilla-suited Italian count and the dark-suited Englishman made an odd couple as they crossed the squalid, potholed street.

Squillante entered The Mango, glanced around, and smiled as he spotted Parnelli. Boom Boom rose and the men exchanged greetings.

"What would you like?" Parnelli asked Glenn.

"I'll have a Cook's lager, thank you."

"And you, Aldo?"

"The same."

Boom Boom held up his beer bottle and motioned "Two more" to the bar girl.

"I rarely visit this side of the island," Glenn said. "The drive has become impossible."

"Better here than your office," Parnelli replied.

"Yes, of course. A typical tourist trap—a good spot for this sort of business."

The waitress served the beers and smiled at Parnelli. "If your friends want to see Tangorora, I make special price."

"I'll let you know."

They clinked their beers and drank from the mouth of the bottles, as was the custom on the island. Another waitress served them a large bowl of sliced shark meat marinated in a blend of coconut milk and lime juice.

"Have you tried our shark meat?" Glenn asked Parnelli.

"I'm not a fish person."

"It's quite good, actually." The Englishman stuck a toothpick into a slice of the red meat and chewed it slowly, savoring its gamy flavor. There was an awkward moment of silence as each man waited for the other to deal the opening card.

Count Squillante eased the tension. "Salvatore, I think Mr. Glenn would like to see the collateral."

Parnelli removed a manila envelope from inside his jacket and slid it across the glass-topped bamboo table.

"That's a transfer to escrow of twenty million shares of Gemstone common."

Glenn examined the document and said, "This is worth slightly more than eight hundred million dollars. You're short two billion."

The gaunt Englishman was playing hardball, but Centurion had the fiscal clout, so for the moment Boom Boom contained his anger. His voice was calm and businesslike.

"I'm buying another forty million shares of Gemstone through Sirocco—that puts us over two billion dollars in aggregate. When this deal is done you'll make no less than twenty-five million for just putting up paper." Boom Boom paused, and with a touch of sarcasm added, "This is one of Centurion's cleaner deals."

Squillante nervously lit a cigarette and hoped the volatile Parnelli would not explode.

Glenn tucked the transfer document into his briefcase and calmly asked, "From whom do you propose to raise the funds to purchase the additional forty million shares of Gemstone?"

"Cintra," Squillante quickly interjected, noticing Parnelli's cheeks beginning to flush. "It's all arranged, Charles."

There was a sudden blast of percussive music that had its roots in West Indian reggae.

"Cintra . . ." mused Glenn. "That means Pakistani heroin money, Sheikh Awadi's petrodollars, and Colombian narco-dollars."

"What's the difference?" Parnelli asked testily.

"None whatsoever," Glenn replied. "Here's your loan guarantee."

He handed over a Centurion insurance bond in the amount of $2.5 billion consigned to Sirocco Film Distribution Company. "There is one other item," Glenn said. "My partners need to know the name of the end-user bank."

"City National Chicago."

"Fine."

Glenn lit a Rothman's cigarette.

Squillante fanned himself with his hat.

Parnelli swallowed his beer and drew on the stogie. The pretty bar girl was smiling at him, still hustling the delights of Tangorora.

After a moment, Glenn asked, "What's in this for you, Mr. Parnelli? It can't simply be running a film studio—can it?"

Boom Boom felt a ball of heat rise from his belly to his throat. "What's in it for me?" He smiled derisively. "Look around. Fresh air, fresh flowers, fresh fish, fresh pussy." His face discolored, turning a reddish purple. "How the fuck is it your business? Where do you come off asking me that?"

Squillante squirmed and said, "Charles was making small talk."

"Mr. Parnelli is quite right," Glenn said apologetically. "His financial stake in this enterprise is none of my business. I was simply curious. We're all partners." Glenn smiled. "And this *is* a clean deal; for that I thank you, my dear Count."

"I merely bring people together." Squillante shrugged off the compliment.

"Nevertheless you've earned your fee. For Centurion this represents a highly profitable arrangement."

"Fucking right," Parnelli remarked. "This is as clean as it gets."

The tropical night had descended and old-fashioned street lamps flickered on, casting a shadowy light along Elizabeth Street.

"Well, I got a long ride back to the Beachcomber," Parnelli said, getting to his feet.

"The car will come for you at eleven A.M. sharp," Squillante reminded his partner.

"I'll be ready." Parnelli nodded and shook Glenn's hand. "A pleasure doing business with you, Mr. Glenn. You know, in our line of work I figure you're way ahead of the game if you turn your car on in the morning and stay in one piece. *Ciao*, Mr. Glenn."

He then squeezed Squillante's shoulder. *"A domani,* Aldo."

"A domani, Salvatore."

Boom Boom was stretched out on his terrace lounge overlooking the palm-fringed beach, phosphorous sea, and starry night. He wore an open blue terry cloth robe and sipped a rum punch. The bar girl's head was buried between his legs, her mouth and lips doing wondrous things. She was very good and he thought this was the only way a man could stop time. This was the way you beat the Angel of Death. She looked up at him, her lips glistening. "You see Tangorora?"

"Yeah, I see him. He's out there riding a fucking shark."

20

A LUMINOUS MIST SPREAD ACROSS THE FROZEN LAKE AND THE SUR-
rounding snow-capped Alpine peaks glistened in the sunrise.
Standing on the wooden decking of her suite, sipping blood-red
orange juice, Aurora watched the rising sun turn the distant ridges
a shimmering white-gold. Her fur-lined coat was belted over her
pajamas and her breath vaporized in the pure, exhilarating air.

She thought this was the loveliest winter setting she'd ever seen.
The vast amphitheater of ice and snow with its remarkable stillness
seemed frozen in time, undisturbed by man. Even the village of
St. Moritz was insulated from the exterior world; but the hotel
itself was swinging and alive. Its guest list comprised the mega-
rich of Europe. The men were handsome and bronzed by the wind
and sun of the ski slopes. The women were trendy, attractive, and
expensive looking.

Aurora had made copious notes of her impressions—bits and
pieces of color that might be incorporated into the final-draft script
of *Snowblind*. She thought the setting was too good for the story.
St. Moritz was the perfect backdrop for an elegant romance, not
a potboiler.

The sharp double ring of the telephone sounded from the bedroom. Reluctantly she turned from the view and entered the suite.

"Hello?"

"Good morning."

It was Alex Carlino, the director of *Snowblind*.

"Did I wake you?" he asked.

"No."

"How about meeting me in the breakfast salon?"

"Give me fifteen—no, twenty minutes."

She stripped and entered the gleaming tiled bathroom. She opened the shower door and adjusted the faucets until a hot, steamy needle spray played across her shoulders. Soaping herself she thought about the screening of *Midnight* at Walters's Bel Air house. The picture had played well. Jack Wheeler's performance was a gem of underplaying. Despite Wheeler's drinking problem she couldn't fault Walters for recommending him for the role of Kopek in *Volunteers*.

She turned her face up to the spray and recalled something Solish had said to Walters after the screening. It had bothered her ever since she left Los Angeles. She had caught only the very end of it but it was enough. Solish had mentioned something about "the Old Man in the desert."

It registered almost metaphysically. Jerry Blake had seen Walters, Solish, and Resnick in the tony Palm Springs restaurant. A few weeks later Schuller had his heart attack, after which the *Wall Street Journal* item broke about Parnelli's takeover bid. At the same time, *The Volunteers* rose from the dead and was instantly activated. If there was a hidden agenda at play, *The Volunteers* had to be part of it. She wondered if Adrian was in on it or just an unwitting pawn. She was grateful that she didn't know.

She turned off the faucets and stepped out of the shower and, wrapping the oversized, white terry cloth robe around her body, began to towel off her hair. Maybe, she thought, it was simply coincidence. Perhaps there was no hidden agenda. But the "Old Man in the desert" sure as hell wasn't Moses. Still, the possibility that Harry Walters wanted to leave a celluloid legacy was a plausible motive. The Spanish picture could very well be Walters's enduring monument to himself. She dismissed her suspicions as quickly as they had surfaced. These were exciting times. No matter how *The Volunteers* turned out, the mere fact of its production would constitute a major industry happening. And she was part of it. This was not the time for fear. This was the time to ride the tiger.

21

THE OPEN-AIR RESTAURANT WAS SHELTERED BY COCONUT PALMS AND tropical banyan trees. A sultry breeze floated in from the Caribbean and a crescent moon cast a silvery light over the powdery beach. Most of the guests had finished dinner and retreated to the bar-terrace for dessert and drinks. A solitary couple danced to a live trio playing a West Indian version of "Stardust." The woman, in a white evening dress, and her companion, in a white formal jacket and dark pants, reminded Adrian of background extras in an Astaire–Rogers film. He sipped the last of his espresso and thought it admirable that the Jamaica Inn still retained its Old World ambience.

He had arrived from Montego Bay in the late afternoon, gone for a swim and taken a nap, but the residual jet lag still lingered. He probably should have declined the invitation to the screening and dinner party at Harry Walters's the evening before, but he was anxious to see *Midnight*. The film was an honest, uncompromising study of middle-aged male terror and he was glad he'd accepted.

He lit a cigarette and checked his watch; it was almost time. The waiter poured a brandy. "Compliments of the management, boss."

"Thank you." He swallowed the fine Napoleon brandy and no-

124

ticed an attractive young woman with large, sad eyes seated alone close to the dance floor. She crisscrossed the hot end of a cigarette lightly over the glass ashtray in a desultory fashion. She was, he thought, a perfect study of solitude.

Their tables faced each other but during dinner she never glanced at him. Her lack of interest was unusual, in that he was the only unattached male and this was too romantic a setting to avoid casual eye contact.

He swallowed the brandy and chuckled to himself: It's over, baby. The woman was not interested. You're crowding fifty. Your face is scarred. You're not exactly the playboy of the western world. His white dinner jacket was creased and his open blue shirt lent him that bruised Gatsby look that Silvi used to say he wore with misguided pride.

He crushed the cigarette out and thought, No, it wasn't F. Scott, or his jacket, or the purple scar; the woman's narcissistic melancholia had nothing to do with him. She was obviously trying to forget someone or to remember—either way it was a losing proposition. He rose and proceeded to tip the waiter, headwaiter, busboy, and maître d'. As he passed the lonely lady their eyes met and she smiled a sad, knowing smile that seemed to convey a kindred sense of loneliness.

At the hotel entrance, the handsome ebony face of his driver greeted him.

"Good evening, boss."

"Good evening, Robert." Adrian opened the rear door of the green '56 Cadillac and got in.

Robert sat behind the wheel, switched the ignition on, and took a .38 revolver out of the glove compartment and placed it on the seat beside him. Driving on the left side of the road, English-style, the vintage Cadillac squeaked its way down the macadam driveway toward the main road.

"What's the gun for?" Adrian asked.

"This is ganja country, boss."

"You think that thirty-eight will help?"

"It won't hurt, boss." Robert smiled, revealing a black space where his two upper front teeth should have been.

The radio played a lively reggae and Adrian settled back and watched the headlights reflect off the passing jungle foliage. God, how he had missed all this. These pre-production trips to never-never land. The first-class flights. The waiting limos. The great hotels. The exotic locations and that mad army of movie magicians coming behind him. It was a wondrous escape into a world of make-believe, and if you had been lucky enough to have experienced the ride when you were young, you were never the same again because the magic never left you. This jungle road was only the beginning of a surreal trip into an uncharted dreamscape. It was a journey that defied prediction.

The engine strained as the big sedan struggled against the incline in the road.

"You sure you know where the villa is?" Adrian asked.

"Yes, mon. My wife's sister cooks for Mr. Paul."

"The fellow at the desk said the villa was secluded," Adrian said.

"You got to know the road through the jungle. Don't worry, mon."

They followed the climbing blacktop road for fifteen minutes before turning sharply onto a muddy track snaking through the rain forest. The car windows were open and the moist balmy air carried the sweet fragrance of jasmine. Illuminated briefly in the headlights, a stream of insects, like flecks of neon, splattered against the windshield. The high-brights penetrated the darkness and every so often the eyes of an animal would shine at them and quickly disappear.

"You care for some rum, Mr. Adrian?"

"No thanks, Robert."

"Ganja?"

"Maybe later."

"Mr. Paul don't ever leave the villa."

"So they tell me."

"He's hid'n out from U.S. law, that's what my wife's sister think."

"How come you don't have seat belts?" Adrian asked.

"Saint George protects me and my passengers."

Adrian sighed. If they hit something he'd be instant company for Robert. But why worry? Years ago he produced a TV series in the jungles of Veracruz. The series was aptly titled *Trader Jim*. After two years of grinding the show out he came to understand that in Third World countries a mystical logic governed daily life and lent an inexplicable confidence to dangerous undertakings. Everything took second place to custom. You never fooled with tradition. You either went with it or you didn't survive. It took eight years and 54,000 lives in another jungle before America's ruling junta realized that simple fact. You don't defeat jungle people with Agent Orange. You don't deter them with massacres. You don't impress them with Hueys or F-14's. The jungle was their place and the white man was nothing more than a pale blur in their long history.

Adrian sighed heavily and his thoughts wandered to the screening of *Midnight* at Harry Walters's and to the dinner that had followed. They had been seated around a huge oblong table. A mysterious white-gowned woman prayed to a combination of Yahweh and Christ for Gemstone's continued success. Her head bowed in feigned prayer, Aurora had whispered, "I feel like an extra in a Pasolini film."

The group had included Ray Smalley, Irv Wexler, Frank Solish, Jerry Blake, Burt Klein, and two rival studio chiefs. Eddie Beaumont showed up with one of his former wives—a handsome good-natured woman. Walters had been in constant motion, seeing to it that everyone's plate was full and the wineglasses brimming.

The mistresses and girlfriends engaged in conversation but the wives were silent. Hollywood wives were respected only as customers. They traveled a lonely gilt-edged path from Rodeo Drive boutiques to The Bistro Garden, to reluctant attendance at premieres, like so many dress extras. Their children were gone or, if at home, treated them contemptuously. Only the strongest survived with their sanity intact—others turned into shrikes, dykes, or vegetables. They were casualties of fool's gold, of a pressured, seductive life-style they neither enjoyed nor understood.

Robert suddenly hit the brakes, throwing Adrian against the front seat. A huge wild boar stared at the headlights then trotted across the road.

"Make a fine jerk-pork," Robert said. "Sorry about the stop, boss."

"How much farther?" Adrian asked.

"Five minutes. The villa is up there; you see that waterfall?" A small stream of moonlit silvery water cascaded down a series of outcroppings. "Mr. Paul's place just up there."

As they proceeded up the steep, winding road, the smell of woodsmoke filled the car. "What's burning?" Adrian said.

"Coca leaves. People growing coca up here."

An enormous boulder marked a fork in the road. Robert swung the wheel to the right and they chugged up a forty-five-degree incline and saw flaming torches atop either side of tall iron gates.

A smiling stocky man wearing khaki shorts and cradling an AK-47 was stationed in front of the gates. The Cadillac rolled to a stop and the security guard walked up to the driver's side and spoke to Robert in Jamaican patois. After a brief exchange, he nodded and opened the gates and the Cadillac strained up another steep incline.

The villa's ochre-colored walls reminded Adrian of those sprawling Roman palazzos on the Via Appia. He got out of the car and was greeted by a comely black girl wearing a bright blue tie-dyed cotton dress. She nodded politely at the driver and said something to him in native patois. She bore a striking resemblance to those remarkably fine-featured Ethiopians. Her blue-black hair splashed across her wide shoulders and the dress was tightly wrapped around her curves.

"Follow me, Mr. Adrian," she said.

They climbed a serpentine path toward a high bluff. The jungle crowded the narrow walkway and the high chatter of crickets was punctuated by the occasional shrill cry of a night bird. The girl trailed the sweet scent of jasmine perfume and swung her hips seductively. He wondered if she was putting him on or whether it just happened that way. He smiled, thinking he had walked endless jungle paths but never with an escort like this. As they neared the top of the stairs, he heard the distinct sounds of Miles Davis's horn filling the jungle night—the number sounded oddly familiar with its Castillian riffs.

They reached the summit terrace, and like the proverbial genie, an immense bald-headed Polynesian stepped out of the shadows. His belly was the size of a Sumo wrestler's and hung below his belt. His arms were as thick as a normal man's thighs.

"This is Sami," the girl explained. "He looks after Mr. Paul."

The circular terrace was ringed by wrought-iron spikes. An oval swimming pool was illuminated by underwater lights that painted the water a celery color. Torches on tall posts burned brightly; their flames danced in the balmy breeze and far below, the amber lights of Ocho Rios blinked through the dense foliage. Adrian suddenly caught a strong whiff of sweet-smelling ganja.

"Hey, baby!"

A smiling Paul Scott was coming toward him. He hadn't lost his boyish good looks. His face was deeply tanned and his eyes glowed in the torchlight. He wore cutoff jeans and a T-shirt imprinted with a naked girl whose feet dangled over a musical note with the word *harmony* emblazoned in red cursive writing. A joint of ganja dangled from his lips.

They hugged one another, parted, and Scott said something to the girl. She nodded and left.

"Her name's Melanie," he explained. "She makes a great rum drink: coconut milk, papaya juice, cinnamon, a touch of coke and white rum, a kickass drink, man." Adrian remembered that Scott used the vernacular of a jazz musician whenever he was stoned.

"That big fellow you met at the top of the path is a Samoan," Scott said. "He weighs close to five hundred pounds; a tough cookie and loyal." He handed Adrian a joint. "Take a hit. It's great dope, man."

Adrian took a drag, held the smoke in his lungs, let it out, took another hit, and almost instantly felt the tension ease. He handed the joint back to Scott.

"You haven't aged," Adrian said. "Not a line."

"Time is just a fucking mirror, man. You see what you want to see. Recognize that tune?"

"It's Miles before the fall—something about Spain."

"Close. It's called 'Sketches of Spain.' I thought it would be an appropriate overture. I've got Goodman behind him." He paused and, glancing seaward, said, "Look at that." A cruise ship, its lights ablaze, was steaming north across the placid, moonlit Caribbean.

Scott turned back toward the main house and waved his arm expansively. "Is this nirvana or what?"

They walked around the pool and sat opposite each other at a candle-lit table. Melanie appeared out of the shadows carrying two glasses of iced rum. She swished her way up to the table and handed them the foaming drinks.

"Tell me if it's fine, Mr. Adrian."

Scott sipped it, savoring the unusual tangy flavor, and nodded. "It's fine." She smiled and left.

Scott toasted. "*Skoal,* pal."

"Skoal."

They clicked glasses and sipped the strong potion.

"Terrific drink," Adrian remarked.

They sat silently for a moment watching the dancing shadows thrown by the torches and listening to Miles fill the night with jazzy Spanish riffs. Adrian thought that Scott may have had the last laugh on the industry; there was definitely something to be said for the seclusion of Ocho Rios.

Scott snapped his fingers and shouted, "Where's that baby?! Where's that Honeybear?" The banyan leaves rustled and a big red cat with emerald eyes bounded out of the undergrowth and jumped up into Scott's lap. He stroked her gently and she purred loudly.

"Great creatures, man. You can't buy them. You can't con them. They either dig you or ignore you. Their affection is not for sale."

"She's a beauty," Adrian said.

"Her name's Honeybear. She was maybe two weeks old when I found her cowering in a hallway at Sixtieth and Third. It was a raw day, man. I took her home, got her shots, got her fixed and cleaned up. She never leaves me. Sleeps on my pillow."

The mellow music was suddenly shattered by a chorus of screeching night birds.

"The birds have spotted Honeybear," Scott explained and swirled the ice in his glass. "Is this a drink or what?"

"Terrific."

"I can't tell you how happy I am for you, Adrian. When Klein phoned and told me about the project I was thrilled for you. This is important, man. *Volunteers* could be something."

Adrian felt a rush of euphoria—maybe he wouldn't have to convince Scott to direct the picture.

"I hadn't read the script in a long time so Klein sent me the last draft. He said you wanted to rap about it—I said okay if Adrian comes alone. Why not? We share a common history with the project—all those years trying to get it on. So I made an exception. I never see anyone from the business. But you're different, man. You're special, and so is the project."

"I appreciate that, Paul."

Scott's eyes suddenly clouded. "Sorry, I shouldn't have offered you the ganja. I forgot the Monkey."

"It's okay. I'm clean. The ganja is cool."

The red cat sprang off Scott's lap, sailed through the air, and disappeared into the thick foliage. "She's hunting," he said. "Either smelled or heard an animal."

The music changed abruptly and the Goodman Quartet played "Moonglow."

"You remember when we made the picture based on your play?"

"Sure," Adrian said.

"We made it for a million-three," Scott said. "TV money, for Chrissake. I shot it in thirty-two days—used the Cinemobile. Small crew. Jimmy Crabe lit it with cigarette butts. We couldn't afford any fill light so Jimmy bounced key light off cardboard—remember?"

"I remember."

Scott rose, and stared off at the sea. "Jimmy was brilliant. He lit the picture like a Degas—a fluid liberation of suffused light. You could have put a frame on every shot." Scott sighed. "Christ, hard to believe Jimmy's gone."

"He was a terrific guy," Adrian said.

"That picture could open today and bury everything," Scott said. "But remember, they played it in select theaters—let the word of mouth spread. The audience can help you, man. They're part of it. They're not aliens from another planet. They're us out there in the dark. They're troubled, fucked up, looking for something they can groove with."

Scott's eyes glowed in the torchlight. "Today pictures are played off instantly," he said. "Two thousand screens. Three weekends and it's over." Adrian noticed beads of sweat forming on Scott's forehead. He was heating up. The combination of rum and ganja stoked his demons. "You know the shit they're making, man. They're dealing from the bottom of the deck to the bottom of the audience." Scott shrugged. "Maybe they're trapped. Maybe everything important has been said."

"They're only interested in home runs," Adrian said.

"Every moronic film is diagnosed by film students, cable mavens, and Kael's disciples. They analyze the star's navel, man. I saw a cassette on a plane—a movie about a teenybopper dancing in a steel town bar and in reel six she's in the Leningrad Ballet. From Scranton to Leningrad in one fucking cut! The audiences are so numbed out they go with it. I had to split the scene. They were

STEVE SHAGAN

coming for me—the killer cunts and cocks, they wanted my soul, man."

Adrian began to see things in a blurred surreality triggered by jet lag, spiked rum, and ganja. It was a tropical Rorschach: flaring torches, crickets, night birds, the five-hundred-pound Samoan, the guard with the AK-47, Melanie and the big red cat and Goodman's lilting clarinet and the once-great director swacked out of his mind, confessing and seeking absolution in the same breath.

"Honeybear is the only living creature with whom I enjoy a loving relationship," Scott said suddenly. "People think Julia broke me down—not true. She's a trip but she's cool. The soul thieves busted me. But look, I've got food, drink, music, great dope, and"—he leaned across the table, the sweat trickling down his face—"I still make movies, Adrian," he whispered.

"That's right. I make them in my head. That's how I keep them. They can't vacuum my brain. They can't change my cut. They can't fuck with my vision. They can't hang my soul in their Bel Air toilets. That's how they get off. They make a trophy out of your soul. They even turn your obituary into a review."

"It's the system, Paul."

"If they knew that I was hip to their action they'd put a hit on me. But I'm cool because they don't fucking know what a director does. They don't know that you have to watch a hundred bodies to expose a frame of negative and if the flute comes in a quarter note late at measure thirty-six, bar one hundred, you're fucked. A director's got to spot that shit, man. A flaw leads to a flaw. They pile up. You have to know what every gesture means to the audience. That's a popcorn-eating monster out there in the dark. You have to hold their attention, man. If they eat your soul how the fuck are you gonna hold the audience? You're dry. You're burned. Empty . . ." His voice lost its speed and turned melancholy. "You're nothing."

There was a sudden rustling in the foliage on the jungle side of the fence and Honeybear strutted onto the terrace and dropped a twitching lizard at Scott's feet. He tossed the lizard over the railing and petted the cat.

"Thanks, baby."

Honeybear jumped up on the table and stared at Adrian.

"I know you've got to do this picture," Scott said. "I understand

132

the alchemy—the highs and lows of a longtime dream. I reread the screenplay. It's a great piece. I'll help you if I can."

This was the moment.

"Harry Walters sent me to see you, Paul. The picture is Walters's legacy. He doesn't care about budget. He wants to make a memorable film. He wants to remind the community that there once was a Magic Lantern. I didn't come here to rap or seek advice." Adrian took a deep breath. "I want you to direct *The Volunteers.*"

There was a beat of silence before Scott shouted in patois.

The Samoan appeared and without a word instantly wrapped his tree-trunk arms around Adrian, carried him off the terrace, down the serpentine path, and dumped him into the Cadillac.

Adrian stood naked on the stone veranda overlooking the sea, feeling as though he'd been on an all-night roller coaster looping through tunnels decorated with luminous Daliesque apparitions.

He had returned to the hotel around midnight and found the lonely lady drinking alone in the bar. She taught art history at Duke University and had been divorced six months ago. After two rum punches they left the bar, removed their shoes, and walked along the surf line. His neck throbbed with the familiar pain caused by the embedded shell fragments but the sensation of his bare feet on the cool sand was soothing. They climbed the crest of a high dune and after a moment of staring pensively at the phosphorous waves she said, "I absolutely ache for a man."

They went up to his room, smoked the last of the ganja, and made love. It was slow, interesting, and wordless. In a curious way it was an exorcism of mutual loneliness. Afterward, she had fallen into a deep sleep.

He took a final hit of a joint and tossed the butt onto the beach below. He went into the bathroom and swallowed a Dalmane and crawled into bed alongside the lonely lady. She stirred slightly and he felt the warmth of her body. He slipped into a fitful sleep.

He was on the point with Patterson, leading the grunts along a footpath in the jungle canopy above Firebase Kelly. He was a captain attached to Military Intelligence Group, First Field Force Headquarters Group at Nha Trang. The patrol's mission was simple. They were bait. The purpose of their night stroll was to provoke an attack and reveal the position of the elusive 344th North Vietnamese division. The patrol was dead meat.

The surrounding jungle was a noisy cacophony of chattering monkeys, buzzing insects, screaming night birds, and the occasional roar of a prowling tiger. They walked deliberately, measuring every step. It was a moonless night and sporadic sheets of rain burst from the reddish sky.

They had penetrated the sloping canopy for half an hour when the animals suddenly fell silent. Patterson screamed as a booby trap shot a spear through his chest. He vomited a bubble of blood and fell. The men dropped. Their M-16 safeties clicked off.

The mortars came in. Whining. Smashing. Flat crack. Yellow explosions filled the night with shrapnel. Mortar bursts increased, and tracers, like luminous slivers, sprayed them from all sides. Adrian called in air support and then the tree behind him exploded. Fragmented. Warm blood seeped out of his helmet and ran down his face. There was a loud crack. He screamed and bolted upright in bed.

The lonely lady sat up wide awake, her breasts exposed, her eyes transfixed, staring at the five-hundred-pound Samoan.

Sami had smashed the door down. Behind him stood Paul Scott. Ignoring the stunned woman, Scott walked quickly to Adrian.

"I want Federico Rossi on camera and Anna Maria Quintana to do the production design. I want to shoot everything in Spain. I want the old Warren Beatty suite at the Beverly Wilshire while we're in pre-production. Honeybear goes with me, and her vet, Dr. Didden, goes to Spain. See if you can get Wheeler for the part of Kopek and Julia to play Rebecca. I want to shoot in thirty-five, then blow it up to seventy for select theaters. Reserved seats. No fucking two thousand theaters."

He hugged and kissed Adrian. "We're gonna make a great picture, baby!" He turned and strode out. The Samoan placed what was left of the door against the wall.

"My God, what was that!" the lonely lady gasped.

Adrian shrugged. "Just making movies . . ."

A Filipino waiter brought them platters of salmon, sturgeon, whitefish, and dishes of coleslaw, pickles, and olives, while the Mexican maid filled their glasses with a chilled white wine. Harry Walters had picked up the food from Nate 'n' Al's deli in Beverly Hills.

Frank Solish ate in small careful bites, his gums still sore from the periodontal surgery.

Wexler and Smalley ate voraciously, their appetites stimulated by the long drive from L.A.

Leo Resnick spread some cream cheese on half a bagel and carefully laid two strips of pink nova on top.

Walters sipped his wine and stared off at the scruffy desert floor dotted by surreal patches of green golf courses and ice-blue squares of swimming pools.

Below them, on the circular terrace, Magda von Stellhoff swam swift laps in the oval-shaped pool.

"I seldom see a movie," Resnick mused, "but I had to see *Bugsy* out of curiosity. I had Juanita pick up the cassette." He chuckled and shook his head in disbelief. "They made the Bug into a visionary with a big vocabulary. Benny was an icepick man. He killed maybe thirty people." Resnick sipped his Classic Coke before continuing.

"The nickname 'Bugsy' was well deserved," he said. "Ben was a heavy hitter in Murder Incorporated. Used to hang out in Midnight Rose's candy store at the corner of Saratoga and Livonia in Brownsville."

The men exchanged glances of impatience; they had no choice but to listen to the Old Man's reminiscences. Leo squeezed some lemon juice on several thin slices of sturgeon and placed them carefully on a half bagel. "I remember when Ben took a contract to hit a guy in Philly. Moey Amberg drove him down there. Siegel follows the contract into a movie theater on Walnut Street. He sits one row behind this guy. Everyone's attention is on the screen— a Hedy Lamarr picture, *White Cargo*.

"The Bug sticks an icepick into the contract's ear. The guy's head drops onto his chest like he fell asleep. Ah, this is marvelous sturgeon.

"The lights come on, the show changes. The Bug stays to see the picture a second time. Moey Amberg finally comes into the theater, spots Ben, and pulls him outside. He says, 'What the hell are you doing hanging around with the stiff.' Ben says, 'I love that Viennese cunt'—meaning Lamarr. He was crazy all right, but a visionary? Christ, Moey Dalitz and Tom Hull were operating El Rancho Vegas on the strip long before Siegel left Brooklyn."

"I liked the picture," Solish said.

"So did I," Leo said, "but it's nonsense. You're a Brownsville kid, Frank. Read the book *Murder Incorporated.*"

He waved the bagel toward the pool terrace below. "Look at Magda. Look at her cut through that water. I invited her for a few weeks."

"I don't mean to rush," Wexler said, "but I've got to make the three-thirty commuter flight back to L.A."

"You're right, Irv. Forgive my indulgence. Siegel, Murder Incorporated, it's all ancient history. You grow old and you drift into old business."

Resnick glanced at Solish, who grimaced as he chewed.

"What's wrong, Frank?" he asked.

"Bridge is killing me."

Wexler quickly said, "Harry, why don't you bring Leo up to speed."

Walters pushed the sunglasses atop his head, swallowed some wine, and said, "We have Paul Scott. I'm working out the nuts and bolts of his deal with his attorney."

"Don't haggle," Resnick cautioned.

"I'm not. Scott's fee is settled at three million, plus six thousand a week for location expenses."

"What did Summers have to say about his meeting with Scott?" Resnick asked.

"Not much. He indicated that Paul was high-strung and angry at the business. He alluded to Scott's odd behavior, but attributed it to drugs and rum."

"Sounds like our kind of guy." Solish smiled.

"Maybe. But there's another side to Paul Scott. When he appeared in Adrian's hotel suite he was in total command. He had the screenplay committed to memory. He even suggested casting Wheeler and Julia Castle. He ticked off his choice of technical crew people and demanded the old Warren Beatty suite at the Beverly Wilshire. He also insisted on taking his cat to Madrid along with the animal's vet. All of which indicates that he may be unstable but he's still capable of coherent thought."

"Are you suggesting that he might perform?" Resnick asked.

"It's possible," Walters acknowledged. "I've worked in the theater with absolute madmen and they've performed brilliantly; but of course, they had my total support. This is much different. We'll back the production fiscally but at the same time we'll do what we can to subvert the enterprise. And let's not forget Adrian Summers's historic emotional problems. We should be fine. In my view, once the pressure builds, both men will crack."

"We've got to be very careful about the cat's vet," Solish cautioned. "If that story gets into print we'll have given the game away. The world will know that we've hired a lunatic."

"Not to worry," Wexler said through a mouthful of whitefish. "The cat's vet will be charged to the production as the company doctor. The cat's name will not appear on any official documents."

"The cat doesn't bother me," Walters said. "Directors and actors bring enormous entourages to film locations: maids, mistresses, chefs, chauffeurs, makeup, bodyguards—the cat is simply Scott's pet. Period. We just have to disguise the fact that Honeybear has her own doctor in attendance."

"Who the hell is Honeybear?" Solish asked.

"The cat's named Honeybear." Walters sighed.

"Is Summers on his way to Madrid?" asked Resnick.

Walters nodded. "Where he'll be meeting Beaumont and Aurora."

"She worries me," Solish said. "She's tough and smart and if she gets suspicious she'll turn on us."

"No she won't," the Old Man said with assurance. "She'll exercise her stock options and make a financial killing."

"How can you be sure of that?" Wexler asked.

"Because I've survived a lethal enterprise for almost eighty years. I survived because I know people. I know how they act and how they think. Aurora is a lonely woman. She won't jeopardize the only meaningful situation in her life—her work. Her position at Gemstone lends her the stature she enjoys in the industry. She'll do what's best for Aurora Flint. You can sleep on that." He paused. "This is marvelous sturgeon."

"When do we make our official announcement?" Solish asked.

"As soon as all the principals are in place," Walters replied.

"I suppose you fellows noticed," Smalley said, biting into a pickle, "Gemstone stock is trading in a narrow range since the initial rise on Micky Dutton's plant."

Walters turned to Wexler. "Irv, are you certain Boom Boom's insured the three billion?"

"Absolutely. I've got a fax copy of Centurion's bond. He's addressed every detail. Sirocco Films will tender at seventy-five dollars. The offer will have been bonded and registered with the SEC. At the appropriate time Parnelli will withdraw the offer; by then we'll have sold at the top and cashed in."

"What basis does he have for withdrawing the offer?" Walters asked.

"The fierce resistance to Parnelli's unfriendly takeover by Gemstone's officers."

"Not bad, Irv," Walters said, "but actually it's no different than any other failed corporate takeover attempt. The raider got cold feet and withdrew."

"I've always wondered why they call him Boom Boom?" Smalley asked.

Licking a spot of cream cheese from his finger, Resnick said, "Legend has it that when Sal was a kid his favorite pastime was hitting his brother over the head with a hammer—the kid brother called him Boom Boom and it stuck."

"Have you seen his latest interview in *Money* magazine?" Solish asked. "He took off on the Hollywood Jews again—how they're trying to keep his company from becoming a major industry player."

"Let him talk, Frank," said Resnick. "He's a fiscal wizard but in the general scheme of the Combination he's small potatoes. When it's over, I'll speak to him."

"Well," Smalley said, "if it all falls into place we'll be shipping a full complement of crazies off to Spain. There won't be a Gemstone stockholder who'll balk at a seventy-five-dollar takeover price."

"I agree. You set it up brilliantly, Harry," Wexler added.

Walters shrugged. "I happened to remember Adrian Summers's screenplay. Everything flowed from that."

Their attention was suddenly diverted to the lower level pool. Wearing a topless string bikini, Magda climbed out of the water, picked up a towel, and wrapped it around her hair in a turban. She put on a pair of oversized reflective sunglasses, creamed her face, shoulders, and jutting breasts, and stretched out on a poolside lounge.

"You know something," Walters said reflectively, "Magda would be perfect for the Swiss ski instructor in *Snowblind.*"

"Get an actress, Harry," Resnick said. "Before this is over we may need Magda's natural talents."

"Especially if we get Richard Bryan to play Abrams," Smalley added.

"Magda may not be enough," Solish suggested. "We might have to send a dealer over to Spain."

"No!" Leo exclaimed. "This man Summers must not be seduced or subverted by drugs. I will not cross that line."

"With all due respect, Leo, we crossed a line with Max Schuller," Solish said.

"That's different!" Resnick countered. "The man was drenched in blood; an unrepentant Nazi. When Schuller was only eighteen he was already an oven commander at one of the death camps. The man murdered innocent women and children."

Leo rose and stared out at the burnished desert vista. "This man Summers has suffered a loss from which there is no relief, no redemption, no salvation. No man should bury his own child. We can use Summers to our advantage but no drugs, and when the payoff comes we'll give him a taste of the proceeds." He paused. "I'm going in now to watch the Lakers."

Pre-Production

ADRIAN SWUNG THE RENTED SIAT ONTO THE SHOULDER OF THE CLAY road and parked. Eddie Beaumont passed him the thermos and they shared a cup of the strong, sweet coffee. Nothing moved on the single-lane road traversing the silent battlefield.

They got out of the car, walked up an embankment, and watched as the vast honeycombed trench system came into focus out of the rising morning mist. The Jarama Valley had been a relentless killing ground from the summer of 1936 to the fall of 1939. The scarred landscape had been the southern hinge of the Republican lines. The men who had stood fast in these trenches had prevented Franco's Fascist forces from cutting Madrid's lifeline to the port of Valencia.

The American volunteers of the Lincoln Brigade had seen their first action here, and for many their last. They had faced heavy artillery, aerial bombardment, tank thrusts, and relentless infantry assaults. It was here, in the Jarama Valley, that young men and women from over fifty different nations had volunteered their lives and fortunes for a single ideal—freedom. They recognized, long before their own governments, that fate had chosen Spain as the crucible in the struggle against fascism. Adrian had centered his screenplay on these volunteers, dramatizing their sacrifice.

Beaumont pointed off toward a hill marked by a grove of olive trees starkly etched against a whitening sky. "That's Suicide Hill," he said. "The Lincolns were ordered to take the summit against seasoned entrenched Fascist troops. It was like Pickett's charge at Gettysburg; the Americans lost two hundred men in less than a minute."

"You feel like going down there?" Adrian asked.

"Why not?"

"Well, you're not twenty-five anymore."

"Listen, pal, you're talking to a man who's survived six marriages, legions of lawyers, batteries of accountants, and a lifetime of outrageous story conferences."

Adrian smiled. "I shouldn't have asked."

Leaving the road and using embedded rocks as footholds, they made their way down into the lateral trench. Cavelike chambers had been carved out of the trench wall. The sandbagged dugouts had sheltered the troops against enemy fire and the elements.

As they entered a dugout, Beaumont snapped his lighter on. The chamber's red clay walls were carved with the initials of tourists. The floor was spotted with goat droppings and the place smelled of decay and urine. The dugout was deeper than it first appeared. Adrian guessed that perhaps twenty men could have occupied a single chamber. It was almost inconceivable to think that thousands of men had survived for three years in these caves and trenches under constant artillery and infantry assault.

Leaving the dugout they followed a parallel trench that curved its way to the base of Suicide Hill. Climbing steadily, they reached the summit in less than twenty minutes. Standing in the shade of the olive trees they were caught up in the undisturbed silence of the battlefield.

"I would have refused," Beaumont suddenly said. "Even if Christ himself had ordered me to take this hill, I would have refused."

"How would you handle this battle in the rewrite?" Adrian asked.

Beaumont's eyes crinkled and narrowed against the sun. "Paul Scott and the production designer will have to answer that one. I'll write it full: armor, uniforms, concertina wire, tanks, artillery, field hospital, softball field, basketball hoops, mobile shower vans, et cetera. Since all the principals work here we can't cheat.

"I'd make the first battle a night sequence: star shells, tracers, artillery flashes—that kind of thing. Night covers a multitude of sins." Beaumont shrugged. "Of course it's up to you and Scott."

"Do what you think is right, Eddie. You have more experience than anyone on the picture."

"Well, no matter what sort of technique Scott employs—cutting in newsreels, front projection, long tracking shots in trenches—you'll still need a second-unit camera crew for weeks just to get action cuts. It's very rich, Adrian."

"Walters said money is irrelevant."

"I'm too old to believe that. Money is never irrelevant. The men who died here were irrelevant but not money. Nothing in business, politics, art, or love is as relevant as money. Believe me, at some point the dagger will be out—cut this—cut that. I hope I'm wrong, but history says otherwise."

They descended Suicide Hill and walked back to the dirt-topped road and got into the Siat and rolled the windows down. Adrian switched the ignition on, shifted gears, and the small sedan rolled north. They passed a kilometer stone with a fallen sign that read "Perales."

"The bridge should be just up ahead," Adrian said. "Remarkable, Jarama is only thirty minutes from the heart of Madrid."

"That's precisely why Hemingway and most of the journalists, including yours truly, romanticized the war—the cafés, the music, the camaraderie, only minutes from the killing ground. The siege of a great city almost always assumes a romantic tone."

They took the fork left and slowed as a horse-drawn cart appeared up ahead. Adrian waved to the old man sitting atop the wagon and pulled up alongside the cart. The man's face was raw, seared by sun and wind. His eyes were black; gray stubble covered his red cheeks. He had been just a boy when the battle raged all around this valley.

Attempting to communicate in his limited Spanish, Adrian asked for directions to the bridge. The old man stared down at them while the horse whinnied and switched its tail against a cloud of flies.

"Donde el puente Pindoque?" Adrian repeated.

The old man clucked to his horse. The wheels creaked and the wagon passed. Adrian gunned the car, downshifted, and swung onto the road leading to the Madrid highway.

"Franco's been dead for fifteen years and the old people are still afraid to discuss the war," Adrian observed.

"I warned you," Beaumont said. "You'll have problems. Our own Civil War ended over a hundred years ago and they still fly the Confederate flag in half a dozen states. Comparatively speaking, this war was only ten minutes ago."

They entered Madrid through the Porta del Alcalá and threaded through the heavy noon traffic toward the Gran Via.

"What time did Aurora get in?" Beaumont asked.

"The concierge said she checked in after two A.M. Her flight was delayed." Adrian paused. "You two will get along fine."

"You told me that she thought I had died."

"Well," Adrian said with a smile, "there was some general confusion between you and Larry Beaumont, the character actor."

Beaumont stared off at two pretty girls walking arm in arm.

"Aurora once offered me a job—years ago, when you both worked at CBS. She wanted me to write an adaptation of Ken Shelby's novel *Twilight's Angels*. It was a generous offer but I turned it down."

"Why?"

"First place I was going through my third or fourth divorce and my attorney advised me not to make any deals until the thing was final; but Aurora was willing to wait."

"What happened?"

"You ever read Ken Shelby's stuff?"

"No."

"He sells a lot of books but I don't know if anyone reads them. They have great covers—have to give him that. And he's smart. He always writes the same story. A young girl, usually virginal, inherits a diamond empire and the board members want to kill her, fuck her, or both."

"What's wrong with that?"

"Nothing if you forgive the repetition of plot and denouement. The climactic scene never varies. It always takes place in the Franz Josef suite at the Palace Hotel in Salzburg. The girl is rescued at the last second, her virginity intact."

"Sounds commercial to me."

"In novels, not movies."

Adrian turned the Siat into the semicircular entrance of the Palace Hotel and gave the doorman the keys. Beaumont waited while

146

Adrian went into the lobby and asked for his messages. The concierge handed him a note from Aurora. She would meet them at Chicote's for lunch.

"Feel like walking to Chicote's?" Adrian asked Beaumont. "It's a beautiful day."

"Let's go."

The Gran Via teemed with life—upscale life. The women were attractive and fashionably dressed. The men wore dark well-cut business suits under light topcoats. They spoke in quiet but rapid Castilian Spanish. The traffic flowed with a mix of Mercedes, Jaguars, and the omnipresent Siat—the Spanish version of the Fiat. Smartly uniformed police saluted tourists asking for directions. The sidewalk cafés were crowded with customers reading newspapers, sipping coffee, and people-watching. The cascading water in the magnificently carved Cibeles fountain sparkled in the March sun.

It seemed to Adrian that the formal sadness that had shrouded Madrid during Franco's regime had been discarded; the once somber city was now a trendy, throbbing metropolis.

"Imagine this boulevard under shell fire from siege guns and German bombers," Beaumont said. "The Palace and Ritz hotels converted to hospitals, the militia women manning antiaircraft guns, the sandbagged storefronts, ambulances tearing through the streets, buildings blazing, trams loaded with soldiers on their way to the University front. How do we re-create all that?"

"I saw some interesting sketches," Adrian said. "Hopefully the production designers can build the Gran Via and the University front on the backlot of the old Brontson Studios."

"Paul Scott better be on his best game."

"He'll be fine, and Walters gave me his word that we'll have total support."

"You'll need it."

24

CHICOTE'S HAD BEEN THE PUB OF THE SPANISH CIVIL WAR—THE PLACE
to have a drink, a sandwich, a dance, a stolen kiss. It was a
hangout for battle-weary soldiers and the favorite watering hole
of Hemingway and the corps of international journalists who covered the conflict. It was also the haunt of spies, secret police,
prostitutes, and Soviet commissars, who enjoyed special status
since Russia alone sold arms to the Spanish Republic. At one time
or another during the three-year siege of Madrid, anyone who
played a significant role in the drama had had a moment in
Chicote's.

The place had been restored and refurbished, but its contoured
booths, Art Deco lamps, and immense blue mirror were precisely
as they were in the summer of 1936. The maître d' remembered
Beaumont and they were shown to the number one booth at the
center of the oblong room. Beaumont ordered martinis and they
toasted one another in Spanish: *"Suerte"*—luck, while the waiter
served them a platter of tapas.

"It's a hell of a cut, from Jarama to Chicote's," Beaumont said.
"The popular song during the siege was 'Madrid.' It was sad and
haunting. The other songs were American: 'The Music Goes
Round and Round,' 'Night and Day,' and 'These Foolish Things.'
The bar was always jammed, and the mirror reflected blue faces.

See that booth?" Beaumont indicated one at the rear. "That was Hemingway's. He usually had at least two pretty girls with him."

"I wish I had met him," Adrian said wistfully. "I would have asked him why in *The Sun Also Rises* Lady Brett kept saying 'I require a bath.' "

"Maybe she needed one."

"I don't think so. Everything she said or did was tossed off. The only line she had that seemed 'written' is the one about needing a bath."

Beaumont chewed the martini olive and thought, what the hell, he might as well tell Adrian what was bothering him.

"It's really none of my business," he said. "I'm a hired hand, but I care about the project and I care about you. And this beak of mine smells trouble."

"Why?"

"Every studio in town is cutting corners and here we are designing a picture that has to gross two hundred million to break even. I'm not saying it can't be done, but the odds are lousy." He shook his head and sighed. "There's a hidden agenda somewhere."

"I don't care, Eddie. I want to make this picture. Nothing else matters."

Beaumont started to say something but Adrian interrupted and his voice brightened, "Here's our girl."

For a few seconds, Aurora stood silhouetted in the backlight of the open door. As she stepped inside, the maître d' greeted her and escorted her to their table. She wore a camel coat over a tailored black jumpsuit with a wide belt and gold buckle. Adrian thought her figure had never been more alluring. She had a certain understated verve—a sense of expectancy.

The men rose and kissed her cheek.

Pointing to their martinis, Aurora turned to the maître d'. "I'll have one of those."

"En seguida, señorita."

The recessed ceiling lights etched her high cheekbones and her recently acquired Alpine tan complemented her light gray eyes and the mass of cherry-red hair that fell across her shoulders.

"I'm starved," she said, spearing a piece of tuna. "Fucking Swissair; thought we'd never leave Zurich. The word was they were looking for a terrorist. For a while I thought it was our erstwhile corporate gobbler—Boom Boom Parnelli—Sal the Snake;

149

or one of his Saudi associates." She smiled. "The delay turned out to be a flat tire."

"You look swell, Aurora."

"No one says 'swell,' Adrian."

"Someone else told me that."

"We've just come from Jarama," Beaumont said.

"And?"

The waiter served her martini and they toasted the picture.

Adrian said, "Someone's gonna have to come up with a lot of money—Jarama is a movie all by itself."

"I spoke to Walters late last night," Aurora said. "He asked me to remind both of you not to be intimidated by costs—write it full." She proceeded to devour the entire serving of tapas. "Walters is still crowing over signing Paul Scott," she said, chewing on grilled shrimp.

"Wasn't easy," Adrian said. "Paul didn't take the commitment lightly."

"This has to be a first," she said. "I mean taking Honeybear to Madrid with her own veterinarian."

Beaumont shrugged. "Just make believe Scott had two or three kids, nurses, nannies, et cetera."

"Eddie's right," Adrian added. "Scott has a cat; other people have babies, lovers, dealers, whatever."

"And you're off to Rome tomorrow," she said.

Adrian nodded. "Eleven A.M. Alitalia."

Beaumont thought she was sending Adrian subtle signals. He knew about their past fling, and his years of combat in the marital wars told him that she was tracking her prey.

Adrian checked his watch. "Come on. Drink up. We've got to get out to the studio."

"Not me," Beaumont said, signaling for the check. "I'm taking it easy."

The waiter presented the bill and Aurora quickly laid her Platinum card on the bill plate. "Studio charge. Mama pays."

The maître d' came over and said, "Your car is here, *señor.*"

"Ask Mr. Tello to come in," Beaumont suggested.

"Don Alfonso does not patronize Chicote's," the maître d' replied. "His father was killed fighting for Franco against the Republic."

Aurora smiled at Adrian. "You picked a hell of a man to be in charge of Spanish production."

"Ray Smalley assured me," Adrian said, "that Don Alfonso Sanchez Tello is the best production manager in Spain."

"That's true," Beaumont said. "He was in charge of Sam Brontson's pictures—I'm talking about the heydey. Big-time pictures. Don Alfonso's as good as they get."

Aurora signed the bill, adding a generous tip. They rose and she said, "We'll drop you at the hotel, Ed."

"No—I'll walk. But first I'll introduce you to the Don." As they walked to the door Beaumont said, "I'll have to assure him that we're making an honest attempt to dramatize sensitive aspects of the war. He'll be all right—besides, he owes me one."

"What for?" Aurora asked.

"One night in Segovia I saved him from the wrath of his long-suffering wife. The Don was having a fling with the wardrobe lady and I interceded. His wife burst into the hotel like a Mura bull charging the cape. There were no nine-one-ones to call and I had to . . . Hell, it's a long story."

The black Mercedes was parked in front of Chicote's. The driver sat behind the wheel and Don Alfonso, a broad-shouldered, middle-aged man, was seated up front in the passenger seat. He heard Beaumont shout and got out of the car.

Alfonso was tall with horsey features and troubled eyes that instantly brightened when he saw Beaumont. He hugged the bereted writer. *"Madre de Dios,* Eduardo—how can you write this Communist shit? You must be in need of money. Another divorce?"

"Bingo—as they say. I assure you, Don Alfonso, neither Mr. Summers nor Miss Flint are Communists. They are many things, but not Communists."

Eddie introduced them. Handshakes were exchanged and Alfonso addressed Adrian: "I have my own feelings, of course. Our Civil War was complicated, *señor;* but I accepted this assignment because whatever its politics, the story is about Spain and we must be honest. The period, the people, the sets—everything must look authentic. I can assure you of my cooperation."

"I appreciate that. Tell me, who did those marvelous sketches of the Gran Via?"

"Pepe Rodriguez Granados."

"Only the best production designer in Spain," Beaumont said, "maybe in Europe."

"Scott's bringing someone from London," Adrian said.

Don Alfonso shrugged. "That's every director's choice, but at least we will have made a beginning and from Pepe's work the studio will get an idea of money, size, and time." He embraced Beaumont. "I'll see you tomorrow, *cabrón.*"

"We're almost there," Don Alfonso told Adrian and Aurora. They had taken the auto-route north, speeding past drab-looking housing developments. "You'll see that Pepe has made detailed blueprints for re-creating the Gran Via and the University front. You will have a good idea of what is possible. I have great admiration for the films of Paul Scott. You're very fortunate to have him."

They turned off the expressway onto a side road marked with a sign that read "Estudios España."

Aurora squeezed Adrian's arm. "I can't believe we're here—together—I feel high."

"It's that Alpine air." He fingered the pearls at her throat. "They look expensive."

"The boys that made *Midnight* gave them to me. They have a new script in development called *Thirty-Eight*—about a woman alone at thirty-eight."

"Close to home?"

"Very."

Pepe Rodriguez Granados was a muscular, handsome man in his late sixties. His ingenuous smile seemed at odds with his intense black eyes. They were grouped around a large table studying his blueprints, while the production designer explained the basics in halting English, leaving the more intricate details of his designs to be translated by Don Alfonso.

"You will see and understand better when we walk the back-lot," Pepe said. "We can re-dress the Gran Via as it has gradually suffered more damage, but more important"—he pulled another mechanical drawing from under the top sheet and spread it before them—"here you have the Gran Via transformed to the Diagonal in Barcelona for the farewell parade."

"It's a wonderful concept, Pepe," Adrian complimented him.

"Of course the director and his production designer will have their own ideas," Pepe said, "but I wanted to give you at least an impression of what is possible."

"It's more than an impression," Adrian said. "It's terrific work."

"Gracias, señor." Pepe smiled.

"The University front will be a permanent set in a separate area—with a park," Don Alfonso said. He motioned to Pepe and the designer rolled up his blueprints.

"As to the various ministries in the screenplay, we can find practical exteriors and some interiors," Alfonso explained. "We can use the Palacio Real to double for the war ministry, but the Prado museum may be a problem; they forbid strong lights on the paintings."

"Scott may want to build a wing of the museum on a stage," Adrian said.

Don Alfonso nodded. "My feeling is we must immediately place a rental deposit on a minimum of eight stages and lease the entire backlot for the life of the production."

"That's why I came over early," Adrian said. "I opened the production account at Banco de España. You can issue checks. Miss Flint will be staying for a while. She and Eddie Beaumont will pin down the critical locations."

Their coat collars were turned up as they strolled the backlot. The sun had descended and a cold wind blew down from the nearby Guadarrama Mountains. They passed an abandoned Western street, a New York street, the Place des Vosges in Paris, and a forlorn South Side Chicago street circa 1930.

They crossed a set of railroad tracks and entered a wide street lined by two-story buildings, shops, cinemas, sidewalk cafés, and a post office. There was an amorphous European quality to the street; it could have been Brussels or Oslo. At the north end, a broad cobblestoned avenue could be seen.

"Up there, *señor*," Pepe Granados said, "is where the Gran Via will begin."

They reached the cobblestoned avenue and were surprised by its width and length. Adrian guessed it curved northward for at least a thousand yards. Ramshackle four-story and five-story building fronts had been erected on either side.

Pepe said, "This is where the tram tracks will begin. The Calle de Alcalá will intersect here at the Banco de Viscaya. We will duplicate the fronts of the Florida and Palace hotels, the shops, the Teléfonica Centrale, the office buildings, and Chicote's. The cinemas can be spotted wherever the director wishes. The Gran Via will extend northward to the park and University front."

Don Alfonso said, "We've re-created Moscow here and also Berlin in ruins. We have excellent people. The dressing, of course, is again up to Paul Scott and his art director."

Don Alfonso continued talking as they walked the length of the avenue. "I must have a list of period trucks, armored cars, trams, ambulances, taxis, cars of the war ministry, double-decker buses, and motorcycles." He proceeded to delineate the moving and stationary dressing necessary for authenticity, both exterior and interior.

At the top of the rise, Pepe opened his arms to an expanse of park dressed with live linden, maple, and pine trees. "This will be the Casa de Campo. The University buildings will be behind and above the park."

They stood quietly for a moment, the cool wind ruffling Aurora's hair. Adrian turned to Pepe and Don Alfonso. "You've done a thoroughly professional preliminary layout. Now, it's up to us to get our act together."

"And fast," Aurora added.

"Can Miss Flint take these plans back to the studio with her?" Adrian asked.

"We can fax them," said Pepe.

"I don't want studio production people commenting on raw plans coming over a fax," Aurora said. "I'll take them with me."

"As you wish," Don Alfonso said.

Adrian shook hands with the Spanish designer. "Thank you, Pepe. We'll be well served to have you on the picture."

Don Alfonso dropped them back at the Palace Hotel and told them to keep the driver and car for the evening.

"Tell me, Don Alfonso," Adrian asked, "it's been ten years since I was last in Madrid. Is the Casa Paco still good?"

"Absolutely!" He smiled. "I'll arrange for your table."

CASA PACO ENJOYED A WELL-DESERVED INTERNATIONAL REPUTATION for the finest grilled steaks and chops in Madrid. Adrian thought there was something fateful about the old restaurant; it had opened for business in mid-July of 1936—the very week the Civil War began. The room was crowded with Madrileños and Europeans; there were few tourists on the second floor of Casa Paco.

The scent of Aurora's perfume was almost lost in the prevalent odors of garlic, onions, and tobacco.

"Amazing that people still smoke in Europe," she said, "and almost exclusively American cigarettes."

Adrian shrugged. "The Colombians ship us coke and we ship cancer to Europe—business as usual."

Aurora sipped some wine and indicated a meat dish being served to a crowded table presided over by one of Spain's famous toreros. "Wonder what that dish is? Looks great."

"Bulls' balls."

"What?"

"Bulls' balls—they're considered a delicacy."

"Ugh." She gasped and said, "Adrian, do you remember the lion's balls?"

"Do I remember?" He smiled. "The lion's balls have never left my consciousness."

"I never worked directly on *Trader Jim,*" she said, "but the story rippled through the network. I always wondered if it was true."

"It was true all right," he said, refilling her glass. "We were, as you know, making that Tarzan ripoff at Churubusco studios in Mexico City and locations in the jungles of Veracruz. We never had scripts and were only minutes ahead of an airdate. We were set to shoot a segment that pivoted on Trader Jim fighting a rogue lion. It was the only script ready to go. Now our lion, Major, was a pussycat. No teeth. No claws. Swacked out on Demerol. Poor Major could barely growl. The day of the fight a bug invaded his testicles and they swelled. I don't mean a slight swelling. Major was in one cage, and his balls were in another cage supported by a child's wheelbarrow. We were on location in the jungle. I finally got to a small village with a telephone and with great difficulty placed a call. Cut to Harry Walters in his office, Madison and Fifty-eighth—it's snowing in New York."

"Nice cut."

"I thought so—anyway, Harry says, 'Adrian—how are you, my boy.'

" 'Not so good,' I reply and proceed to explain the problem."

Aurora took small cautionary mouthfuls of wine, not wanting to burst into laughter and shower Adrian with red Rioja.

"Harry says, 'What about Major's stand-in?' I say, 'She's a lioness and hates Trader Jim's guts. She growls when his car enters the studio gates. He refuses to fight her.' 'I see,' Harry says, and asks, 'What else have you got?' I went down the list: Panther—'No good, can't see it.' Ocelot—'No, too exotic.' Gorilla—'No, people like gorillas.' A python—'No, snakes are a turnoff.' " Adrian paused. "You realize the network's riding on this conversation—we were the lead-off Saturday night show."

"I remember—*Trader Jim* was big time."

"Right—so finally, reluctantly, I said we have a very young tiger. Harry says, 'That's it, Adrian, have Trader Jim fight the tiger.' I said, 'Not so fast, Harry.' 'Why not?' he asks."

Adrian refilled both their glasses. " 'Because there are no tigers in Africa,' and Harry replies, 'No one knows that. Use the tiger.' 'But, Harry,' I say, 'we play to twenty million people. Someone out there, a child, a schoolteacher, a high-school graduate, a zoologist, an anthropologist, a critic, someone will call us on it and make us the laughingstock of African kiddie shows.' Harry insists, 'Adrian, I guarantee, we will not receive a single complaint; have that imbecile fight the tiger,' and he clicked off. And you know what?"

She smiled. "He was right."

"As rain—no one in America watching CBS between seven and eight P.M. on Friday night knew that tigers do not exist in Africa."

"You know what? Neither did I."

"By the way, Major recovered and spent his remaining years on a farm in the Valley."

After dinner they decided to see flamenco at Zarazuella. They were seated at a comfortable banquette and ordered Fundador brandy. They were mildly drunk but enthralled by the sensual heel clicking, hand clapping, clicking castanets, and authentic Arab lyrics. When the dancers stopped, the break was filled by a virtuoso guitarist who sat on a stool in a red key light and played spellbinding classical Spanish guitar.

In hushed tones, Aurora proceeded to tell Adrian of her fears. She ticked off the recent events, concluding with Solish's line about "the Old Man in the desert."

"Sounds like the Emir of Kuwait."

"It's Leo Resnick."

"You think?"

"I think."

"So be it. Let them screw the stockholders, the theater owners, the unions, or whoever it is they choose to fuck at this particular moment. I just want to make the picture." He kissed her cheek. "You look swell. Not terrific—swell."

"No excuses tonight," she said. "You're single, I'm single." She stared deeply into his eyes. "Can I trust you with an awesome secret?" She traced the line of the scar on his cheek and kissed him softly. "You broke my heart."

"Now, now . . . that's a 'was.' Can I trust you with a stream of momentous secrets?"

"I've got everything crossed."

He proceeded to relate in precise detail his evening in Ocho Rios with Paul Scott, Honeybear, the five-hundred-pound Samoan, the ganja, the cocaine-spiked rum, the lonely lady, and his hotel room door being splintered and smashed. And Scott, ignoring the shocked lonely lady, kissing him and saying, "We're gonna make a great picture, baby."

Aurora laughed until tears streamed down her cheeks. She gasped for breath, swallowed some Fundador, and grabbed his arm. "No more, enough. That's as rich as Julia Castle being gobbled under the table at Cannes—no, it's richer. I guarantee that lonely lady will never forget her Jamaican tryst. Somewhere walking around the Duke campus, a history of art professor is suffering a recurring nightmare of a five-hundred-pound Samoan and a whacked-out director telling you he wants Warren Beatty's old suite at the Beverly Wilshire."

"It was one of those scenes," he said. "How about another brandy?"

"Let's go home, Adrian."

He opened the door to her suite and followed her inside.

"No lights," she slurred. "When I'm this drunk my eyes tend to cross." She leaned into him, curving her body against his. Her arms encircled his neck and she pulled him to her, kissing him deeply. She parted and smiled wickedly. "You know what my true ambition is?"

She staggered slightly and he said, "Get undressed."

"Listen, damnit! I've never told this to a soul."

"Okay."

She tossed her red hair. "I want to be the first woman to be fucked in outer space. In one of those space shuttles just floating weightlessly, and it's on TV. CNN to the world and"—she tottered—"and you know who I'm fucking? Not one of those astronauts, oh no . . ." She swayed and he reached for her. She pushed his hand away. "I want that five-hundred-pound Samoan . . . You see, in outer space he'd be weightless."

She fell onto the bed and passed out.

He undressed her, tucked her in, and scribbled a note on her bureau. "Your secret is safe with me. Had a great night. I'll be at the Hassler in Rome. Take care of Eddie. *Suerte.*"

26

SAL PARNELLI AND IRV WEXLER HAD TAKEN A HELICOPTER FROM THE Luxembourg city airport, landing on the pad adjacent to the gardens of Le Royal Hotel. The check-in procedure had been fast and professional.

They showered, dressed, and went down to the ornate dining room with its exquisite chandeliers and its painted cherubs dancing across the vaulted baroque ceiling. In the background a string quartet played Brahms.

Wexler ordered a bottle of Bernard Massard '67 and turned his attention to the elaborate menu. Parnelli scanned the room, taking in the well-dressed Common Market bankers and their bejeweled wives and mistresses. His slow sweep of the room stopped at a candlelit table where two stunning blond women were sipping champagne and staring into each other's eyes.

"Take a look at those two cunts," Boom Boom said. "I'll bet they're Swedish high divers."

"Probably," said Wexler.

The waiter popped the cork and poured a small amount of champagne into Wexler's glass. He took a sip and nodded. The waiter then filled their glasses and placed the sweating green bottle in a silver ice bucket.

Wexler ordered smoked salmon, truffles, and grilled mountain trout. Parnelli ordered pork chops and a first course of smoked Ardennes ham.

"Some fucking country," Boom Boom said. "The whole thing is as big as Queens and they got more hot money stored here than in Switzerland and Panama put together. They got the best cosmetic surgeons in Europe. They take fallen asses and make them like new. Think of it, Irv—a country based on hot money, chocolate, and fake asses."

"Sounds like Aspen."

"No . . . Aspen's movie people. This is Heidi with a fake ass."

Parnelli continued his critique of the duchy until the waiter served their first course. They ate in silence, washing the food down with champagne. From time to time, Boom Boom's agate eyes shifted from Wexler to the two blondes.

"Sal," Wexler said.

"Yeah?"

"I want you to know that we're all delighted with the job you've done. The Old Man wanted me to give you his compliments."

"He better put his compliments on hold. I'm depending on Squillante to come up with another eight hundred million dollars. I'm stretched out and my deal isn't set."

"Sure it is. When you pull the plug on your offer you'll walk away with no less than forty million."

"Where's that written?"

"Nothing's written. No one has anything on paper. The deal is the deal. It's guaranteed by Leo Resnick."

The waiter removed their plates, served their entrées, and refilled their glasses.

Somewhat subdued, Parnelli said, "I hope I can keep everything zipped up until that Spanish disaster starts shooting."

"Careful, Sal, there are certain things we don't mention. Gemstone will announce *The Volunteers* with great fanfare, and when the picture goes out of control you'll tender the offer. That's all you have to know."

Boom Boom studied the scholarly looking business affairs director. He disliked and mistrusted Wexler but understood they were inexorably tied together.

"You're right, Irv." Parnelli sighed. "I'm just a little tired. This is a complicated deal, and since my company is out in front of the scam I get a little nervous." He pushed his plate away and finished his champagne. "I want to go to the casino, throw some dice."

Wexler took an envelope out of his jacket and slid it across the table. "Two thousand in Swiss francs."

Boom Boom fingered the envelope and eyed Wexler suspiciously. "What for?"

"Petty cash charged to a Gemstone picture called *Snowblind*. Actually it's for your dessert."

"My what?"

"Those two Swedish divers holding hands over there are yours. When you're through with the casino, just knock on the door of suite eight-oh-six."

"You're kidding . . ."

"No. They're a gift from Gemstone Pictures."

Parnelli smiled. "You're full of surprises, Irv."

"I'm just an accountant. Lew Freeman recommended the girls. According to Lew those two dykes have more tricks than a tank full of dolphins."

Wexler signaled for the check. "If I were you, I wouldn't bother with the casino."

"What are you gonna do?"

"Take a stroll—go to Le Grille. Have a sip of Meewan."

"What?"

"Meewan. Liquid gold made from the residue of last year's grape harvest. Supposed to be an aphrodisiac. I can't testify to that, but it tastes great. After the Meewan, I'll go to the Parfumérie and buy a few ounces of something special for my wife."

"Then what? I mean it's early."

"I'll walk back and go to bed. Tomorrow morning I'll deposit a copy of that Centurion bond in the Gemstone vault and fly home."

Wexler signed the check, adding a sizable tip, and slipped the waiter a note. "For that table," he said, indicating the two blondes. "Not bad, eh, Sal." Wexler leaned across the table and in a clipped, cold manner said, "I've been chosen as the liaison man, so if you see, or hear, or think of a problem along the way, you call me—not Solish, not Walters, not Resnick. I'm your contact with Gemstone. You call me."

Parnelli nodded, surprised at the accountant's assertive tone.

"Enjoy your dessert, Sal." Wexler rose. "See you in the morning."

Parnelli unwrapped a thin Sicilian stogie, bit off the end, and spat the shred onto the priceless Persian carpet. The busboy struck a match and held it for him. He blew a cloud of smoke and slipped the boy a ten-franc coin. He was still somewhat thrown by Wexler's authoritarian attitude. The pasty-faced accountant might be tougher than he looked. Sometimes those Hebes came tough. Crazy tough. He remembered the stories of Murder Incorporated: of Phil Strauss, Siegel, Reles, Marty Goldstein, Charlie Workman— tough fucking Hebes. There was an icy Jew behind Wexler's steel-rim glasses. Ah . . . , he sighed, in the end it was all bullshit— Hebes and Wops were the same people. Mediterranean people. Emotional. Hot-blooded.

He snapped his fingers at the waiter.

"Yes, sir?"

"Let me have a Meewan."

"With pleasure, sir."

He sipped the golden liquid and suddenly froze. He had forgotten the blond duo's room number! He'd have to wait in the lobby for Wexler to return from his stroll. How the fuck could he forget a thing like that? Jet lag. Rarotonga. The bar girl. Seeing the god of fertility took something out of a man.

ADRIAN STEPPED OUT OF THE MARBLE LOBBY OF THE HASSLER HOTEL, nodded to the doorman, and got into the rear seat of an enormous white limousine with smoky windows. The cool air-conditioned interior contrasted sharply with the unseasonably warm March day.

"Cinecittà?" the driver asked.

"Yes, please."

The limousine had been provided by Sid Zarcoff, the producer of Jack Wheeler's biblical miniseries, and the courtesy was not purely altruistic. Zarcoff knew that Wheeler had a long-standing relationship with Adrian and the producer hoped Adrian might exert a calming effect on his recalcitrant star.

As the limousine rolled down the steep curve of the Trinità del Monte, the driver said, "Signore Zarcoff will be pleased to see you. The problem with Signore Wheeler is very grave."

"So I understand."

The driver shrugged. "All actors are difficult, eh? Who knows what makes them *pazzo.*"

Adrian did not respond. Seasoned movie people did not engage in dialogues with drivers. Almost without exception, chauffeurs assigned to principals on any picture were fountainheads of gossip.

As they circled the Piazza del Popolo Adrian noticed one of his favorite Roman cafés—Rosati's. He and Silvi shared fond memories of the sidewalk trattoria. It was a good place to have a drink and contemplate the Roman ruins directly across the piazza in the Borghese gardens.

The limousine swung around the Egyptian Obelisk and headed toward the Tiber. The sluggish river shone like burnished silver in the radiant sunlight and the stark, leafless maple trees seemed to belong to another season. Adrian leaned back, loosened his tie, and thought about Aurora and their last night in Madrid. Despite her power position she maintained a certain honesty that somehow withstood the hypocrisy of the business.

"Care for the English paper?" the driver said.

"Yes—thank you."

He glanced at the familiar news items in the *International Herald Tribune:* famine in Nigeria, firefights in Slovenia, rumors of an Iranian nuclear bomb, Israeli jets over Damascus, and in Germany, neo-Nazi thugs attacking Asian refugees.

As they drove past the gated, ochre-colored villas along the Via Appia, Adrian lowered the window, remembering that one could still see the iron grooves impressed into the cobblestones by Legionnaires' chariots returning to Rome from the far reaches of the Empire. This ancient road ran from Rome to Anzio—to the military cemetery—to his father's grave.

The studio security guard waved them past the main gate and they proceeded slowly along a broad street lined by storefronts. Cinecittà was one of the most complete motion picture studios in Europe. Its soundstages were huge, the lighting facilities hi-tech, the backlot expansive, and the technicians first class. Adrian hadn't been here since '78 when he was flown over by United Artists to do a fast rewrite on a spy thriller.

The driver made a sharp left at the corner and they came to a stop in the shade of a soundstage. Both sides of the street were lined by a fleet of diverse vehicles: trailers, generators, honeywagons; electric, grip, makeup, wardrobe, and camera vans. Adrian got out and glanced at Nubian slaves milling around a catering truck; close by, camels, donkeys, and goats brayed for a handout.

"This way, *signore*," the driver said, opening the heavy stage door.

Once inside, it took a moment for Adrian to absorb the bizarre scene occupying the cavernous stage. An immense cyclorama depicting undulating sand dunes painted to what appeared to be infinity was joined by a foreground ledge to an earthen hill rising up from the stage floor. Huge papier-mâché boulders rested on the protruding ledge.

In the center of the stage, a magnificently carved golden calf glowed under the hot lights. Hundreds of Israelites wearing goat-skin costumes were joined by dancing girls and slaves. Pitched tents were cleverly positioned to blend into the cyclorama. Cooking fires burned. Wine casks were filled. Camels, donkeys, and goats were tended by children.

Walking through the maze of electric cable and grip equipment, Adrian noticed a large camper-trailer parked in the semidarkness at the rear of the stage. The trailer had to be Jack Wheeler's. So as not to be annoyed by cast or crew, stars usually insisted that their trailer–dressing room be placed onstage.

A worried-looking young man approached Adrian and asked, "Are you Signore Summers?"

"That's right."

The boy quickly crossed himself, whispered something in Italian, and said, "Please come with me." He followed the tense youth across the stage.

The first, second, and third assistant directors huddled with the director—a grim-faced man who chewed viciously on a wad of gum. The portly Zarcoff was listening sympathetically to his director and shaking his head in dismay.

The young man escorting Adrian tripped over a baby spotlight and bumped into a costumed dancer, causing her to spill hot coffee on her skirt. She cursed him loudly in Roman street slang. Zarcoff turned toward the commotion and a grin creased his face as he saw Adrian.

"Long time, baby." Zarcoff smiled, shaking hands, and turned to the gum-chewing director.

"Adrian, this is my director, Tony Witzer."

Witzer extended a clammy hand and sighed. "I hope to Christ you can help us. I'm dealing with a certifiable madman." The director snapped his gum and went back to his waiting assistants.

Zarcoff moved Adrian away from the extras and the spitting camels. "How long has it been?" the producer asked.

"Oh, '76 or '77—we had adjoining bungalows at Fox."

"That's right—my God, what a memory."

"How could I forget," Adrian said. "You were balling a screamer."

"Right! Margie something. An Irish kid—terrific. Got her out of the typing pool. What a find." He paused and tossed the cigar stub into a half-full coffee container. "Everything okay? The driver? The hotel suite?"

"Perfect, but Gemstone's paying my bills."

"Nonsense."

"No—I'm here to see Jack about *The Volunteers*. It's official business. My trip is charged to the picture."

"Listen, Adrian, you fought the TV wars. You can empathize with my problem. We're eight weeks from an airdate with thirty shooting days still left. I've got a second-unit crew shooting in Israel and we're cutting behind the picture. But it's touch and go—I've got to release this thing at Easter. It's a locked airdate. I miss it and I'm in Chapter Eleven. We've started shooting Sundays. You have any idea what that costs?"

"Probably enough to feed Peru for a month."

"You got it. Wheeler is killing us."

"Booze?"

"No . . . He seems to have that under control. Once we got past the Stolichnaya I thought we were okay. I was wrong—he's driving us crazy with this motivation crap."

"Character motivation for Moses?"

Zarcoff nodded. "He claims there's no motivation for Moses to break the tablets. You go back a long way with him. He did your play years ago. He respects you. I know you have your own business with him and I'm thrilled for you; but if you see an opening, for Godsake help me."

"I'll do what I can."

"Thanks, sweetheart."

The first assistant called places and sent the second assistant to alert Jack Wheeler.

In what appeared to be a well-organized set the first and second assistants assembled the Israelites around the base of the golden calf. The dancers and drummers circled the periphery. Torches outside the tents were lit. Wranglers positioned the camels, goats, and mules. The director mounted his seat on the crane and the boom arm rose.

The second assistant shouted up to the director. "Tony!"

"Yes?"

"Wheeler's on his mark."

"Okay—let's go."

A prerecorded drumbeat filled the stage and costumed drummers pounded on their fake drums. Adrian thought the syncopated rhythm sounded suspiciously like Gene Krupa's famous drum solo on "Sing, Sing, Sing."

Various commands boomed across the set.

"Torches burning!"

"Background stand by."

"Effects stand by."

Tony Witzer shouted down through an electric bullhorn.

"Lightning!"

A bolt of electric blue lightning zigzagged across the cyclorama.

"Thunder!"

A clap of thunder pealed across the stage.

"Okay, stand by!" Witzer said and turned to the choreographer. "Let's get that frenzy going, Francesca!"

A slim woman wearing a black hat, black shirt, and white tie shouted instructions in Italian to the Israelites.

Witzer aimed his amplified megaphone toward a huge papier-mâché boulder halfway up the earthen rise.

"Ready, Jack?"

"Let's shoot the fucker!" a resonant voice responded.

"End slate all cameras!" the first assistant shouted.

"Okay?" Witzer asked.

"Ready!" the first assistant replied.

"Let's roll."

The camera operators shouted in succession:

"Camera one speed!"

"Camera two speed!"

"Camera three speed!"

"Scene forty-eight-A—take twenty-two!" the soundman exclaimed.

"Action!" Witzer commanded.

The dancers waved their arms and performed sensuous bumps and grinds. The Nubian slave girls joined in. Lightning flashed across the cyclorama—thunder echoed.

"Moses!" the director shouted.

Wearing a purple velvet robe, Jack Wheeler appeared from behind the boulder. A mane of snow-white hair fell across his shoulders and the point of his beard touched a gold medallion on his chest. He held a wooden staff in his left hand and the tablets were cradled in the crook of his right arm. His eyes blazed with anger as he surveyed the blasphemous scene below. The first assistant signaled the lead dancer and, one by one, as the frenetic dancers became aware of Moses's presence, their movements slowed and ceased. The playback was out. The drummers stopped beating their prop drums. All eyes turned upward toward Moses.

His face crimson with anger, Wheeler gripped the tablets with both hands and raised them above his head.

Zarcoff chewed his lower lip.

The director crossed himself.

The assembled dancers, technicians, and even the animals fell silent, all staring at Wheeler—waiting for him to smash the Commandments.

He held them high, poised to bring them down.

Witzer shouted, "Come on, Jack! You can do it, sweetheart! Break 'em! Break 'em, baby!"

Wheeler remained transfixed, the tablets trembling in his upraised hands.

"Should we keep rolling?" the first assistant asked Zarcoff in a hushed voice.

"Ask Witzer," he snapped. "I'm not the fucking director."

Adrian couldn't help smiling at the bizarre standoff.

"Save it!" the director shouted.

"Lunch!" the first assistant announced. "Cast and crew one hour!"

Wheeler came down the earthen rise and handed the tablets to a prop man. "I'll keep my staff, Gino."

"What the hell is wrong, Jack?" Witzer asked.

"I've been telling you what's wrong for weeks. There's no motivation for Moses to break the tablets."

"We have a locked-in airdate," Zarcoff said.

"Moses wasn't concerned with airdates. He was delivering God's word, not Nielsen ratings!"

"Heston broke the tablets," Witzer offered.

"Yeah, and it took a chariot race to revive his career."

Zarcoff sighed and turned to the first assistant. "Take Jack over to Mr. Summers."

Staff in hand, Wheeler followed the assistant.

Zarcoff put his hand on the director's shoulder. "Maybe we should just cut from Moses with the tablets raised to an effect shot of the calf melting."

Witzer shook his head negatively. "It's not the same, Sid. Maybe Summers can reach him."

Jack Wheeler greeted Adrian warmly, setting his staff down in order to give him a bear hug. After the bone-crushing *abrazo* the star whispered, "Let's get out of here—the stage is loaded with Zarcoff's spies."

Once outside they walked past extras and technicians seated at portable tables eating pasta and drinking cheap Chianti. Wheeler maintained silence until they reached the sunbaked Western street. The dirt street was dressed by storefronts and smelled of horse manure and urine.

"I'm thrilled for you, Adrian," Wheeler said. "The Spanish script was always great but I never thought you'd find the financing."

"Neither did I." Adrian paused, squinting against the bright sun. "We've signed Paul Scott to direct."

"No shit?"

"No shit."

"I thought he was committed."

"No. He just dropped out for a while."

"Well, let me tell you something; on his best day Paul Scott is terrific, not like these TV traffic cops. Who else have you got?"

"I'm going to meet with Julia Castle in New York. She's doing a play but her agent recommended the script to her. I think we'll get Richard Bryan, and Mayo Morosco's been mentioned."

"Morosco!" Wheeler exclaimed. "He hasn't acted in years. He was hooked on schmeck! His nose collapsed. I understand he's lost line retention."

"Gossip, Jack. Malicious gossip. They don't call him 'the Genius' for nothing. The man single-handedly changed the traditional method of film acting."

Wheeler nodded. "We worked together in Durango years ago. Jesus, if you get a healthy Morosco and fill in those British, French, and Italian roles with solid character people, you've got lightning in a bottle."

The hot sun was melting the pancake makeup on Wheeler's face and brown rivulets ran down the burly actor's cheeks, staining his white beard.

"We may be able to assemble a group of superb actors," Adrian said, "but yours is the critical role, Jack. You're the conscience of the piece."

"I have a few ideas about the role—nothing major—touches."

"Hold on to them. Eddie Beaumont's doing a polish."

Wheeler smiled. "Is that old whoremaster still alive?"

"Just wrapping up his sixth divorce."

"Amazing. I love Eddie." Wheeler picked up his staff. "Fucking hot in this robe. When do you need me?"

"We start principal photography in sixteen weeks."

"Call my agent. Make the deal."

"Swell."

"What?" Wheeler asked, puzzled.

"Terrific," Adrian quickly corrected himself.

"Oh, yeah . . . how's Silvi?"

"Fine. Listen, Jack—I saw *Midnight*, you were marvelous."

They started walking toward the far end of the street. "On the level?"

"Absolutely. One of your finest performances."

"I liked those two kids who wrote and directed."

"You did a hell of a job."

"Thanks. You know I haven't had a drink in seven months."

"So I understand."

"What about you?"

"I've been clean for five years."

"I've got to admit I miss the juice. I hate it but I miss it."

"My therapist said we despise the things we need."

"Ah, bullshit." Wheeler put his huge arm around Adrian's shoulders. "We're rummies and junkies. We need to get loaded. So fucking what? Listen, have some lunch with me in the trailer."

"I can't, Jack—we'll do it in Spain."

"I don't know what to do about the tablets," Wheeler said pensively. The star's entire face seemed to be melting into his beard.

"What's the problem?" Adrian asked.

"Moses is ninety-three. He was up on that fucking mountain for forty days and nights. God had told him that the people were worshipping graven images, so Moses had had a lot of time for his anger to dissipate—right?"

"Makes sense."

"His sacred mission was to deliver those tablets to the tribes. If he breaks them how can he be certain that God will take another meeting with him? Besides, it's a bitch of a climb back up that mountain. Got a cigarette?"

"No. I'm trying to stop."

"Never mind. Anyway Moses knows the people are rock'n and roll'n around that golden calf—right?"

"Right."

As they reached the corner a Wells Fargo wagon pulled by four white horses careened into the Western street, shrouding them in a cloud of red dust.

"Sons of bitches!" Wheeler said, brushing the dirt from his robe. "Give these greaseballs a stagecoach and they think they're in ancient Rome. I can't wait to get back to New York." He wiped the runny makeup with the sleeve of his robe.

They turned the corner and strolled toward the stage.

"I don't mean to be a pain in the ass," Wheeler said, "but Zarcoff and that asshole director are treating the Bible as if it's gospel—the whole thing is nothing more than legend."

"Trouble is," Adrian said, "legend is more durable than fact."

"Does that mean I'm stuck with this scene?"

"No." Adrian sighed. "You're a star, Jack—stars are never stuck with anything but alimony."

As they approached the stage a cluster of Nubian slaves were grouped around the caterer's truck finishing their spumoni. Adrian thought it was now or never. "It's none of my business, Jack, but Zarcoff is not wrong. The motivation is apparent."

"Where?"

"The heat, his age, the fatigue, the disappointment, the sacrifices he endured leading the Hebrew tribes out of Egypt. Moses just lost it. He blew up. Play the rage. The whole thing is operatic anyway.

You're a facile artist. Use your body. Use your eyes. Have them shoot chokers of your eyes. You'll sell it. Break the tablets, it'll play."

"Think so?"

"I'm positive."

They reached the white limo and shook hands.

"I'm thrilled to have you in the picture, Jack."

"Thanks for coming to Rome to see me. And, Adrian, I promise I won't fall off the wagon."

"I know that."

The burly actor turned abruptly and opened the heavy stage door, went inside, and made a beeline for Zarcoff.

"Let's shoot this fucker, Sid."

Adrian had the driver take him to the U.S. Military Cemetery at Anzio-Nettuno. He checked the grave registration directory and followed the security officer along the neat grass lanes between rows of crosses and Stars of David.

"Just down this aisle," the officer said. "Last one to your left."

Adrian reached the grave and placed a single rose at the foot of the cross.

He straightened up and stared intently at the engraved inscription:

CAPTAIN FRANKLIN SUMMERS
325TH REGIMENT—34TH DIVISION
10/25/20–2/28/44

He wondered what sort of man his father had been. What were his ideas? His dreams? His visions? He thought of the improbable set of circumstances that had caused his father to die on the nearby beach.

After a while, he glanced off at the endless lines of crosses and thought about the other men who had suffered the same fate. They had been kids, carrying wallet-size photographs of people and places, mementos of remembered beauty shattered in the millisecond of a shell-burst. There was nothing left but this manicured piece of Italian earth at the edge of what had become a popular summer resort.

Walking out between the rows of crosses, Adrian marveled at

the bizarre power of time, how its passage managed to transform enemies into allies and battlefields into resorts.

The limousine parked near the Egyptian Obelisk in the center of the Piazza del Popolo. Adrian tipped the driver generously and thanked him for the trip to Anzio.

"My pleasure, Signore Summers. I'll pick you up at nine. The morning traffic to the airport is heavy."

"I'll be ready."

The twilight suffused the lights in the cafés surrounding the piazza and the insistent roar of traffic had subsided. Adrian circled the Obelisk and entered Rosati's.

He followed the waiter to a table and ordered a Campari and tonic and a dish of olives stuffed with anchovies.

The sidewalk café was crowded and lively. There were animated Swedish girls, escaping the cold and darkness of their native land. Wealthy Milanese businessmen listened attentively to their German mistresses. A noisy smoke-wreathed table of cinema writers argued the merits of Fellini's latest film. A famous black diva laughed loudly at something her conductor had whispered.

The waiter served the Campari, and Adrian sipped the sweet, rose-colored liqueur and glanced at the floodlit Roman columns. They were like luminous sentinels reminding the twenty-first century of the inevitability of ruins.

Adrian had a special fondness for this ancient city with its fallen columns, ochre walls, and African trees. It was a city of ghosts and mystery, of noisy Vespas and quiet, dark side streets, of marble remnants of ancient glory guarded by legions of wild cats.

He popped an olive into his mouth and tasted the salty anchovy. The amplified stereo played an Italian love song that instantly reminded him of Silvi. He would never lose her. She was his Girl in the Summer Dress. It was impossible to visit familiar places and not be haunted by her. He remembered a younger version of himself and Silvi crossing this same piazza—he'd say something funny and she'd hang on his arm, her head thrown back in laughter. It was not easy to be alone in old familiar places.

But soon he would have lots of company: actors, agents, wives, nannies, an army of movie magicians. They would descend into an alien society and cling together, sharing their most intimate secrets, but as soon as the film was over, it would be as if the shared intimacy had never occurred. One never spoke of indiscretions that had taken place on distant locations—silence was the ancient and honored code of location shooting.

THE LIGHTS ROSE IN THE SCREENING ROOM.

Harry Walters stretched.

Ray Smalley scratched his head.

Aurora rubbed her eyes.

"When do they score?" Walters asked Smalley.

"Two weeks. Trummel wants to use Sonny Rollins."

"To do what?" Aurora said.

"Write the score."

"Rollins is a great jazz virtuoso but he's never composed a film score," she said.

"He'll probably come up with a music track that deserves a better picture," Walters said.

"I like the picture," Smalley said. "I'll bet it goes through the roof."

"You may be right," Walters admitted. "Solish's salesmen love it."

"The girl is really smoked," Smalley said, referring to Tracey Warren's sensuality. "That scene where she kneels down and unbuckles the stockbroker's belt and unzips his fly."

"The zipper opening will have to be cut," Walters said. "The belt buckle is a hard 'R' but the zipper's an 'X.' "

"Too bad," Smalley sighed.

"It's sexier without the zipper," Aurora said.

Walters nodded. "I agree. When was the last time we made a 'P.G.'?"

"This one started off as a 'P.G.,' " Smalley said. "But once they cast this actress we forgot the rating. Tracey Warren does not have Parental Guidance tits—not to mention her keister."

"She certainly has all the right curves," Aurora conceded.

"Jealous?" Walters asked with a smile.

"A little."

Walters and Aurora walked through the dark, deserted studio streets. "You seem depressed," he said. "What is it?"

"Spain."

He squeezed her shoulder affectionately. "Be careful, honey. I'm no authority in matters of the heart, but Adrian is a wounded, complicated man. His years with Silvi are not going to disappear. Now that he's back in action he'll probably——"

"Harry, please," she interrupted. "I appreciate your concern but honestly I'm not in love with him."

They walked past the entrance to the Ritz Hotel in Paris and entered a Mexican plaza.

"How's Eddie Beaumont doing?" asked Walters.

"Fine. We went to Belchite. The whole town is still in ruins. Pretty eerie walking through it—nothing's been touched since '37. We can build fronts, then shoot the ruins."

"Good. Adrian phoned me from Rome. Wheeler's committed to the project. I'd like you to call his agent and make his deal."

"Who represents him?"

"Jerry Blake."

"God, that agency has everybody. Their power is killing the business."

"For the moment, but it'll pass. Power is transient because the power broker molds his disciples in his own image, creating a pool of pretenders to the throne. Inevitably one of the pretenders will either replace the king or build his own empire."

As they approached the administration building, Walters casually said, "I spoke to Mayo Morosco's agent."

"The Genius?" she said, somewhat surprised. "For what role?"

"General José Miaja."

"Of course! It's a fantastic idea." She paused. "But Morosco hasn't worked since *Overlord*. That's six years ago."

"I know. But I got the distinct impression from his agent that Morosco needs money. In any case, I sent him the script."

"They say the Genius is into some bizarre religious sect."

"Everybody's into something," Walters said with a smile.

They entered the old ramshackle building and walked down the hall of "dead actors" to Walters's office.

"What's up, Gloria?" he asked his imperious secretary.

She read the names in a flat monotone: "Solish, Burton Klein, Trummel, the Chipmunk for you, Aurora, and . . ." She peered over her glasses at Walters and, in a tone laced with triumph, added, "Your wife would like to know what time to expect you."

"Tell her to meet me at The Grill at eight-fifteen. I'll phone Klein and Solish first thing in the morning."

Walters held his office door open for Aurora and they went inside.

"A drink?" he asked.

"Sure."

"Scotch?"

"And soda."

"Want to join us for dinner?" he asked, fixing the drinks.

She would have said yes but Walters's catatonic wife was too much to bear. Aurora had a difficult time with people who seldom spoke.

"No thanks. I'm going home—stick some low-cal lasagna in the micro and get into bed. I'm worn out."

"You did a terrific job putting *Snowblind* together, then going on to Spain and getting things organized. By the way, those set-design prints look great."

He handed her the Scotch.

"Cheers," he said.

"Cheers," she replied.

"I don't see how we can improve on the Spanish production designer," she said. "He seems to have a dynamic overview of the whole mad enterprise."

"Not so mad." Walters swallowed some Scotch. "We're stepping out in the grand manner at the right time."

"Maybe, but from Adrian on down: Scott, Wheeler, Bryan, the Genius, Julia Castle, and foreign stars—it's as if we're moving nitro on a hot night in South-Central L.A. The project's a live grenade, Harry."

"Any film that employs truly gifted people is a live grenade. You've got to be innovative in order to survive. The audience represents conformist citizens living in a restrictive, conservative society. We have to go against that. The audience wants to escape that straitjacket of conformity."

"Harry . . ."

"Yes?"

"I may be out of line but I have to ask you." She sipped her Scotch. "At your house—three, four weeks ago, I heard Frank Solish ask you about 'the Old Man in the desert.' Who was he referring to?"

"Leo Resnick." He dropped the name without a second's hesitation and said, "Why do you ask?"

"Just wondered."

"Frank's always been fascinated by gangsters," Walters said. "Some months ago, we had dinner at Le Vallauris in the Springs. Resnick was in the restaurant. Frank wondered if I had seen the Old Man again."

"Oh," she said, feeling foolish for having asked.

"Listen to me." He paused. "Exercise your Gemstone stock options."

"Why?"

"I have a feeling the stock is in for a significant rise."

"You mean the Parnelli takeover thing?"

"That and the fact that we're undervalued and have a strong lineup and a profitable television operation—just do it."

"I don't have any cash," she said.

"I'll have Wexler cut a check for a hundred thousand. Call it a bonus."

"You will?"

"Absolutely—it's long overdue. There's no price on your contribution to Gemstone's success."

Suddenly, impulsively, she grabbed him and kissed him.

They parted and he smiled. "Is that the one-hundred-thousand-dollar special?"

"What do you think?" she said warmly.

She strode to the door and left. He swirled the ice in his Scotch, glanced up at Ava's poster, then shook his head and murmured, "Nitro on a dark night in South-Central L.A. . . ."

He sat at his desk and lit his fifth cigarette of the day. He'd have to speak to Frank and remind him to be careful around Aurora. She was smart as a whip. He had answered her query about Resnick without hesitation and believed every word of it.

He learned long ago never to lie unless you can buy it yourself. Aurora's bonus was an insurance policy. If it came down to cases, she'd protect her pocketbook. And with a little luck, she'd double her money by July.

He swallowed some Scotch and thought about the ethics of his actions. Only desperate men launch desperate schemes and he was neither desperate nor mad. His decision to subvert the Spanish picture and promote the stock swindle represented a classic case of means justifying ends. The industry was in need of a renaissance and only a renaissance man could bring it about. When it came to the preservation of an art form, ethics were irrelevant.

He finished his drink, snuffed out the cigarette, and pressed the intercom.

"Yes?"

"See if you can reach Adrian Summers at the Mayfair Regent in New York."

29

ADRIAN TURNED HIS OVERCOAT COLLAR UP AND TIGHTENED HIS CASH-
mere muffler. The cold night wind and dancing snow flurries
seemed surreal, dreamlike. In only seven hours a summery day in
Rome had been transformed into a wintry Manhattan night.

He left the theater after the final curtain and was standing under
the marquee looking west on Forty-fifth Street, admiring what
appeared to be an Impressionist painting: streaming lights, illuminated snowflakes, rising clouds of underground steam, the va-
porizing breath of police horses, glistening limousines, and excited
audiences leaving their respective theaters.

He was struck by an overwhelming sense of nostalgia. He had
been a young, successful playwright in a theater on this very street,
and he vividly recalled that heart-stopping moment when the curtain
rose. Nothing in film could equal that frightening, magical moment.

He glanced up at Julia Castle's name glowing above the marquee. She had somehow climbed the mountain; it was one hell
of a ride from that West Virginia coal town to these bright lights.

The theater doors were suddenly flung open and the exuberant
playgoers rushed out. Adrian managed to elbow his way through
the crowd to the Shubert Alley stage door. Once inside, he
brushed the snowflakes from his overcoat, loosened his muffler,
and gave the stage door guard his name. The man checked a list

of approved names and nodded. "Upstairs, first dressing room on your right."

He climbed the worn concrete steps, still thinking of Julia's performance. Her incredible beauty was a handicap on stage, a challenge she had to overcome in order to become the character in the play. Her performance had been mesmerizing. No playwright could have hoped for a finer rendition of his work.

Groups of well-wishers stood outside the various dressing rooms. A young man wearing an usher's uniform guarded Julia's closed dressing room door. Adrian excused himself as he moved through the circle of visitors and gave his name to the usher. A flash of recognition lit up the youth's eyes. "Miss Castle's expecting you. Go right in."

She stood before a full-length mirror wearing an open black silk kimono. Her small, straight nose crinkled as she vigorously brushed her white-gold shoulder-length hair. Her high, sculptured cheekbones contrasted seductively with her soft, full mouth. Her tall, curvy figure was perfectly proportioned. The open kimono revealed long dancer's legs that tapered down to delicately shaped ankles.

She caught a glimpse of him and turned around. A devilish smile appeared on her lips and she approached him slowly. Even without makeup her complexion was flawless. Her amber eyes radiated a sense of danger. They were tiger eyes and she knew how to use them.

She kissed him softly on the mouth. "Shame on you—standing there, spying on me."

"It's been a while." He smiled. "I had forgotten how outrageously beautiful you are."

"The hell with that—what about my performance?"

"You were terrific." He remembered not to say "swell."

"Really?"

"Yes . . . really."

"Let me throw something on. I'm absolutely starved."

She slipped off her kimono, turned to him, and raised her arms in a Diana-like pose. She was wearing only silk panties. "What do you think?"

He smiled. "I think this is close to sexual harassment."

"Remember when I did that bit in *Trader Jim?*"

He nodded. "The nurse in the jungle."

"In those days I'd flop for a pastrami sandwich and a ticket to the Kahala Hilton. Have a drink. I'll only be a minute."

She disappeared behind a dressing screen. He crossed to the bar and poured himself a few fingers of brandy. Nothing she said or did surprised him. She acted out of a childlike arrogance triggered by her extraordinary beauty.

"Adrian?"

"Yes."

"You're not kidding me about my performance?"

"Not at all. You were that funny-sad girl and somehow managed to overcome your beauty."

"That's what the fellow on the *Times* wrote. You wouldn't think they'd review my genetic luck. I mean what the hell does beauty have to do with acting?"

"Nothing—but it's there. It was a stunning piece of work, Julia."

"I'm scared to death on that stage. Terrified. But I was determined to bring this off. I studied until I dropped. I haunted the Actors Studio. I learned how to find that critical moment in a scene, that second or so that demands total concentration."

She came out from behind the screen wearing black cashmere slacks, a turtleneck sweater, black leather boots, and, except for her pink lipstick, no makeup. She held an open diamond bracelet in her hand.

"Help me with this. My producer gave it to me and I can never close the fucking clasp."

Adrian clicked the latch shut and shook his head admiringly. "That's some gift."

"Well, why not? I made a fortune for him."

She picked up her vicuna coat and pulled on her gloves.

"How's about Patrice's in Little Italy?" she said.

"Sure."

"You just came from Rome, you're probably sick of pasta."

"Patrice's is fine."

"It's selfish of me but I'm dying for zuppa di vongole, fried calamari, and ziti." She tossed her pale-gold hair and stared deeply into his eyes.

"Are you all right, Adrian?"

He knew what she was referring to. "I've been clean for years."

*　　*　　*

182

They ran the gauntlet of admirers, Julia nodding and smiling along the way. The doorman held the stage door open. The limo was waiting in Shubert Alley. They climbed in and settled back in the spacious leather seat. The driver closed the door and got behind the wheel.

"Patrice's," she said. The limousine rolled out of Shubert Alley, turned right, and headed west. "God, it's beautiful," she said. "The snow, the lights, the steam—the whole New York thing." She squeezed his hand and looked out of the window. Her profile could break your heart, he thought.

"Oh, Adrian," she said, turning to him. "This has been an incredibly joyous time for me. It's not like film. You're not playing to a lot of fucking equipment. The audience is really there waiting to be seduced. At first they're arch, reserved, 'show me—live up to your reviews, you bitch.' About five minutes in, there's a very rough, unexpected line. When she says to the priest, 'I can do something for you God can never do. I can give you'—"

"I remember," he interrupted, holding up his hand.

"When I hear them react I know I've got them. Then she breaks down and cries. She's such a cunt, isn't she?"

"She's human. It's a very well-written character."

"And you're a very bad boy."

She was thrown up against him as they swerved around a truck that had run a light on Hudson Street.

"Why am I a bad boy?"

"Going to Ocho Rios—seeing Paul."

"Let's discuss it at dinner."

"I'm absolutely famished, but I've been watching my weight. I was overweight in *Legend.*"

"You look great."

"Everyone looks great in footlights."

"I saw you practically naked a few minutes ago. You're in the best shape of your life."

She kissed his cheek and her eyes grew pensive.

"I heard about you and Silvi breaking up."

"We're still close."

"When I was practically hooking to stay alive she was very kind to me. She's not only beautiful, she's got that special thing, that empathetic kindness—it's just there."

They crossed Canal Street and entered Chinatown.

"I had a cheerleader," she said suddenly.

"A what?"

"A pom-pom girl. We were on the road trying out the play—regional theater—in Salt Lake, I guess. They had this parade for me. A promotion for the play. I saw this girl tossing a baton and striding like a Thoroughbred filly."

"How old was she?"

"I don't know—seventeen, eighteen. We had a lot of fun. I always wanted to be a pom-pom girl. But I never went to high school. I started working the day I learned to walk. Christ almighty, what a dreadful time that was. My father used to come up from that fucking mine spitting blood and covered with coal dust.

"Poverty killed my mother. Good things happened for me too late to help her, but I've taken care of my father. No medals. It's been a joy."

Adrian smiled. "You probably ruined that cheerleader."

"Are you kidding? She wore me out. You'd be surprised at what's out there on the prairie." She squeezed his hand. "The Spanish script is marvelous. I love the role, but I can't do it."

"Let's discuss it after the calamari."

"I've always been taken with you, Adrian—I mean interested. I wonder what you're like under that Jay Gatsby cool."

"What's that perfume you're wearing?"

"It's called Maja—it's Spanish. I wore it for you."

Patrice's played to a special late-night audience: jockeys, fighters, journalists, a few local artists, an opera star, and, seated at a table flush with the wall, a major capo in the Lucchese family with his bodyguards and two chorus girls.

From the moment they entered, the conversation in the restaurant had diminished; all eyes were on Julia. Oblivious to the attention, she ate voraciously, dipping her bread into the clam soup, popping fried calamari into her mouth, and swilling Chianti while still managing to conduct a monologue.

"As I said, the screenplay is fabulous and the role of Rebecca is marvelous, but having Paul direct makes it impossible for me. I can't work with him."

"Why not? He's a brilliant director. A little crazy. But a genius."

"You're wrong," she said. "He's neither crazy nor a genius. He's an artist and some of his stuff works and some of it doesn't. Paul's gift is his incredible retention. He can be shooting out of sequence but in his head everything's in sequential order. He hears the score and sees the edited film as he's shooting. He's on the stage, but in his head he's in the theater with the audience watching the finished movie."

She pushed the soup bowl away, wiped her fingers, and swallowed the blood-red Chianti.

"Clams were sensational. Don't let Paul touch the script. He's not a dramatist, but he's the perfect director for *The Volunteers*. I wish I could do it."

The strong wine combined with jet lag made him impulsive. "Paul has suffered," Adrian said, "and he deserves a shot."

"Suffered? Suffered?" Her tiger eyes flashed. "Don't be fooled by his dropping out with his cat. He has a great sense of self-promotion.

"That whole thing in Cannes, years ago—the French girl going down on me under the table. It was staged. She never touched me. The Italian count was an out-of-work actor. Paul thought the story would break me out. Scandal is box office. What a joke. I was young. He was my mentor. But Paul Scott suffering? That bastard had a fling with Astra Collins, for Chrissake."

"What's wrong with that? She's an attractive, successful agent."

"Listen." She rubbed her hands with childlike pleasure as the steaming ziti was served. "Astra Collins has had her legs in more stirrups than Willie Shoemaker."

The waiter refilled her wineglass as she dug into the baked pasta. Adrian sipped his wine. "I've heard stories about Astra, but you hear things about everyone."

"I'm not jealous. Not in the least. But I lost all respect for him."

"Listen to me, Julia. We've got Jack Wheeler, Richard Bryan, and"—he paused dramatically—"Mayo Morosco."

She turned to him, a fork full of ziti suspended in midair.

"The Genius?" she said reverently, lowering her fork. Adrian knew he had her.

"The Genius . . ." she whispered, and glanced off at the famous Italian tenor who raised his glass and toasted her loudly.

"*Brava*, Signora Castle. I saw your play!"

She smiled, raised her glass, and returned the toast, "*Bravo* to you, maestro!"

The Lucchese capo said something to the waiter, who nodded and hurried off. Adrian could have murdered the opera star for disturbing his pitch but his anxiety was groundless. Julia moved closer to him, her thigh pressing against his. She traced the scar on his cheek with her forefinger.

"Who's the director of photography?"

"Paul wants to use Federico Rossi."

"Oh Jesus! Federico Rossi," she said admiringly, "and Mayo Morosco, Jack Wheeler, Richard Bryan . . ."

"And Julia Castle." He smiled.

"What about all the foreign roles?"

"We're trying to get the top people."

"I want a cannoli," she said with childlike petulance.

The waiter returned, holding a bottle of grappa.

"A *digestivo*," he said. "Fine imported grappa—compliments of Don Vito." He indicated the Lucchese capo.

Adrian waved to Don Vito and out of the corner of his mouth whispered to Julia, "Smile at him, for Chrissake." She showed her pearlies and tossed her golden mane while the waiter poured the grappa into two thin-stemmed glasses.

"You'll own this place if you're not careful," Adrian said.

They sipped the strong colorless liqueur and felt it smoke its way down.

"Adrian . . ."

"Yes."

"You tell that sonofabitch Paul, no fucking chokers unless Rossi uses a long lens. I don't want to compete with the background."

"Okay."

"My God . . . Morosco, Wheeler, Rossi, and that little shit Bryan. I despise him but he's a fine actor. And Paul, my Paul having an affair with that tramp, then running away with Honeybear. She's my cat, you know."

"Paul said he found her on Third Avenue."

"She's my cat," Julia said stubbornly.

The waiter served the cream-filled cannoli and she picked it up and bit into the crust. "I've read all the Greek playwrights, and Stendhal, Schiller, Baudelaire, Rousseau, and, of course, Shakespeare." She licked the cream from her fingers. "I could even play the Mad Dane. Who needs balls to do Hamlet? I never went to school, but I've memorized entire passages of F. Scott, Hemingway, Melville, Jack London—" The names poured out of her in a determined "I'm somebody" burst. "I've studied, Adrian. I've given it everything I have."

In that moment, with the wine and grappa, the smells of garlic and tobacco and Julia's heady Spanish perfume, Adrian, sitting thigh to thigh with this dazzling, troubled girl, loved her. He loved them all, the artists, actors, painters, composers, writers—all the wounded angels.

"What is it? Why are you staring at me?"

"I'm sorry," he said. "It's a deal; no chokers unless Rossi uses a long lens."

She was strangely silent during the drive back uptown. Her head rested on the pillowed leather top, her eyes wide open, staring.

"Anything wrong?"

"I was just wondering."

"About what?"

"Did all that really happen? I mean in Spain, during the siege."

"Yes. It happened."

"There are some scenes that made me cry. When those trains meet, the wedding, the final defeat at the Ebro—and the farewell parade in Barcelona."

She turned to him. "I'm thrilled to be a part of it."

The limo parked at a three-story brownstone on East Sixty-fifth Street.

They got out and dashed to the entrance as the snowflakes played across their faces.

At the door, she turned to him and kissed him deeply, sensually. He felt himself heating up as they parted. She kissed him again quickly, lightly, and disappeared inside. He stood there for a moment, tasting her lipstick and sensing her perfume.

The door suddenly opened. "I want my own makeup man and wardrobe lady. Approval of all still shots and publicity releases. Have a safe flight home, and give Paul a hug for me."

He got back in the limo and thought about her. She was the girl in any Cole Porter song but God help those who fell in love with her. She was fighting her beauty, her past, her legend, and her success.

He smiled, thinking that after all his meticulously rehearsed speeches during the flight from Rome, the nickel had dropped when he mentioned Mayo Morosco. Legends loved legends.

30

FRANK SOLISH FELT UNEASY AS HE RODE UP IN THE PRIVATE ELEVATOR.

He had lunched with Salvatore Parnelli and, over espresso, Boom Boom had casually remarked, "Squillante's having trouble finding an additional eight hundred million. If the Count doesn't come up with it, Centurion can void their bond."

Solish got off the elevator at the penthouse level and walked down the thickly carpeted hall, wondering whether to alert Walters and Resnick to the problem, but decided against it. Wexler was the point man on the fiscal end of the scam. Fuck it—let Irv worry about the Wop.

Since assuming the role of CEO, Solish had been inundated with bureaucratic red tape. His marketing expertise had been diverted by the maze of corporate operations. He sighed, thinking maybe Resnick had put the nail on Schuller prematurely—wearing the mantle of CEO had been as thrilling as growing another hemorrhoid.

He turned the corner and saw the polished oak doors embellished with the raised gold letters CHARLES LEVITT AND ASSOCIATES. He detested these endless sessions with Gemstone's accountants. They pressed him relentlessly for answers to a wide range of subjects: projected grosses of current pictures, both domestic and foreign, TV syndication revenue, the effect of foreign currency

189

fluctuations against the dollar, carry value of projects in the pipe-line, writeoffs on abandoned scripts, on and on. The grilling would not end until late this evening.

Well, he'd stay overnight at the St. Regis. He hadn't used the Waldorf corporate suite since Schuller's demise. Resnick had made a strong case for removing the unrepentant Nazi CEO, but murder exceeded Solish's limited ethical strictures.

He opened the heavy oak door and entered a spacious, softly lit wood-paneled reception area. A large sepia-tone photograph of Wall Street, circa 1912, hung on the wall behind the reception desk.

A homely, dark-haired receptionist answered the phone in a singsong Brooklyn accent, "Levitt and Associates—just a moment, puleez."

Paying no attention to Solish she continued her ongoing phone conversation. "He was nice—yeah—but he had a funny smell—like pine needles. All he talked about was Woody Allen. I said to him, listen, are you in love with Woody or what?"

Solish cleared his throat, coughed, and with undisguised annoy-ance said, "Miss—Miss, can you hold that for a minute?"

She glared at him. "I'll talk to you later, Janet." She hung up and picked at a pimple on her chin.

"Yeah?"

"Frank Solish to see Mr. Levitt."

She pressed a button on the console. "Nina? The guy is here to see Charlie—okay."

She pressed the disconnect button and, without looking up, said, "Have a seat."

In that second he lost it, he lost it all: the scam, Parnelli, the board, Resnick, Gemstone—all of it. A ball of heat scorched his throat.

He shoved the phone console out of the way and leaned across her desk, his face close enough to count the hairs on her mustache, and in a false friendly tone he said, "How did you know my name?"

She stared at him with a mixture of surprise and fear. "What?"

"I want to know how you knew my name."

"I don't know what you're talking about. I told you to take a seat."

"Tell me how you knew my name. I have a very unusual name: how many people do you know that are named 'The Guy'?"

"What?"

"You hoid me, sweetheart." He said "hoid" instead of "heard"—this cunt would set him back six weeks at Berlitz. "Look, if you say 'The Guy is here,' it means I have no identity—I'm nothing, which means Charlie Levitt is less than nothing."

Her eyes turned wary as she wondered about the best route of escape. "Would you please get out of my face."

He straightened up. "My name," he gasped, choking on his rage, "my fucking name, is not 'The Guy.' It's Frank Solish. I'm CEO of Gemstone Pictures and I'm here to see Charles Levitt, who happens to be my accountant."

"You're a crazy person—get away from me."

"I'm a client. I pay this firm a ton of money. They work for *me*, which means *you* work for me too. That's not hard to understand, is it, honey?"

"Don't call me honey. I'm not your honey."

"Well, at least you got that right."

He started for the door.

"Frank!"

He turned to see a balding, harried-looking man.

"Where are you going?" Levitt asked. "The whole team's waiting for you."

"Not for me. My name's Frank Solish. The team's waiting for someone named 'The Guy.'"

"The Guy?" Levitt asked, incredulous. "What guy?"

Solish pointed to the secretary. "Ask her."

"What's she got to do with this?"

"So long, Charlie."

"What do we do with the annual report?"

"Shove it up your ass!"

It was a bright sunny day, a pleasant harbinger of spring. But as Solish walked up Chambers Street he couldn't shake his anger. "The Guy" stuck in his throat and burned a hole in his stomach. He had made it. He wasn't the street urchin in Dr. Graff's chair. It was too late to accommodate "The Guy." He was Frank Solish, CEO of Gemstone Pictures, and he had walked out on the annual report. Walters would be upset. Wexler would be beside himself. There would be astronomical time charges for the assembled accountants. Fuck it. He had paid his dues. He had a name.

31

THE SALON OF PAUL SCOTT'S SUITE AT THE BEVERLY WILSHIRE HOTEL had been converted into a motion picture production office. Pepe Granados's blueprints of the Gran Via and the University front were spread across a huge marble table and several cans of cat food held down their curled edges.

The screenplay had been broken down into individual scenes summarized on five-by-seven index cards pinned to a large corkboard. Aurora was seated at an ornate desk making copious notes while Adrian and Eddie Beaumont reviewed the abbreviated scene cards.

Paul Scott and the American production manager, Fred Glickman, sat on the floor studying a production board that displayed thin multicolored quarter-inch cardboard strips detailing the shooting schedule. Each strip contained an amazing wealth of information: whether the scene was day or night; interior or exterior; the time and scenes in which various actors worked; the gender, age, and number of dress extras; vehicles; props; livestock; wardrobe; special effects; and cover sets in case of inclement weather. Once the director approved the production board schedule a budget could be made. The strips could be moved and reinserted at any place on the board should production problems dictate a switch to an earlier or later date.

Despite his reputation as a petty thief who accepted kickbacks, Fred Glickman worked on world-class pictures. His larceny was overlooked by virtue of his talent. Glickmen knew how to organize and cope with the arcane details that comprised a day's shooting. He always anticipated a worst-case scenario and operated on the realistic theory that what could go wrong would go wrong. He was responsible for providing the director with every minuscule detail required for a day's shoot. Glickman's production expertise more than compensated for his larceny.

Perched atop a tall French armoire, ignoring the activity below, Honeybear busily licked her luxurious red fur.

"I need five days for that train sequence," Scott said to Glickman. "I'll never make it in three—too many extras, too many effects; besides all the principals' work. It's the emotional punctuation of act two, and demands a lot of coverage."

"Okay," Glickman said, sliding the strips out and setting them aside—two more strips would be added.

"Got that, Red?" Scott called to Aurora.

"Got it."

She noted the scene number and added days. It seemed to her that Scott's boyish good looks were fading under the pressure of the approaching start date.

"I can modify that scene if it will help," Beaumont offered.

"No," Adrian replied. "Paul's right. It's a critical scene. We can't cheat that one."

"What about the University front?" Aurora asked.

"That sequence demands night-for-night," Scott said and turned to Adrian. "Is that okay with you?"

"Sure—no problem."

"Let me change those day strips to night," Glickman said, pulling the white strips and inserting blank blues to be detailed later.

"Pepe Granados's blueprints are terrific," Scott said. "I'd like to use him."

"I thought you wanted Tony Frazer," Adrian said.

"So did I, but Pepe's designs are sensational and he's Spanish. He knows what actually happened in '36 and what we have to re-create."

"His English is limited," Aurora cautioned.

"Maybe, but not his talent. Let's sign him as production designer, and Fred"—he turned to Glickman—"I want Federico

193

Rossi in Madrid three weeks before we start. I'd like him to shoot tests of key sets, exterior and interior."

"Rossi's expensive."

"Get him," Adrian ordered. "You never lose money rehearsing."

"Suits me," Glickman said, smoothing his Vandyke beard.

"Is our European casting lady on the case?" Scott asked.

"She'll meet you in Madrid," Aurora replied. "She has offers out to all of your top choices. I almost forgot, she wants to know whether to make an offer to Claudia Grimaldi for the part of Carmen."

"I think we should use a Spanish actress," Scott said. "If we can find one that can handle it. I mean this is the *Spanish* Civil War. Honeybear! Come down here, baby!"

The red cat ignored him and continued to lick her paws and rub them across her face.

"She's always bathing," Scott said.

"Like Lady Brett." Adrian smiled.

"Like who?" Scott asked.

"The female lead in *The Sun Also Rises*," Beaumont explained. "Adrian's fascinated with Lady Brett's continuing desire for a bath."

Scott stretched, sipped some orange juice, lit a cigarette, and asked, "Where are we with principals?"

"We've signed Wheeler," Aurora stated. "We're in negotiation for Julia Castle. We're ready to sign Richard Bryan but he insists on meeting with you before we close."

"Where and when does he want to meet?"

"It's up to you. He's finished shooting *Wetworks*."

"I don't want to get into a pissing contest with him. He's a fine actor but a major ball breaker."

"Is he off the schmeck?" Glickman asked. "I did *Outrigger* with him in Hawaii—he was flying."

"He's clean," Adrian said. "We checked with Warner's—no trouble on *Wetworks*. No schmeck. No booze. He jogs, eats veggies, new wife, new philosophy."

"What about his overactive libido?" Scott asked.

"His satyriasis is apparently in remission," Aurora said.

"Let's hope so," Scott said. "What's the word on Wheeler?"

"On the wagon but a pain in the ass," Adrian replied.

"The Moses story is priceless," Beaumont said, then remarked,

"Although when you think about it, Wheeler's not altogether wrong. I wouldn't climb up Mount Sinai twice and I'm not as old as Moses."

Scott walked over to Beaumont and squeezed his shoulder affectionately. "You did a fine piece of work on the rewrite. The politics of the war are simplified. The love story is poignant, not soapy. The structure is solid. I'd like you to accent the principal theme—that is, if Adrian agrees."

"What do you have in mind?"

"I think we have to see, hear, or feel that losing the war was not the ball game for the volunteers. The fact that they were there, that they risked it all for something they believed in, is victory enough. The audience has to feel the passion of those kids—without speeches. You've got to find a way to dramatize that theme without schmaltz. Also remember to emphasize that the first time white and black American soldiers were fully integrated was in Spain—in the Lincoln Brigade. I think that's important, Eddie."

"I'll do my best," the veteran screenwriter said.

"Rossi will light each scene for effect," Scott continued. "Soft amber tones, silhouettes and backlight. A feeling of the last chance, last kiss, last song—the art direction, the music, the staging, will work toward that same end, but we need your help, Eddie."

"It's dicey—one word too many and we're back to *The Fighting Sixty-ninth.*"

"They *were* the Fighting Sixty-ninth," Adrian interjected. "Spain happened only fifteen years after World War I. Don't be afraid of it, Eddie. There was still a certain innocence in the world."

"What about the negative?" Glickman asked.

"We ship it to Hollywood after we develop it in Madrid," Adrian said. "We'll print two sets of dailies. One set stays in Madrid for editing. We'll cut as we shoot. The second set can be shipped to the studio with the negative."

"How reliable is the lab in Madrid?" Scott asked.

"The best in Europe," Beaumont said. "Phono España developed all of Sam Brontson's pictures. We never lost a foot of film; their one-light dailies looked like timed prints."

"Fine with me," Glickman said.

"When do we see the Genius?" Scott asked.

"Walters is working on it with Morosco's manager," Aurora replied.

"They say he's lost his line retention," Glickman said.

"Fuck it," Scott snapped. "We'll use cue cards or loop him. His presence is priceless."

"You're the boss." Glickman shrugged. "Do you intend to shoot in seventy millimeter?"

"No. We'll blow up the thirty-five millimeter for the reserved-seat prints."

"Not that it matters, but is anyone hungry?" Beaumont inquired.

"Why don't you, Aurora, and Fred go across the street to The Grill," Scott suggested. "I have to speak to Adrian alone."

"I love The Grill," Aurora said. "Best Cobb salad in town."

"Don't we need reservations?" Beaumont asked.

"No," she said, getting to her feet. "I've been a loyal customer from the day they opened. The boys always take care of me."

They started for the door and she glanced back at Adrian. "See you after lunch?"

He nodded. "At the studio."

Once the door closed, Scott walked over to Honeybear. "Want some Puss 'n Boots?"

The cat's ears pricked and she meowed loudly.

"Come on," Scott said, picking her up.

Adrian followed them into the kitchen. Scott opened a can of cat food and served it to Honeybear.

"How about a drink?" Adrian asked Scott.

"Stoli on the rocks?"

"Make it a double."

Scott proceeded to fix Adrian's drink, then poured himself a glass of white wine. They went back into the salon and sat down on opposite sofas.

"Now, tell me about Julia," Scott said.

HARRY WALTERS CLOSED THE PLASTIC LID ON HIS KEVIN COSTNER salad, sipped the last of his Amstel Light, and lit his third Sherman. He studied the names on his pad: Paul Scott, Jack Wheeler, Richard Bryan, Julia Castle, and Mayo Morosco with an asterisk. They hadn't yet closed with the Genius, but his manager indicated that Morosco could be had for the right price. Walters then shifted to the list of possibilities for the foreign roles—taken altogether, it would be a remarkable cast.

He felt the kick of nicotine and a curious thought struck him: suppose all these emotional cripples controlled their demons long enough to make it through the shoot? What then? The picture might turn out to be a . . . The flat buzz of the intercom interrupted his train of thought.

"Solish returning," Walters's secretary announced.

"Hello, Frank."

"What's up, Harry?"

"I received a frantic call from Charlie Levitt. He said you walked out of the annual report meeting—something to do with his receptionist."

"That's right."

"Want to discuss it?"

"No. Charlie's coming over to my office tomorrow at noon. We'll get the report done."

"Do you want Wexler at the meeting?"

"Wouldn't hurt."

"I'll ask him to take the red-eye."

"Okay."

"You sound tense. Is everything all right?"

"Parnelli may be having fund-raising problems."

"You better alert the Old Man."

"I already have."

"Good."

"We ran *Backwash* for three hundred exhibitors. They ate it up. That cunt is sensational."

"You mean Tracey Warren?"

"Yeah. She's terrific. Sex just oozes out of her. Trummel did a hell of a job. There's only one scene that played flat."

"Which one?"

"In that tropical bar. It's a blatant lift of *Casablanca.*"

"We couldn't shoot it on the water," Walters explained.

"The dialogue is shit—who wrote it?"

"Trummel."

"He should stick to directing. It's gonna be a smash anyway. The girl makes it work. Where'd you find her?"

"Aurora spotted her in a soap."

"We ought to wrap her up."

"I'm working on it."

"Is it true that Summers got Julia Castle?"

"We've closed the deal."

"Hell of a cast—what about Morosco?"

"Looks good. The boys are going to meet with him." Walters paused. "When are you coming out?"

"I don't know."

"I think you should be here for the announcement."

"If you need me, I'll be there."

"It would help."

"You got it."

"Frank, talk to Bill Trinz, he's Julia Castle's play producer. Try and get him to spring her for a few days. It would be terrific to have her at the announcement party."

"Talk won't do it, Harry. Julia's stand-in won't sell any tickets. Trinz will want us to make up the difference."

"It's worth it."

"I'll have lunch with him—tell him we're interested in buying the play for a feature."

"Good idea. How's Doris?"

"The usual complaints."

"Give her my best and take care of yourself."

Feeling uneasy, Walters hung up. His longtime colleague was clearly suffering severe emotional stress. According to Charles Levitt, Frank had lost control in a disagreement with the receptionist—she had referred to him as "The Guy." The remark probably triggered some demon out of Frank's impoverished past, Walters reflected. Solish was a superb salesman who had clawed his way out of the Brownsville ghetto, and his hellish childhood had left him insecure and scarred. Now, finding himself at the very edge of a fabulous score, it was only natural that he feel the pressure. Still the blowup with the receptionist and that tidbit about Parnelli were not good news. Well, Resnick would handle it.

The intercom buzzed.

"Yes, Gloria?"

"Miss Flint, Charlie Morton, and Jerry Dicola."

"Send them in." Walters walked to the bar and poured himself a Scotch on the rocks.

The door opened and the Chipmunk and Dicola accompanied Aurora into the office.

"Anyone want a drink?" Walters asked.

Aurora declined. "Not for me."

"No thanks," Morton said.

"I'll have a finger of vodka," Dicola said, "on the rocks."

Walters fixed the drink and handed it to Dicola.

"Here's to the Ball Crusher," the horror writer toasted.

Walters exchanged a quick glance with Aurora, who bit her lip, trying not to smile. "The Ball Crusher," Walters toasted. He sat down and indicated the chairs in front of his desk. "Have a seat, fellas."

He hadn't seen Dicola in a while and had forgotten how startlingly grotesque the man was. Folds of skin drooped from a boneless face. His flat nose seemed to be made of blue clay and his thick-lensed glasses magnified and distorted his eyes.

"Well, I read the treatment," Walters said to Dicola. "You've taken Aurora's one-liner a long way."

Morton felt as though the sun had risen for him alone. He

smelled a development deal. Aurora watched the scene unfold with a bemused look. She liked Morton but didn't want to be caught dead anywhere near this project.

"I like the fact that we lose the ball crushing over titles," Walters remarked.

"That was Jerry's idea," Morton said, deferring to his writer.

"Yeah . . . well, I said to myself," Dicola expounded, "what could be driving this crazy broad to squeeze balls—and den it hit me." All his years in California had not diminished Dicola's heavy Mulberry Street accent. "It hit me right in da bonzo. I knew we needed a subplot and it came to me out of da blue. What we needed was"—he gulped the vodka—"a fuck'n killa cult."

There was a sudden silence as Dicola waited for Walters's reaction.

"Seems to work—don't you agree, Harry?" Morton said tentatively.

"I haven't read it all the way through but I don't want to lose our title," Walters said.

"Not to worry," Dicola said. "We'll still call it *Basic Desires.*"

"I love the title," the Chipmunk hastily agreed. "We're not going to lose that title."

"What does this killer cult get into?" Walters asked.

"Devil worship," Dicola replied. "People love that shit. Blatty made a fortune with it, God bless him. Remember the Senate hearings on that black judge a few years ago? Remember that candy-ass Senator Hatch waving Blatty's book in the air and wanting to know who put the cunt hair on the Coke. Geez, what a plug for Blatty, God bless him."

Walters smiled. "Devil worship certainly has its devotees."

"We'll steal a piece of *Rosemary's Baby,*" Dicola said. "And have our girl knocked up by the chief of the killa cult; opens it up for a seekel."

"A what?" Aurora asked, perplexed.

"A sequel," Morton interpreted.

"That's what I said, a seekel," Dicola repeated.

"Yes, you did," Walters agreed. "Am I correct in assuming you've consented to omit your middle name from the screen credit?"

"Yeah—what the hell, if it bothers you, fuck it. I only use it to please my mother."

"Good." Walters rose. "Start writing, Jerry. I don't mean to cut you fellows short, but I'm running behind schedule."

"No problem." The Chipmunk rose and smiled. "We've got a lot of work ahead of us—let's go, Jerry."

Dicola finished the vodka and wiped his lips with the back of his hand. "Nice see'n ya again, Harry. I'll give you a dynamite script. You can sleep on it."

"I know that. When it comes to horror—you're the best."

The Chipmunk hustled the pudgy writer out and closed the door softly behind him.

"It's very kind of you, Harry," Aurora said, "giving Morton a development deal. The poor man is a walking sight gag—everyone has a laugh at his expense."

"He's a decent guy." Walters paused. "What's happening over at the hotel?"

"Glickman's boarded the screenplay for a hundred forty-five days of principal photography, and sixty days of second unit."

"What about post-production?"

"John Carr is going to set up an editing room at the hotel in Madrid. He'll have a crew of sound and picture cutters. They'll edit behind the shoot. Paul thinks he can have rough cut five weeks after we wrap. We've got a fighting chance to make Christmas for Academy consideration."

"I did some checking," Walters said and proceeded to read from a notepad. "*Spartacus* was made in 1960. They shot one hundred sixty-seven days and constructed a hundred major sets; the cast and crew numbered in the thousands, the stars included Kirk Douglas, Tony Curtis, and Olivier. They used twenty-seven tons of armor, weaponry, chariots, and five thousand pieces of wardrobe. What do you think it cost all in?"

"How would I know? I was still in my crib."

"Take a guess."

"Twenty mil?"

"Twelve."

"God . . . Twelve for all that."

"Translate those 1960 dollars to 1993 and the same picture would cost sixty million with all the breaks. That's pretty much where I feel we're going to be."

"With luck."

"Right—with luck. How are Scott and Glickman getting along?"

"No problems yet—of course Paul will actually be depending on Don Alfonso, the Spanish production manager."

"Well, between the two he should be well served. How's the casting going?"

"Europe's underway and Paul's planning to meet with Richard Bryan. He's worried about Bryan's past peccadilloes, but they know each other. I think it'll work, and right about now, Paul and Adrian should be on their way up to Mulholland to see the Genius."

"What's Beaumont doing?"

"Working on script changes." Aurora shook her head in disbelief. "I still can't believe Adrian sold Julia on doing the picture."

"Why not? By the time we need her she'll be out of the play, and Rebecca is a great role."

"I know, but being directed by a man with whom she shared a stormy five-year marriage is a little much."

"When Paul says 'action' there's only the camera and those tiger eyes of hers. Julia knows exactly what she's doing."

Aurora nodded. "She's as hard as she is beautiful, but it's still a tense situation."

"No question, but volatility creates a certain dynamic. They're all high-strung but so are great Thoroughbred race horses. What's happening with Honeybear?"

"She seems fine. But her vet, Dr. Didden, wants to bring his wife and daughters to Madrid."

"For the entire shoot?"

"He didn't say."

"Well, what can we do? According to Adrian, that cat is everything to Paul. Honeybear and her vet in Madrid is a cheap insurance policy."

Aurora said, "We've booked Chasen's private dining room for Tuesday evening and Herb Stoner's reserved double-truck space in both trades. Be nice if Frank could come out for the announcement."

"He will. Jesus, that reminds me." Walters pressed the intercom. "Yes?"

"Irv Wexler, please," Walters said. "Aurora, fix me another Scotch, will you."

She took the glass, thinking that lately he'd been drinking more than usual.

"Wexler," the secretary announced.

Walters pressed the speaker button.

"Irv—big favor. Very important. Can you take the red-eye tonight and help Frank through the meeting with Charles Levitt tomorrow morning?"

"I had other plans, but if you think it's important . . ."

"It's vital."

"I'll be there."

"Thanks, Irv."

Walters released the speaker button as Aurora handed him his drink.

"I'm worried about Frank," he said reflectively.

"Maybe this CEO thing doesn't agree with him," she offered.

"You may be right. Frank is essentially a salesman."

"How did the exhibitors react to *Backwash?*" she asked.

"Apparently they loved it. The critical kudos went to Tracey."

"She steals the picture," Aurora said. "I hated the goddamn script and I despise Trummel, but I have to admit he captured a film-noir quality. It's going to sell tickets."

Walters nodded and raised his glass. "Here's to sweaty young ladies in anal floss"—he smiled—"and killa cults."

"And castles in Spain," she said pensively.

ADRIAN'S SILVER BENTLEY HALTED AT THE SPIKED IRON GATES. REACH-ing through the open window, he pressed the speaker button on a low stanchion.

"Yes?" a female voice responded.

"Paul Scott and Adrian Summers."

"Thank you, please to wait," she said with an Oriental inflection.

"They say he's into some weird Eastern sect," Scott said. "They believe in reincarnation and Morosco's determined to come back as Fanny Brice."

The gates swung open. They drove up a winding road, passing security guards, pulled into the circular driveway, and parked in front of a white neo-Palladian mansion. An attractive Oriental girl wearing a saffron-colored sari greeted them. She bowed and handed each of them a mauve-colored flower.

"From Blazil—glape frowa," she explained. She turned to the huge mahogany entrance doors and spoke a single word into the speaker—the word was in a strange language and sounded like "tukumakahai." The doors creaked open.

A vaulted portico led to a long marble hall bisected at its center by another corridor. The girl stopped at the fork in the hall and turned her palm left. "Please to go in." She bowed and dis-appeared.

They entered an immense room with a skylight built into the vaulted ceiling. The furniture was made of heavy bamboo and upholstered in silk of various shades. Tropical plants were in every corner. A sign on the wall drawn in red crayon with block letters stated, *"No Smoking. No Drinking."*

An ornate teak bookcase covered one wall and a bank of stereo equipment was built into the opposite one. From the distance they heard a faint mantra chant which sounded like "Cola . . . Cola . . . Mento-Cola . . ."

They waited apprehensively in the center of the exotic room in the soft sculpted light filtering down through the skylight. After several minutes they heard a shuffling sound, an eerie rustling. Scott turned pale, pointed, and gasped, "Holy shit!"

Crawling into the room was a huge, brilliantly colored snake. Walking calmly beside the reptile, wearing a blood-red toga and a high-coned Mexican sombrero, was Mayo Morosco. His long gray hair fell across his shoulders. His trademark Roman nose was pronounced and his gray eyes were hard. He removed the sombrero, spread his arms expansively, and bowed. "Welcome."

Scott's eyes remained fixed on the slithering reptile.

"That's Ruby, she's harmless," Morosco explained. "She's a rock python. Keeps the rat population down. Good karma. She'll curl up alongside that banyan plant." He gestured toward a large sofa. "Sit down, fellows." He paused and smiled. "You look well, Paul."

Scott's color was beginning to return and he nodded, still eyeing the snake. "I'm fine."

"And how goes it with you, Adrian?" Morosco inquired.

"It goes well."

"A Coca-Cola?"

They declined.

"Would you object to my taping this session?"

"Okay with me," Scott said, somewhat relieved after seeing the reptile curl up by the banyan plant.

"I have no problem with taping," Adrian agreed.

"Good. I like to record things because my memory bank has grown faulty."

The Genius swept across the room and activated a switch on the recorder. He returned, carrying a bowl of cashews, and sat

205

down opposite them. "Now, tell me why this screenplay is so anti-Franco."

Scott deferred to Adrian, who described with knowledgeable accuracy the centuries of dictatorial rule by Spain's church, state, and nobility; after eight hundred years of this tyrannical oppression, the dream of a duly elected Republic was finally realized. He traced the rebellion by Franco and other Fascist generals against the Republic and detailed Hitler and Mussolini's military support for Franco, and the western democracies' failure to help rescue Republican Spain.

From time to time, the same Oriental girl wearing a white kimono entered and whispered in Morosco's ear.

"Why did General Miaja abandon Madrid to Casado?" Morosco asked. "He had to know it was a sellout."

"Once Chamberlain caved in at Munich, Miaja felt the Republic's last chance for Allied help was gone," Adrian explained. "His soldiers were out of ammunition, fuel, medicine, and hope. He had wanted to negotiate a surrender with dignity and believed General Casado to be an honorable man. Unfortunately, Casado was a treacherous bastard."

Morosco popped cashews into his mouth, sipped tea, and said, "And I'm to take your word for all this? The war was complicated and passionate. You sound opinionated. You sound like a professional propagandist."

Scott spoke out before Adrian could respond. "We're not on trial here, Mayo. The script is not going to change. Adrian's related the events as he understands them, but he isn't a history professor. He's a writer, and this is his impression of those events. You want to play the role of General Miaja as it's written, fine—if not, we'll work together another time."

Paul's forcefulness was a good sign, Adrian thought. While Morosco had addressed his questions to Adrian, he was in fact testing the director's commitment to the existing screenplay. It was an old ploy, and almost always succeeded; if the director was hungry enough he could be manipulated.

Morosco's gunmetal eyes worked Paul Scott over.

The reptile stirred; its head rose up out of its coils.

A tall bearded man wearing a saffron-colored robe entered and handed the Genius a pipe and held a match over the bowl while Morosco puffed, sending clouds of bluish smoke up toward the skylight. The sweet, aromatic odor of hashish wafted across the room.

"This is my guru, Dr. Sindi," Morosco said by way of introduction. The guru nodded and left.

"Do you have Jack Wheeler?" Morosco asked.

Adrian nodded. "He's signed."

The Genius grunted and placed the pipe on the glass-topped coffee table. "Hell of a chess player, Wheeler. I worked with him years ago in Durango. He got drunk one night and pissed in a Mexican *pistolero*'s sombrero. It was a wild night. He almost caught a bullet, but you have to admire a man who has the courage to piss in a bandit's sombrero." He chewed a cashew, relit his pipe, inhaled deeply, and said, "Is Wheeler off the sauce?"

"He's been on the wagon for seven months," Adrian replied.

"How about you?"

"I'm clean."

"Terrible thing, heroin. I prefer opium suppositories. Who else is committed to the project?"

"Richard Bryan, and Julia Castle," Scott replied.

"Bryan keeping his cock dry these days?"

"So we understand," Adrian said.

The Genius got to his feet, crossed the room, and snapped off the tape recorder.

"When do you need me?"

"On or about July fifteenth."

The great actor faced them. "I have to have Dr. Sindi, my servants, my wardrobe, my makeup, and Ruby, my snake." He picked up a bell and shook it. A turbaned child-woman appeared.

"Dawn will show you out." For the first time, Morosco smiled. "Oh, Adrian, there's something I've been meaning to tell you."

"What's that?"

"There are no tigers in Africa."

THE FISHNET WAS A COZY RESTAURANT PERCHED ATOP A HIGH BLUFF overlooking Paradise Cove. Adrian and Silvi were seated at a window table with a splendid view of the languid, moonlit Pacific. A pianist played the final chorus of a current show tune and effortlessly segued into "Rose Room."

Silvi's jet-black hair shone in the candlelight and her dark eyes reflected merriment. She had just tossed her head back and laughed. He had forgotten how sweet and bouncy her laughter sounded.

"I don't know how you top a topper," she said, "but somehow Paul's Samoan is capped by Wheeler's Moses, which in turn is topped by Morosco's snake and whispering ladies in orange togas." She paused. "By comparison, Julia Castle is pure Valium."

Adrian nodded. "I thought Julia had it together."

"What about the Mormon pom-pom girl?"

"Well, no one ever confused Julia Castle with the Virgin of Guadelupe."

"Remarkable," Silvi said, "that Morosco remembered the tiger in Africa."

"Apparently *Trader Jim* was one of his favorite TV shows."

"I must say it's a talented package, Adrian, but a little short on sanity. You're in a difficult situation. You're the producer and if the thing blows up, you'll pick up the pieces."

"Yes and no—once we start shooting, Paul's got the ball. I can support him, but the director makes the movie. He's on the cross."

"Paul is not exactly a pillar of strength."

"You'd be surprised. He stood up to Morosco."

"With this group he's going to have to be Superman."

"One of Paul's attributes is his meticulous preparation. He comes to the set ready to shoot and the actors respect him."

"Are you satisfied with the studio's attitude?"

"Walters has assured me of his total support for the project."

The waiter cleared their dishes and they ordered espressos.

"Is Richard Bryan behaving these days?" she asked.

"Apparently. New wife. No coke. Calm. Professional."

"Well"—she smiled and tossed her hair—"maybe it will all work. Just don't jeopardize your health."

He stared at her, thinking that she was totally alluring, even more so now than when they first met. He recalled in vivid detail the first time he had seen her on a runway at a fashion show— tall, striding out in a silk print summer dress—a standout among all the pretty shills selling the designer's creations. At the end of the runway she pivoted and shot him a look that he had never forgotten. It was a snapshot of desire and promise. Indelible. Click. In those days, they lived together in a walkup apartment in the East Village. One of those prewar red brick tenements with a fire escape zigzagging down the face of the building. They were desperately in love and happy in that tiny apartment with its Murphy bed and Pullman kitchen. It was another lifetime and yet it seemed five minutes ago. The years blurred, defying definition.

"Tell me about Rome," she said.

"After Moses, I visited Anzio—not much to say about that. I got back to Rome and went straight to Rosati's. It was dusk, the ruins were lit up in the Borghese Gardens, and the Obelisk looked as pristine and majestic as ever." He sipped his coffee, then said, "It wasn't easy to be there alone."

"But you managed."

"Silvi . . ."

"Let it go, Adrian."

"Promise me one thing, at some point during the production you'll come to Madrid."

"If you really need me I'll come, but I don't want to plan anything in advance." She sipped her sambuca. "How's Eddie doing?"

"He's fine."

"Listen to him. He's the grand master. He's seen it all and heard it all."

"Everyone thought he had died."

"Probably thought the same about you. They bury their dead warm in this town. I saw your friend Aurora Flint jogging along the beach with her dog. Have you been out to her place?"

"No. She lives with a TV director."

"I'll bet."

"Come on, Silvi, I'm not interested in Aurora."

"Not now—but"—she raised the thick colorless drink—"there was a time."

"No—not really."

"It doesn't matter. You were, all things considered, not a terrible husband. I just . . . ah hell, what does it matter now?"

The pianist played "Here's That Rainy Day."

"Listen," she said, covering his hand with hers, "remember when we saw Benny Goodman at Carnegie Hall? He played that tune and put us away."

"Benny took no prisoners."

She squeezed his hand and said, "I can't change the past, but know that I'm here if you need me."

He dropped her off at the beach house, kissed her good night, and promised to call. Driving back to town the traffic was sparse and off to his right the sea shimmered in the pale moonlight. The car stereo played an old Tony Bennett tune. He slid the window down and the salty sea breeze rushed in, bringing with it another flood of memories.

The drive along the coast reminded him of other beaches, and other seas, of Ischia, and the multicolored lights of Porto Canto, Algeciras with Gibraltar lit up in the bay, and the twinkling lights of shrimp boats off the Costa del Sol, balmy tropical nights driving down to the Florida Keys with the top down, and a sidewalk café at the Place de l'Opéra, the cloister near the Roman Forum with its sparkling fountain that seemed to demand silence.

A CAST OF THOUSANDS

And all the nights and applause and awards, and the weddings, funerals, flowers, anniversaries, birthdays—and then the fall, Needle Park and stoned Vietnam veterans wandering in and out of the house. And Silvi understanding, and then Timmy. And all of it, the good and the bad, fading into bits and pieces of memories, each with its own special light.

35

THE COFFEE SHOP WAS LOCATED AT THE CORNER OF BRIGHTON WAY
and Camden Drive. The place was a thriving anachronism—a family-
run luncheonette that would have been more suited to mid-
Manhattan than Beverly Hills. Formica-topped tables were
jammed together and set with paper napkins. Counter seats faced
the open kitchen. The food was fresh, the portions generous, and
the prices reasonable.

Its regular customers were mostly secretaries, receptionists, and
paralegals. The movie people had their breakfast meetings else-
where and the omnipresent Iranians did not understand an all-
American coffee shop.

The coffee shop was the perfect place for Walters and Mickey
Dutton to meet. They ordered the $5.95 breakfast special: fresh
orange juice, two eggs, toast, hash browns, four strips of crisp
bacon, and a pot of hot coffee.

"We're really going to hell in a hurry this morning," Dutton
said.

"I don't think an infrequent dose of bacon and eggs ever killed
anyone," Walters replied. "We've become fearful of everything
from sugar to sex—give yourself a break, Mickey."

"With my cholesterol count I'd have been better off with coffee
and juice at your house."

"I try and keep my business away from the house. We have occasional parties, but I long ago realized that having business meetings at home was unfair to Carla. She felt reduced to the role of a servant tiptoeing her way through pressure conversations."

The waitress refilled their coffee cups and moved to the next table.

"I need a fresh item to keep the Parnelli story hot," Dutton said.

"What kind of an item?"

"A progress report. I've got a terrific contact on *Money* magazine. All I need is a quote."

"I've got one for you," Walters said.

"They'll call Parnelli for confirmation," Dutton cautioned.

"He'll confirm."

Dutton swabbed at the yolks of his eggs and smiled. "It's a pleasure doing business with you, Harry." Walters thought the publicist's capped smile was a shade too white.

"Here's the quote, Mickey."

Dutton took out a miniature tape recorder, placed it on the table, and pressed the Record button.

"Shoot."

"A spokesman from Sirocco Films International announced yesterday that its CEO, Salvatore Parnelli, had raised two billion dollars and is expected to have the additional eight hundred million dollars within ninety days, at which time he will file a notice of intent to acquire Gemstone Pictures. The takeover price will be announced at the time of the SEC filing."

"Perfect," Dutton said, snapping off the recorder and slipping it back into his pocket. "Once this breaks, you and Solish should issue a rebuttal—keep the pot boiling."

Walters nodded. "I'll have Herb Stoner issue a written denial for an all-media feed."

"You know, it's odd," Dutton said reflectively. "MGM is in bed with the French; Columbia and Universal sold out to the Nips; Fox is owned by an Australian conglomerate. Gemstone is one of the few surviving American film companies. We should reflect that in our rebuttal—sound a note of patriotism."

"Flag waving never hurts," Walters agreed. "By the way, I signed your first check last Tuesday."

"It's already been deposited—very generous, Harry. Maybe a

little excessive. I mean that's a lot of bread for promoting Tracey Warren. Stoner might be suspicious."

"Why? You're not just polishing her image; you're augmenting our efforts to market *Backwash*. We've employed outside publicity agencies in the past."

"Is the picture any good?"

"It works."

"I hope so because I've nailed a five-page layout featuring Tracey in *Playboy*'s May issue. The magazine will be on the stands in April in synch with the picture's release." Dutton smiled. "You ought to see that young lady in the buff."

"I have. Stoner showed me some proofs."

"If she's handled right she's got a shot to be a star."

"I'm not so sure."

"Why not?"

"Her eyes are flat. Dead. You've got to have eyes. I hope I'm wrong. We signed her production company to a three-picture deal."

"Eyes or no eyes, she's got a smile that would burn a hole in a ceramic Madonna. She's a major pussycat."

"That she is."

Dutton lit a cigarette. "This bother you?"

"No. I use five a day."

"You know something," Dutton said, "you're putting together a sensational cast for *Volunteers.*"

Walters stared at the handsome graying publicist and nodded. "It is quite a company. A wealth of talent, as they say."

"If you're not careful," Dutton said, "you might have a hit."

"Fine with me. Once we've cashed in, who cares? We have to subvert the film until the takeover bid is filed. After that"—he shrugged—"the picture is irrelevant."

"Suppose Boom Boom has trouble?"

"There are very wise heads on this thing, Mickey. Your job and mine is to create an aura of chaos around the making of the picture, and we may not have to invent all that much. Anytime you design a movie where everyone in it from the producer on down is at the edge, and you drop them into a foreign setting under pressure conditions, the whole thing could go up in smoke—and yet, no one can question the legitimacy of my choices. Everyone in it has at one time or another demonstrated great artistry."

"Maybe so, but you better make damn sure that Madrid location is a closed set. I don't want to be planting disaster stories and have some journalist visit the location and discover that things are more or less orderly."

"Everyone we've signed has 'closed set' written into their contract—don't worry about it."

"What about Aurora? She'll see the dailies. She'll see production reports. She might sniff something out."

"I'll take care of Aurora."

Dutton was surprised at the sudden hard edge in Walters's voice.

"Hi, Mickey," a lilting feminine voice greeted Dutton.

He glanced up at a statuesque redhead and recognized her instantly. She was one of the world's leading fashion models.

"Margo!" Dutton said, starting to rise.

"Sit, sit. I've got to scoot."

"Say hello to Harry Walters."

"Hi—Margo Forbes."

"Would you care to join us?" Walters asked.

"No thanks—I've got to get my face on. We're shooting a layout at Hermès on Rodeo." She paused. "Aren't you the chief of Gemstone Pictures?"

"More or less." Walters shrugged.

"You know, it's strange"—her tongue darted across her curvy lips—"I saw your reflection in the mirror and I felt my heart stop. I could have sworn you were Peter Lawford. I'm certain other people have said the same thing."

"It's tapered off since Peter died."

She edged closer to the table, her pelvis curving toward Dutton's face. "Give me a ring, Mickey, I'm at the Bel Air."

"Sure."

She displayed a sudden, dazzling smile. "Nice meeting you, Mr. Walters." She pranced out like a Thoroughbred filly stepping out onto the track.

"Interesting girl," Walters said.

"I can arrange it," Dutton offered.

"No thanks, Mick. I was never a hit-and-run man. I've always required a touch of romance." Walters rose and laid a twenty-dollar bill on the check. "Back in my theater days there was a

215

girl . . ." He shook his head. "I created a whole myth about that girl."

"What happened?"

"She was a dancer." He said "dancer" as though it was a fatal disease.

Once outside, Dutton asked, "Where are you parked?"

"On Bedford."

"I'll walk you."

"We're running a double-truck ad in Monday's trades officially announcing the production of *Volunteers.*"

"I'd like to see a proof."

"I'll send one over to your office. It's first class."

They reached Walters's VW Jetta.

"You enjoy driving that thing?" Dutton asked.

"Suits me. I'll see you at Chasen's."

"Is it okay if I bring Tracey Warren?"

"That's a bad idea. Julia Castle may fly out for the announcement party. I don't want another actress's face in front of those Nikons." Walters got behind the wheel, rolled the window down, and said, "Why don't you bring that model—what's her name?"

"Margo."

"Perfect. She'll dress up the party." Walters turned the ignition on. "Take care, Mickey."

Dutton watched the silver-blue Jetta pull away from the curb and ease into traffic. He shook his head, thinking only Harry Walters could get away with driving a Volkswagen.

36

RICHARD BRYAN WAS A SHORT, BALDING MAN WITH LIVELY EYES AND a friendly smile. As an actor he managed to convey an on-screen image of boyish innocence. He appeared in film after film, driving himself with remorseless determination. In a business famous for heartbreak, Bryan had a decided edge on the competition—he had no heart to break.

In a relatively short period of time, he had parlayed a supporting role in a Neil Simon comedy to stardom; but at the height of his popularity something happened—his shining star grew dim and extinguished itself. His unbearable ego and uncontrollable satyriasis had coalesced—a combination that caused him to become too difficult to handle. On stage, he would rage and rant at the slightest provocation; offstage, he would chase anything with a hole in it. Bryan had only two prerequisites; his victims had to be female and breathing.

Photographs taken of Bryan's actions at an orgy had circulated in the film community, confirming the old adage that one picture is worth a thousand words. He became the subject of dinner jokes on the Bel Air circuit and by clever innuendo the butt of a classic *Saturday Night Live* comedy sketch. He soon found himself on the invisible blacklist, joining those fallen angels who for one reason or another were categorized as unemployable.

In the winter of '87, against all prevailing advice, Harry Walters signed the discarded former star to the male lead role in a romantic comedy set on the picturesque island of Ischia off the southern coast of Italy, and while the considerable talents of Magda von Stellhoff were eventually required to calm his raging libido, the afflicted actor managed to finish the film in style. The picture was a box office smash, and Walters assumed a fatherly interest in the troubled actor's future. The studio chief arranged Bryan's admission to a clinic in Liechtenstein and secured the services of a renowned specialist in the treatment of satyriasis.

After months of intensive and often painful therapy, the doctor pronounced Bryan cured and prescribed a strict physical regime for the reborn actor: three miles of jogging a day, two hours of weight lifting, long afternoon walks, no smoking, no alcoholic beverages, and absolutely no drugs. Slowly but steadily Bryan's career revived and a forgiving public once again bestowed stardom on their resurrected screen idol.

Harry Walters called in the IOU, not too subtly suggesting that Bryan join the cast of *The Volunteers*. The actor promptly agreed to play the role of Abrams but requested a meeting with Adrian Summers and Paul Scott prior to actually signing the cor.tract.

Wearing jeans and a T-shirt, Bryan waited patiently on the cream-colored sofa in the Beverly Wilshire production office. Aurora was on the phone talking to Mary Barton, Gemstone's London casting director. Paul and Adrian were studying a scene card involving the characters Julia Castle and Bryan were to play.

"This is a killer scene, baby," Scott said.

Adrian knew at once the director had taken a hit of grass.

"The thing is," Scott continued, "you go one beat over in this scene and you're into soap."

"You want Eddie to rewrite it?" Adrian said.

"I'm not sure. The scene is cool. Underwritten. Tossed away. It's opaque. Weightless. But I'm gonna have to walk on water. The audience has a built-in schmaltz detector—they can smell schmaltz."

Aurora clicked off with London, pushed the blinking button, and called out, "Adrian."

"Yes . . ."

"Your secretary's on: Trummel's called twice, and Morosco's

guru, Dr. Sindi, called, *and* your favorite agent and mine, Jerry Blake."

"It can all wait," Adrian said.

"Hey," Bryan said, "if you guys are too busy we can do this at the studio."

"No . . . no . . ." Scott said, "we're with you, man." The weary director sat down opposite Bryan while Adrian remained standing. "Sorry to keep you waiting," Scott added, "but we're going fast and this thing is a monster."

"Hey, don't apologize. I'm not blind. You fellows are planning a war. I don't want to be a pain in the ass."

"Don't worry about it. We always have time for you," Adrian said. "By the way, you look great."

"I should. I run three miles every morning. I don't mean jog— I mean run. And no booze, no coke, no strange pussy." He smiled sheepishly at Aurora. "Sorry, baby. No sexual harassment intended."

"None taken," she said.

"I got married last summer, a Korean girl," Bryan said. "I've never been happier. New life. New wife. New agent. I finally left Fats Axelrod. Who are you with, Paul?"

"I have no agent," Scott replied. "My attorney Burton Klein handles all my business."

"I heard you disappeared," Bryan said matter-of-factly.

"That's right. I had to lay out for a while."

"I understand—Julia must have been a handful."

"Wasn't Julia. It's the scene. It's making movies, trying to expand the form. No one dug my action. So I laid out."

"Well, the important thing is we're all here. Alive and well, and on the edge of something great." Bryan smiled ingenuously and got to his feet. "This is a terrific project, just terrific."

He paced in a tight radius, waving his arms, using his hands to accent his words. "The role of Abrams—Christ, I don't know what to say . . . It's an actor's dream. I just have to get you——"

A hissing blur of red fur hurtled down from the armoire and, with claws extended, struck Bryan's neck, dug in, and bounded off.

Bryan screamed. His hand flew up to his torn flesh. The color drained from his face. His eyes were glassy as he stared at his bloodstained fingers.

The swiftness of Honeybear's attack stunned the others, and for a few seconds no one moved or spoke.

Bryan looked up from his fingers and in a hoarse, reedy voice croaked, "What the fuck was that?"

"Aurora!" Adrian said. "Call the desk. We need iodine, peroxide, a tube of Neosporin, and some Band-Aids. Tell them it's an emergency." He turned to Scott. "Do you have any alcohol in the bathroom?"

"There's a bottle of bay rum."

Adrian hurried out of the room.

Scott moved Bryan to a chair. "Jesus, I'm sorry, man; you must have excited some jungle instinct in her."

"Maybe it was the pacing and arm waving," Aurora suggested. "She's always been the perfect house cat."

"That was no house cat," Bryan snapped. "That was a fucking tiger."

Aurora stood over Bryan and applied tissues to the serrated scratches. "Cats don't take kindly to change," she said. "There's been too much activity here."

Bryan glanced up at her and their eyes locked. Aurora thought the actor had sent a signal but quickly dismissed the thought; this was the new Richard Bryan.

Adrian returned and handed a wad of gauze and a bottle of bay rum to Aurora, who promptly applied the antiseptic to Bryan's neck.

"Ouch!" he protested.

"Sorry," she said, dabbing lightly at the fiery scratches.

"I don't know what to say," Scott said apologetically. "She's never done anything like this before."

"I'll survive," Bryan said. "It just scared the hell out of me."

"Well, the bleeding's stopped," Aurora said.

Chimes sounded and Adrian opened the door, and took a plastic bag from the bellboy. He tipped the boy and handed a small bottle of iodine to Aurora. She dipped the applicator into the dark fluid and cautioned Bryan: "This will sting." She carefully painted the iodine into the raw ridges. Bryan winced but did not complain.

"That should do it," she said, and peeled a Band-Aid.

"Leave that Band-Aid off," Adrian said. "This sort of wound heals faster when it breathes."

"It's very weird but those scratches have the look of the stripes of passion," Scott observed. "May be tough to explain to your pregnant wife."

"You're right," Aurora concurred. "There isn't a woman alive who'd buy those scratches as a pussycat attack."

"How about someone pouring me a drink," Bryan said.

"What would you like?" Aurora asked.

"Cognac."

"I'm really bummed out, man," Scott said apologetically.

Bryan waved his hand and shrugged. "These things happen. My former agent Fats Axelrod went out to a Malibu beach party and a Russian wolfhound took a huge chunk out of his ass."

Bryan managed a smile. "Of course Axelrod's got a lot of ass left."

Aurora handed him a snifter of brandy.

"Cheers," Bryan said and swallowed the cognac. "Ah . . . that's better. Anyone got a smoke?"

"Thought you quit," Aurora said.

"Fuck it."

Scott shook a cigarette out of a pack.

"Thanks," Bryan said.

Adrian struck a match and Bryan inhaled deeply. "Ah . . ." He sighed in satisfaction and put his feet up on the coffee table. "Shall we continue?"

Paul and Adrian sat down opposite the wounded star. Aurora leaned against the Louis Quatorze desk.

"I love the role of Abrams," Bryan began, "but it's my gut feeling that"—he stopped suddenly, his eyes apprehensive— "Where's the cat?"

Aurora giggled.

"It's not funny," Bryan snapped.

"You're absolutely right," Adrian commiserated. "Aurora, make sure Honeybear's in the bedroom."

Suppressing her laughter, Aurora hurriedly left the salon.

"Go ahead, Richard," Adrian said.

"I'm glad you got Leroy Belgrave to play McQueen. Belgrave's a big guy and I have a feeling the audience has to sense Abrams's toughness early on. He shouldn't put up with McQueen's anti-Semitic barbs. He should challenge him. Even though McQueen is twice his size, Abrams should go after him. Maybe Abrams boxed in the Golden Gloves and worked on the docks. It's Depression time, after all. The Hebes, the Micks, the Wops, were all streetwise." Bryan rose, sipped his cognac, and with conviction said, "Look, if Abrams has the balls to go to Spain and sign up with the losing side he sure as hell wouldn't take any shit from McQueen, not because he's black—it's just the nature of Abrams's character."

"Where do you go with it?" Scott asked.

"As the film progresses," Bryan continued, "these two men—white and black—grow to love one another so that the last scene has an understated emotional impact. Abrams and McQueen are the sole survivors. All the other guys in the Lincoln Brigade are dead. So at the end, when they're reunited, there's a symmetrical truth to their characterizations. What do you think?"

"Makes sense," said Scott.

Adrian said, "Eddie Beaumont's rewriting; I'll mention it to him."

"Let me talk to Eddie," Bryan suggested. "This is important. After all, I have to create this role. I'm searching for what the great Piscator called harmonic character coherence." Bryan paused and with sudden consternation asked, "Did you say Eddie Beaumont?"

"Yes."

"How can that be? I went to his funeral."

Returning to the salon, Aurora said, "I made the same mistake, Richard. You went to Larry Beaumont's funeral. Eddie Beaumont is alive and well."

"I'm glad to hear that," Bryan said without conviction. "Eddie's a world-class writer—great constructionist. I've gotta see him."

"Aurora can take you to the studio," Adrian said. "We'll call Eddie and tell him you're on your way."

Bryan walked to the mirror and examined the scratches on his neck. "Shit. You guys are right. Sonji's never gonna buy a cat attack."

"Who's Sonji?" Scott asked.

"My wife. I told you she's Korean. I better cover these scratches. Can you have a makeup man meet me in Beaumont's office?"

"No problem," Adrian said.

"I'll need that medicated number-five pancake," Bryan said and, downing the last of his cognac, he flashed a dazzling smile. "Forgetting the feline attack, I'm thrilled to be in this picture—I mean, Jack Wheeler, Julia Castle, and Mayo Morosco . . ."

"We've just signed Pierre Claudon to play Montaigne," Aurora said. "Our London casting director confirmed it. We've also signed Alberto Lescoli to play Commandante Bernini."

"Holy shit . . ." Bryan whispered in awe. "What about Carmen?"

"We're hoping to cast a Spanish actress," Scott replied.

"Makes sense. Well, I'm yours, fellas. I'll give it everything I've got. Working with Julia Castle should be terrific—just terrific."

Bryan followed Aurora to the door, then turned back and smiled. "It just occurred to me. There's another upside to shooting in Spain. We won't have to worry about any cats—*ciao.*"

Once the door closed, Adrian sighed heavily. "That was close, Paul. You never said Honeybear was wild."

"I can't explain it." He turned toward the alcove and shouted, "Honeybear! Come here, baby!"

Not unlike a dog, the big red cat loped into the salon and sprang up onto the bar. Scott walked over and stroked her.

"She's hunted lizards, mice, snakes, but she's never attacked a human being. She must have smelled something on him." He snapped his fingers in sudden realization. "Bryan is in heat! She sensed his heat and went for him."

"Come on, Paul, that's madness," Adrian said.

"Think about it. His wife is in her eighth month. He doesn't play around. His raging satyriasis may be under control but the heat is still there. It's like a bonfire under asphalt. That's what triggered Honeybear's attack. She smelled raw sex."

Changing the subject, Adrian said, "Morosco's guru called again."

"Did you talk to him?"

"No . . . I don't think we should be too available for the Genius and his handlers."

"Is Julia flying out for the announcement?"

"Solish is negotiating with Bill Trinz, her producer. I think he'll spring her for a few days."

"It's been a long time," Scott said pensively. "I hope she's cool. We had a good thing for a while. I suppose I just . . . ah, Christ— who knows? It was complicated, man; but it was lively."

In the descending elevator, Bryan glanced at Aurora and flashed his famous smile. "You look terrific."

"Thanks, Richard. I'm on a very similar regimen to yours. No sex, no booze, no tobacco, no drugs, jogging daily." She smiled. "I'm pure as the driven slush."

Tourists buzzed as they recognized the boyish-looking star crossing the lobby with the attractive redhead.

Bryan took her arm and steered her toward the bar. "I'm off booze but I've got the shakes. I need another cognac."

"It's no wonder. That must have been quite a shock."

"Do you still live at the beach?" he asked casually.

She nodded. "I love it. You get high just breathing the air."

"I miss the ocean," he said. "I lived at Trancas with my first wife." He stopped and snapped his fingers. "Listen, why don't I drive out one morning. We can jog together. Afterward, we can have breakfast at Patrick's and knock around."

"What about your wife?"

"Sonji has to stick close to home. She could drop the baby any minute now. You know way back in those days at CBS, I used to watch you strut around the production office with those goddamn long legs. Drove me crazy. You were something then, but you're dynamite now."

A CARAVAN OF LIMOUSINES DISCHARGED THEIR GOWNED AND TUXE-doed passengers at the entrance to Chasen's restaurant. Brilliant white beams of rotating klieg lights constantly probed the low clouds as if the Luftwaffe was en route to West Hollywood. TV camera vans covered either side of the restaurant's entrance. Police barricades held back the locusts—the celebrity seekers who always surfaced at industry events desperately seeking a glimpse of the stars. They had shrieked at the arrival of Gemstone's television actors, and Dr. Sindi, Morosco's saffron-cloaked guru, had caused a stir, but the arrival of Richard Bryan and his Korean wife triggered a near riot.

Julia Castle had been handled personally and adroitly by Walters. She had flown out from New York on the corporate jet, been chauffeured to Chasen's, and ushered into the service side.

Nikons flashed and whirred as the stream of celebrities arrived. Gemstone's publicity director, Herb Stoner, had seen to all the details: press, police, food, music, backstage setup, and seating arrangements. Professional lighting men from Stagehands Local No. 33 had installed the exterior and interior lights and dimmer boards.

Dignitaries from rival studios received cordial VIP treatment.

In deference to their age, a few surviving veterans of the Lincoln Brigade had been seated early.

Frank Solish entered with two elderly Gemstone board members but quickly dumped them in favor of a vodka martini.

Paul Scott, Aurora Flint, and Adrian Summers arrived in Michael Jackson's favorite stretch limo.

To the accompanying cries of the locusts, a rock group wearing tuxedos roared up on their Harley-Davidsons—the famous group recorded for Gemstone's music division.

Across Beverly Boulevard, a few dazed, homeless people watched the excitement from their makeshift shelters.

Chasen's banquet room was decorated with the red, gold, and mauve flags of the old Spanish Republic. A banner above the curtained stage read "The Volunteers." Black and white photographic blowups of Madrid circa 1936 hung on the walls, and stereo speakers played classical flamenco music.

The buffet table featured platters of smoked Norwegian salmon, steak tartare, and Iranian caviar. A four-foot ice carving of a Lincoln Brigade soldier complete with rifle and bayonet dominated the table. Two additional bars had been set up to service the glittering crowd. Uniformed waiters moved through the room carrying trays of canapés and glasses of Cristal champagne.

The banquet room overflowed with Hollywood stardust: studio chiefs, actresses, actors, directors, agents, writers, composers, attorneys, and a small army of journalists and photographers.

The power brokers' wives wore pricey designer dresses and Cartier diamonds. The girlfriends, most of whom were just out of their teens, wore modish short skirts and beaded blouses. Catty looks shot across rims of martini glasses and gossipy tidbits were exchanged.

The newsmen huddled together—they neither gossiped nor drank, they ate and they listened.

Studio chiefs wearing perfectly tailored Italian tuxedos clustered around the buffet table sampling the hors d'oeuvres, swilling vodka, and discussing a competitor's latest box office disaster with feigned concern. Resplendent in black and white, they reminded Adrian of mating penguins. He watched them with bemused detachment. He could afford to play it chilly now that he had a "go" project.

In the past he would have mingled fearfully, paying respects, drinking too much and talking too much in a vain attempt to disguise his insecurity. Not now. Not this night. He was about to produce an epic film the likes of which had not been seen since the heyday of the silents.

Watching the festivities he thought only those who had fallen from grace and managed to come back truly understood the moral equation of Hollywood: no one had to love you, like you, or respect you; they had to *need* you.

He noticed Eddie Beaumont and Magda von Stellhoff making their way through the milling crowd toward the buffet table. The blond Nordic wunderkind looked smashing in her sexy Ungaro dress; Gemstone's secret weapon was not partying. She was here on assignment. Her target for the night was Paul Scott. Walters thought it unwise to leave the director alone on a night in which he would be in close proximity to Julia Castle. Magda would serve as a temporary but powerful distraction for Scott's loneliness.

Aurora nodded to well-wishers as she made her way across the room to Adrian. "Hell of a party," she said somewhat breathlessly.

"Herb Stoner outdid himself," Adrian agreed.

"Herb was in the trenches but Walters called the signals on this one."

"Where is he?"

"Over there." Aurora indicated the curtained stage.

Walters and his wife, Carla, were standing in the center of a group comprising Frank Solish, Ray Smalley, Irv Wexler, and two of Gemstone's board members. Walters nodded and exchanged polite conversation but Carla wore her usual frozen smile. She neither spoke nor acknowledged anyone's presence—she merely smiled.

"Poor Carla." Aurora sighed.

"This is tough duty for her," Adrian said.

"I've seen her actually tremble in the presence of stars."

"Speaking of stars, where's Julia?"

"Backstage in a makeshift dressing room."

"Has she seen Paul?"

Aurora nodded. "He was with her."

"No trouble?"

"Chilly but civil. Paul is somewhat stoned. He sounds like Dizzy Gillespie. I hope he doesn't fuck things up." Aurora sipped her drink and said, "Look at the newlyweds."

*　　*　　*

Richard Bryan was seated at a small table feeding canapés to his Korean wife. She was a petite, attractive young woman but her belly had swollen to alarming proportions.

"Looks like she's carrying twins," Adrian remarked.

"I guess Bryan shoots bullets," Aurora said. "You know he put a move on me."

"You're kidding."

"No. It was a move—pregnant wife notwithstanding. Once you get to Spain, he'll be all over Julia."

"She'll handle him."

"There's Paul." Aurora indicated one of the bars. "He looks grim. Who's he talking to?"

"His attorney, Burton Klein."

Across the room, Klein shrugged. "Look, Paul, for eight hundred years Spain was an agrarian society. They depended on their animals. They produced generations of veterinarians. I'm certain they have top-notch vets in Madrid."

"Come on, man, Dr. Didden was supposed to be there for the whole gig."

"His partners refused to go along," Klein said. "Didden has an obligation to his practice. I did get him to agree to stay in Madrid for three weeks and interview qualified Spanish veterinarians."

"But Honeybear knows Didden and she doesn't speak Spanish. When she had worms in Jamaica he flew down to take care of her."

"Paul, trust me. Madrid is a sophisticated metropolis—a far cry from Ocho Rios."

A once popular actor now passé and surviving on TV guest shots approached Scott.

"Hey, Paul . . ." The actor smiled nervously.

"Hi," Scott answered, barely recognizing the man.

"Vincent Starrett." The actor reluctantly identified himself. "We worked together on *Deadcalm*."

"Sure—I remember. You look great, man—what's shaking?"

"This and that. I did a bit in a Gemstone picture called *Backwash*. Ray Smalley invited me here." He paused and blurted, "When do you leave for Madrid?"

"Monday."

"I don't suppose—"

"We've got to see Adrian," Klein interrupted, moving Scott away from the desperate actor.

Jerry Blake intercepted them. "Hey, Burt—Paul—hell of a party. I wanted to wish you both the best." He turned to Scott. "I'm thrilled that you're directing this monster."

"Thanks, baby."

Mickey Dutton and the willowy model, Margo, were at the bar talking to the Chipmunk and Jerry Dicola. The horror writer's bulging eyes were fixed on Margo's jutting breasts. Dutton was casing the action. He had a few clients in the illustrious assemblage and would have to do some business before the night was over. Watching the frenetic action, he smiled, thinking of Walters's genius at setting up a monumental scam with such style.

Morosco's guru, Dr. Sindi, wore a silky saffron-colored toga and a white turban. His beard had been dyed snow white.

Richard Bryan spotted Sindi and leapt to his feet.

"Dr. Sindi." He offered his hand. "Richard Bryan. We met last week at Mayo's house."

"Ah, yes."

"This is my wife, Sonji."

"A pleasure."

The pregnant Mrs. Bryan managed a weak smile.

"How come the great man's not here?" Bryan asked the guru.

"Mr. Morosco is meditating. He's inside the samsara—the circle of tranquillity. I am representing him tonight."

"Listen"—Bryan glanced quickly around—"you want to blow a line? Lima White—senfuckingsational."

"Why not?" Dr. Sindi smiled.

Bryan kissed his wife's cheek. "Be right back, honey. Have some more of that steak tartare—terrific."

Aurora nudged Adrian. "There goes Dr. Sindi and Bryan. East meets West over a few lines of schmeck."

"How do you know they're doing blow?"

"They're heading straight for the bathroom. You think Dr. Sindi requires company in order to relieve his bladder? Bryan is supplying him with coke in hopes of ingratiating himself with the Genius."

The ceiling lights suddenly flickered off and on.

Standing on the apron of the small circular stage, Herb Stoner tapped the microphone to be certain it was live.

"Ladies and gentlemen," he announced, "the bar service and buffet are closing. We're about to begin. Please find your seats."

The lights continued flickering as people sought out their tables. Simultaneously, in quick, disciplined, almost military fashion, a crew of waiters removed the buffet table and serving bars.

In the closed stall near the urinals Dr. Sindi snorted from a gold teaspoon. He shook his head and sighed. "Splendid quality, Mr. Bryan. It's almost as exhilarating as Bombay Snow. I feel my mind expanding."

"It's the top of the line, Doc." Bryan took the spoon and filled it with a generous portion of coke. "Happy days." He grinned and snorted expertly.

"Whew . . . wow . . . goes right to my balls."

"Not surprising," Sindi said. "Fine cocaine stimulates the pleasure side of the brain."

"Oh yeah, it hits the brain but it travels right to my nuts. It's probably due to my cloistered life—but"—he socked the tall Indian guru playfully on the shoulder—"I've promised myself a breakout."

The lights had dimmed in the banquet room and with the exception of a few stragglers, everyone was seated. Press photographers from the wire services, newspapers, and magazines knelt at the foot of the stage, their Nikons loaded and ready.

Aurora thought Herb Stoner looked splendid in his new tuxedo. His dark, wavy hair had been expertly shaped. He had lost some weight and picked up a suntan. He seemed in control and composed. She had always liked the harried publicity director, "the Fixer," as he was affectionately called. Stoner fixed everything from writers' strikes to traffic tickets to drug busts and, on occasion, murder. He knew where the bodies were buried.

"Ladies and gentlemen . . ." Stoner began, "and I include the press in that salutation." He paused for a laugh but elicited only a few polite chuckles and continued. "On behalf of Gemstone Pictures, I would like to extend our appreciation for your—"

There was a sudden disconcerting crash of falling tables, clattering dishes, and breaking glass.

Women screamed and men cursed.

230

Whacked out on Lima White, Bryan had tripped over Sindi's toga, knocking the guru into a sheathed woman who went sprawling across a table, spilling glasses of wine and champagne over the seated guests.

Squinting against the powerful key light, Stoner calmly said, "It seems as though we have a minor accident back there—waiters, busboys, please." Red-jacketed waiters, napkins in hand, descended on the soaked guests. Bryan and Sindi smiled their apologies and lurched away.

"Ladies and gentlemen," Stoner continued, "it's my pleasure to introduce Gemstone Pictures' chief operating officer, Mr. Frank Solish."

The curtain parted, revealing a small stage illuminated by overhead baby spots. The diminutive Brownsville street hustler adjusted the microphone and thought, Remember to roll those fucking r's. He waited modestly for the applause to subside.

"Thank you. Thank you. Before I introduce my colleagues I would like to ask your indulgence for a brief moment of silence in honor of Gemstone's late chairman, Max Schuller."

Heads were bowed and a hush fell across the huge room. The seconds ticked off in respectful silence when a sudden amplified shriek shattered the theological moment.

"When does this motherfucking show get up and walk?"

The voice had come from a live backstage microphone and belonged to Julia Castle.

The audience was too stunned to react. Solish raised his head and, in what Aurora thought was his finest moment, spoke with an almost cheerful obliviousness. "And now, it's my great pleasure to introduce a man whom you all admire and respect—a man who has never neglected a worthy industry cause—a man of courage, taste, and vision, my friend and partner, Harry Walters."

Accompanied by a wave of applause, and looking more like a movie star than a studio executive, Walters crossed the stage and warmly shook Solish's hand before moving to the microphone.

"Thank you, Frank, and my gratitude to all of you for your presence here tonight." He moved slightly so that the light played off the silvery touches in his wavy hair. "On or about July fifteenth, Gemstone Pictures will commence principal photography on the most challenging project in its seventy-year history. I am speaking of Adrian Summers's *The Volunteers*, the epic drama of the Spanish Civil War covering the years 1936 through 1939.

"During those years Madrid was the moral heart of the civilized world. The besieged Spanish Republic drew to her side men and women from fifty nations—volunteers who came to Spain of their own free will to fight against the overwhelming forces of Fascist Italy, Nazi Germany, and Franco's Army of Africa.

"The picture is scheduled to shoot for one hundred sixty days, employing a cast of thousands, an international group of stars topped by our own Julia Castle, Jack Wheeler, Richard Bryan, and Mayo Morosco."

The mention of the Genius's name evoked an audible gasp from the audience.

"*The Volunteers* will be shown in seventy-millimeter on a reserved-seat basis in selected theaters for Christmas '94." Walters paused and smiled, his light blue eyes twinkling. "Try and take that over, Mr. Parnelli."

There was a spontaneous burst of laughter and applause.

"I know it's considered prudent these days to avoid big-budget films," Walters continued, "and I can't quarrel with cautionary budgets, but I've always placed my chips on people, not budgets. No one ever left a theater saying it was a lousy picture but it came in on budget. However, as we all know, it takes more than money to make pictures. It takes talent. I'm proud and pleased to introduce Adrian Summers and Paul Scott."

Both men came out to an ovation.

Adrian waited for the applause to subside before saying, "There are a few moments in one's lifetime that remain forever in one's mind. This night is one of those moments. I've been blessed with the good fortune to be associated with Gemstone Pictures and doubly blessed to have the skilled writing services of the grand master, Eddie Beaumont—take a bow, Eddie."

A spotlight picked up the veteran screenwriter looking handsome in his Italian tuxedo. He waved his acknowledgment and sat down beside the wondrous Magda.

"And now—the best man on any stage, my friend, my director, Paul Scott."

Adrian turned and strode off.

Stoned but steady, Scott emerged from the wings and basked in the applause.

Aurora bit her lip, hoping Scott wouldn't drift off into a Gillespie-like monologue.

"It's been a while between pictures for me, but that's cool. Sometimes you do what you do. I mean it takes what it takes—right? I'm doing this picture because I believe in its message—yeah, message—that dirty word. But that's life. We eat, drink, make movies, take meetings and messages. The red light blinks on the answering machine and they got you, baby. This picture is about *something;* and its message is not complicated. It's about putting your life on the frigging line. That's important and rare—at least to me it is.

"But I'm doing this picture for another reason. This is my pal's dream. This story is Adrian's baby. I'll give it all I have and no excuses. I've got the finest people in front of and behind the camera and an open-end budget. That's right—an open budget. These people trust me, man. And now, let me lay on you one of those astonishing talents you'll be seeing in *The Volunteers*. Ladies and gentlemen, Miss Julia Castle."

The applause began as she appeared but almost immediately diminished. People caught their breath and stared. It was as if a priceless Impressionist painting, lost for years, had suddenly been unveiled before their eyes.

She stood in the hot cone of a blue spotlight wearing a shimmering white satin gown that clung to her curves like cold cream. Her shiny pale-gold hair fell to her shoulders and her tiger eyes glowed. The blue light lent an icy translucence to her flawless skin.

The photographers' Nikons whirred and their yellow flashes lit up the stage.

"She's unreal," Smalley whispered to Aurora.

"She, she's something . . ." Aurora murmured.

Carla Walters leaned forward and, studying Julia's gowned figure, sighed, "My God . . ."

Feeling the arctic rush of Lima White, Richard Bryan's fried brain projected Julia into a glittering prismatic blond image that traveled into infinity. Christ, he thought, thirty weeks in Madrid with that golden girl.

Julia wet her lips and, as she started to speak, Bryan's wife stood up and screamed, "It's coming! It's coming!"

233

She collapsed to the floor.

Herb Stoner dialed 911.

Bryan knelt alongside his wife, while Dr. Sindi instructed the writhing woman to breathe.

People rushed over, permeating the air with smoke and perfume.

An elderly man pushed his way through the crowd shouting, "I'm a doctor! I'm a doctor!"

Julia Castle hurried offstage, spotted Walters, and said, "I want you to take me to the airport right now, Harry."

He put his arm around her and hustled her out past the shrieking locusts into the limo. Once inside he kissed her cheek. "You were magnificent."

"Where to, Mr. Walters?" the driver inquired.

"The Bel-Air."

"No. The airport!" Julia shouted.

Walters patted her hand. "It's very late, Julia. You've got two shows on Saturday. Get some rest. Sleep in. Fly back tomorrow."

She stared deeply into his eyes and a small, wicked smile formed at the corners of her mouth. "Did they get the pictures?"

"Of course."

He admired her ability to cut to the heart of the matter. The photographs were the ball game. They would appear in the world press. The rest of the evening was eyewash.

"Is Paul alone?" she asked.

"He's been here for weeks. I've never seen him with a date."

An orange and white ambulance wailed past them on the way to Chasen's.

"Harry, if Richard Bryan so much as touches me I'm off the set."

"I'll talk to him."

They turned right off Santa Monica into Camden and headed north toward Sunset.

"Honeybear is my cat," Julia suddenly announced.

"Is that so?"

He enjoyed the close proximity to this rare beauty. There was no mystery about man's worship of goddesses. In ancient Athens, Julia Castle would have had her own chain of temples.

"She's my cat," Julia insisted with childlike petulance. "And when we get to Madrid, I'm taking her back."

"Julia . . ." He turned his baby blues on her. "I'm thrilled that you're doing this picture."

She kissed him lightly on the lips and smiled a small, intimate smile.

"You're some cutie pie, Harry."

The
Shoot

THE LA SIRENA WAS A FIVE-STORY PRIVATE HOTEL ON THE RESPLENDENT tree-lined Paseo del Castellana. Gemstone's Spanish production manager, Alfonso Tello, had negotiated a contract with the hotel's management—for six months the Sirena's staff and facilities would be exclusive to the film company. The stars, director, and producer would occupy suites, while members of the production staff and supporting actors would be assigned to regular rooms.

The second-floor conference room had been converted to a production office. The walls were covered with pegboards displaying color-coded cards delineating the requirements of various crafts involved in a given day's filming. Production boards with their quarter-inch strips rested on the desks of Don Alfonso and Fred Glickman.

Secretaries had been hired, phone consoles installed, and extra help added to the hotel services. The Spanish hotel staff looked upon the idiosyncrasies of the foreign illusionists with amused curiosity. They ignored the drugs, naked midnight hallway dashes, drunkenness, and squealing toddlers. A sense of camaraderie formed between the film people and their Spanish hosts.

The creative team handpicked by Paul Scott was seated on either side of the conference table.

From Rome came the director of photography, Federico Rossi, and his camera operators.

From Spain, the production manager, Don Alfonso Tello; the production designer, Pepe Granados; the script supervisor, Sarita Montiel; the transportation chief, Raoul Reyes; and the Spanish first assistant director.

From England, the set decorator, Polly Turner; the chief soundman, Ian Holmes; along with the wardrobe supervisor and the casting director.

From America, the special effects chief, Mike Rettig; the first assistant director, Sam Solomon; and the U.S. production manager, Fred Glickman.

Adrian and Paul were seated at the center of the table flanked by Don Alfonso and Glickman. Eddie Beaumont sat beside the pretty Spanish script supervisor.

Everyone had their scripts open to page 136, shot 118-A—a night scene on the Gran Via. Scott conducted the meeting, referring occasionally to marginal notes in his leather-bound script.

"Eddie"—Scott addressed Beaumont—"do these blue pages reflect the latest line changes?"

"Yes. I finished them early this morning and"—he indicated the script supervisor—"Sarita ran them off and distributed them."

"The crane set?" Scott asked Rossi.

The award-winning Italian cameraman nodded. "I have my crew from Rome."

"I'll need a hundred meters of track," Scott said.

"That's gonna take a shitload of Brutes to light," Glickman cautioned. "These Spanish arcs pull a ton of voltage."

"I've arranged auxiliary generators," Don Alfonso said.

"Ian," Scott spoke to the soundman, "this is a long tracking shot with stuff happening in the background as we move with Julia and Bryan. I'd hate to loop this scene. Can we get usable production sound?"

"I would hope so. We'll mike the principals and use directional parabolics on the background crowd-fill."

"How are you fixed, Peg?" Scott asked.

"Julia's outfit is all set," the matronly English wardrobe lady replied. "She wears the nurse's uniform under a khaki-colored trench coat—the one you approved. Bryan will be dressed in the Lincoln Brigade uniform: corduroy trousers, olive-colored sweater, and brown Glengarry cap." She consulted her notes before continuing. "The paramilitary Spanish extras wear blue coveralls and black berets."

"And the civilians?"

"Period clothes as discussed"—she smiled—"over and over."

Scott nodded and turned to Raoul Reyes. "Are you okay, Raoul?"

"Yes, *señor*," the transportation chief said. "Autos, trucks, horse-drawn wagons, yellow trams, bicycles, motorcycles, and green double-deck buses. We have seen to everything."

Adrian watched in admiration as Paul ran down his start-up list with the precision of a pilot checking his takeoff instruments. Scott had committed crew names to memory and by addressing them on a first-name basis had managed to create a subtle sense of equal status and importance.

"How are you fixed, Pepe?" Scott asked the production designer.

"The Gran Via is ready, *señor*," Granados replied. "We finished at four A.M. this morning. I think you will be pleased."

"I'll be pleased just to get out of this fucking hotel." Scott smiled, enjoying the ensuing laughter. "By the way, Federico, which one of your boys shot the Jarama night test?"

"Jose Giron," Rossi said. "A fantastic Spanish cameraman and colleague. We worked together on a co-production in Milano. Giron is a genius at staging second-unit action."

"The stuff looked great," Scott said. "Star shells silhouetting bodies draped over barbed wire. Artillery flashes and phosphorous smoke rolling over the trenches. He made me a believer. How many lights did he use?"

"Two Brutes and six sets of Sun Guns. He shot wide open with a cyan filter and pushed the negative two stops."

Scott turned to Glickman. "We've found our second-unit director."

"We already signed Arty Hansen," Glickman said. "He's due here next week."

"Pay him off," Adrian spoke for the first time. "Don Alfonso will make Giron's deal."

"Leave it with me, *señor*," Don Alfonso said.

"Polly . . ." Scott addressed the attractive and flirtatious English set decorator.

"Yes, darling?"

"Chicote's interior should be dressed just enough to cover the door opening."

"You're not going inside—please, love—not inside."

"Not tonight. Just cover the door opening—okay?"

"I'll do something."

"Eddie?" Scott turned to Beaumont. "I'd like you to be with us. I mean if something flattens out in the dialogue you might get an inspirational thought."

"That'll be a first." Beaumont smiled. "But I'll be there."

Scott glanced at the English director of research. "Joanna?"

"Yes . . ."

"I assume you've checked the costumes, banners, signs, hair styles, license plates, et cetera."

"Righto—everything that works tonight matches my research."

"Good. Any casting news?" Scott asked Mary Barton.

"Wheeler is due in Tuesday along with Morosco, Leroy Belgrave, and the Lincolns."

"And what about our European people?"

"Claudon and Lescoli arrive on the twenty-third. I have two Spanish actresses for you to see for the role of Carmen."

"Tomorrow afternoon," Scott said, then turned to the script girl. "Am I forgetting anything?"

"We have two wounded men being carried into the Palace Hotel just as Abrams and Rebecca come out. Also the wild dogs work."

"Make a note of that, Ramon," Scott said to the Spanish first assistant.

"I already have it, sir."

"Anyone with a problem?" Scott glanced around.

The British soundman, Ian Holmes, spoke up. "Do you plan to use a playback of air-raid sirens, Moorish troops chanting—that sort of thing?"

"Do we have it?"

"I prerecorded a dozen different tracks."

"Sure—let's try it."

"Anything else?" Scott asked.

"The cobblestones must be wet," Rossi said. "And we should see smoke from fires caused by shelling in the background."

"We'll have it," special effects man Mike Rettig said.

"Anyone else?" Scott looked around.

No hands were raised.

"Okay, boys and girls." He smiled. "Remember what Flaubert

242

said, 'Art requires clean hands, composure, and the absence of compromise.' "

The vivacious set decorator, Polly Turner, flashed an engaging smile. "Does that mean we have a shower, a Valium, and piss off?"

"It means we assemble in the lobby in fifteen minutes, drive out to the studio, and see what the Gran Via looked like in the summer of 1937."

39

LED BY PAUL SCOTT, THE INTERNATIONAL BAND OF MOVIE MAGICIANS entered the backlot Gran Via and stood silently in awed admiration. The re-creation of the great boulevard was a stunning achievement in production design.

The imposing Bank of Bilbao with its sculpted gold dome glowed in the sunlight. Cinema marquees advertised Garbo in *Anna Karenina* and the Marx Brothers in *A Night at the Opera*. A banner had been strung across the boulevard bearing the Loyalists' slogan, *No Pasaran*.

Paul Scott wrapped his arms around the Spanish production designer. "It's magnificent, Pepe. And you too, love." He smiled at the saucy English set decorator.

Eddie Beaumont stared at the set misty-eyed. The re-created Gran Via rekindled the memory of the six months he had spent covering the Spanish Civil War as a correspondent for the old *World-Telegram*. He had been a novice, a fresh-out-of-college journalist drinking Fundador and hanging out in Hemingway's second-floor suite at the Florida Hotel.

Adrian whispered to Paul, who nodded and shouted, "Attention, everyone, the boss has something to say."

"I would like to add my appreciation," Adrian said. "I thank all of you for this magnificent achievement."

There was a spontaneous burst of applause.

Adrian followed Scott and his team of assistants to the Chapman crane parked in front of the Palace Hotel. A crew of grips had laid down evenly planed wooden planks to accommodate the Chapman's wheels and ensure a smooth tracking shot.

Scott put his arm around Rossi's shoulders. "We start tight, crane up, and widen on the pullback with Bryan and Castle. The background and foreground action peel into the shot as we take the principals all the way to Chicote's."

Rossi translated for his Italian camera crew.

Scott fixed a viewfinder to his eye, trained it on the boulevard, and slowly changed lens sizes. He handed the viewfinder to Adrian. "Have a look—make believe it's moonlight."

Adrian studied the street through the viewfinder.

"Christ . . . it's sensational, Paul."

"I think we should shoot the rehearsal," Scott said. "All we need is Julia and Bryan."

"That may be a problem. They're not expecting to work until tomorrow night."

"So what? They're in the hotel. They're standing by. What the hell." He smiled and ran his hands through his long, shaggy hair. "We might get lucky."

Returning to the hotel by way of the present-day Gran Via, they experienced a mind-boggling sensation—it was as if they had traveled half a century in thirty minutes. The past and present had collided and coalesced.

They turned into the Paseo del Castellana at the Alcalá intersection. The dappled sunlight coming through the trees painted a camouflage effect over the outdoor cafés.

The caravan of film cars swung around the Fountain of Dancing Dolphins and pulled up at the La Sirena.

Once inside the lobby Paul touched Adrian's sleeve and said, "Let's meet in my suite in fifteen minutes. I'll order two of those great club sandwiches—okay?"

"Fine."

Adrian walked up a flight of stairs to the second-floor production office and asked Glickman's secretary to fax Smalley that they were going to shoot what was to have been a rehearsal.

He then dialed the editor in chief, John Carr, who had been

installed in a suite that had been transformed into a modern editorial facility.

"Cutting room," Carr's laconic voice answered.

"John, this is Adrian. We've decided to shoot the rehearsal. Advise the lab the negative they'll be getting tomorrow morning is not a test and should be treated as the real thing."

"Right."

"When do you think we'll see the print takes?" Adrian asked.

"About six tomorrow night. The ballroom projection facility is all set." The editor paused. "I'd like to come out and watch the shoot tonight."

"No problem. We'll be leaving the hotel at five forty-five."

"See you then."

Adrian hung up thinking, Another solid soldier—John Carr was a two-time Oscar-winning editor.

Paul Scott's third-floor suite was a split-level apartment with a picture window facing the Paseo del Castellana. The walls were papered with lithographic reproductions of eighteenth-century Madrid. The furniture was Italian modern and comfortable. Wearing jeans and a T-shirt stamped "Ocho Rios," Scott padded about barefoot. His youthful demeanor was marred by dark circles under his eyes. The last vestiges of his tropical tan had long since faded.

"Sandwiches are on the table," he said. "Help yourself to the bar. I'm a drink up on you."

As Adrian crossed to the bar, Scott placed a CD into the stereo.

Stirring his vodka and tonic, Adrian caught the unmistakable aroma of ganja but decided not to mention it. Scott had worked tirelessly for the last six weeks checking every department, every piece of rolling equipment from tanks to generators. There wasn't a costume or a prop he hadn't personally approved. He was on top of the pre-production team and had worked closely with Eddie Beaumont on script changes. He had accompanied Adrian to the airport to welcome Julia Castle and Richard Bryan. He was a one-man gang constantly stoking the pre-production process. He had thrown himself into the enterprise with total abandon and yet he never failed to acknowledge Adrian's contribution to story, to securing the deal and signing the key players. Their relationship was one of trust and respect. Paul Scott was neither a juicer nor a shooter and if he required a toke of ganja to cool out, so be it.

Billie Holiday sang "What a Little Moonlight Can Do."

"Listen to Lady Day, man—1935. Just issued. Columbia's ninth CD. The quintessential Billie Holiday." Scott sipped his gin.

"She was all by herself," Adrian said.

"Thank Christ for these re-issues."

"It's a terrific arrangement."

"You know who's backing her?"

"Sounds like Benny on clarinet."

"Right." Scott nodded. "Along with Roy Eldridge, Ben Webster, Teddy Wilson, and Cozy Cole. Sometimes I think I should have stayed with my music. I was doing some good things on vibes; but I fell for Bogart."

"We all did. How's Honeybear?"

"She's cool. Didden got me a terrific Spanish vet. Listen!" Scott exclaimed. "Listen to her articulation. Clean—just off the beat and a touch of vibrato for emotion. No jazz vocalist had a more versatile sense of phrasing." He paused. "Except Sinatra."

There was a knock at the door and Scott shouted, "It's open!"

Julia Castle, followed by Richard Bryan, entered the suite. She wore jeans, a T-shirt, and no makeup. Her pale hair was parted in the center and framed her oval face. Day or night, makeup or no makeup, she was perfection. Scott stared at her as if for the first time.

"Are we disturbing you fellows?" Bryan asked.

"Not at all," Adrian said. "Want to split a sandwich?"

"Thanks—but we've eaten."

"They serve a wonderful cold lobster," Julia said. "The hotel restaurant is damn good. Listen," she said, "Richard doesn't share my concern, but aren't we moving a little fast? How come we're shooting tonight?"

"Sometimes you get very lucky shooting a rehearsal," Adrian explained. "You can be loose. If we miss, we come back as scheduled—it's on the house."

"We can try a few things." Scott finally spoke. "We've got absolutely nothing to lose."

"Except a night's sleep," she said.

Bryan started to say something, then glanced nervously around the room and said, "Where's the cat?"

"In the bedroom," Scott replied.

"You look exhausted, Paul," Julia said. "You better take a nap.

It's going to be a bitch out there tonight. It's a complicated sequence."

"Just a two-shot with atmosphere." Scott smiled.

"When is Morosco due?" Bryan asked.

"Tuesday," Adrian replied, "with Wheeler and the other Lincolns."

"Did you tell Rossi no chokers with anything but a long lens?" Julia asked.

"All taken care of," Scott said. "But there won't be any close-ups tonight. This is an evolving master. The environment wraps around both of you as we track."

Bryan shrugged. "Well, guys, we'll give it our best shot."

At the door, Julia glanced back at Scott and smiled wickedly. "Shame on you, Paul—Astra Collins, for Chrissake. It's a wonder you didn't fall in."

THE POWERFUL CARBON-ARC BRUTES ILLUMINATED THE LENGTH OF THE
Gran Via set. In deference to the occasional air raids the interior
and exterior lights of hotels, shops, cinemas, and sidewalk lamps
were cast in midnight blue.

Seated atop the Chapman crane, Scott set the opening composition of the long tracking shot.

Speaking in Italian to his crew, Federico Rossi corrected the
angle of a key light at the entrance to the Palace Hotel.

The American and Spanish assistant directors reviewed cues and
start marks with the dress extras.

Production assistants stood by ready to cue the rolling stock:
trucks, buses, trams, motorcycles, military sedans, horse-drawn
wagons, and ambulances.

Helmeted Spanish women manning antiaircraft guns were at
their sandbagged emplacements smoking and gossiping.

Spanish paramilitary units dressed in blue coveralls and black
berets carried Soviet-made rifles and lounged in the sidewalk cafés.

The animal trainer fed biscuits to his caged dogs and the street
vendors and metro riders stood by kiosks.

For the past two hours Richard Bryan and Julia Castle had
rehearsed their moves, starting inside the Palace and continuing
down the Gran Via, with extras and vehicles entering the widening

composition. The last run-through had been close to perfect and Scott finally decided they were ready to try one.

The camera grips lowered the Chapman's boom arm. Scott jumped off and grabbed Federico Rossi's arm and whispered something to the cinematographer. Rossi nodded and Scott moved off. Adrian watched him weave through the maze of technicians: whispering, patting, touching, joking, admonishing.

He was not unlike the conductor of a symphony orchestra pulling the composition together, making certain that everyone was in concert. He knew exactly what he wanted from each member of his team. He was the general before the battle, calming and encouraging his troops. The film's fortune was now in his hands. For better or worse, Paul Scott was the engine of the whole mad enterprise.

He again reviewed the propaganda posters and signs with Polly Turner. She smiled. "Don't you trust me, love?"

Paul kissed her cheek and went over to the special effects man, Mike Rettig, and exchanged a piece of information. He complimented Peg Monroe on her costume design. As he walked back to the Chapman, he had a kind word for Don Alfonso and Fred Glickman.

The cobblestones had been hosed down, the arcs struck, the engines on all working vehicles switched on. Paul hugged Adrian and jumped up onto his perch alongside the Chapman's camera. With a microphone wired to strategically placed speakers, his voice boomed and echoed the length of the set. "Stand by. This one will be with film."

The Chapman's boom-arm rose to its full height. Scott stood precariously atop the saddle-shaped seat, a silhouetted figure about to launch his cast and crew on an unpredictable voyage to an uncertain destination.

"Okay, people. Just listen to the assistant directors. You're all professionals—wait for your cues. Hit your marks. Your actions must be real. This is Madrid on a summer night in 1937. The Fascist forces have been held in a long sweeping arc from Jarama to the University. Remember the slogan on the banner, *No Pasaran*—'They shall not pass.' The Gran Via is the principal artery of a great city under siege. A city that refuses to surrender. Now— stand by."

Scott sat down alongside Federico Rossi and, still holding the mike, called down to his Spanish and American first assistants.

"You fellows ready?"

"All set, Paul," Sam Solomon shouted.

"Todo listo." Fuentes waved.

Scott then addressed the chief soundman.

"You all right, Ian?"

"Yes, sir."

"Sam, let me have Julia and Bryan for a minute."

The American first assistant went into the Palace Hotel interior and after a moment the actors came out. Bryan looked smart in his corduroy pants, leather jacket, and Glengarry cap. His left arm was bandaged. Julia's trench coat was draped over her shoulders. Her nurse's uniform was bloodstained.

Adrian shook his head thinking, you could dress her in rags and splatter her with blood and still not diminish her beauty.

"Richard, let Julia come out by herself," Scott said. "Count to ten, then come out and catch up to her."

"Gotcha."

"You okay, Julia?"

"Let's shoot it."

Scott stood up in the seat and, using the mike, said, "All right, here we go!"

A series of shouts for quiet from the various assistants echoed the length of the set. A disciplined stillness fell over the men, women, animals, and machines.

Adrian would always remember this moment—it was as if they were characters in a historic mural, waiting for a magical command that would bring them to life.

A camera assistant held the clapstick in front of a baby spotlight.

"Roll camera!" the first assistant shouted.

The operator on the Chapman flipped a toggle switch on the Panavision camera and pressed his eye to the rubber lens cup.

"Speed!" he replied.

"Roll sound!"

"Scene 118-A—take one."

The camera assistant slapped the sticks together for synch mark and quickly ducked out of camera range.

"Aaaaand . . . action!" Scott shouted.

An olive-colored ambulance with a red cross painted on its roof careened around the corner and screeched to a halt at the Palace Hotel. The attendants jumped out, opened the rear doors, gently lifted two wounded soldiers onto stretchers, and started toward the Palace entrance. Julia came out, glanced at the wounded men, bit her lip, and started walking down the sloping boulevard. The Chapman dollied back with her. A shell burst in the background and paramilitary units raced through the smoke and yellow light.

Wild dogs loped across the glistening cobblestones, buses chugged past Julia on their way to the University front. Trucks trailing artillery pieces clattered along the boulevard.

"Playback!" Scott ordered.

The dull sound of distant artillery echoed, together with Arabic chanting and beating drums.

Bryan burst out of the Palace doors, glanced down the street, spotted Julia, and trotted after her. He caught up to her and they played the scene, oblivious to the enveloping pedestrian and vehicular traffic.

They were halfway down the Gran Via, surrounded by atmospheric action. A convoy of heavy-duty military trucks with their blue running lights on trundled up the boulevard.

Scott signaled the Chapman camera grips to cut the wheels for the parallel move to Chicote's.

They crossed the boulevard just as a shell-burst hit a café some twenty yards off. People fell, screamed, and ran for shelter. Bryan grabbed Julia's arm and they dashed toward Chicote's. Two drunken Lincoln Brigade men stumbled out of the smoke-filled café just as Bryan and Julia entered.

Scott waited fifteen seconds before shouting, "Cut! Print! We go again, right away."

The crane arm was lowered and Scott jumped off and went over to Adrian. "Bryan blew a few lines. But it was pretty damn good. I'll get one more."

"What about the close stuff?"

"Tomorrow night. We can lose most of the extras."

Scott walked to Chicote's and put his arms around Julia and Bryan.

"It was fine. Only two minor things. You forgot to ask her where she was billeted and—"

"Oh shit!" Bryan interrupted, snapping his fingers, angry at himself.

"It's okay. We'll pick it up," Scott said reassuringly. "It was a terrific take. Remember to play the shell-burst—the concussion ring would throw both of you up against the door. We've got to see that."

"That shell-burst scared the pants off me," Julia said.

"The action around the shot was beautifully staged," Bryan complimented Scott.

"Thank you. Now the second thing is subtle but important. You're both giving me four-four. Julia, I'd like you to play a beat off the dialogue, and Richard, play a beat ahead—you're pushing the scene. She's responding. Okay?"

Bryan nodded. "They'll love this back in lotusland."

"Who cares?" Scott said. "This is *our* thing."

The assistants began to reorganize for another take. Scott moved from one key crew member to another, thanking them, praising them, and telling them how to make it better.

Watching the director's frenetic energy pulling it together, Adrian thought back to the night in Ocho Rios when Paul had inexplicably changed his mind and agreed to direct the picture. He had wondered about it but the answer was obvious—it was the Magic Lantern; sooner or later even the most reluctant moth found its glow irresistible.

During his infrequent visits to L.A. Resnick stayed in bungalow 33-E at the Beverly Hills Hotel. The secluded pink stucco structure had a private walkway and was shielded by tropical foliage and cascades of fuchsia-colored bougainvillea.

The sitting room/salon was spacious, bright, and furnished with plush upholstered furniture. Seated behind a desk, Resnick was holding the phone to his ear, listening patiently to his granddaughter's tearful complaints.

Sprawled around the room, fanning themselves with hotel menus, were Salvatore Parnelli, Harry Walters, and Irv Wexler.

"Yes . . . one o'clock. No . . . no . . . I'll take care of it. I love you too. Yes, a tuna salad will be fine . . . 'bye, sweetheart."

Resnick hung up, rubbed his eyes, and glanced up at the revolving ceiling fan pushing the heavy, warm air around. "I'm sorry about the heat," the Old Man apologized, "but I have a problem with air-conditioning."

"It's okay," Parnelli said, mopping his forehead with a damp handkerchief. The Sicilian hustler looked weary and unkempt.

Resnick glanced at Walters and shook his head. "I'm disappointed with Frank."

"The man is exhausted," Walters said. "We have three pictures opening within a ten-week period. He was too tired to make the round-trip flight.''

Resnick smiled derisively. "Too tired—Frank is thirty years younger than me. You're all young men. I'm a hard eighty. I've been working since I was twelve. Right now, there's an arthritic pain starting out of the base of my neck running down my left arm—like a knife inside my flesh. My teeth hurt. My eyes burn at night. I can't sleep more than three hours. I get up to piss two, three times. But I'm here. I take care of business. Look at Sal''— he motioned to Parnelli—"he's been on a fourteen-hour flight from Rome to Chicago to L.A.''

Walters knew that Solish's presence was not critical to the meeting but the Old Man regarded his absence as a lack of respect.

"Frank is over his head,'' Wexler explained. "He never bargained for the corporate red tape that goes with being CEO.''

Resnick stared at the ceiling fan for a long moment before saying, "Tell me about Spain, Harry.''

"They started shooting a day early,'' Walters said.

"Why?''

"Paul Scott decided to shoot what was scheduled to be a dress rehearsal.''

"Have you seen the film?''

"It's en route.''

"No trouble yet?''

"It's on the way in the person of Morosco and Wheeler.''

"Let me ask something here,'' Parnelli said. "What are you planning to do about Aurora? She's in the middle of everything. She could tumble onto the score.''

"She has a hundred thousand reasons to look the other way,'' Wexler replied. "We gave her a bonus and she invested it in Gemstone common.''

"Smart,'' Parnelli said.

"I'm planning to send her to oversee our picture shooting in Switzerland,'' Walters said. "I told you before, don't worry about Aurora.''

"Easy for you to say,'' Parnelli said. "I gotta worry. I'm up to my ass in worry. That's why I asked for this meeting.''

The Old Man swallowed some water and asked, "What's the problem, Sal?''

"I'm still eight hundred million short.''

"What about Charles Glenn at Centurion?"

"They won't exceed their bond."

"What do you propose to do?" Resnick said.

"Shit . . . I don't know—everything depends on Squillante."

"What the hell is a Squillante?" Resnick asked disdainfully.

"Count Aldo Squillante is my main money-mover. He has solid connections to titled Italian money—old money. He's also wired to laundrymen at Banco della Croce."

"So what's the problem?" Walters said.

"The Count ran into a wall. There's a recession in Italy."

"Where does that leave us?" Resnick asked.

Parnelli sighed heavily, got to his feet, lit a dark cheroot, and shook his head. "I wish I could answer that. Squillante is in Palermo meeting with some capos in the heroin cartel. They have a mountain of cash that needs to be washed. Our scam presents them with a ready-made laundry."

"How do you wash it?" Wexler said.

"Banco della Croce wires the eight hundred million to Aflin A.G. in Zurich. It's then transferred to the Bank of Panama, from there to the Caymans to Liechtenstein and finally to Luxembourg, where it's wired back to Sirocco's account at City National, Chicago."

"What's in it for the cartel?" Resnick asked.

"Once we cash in, they get back sixty clean cents on every dirty dollar."

"So in essence," Resnick said, "the heroin cartel pays Sirocco forty percent vigorish to clean their narcodollars."

"You got it."

"That's a pretty steep vig," Resnick said.

"Not when you consider that their cash is being eaten by rats in a Palermo warehouse."

"And Squillante has already effected this arrangement?" Walters asked.

"It's in the works. Negotiating with Sicilians takes time. They always look to beat you out of a few points."

Resnick rose, crossed to the window, and, in a surprisingly quick and forceful move, snapped the curtains closed. He faced Parnelli and his eyes narrowed to gunmetal slits.

"Let me understand something. Are you telling us that the scam depends on this phony count?" Resnick's voice blurred with anger. "This . . . Squillante?"

"I believe he'll deliver."

"I have to tell you," Wexler interjected, "Squillante has fucked a lot of people. I ran a check on him."

Parnelli nodded. "He's screwed civilians. But he would never cross connected people." Boom Boom sucked on the cigarette. "I'm doing the best I can," he said through the smoke. "I'm two thirds there. And let's get something straight; Sirocco is in the limelight—not Gemstone. If this thing gets out of control the Feds are at my door. I placed my chips on Squillante. If anyone's got a better idea, I'm listening."

The room fell silent for a moment. Resnick poured some water into his glass, took a long swallow, and cleared his throat.

"Listen carefully, Sal. If this scumbag Squillante screws us, intentionally or otherwise, I'll have him whacked."

Parnelli sank back down into his chair.

"You tell Squillante," Resnick continued, "if I make one phone call, he's dog food. He'll be called Count Fido."

Walters smiled. Wexler chuckled. Parnelli squirmed.

"I designed this operation," the Old Man said, "I put a lot of time and thought into its execution. There's a very expensive deception underway in Spain—a fraudulent film is being produced, a picture that Harry has set up with great care. We've gone too far and worked too hard to lose this score and I'll be goddamned if we're gonna hold the bag."

Parnelli's black eyes darted apprehensively from face to face.

"Don't you dare tell me your ass is out!" Resnick's voice rose. "I depended on *you*—not on some bullshit count. And if we go under, someone's gonna pay."

Neither Walters nor Wexler had ever seen this malevolent side of the Old Man's nature. Now, with clarity, they understood how this frail octogenarian had made his way to the top of the Combination.

Parnelli crushed out his cheroot and dabbed at the perspiration on his lip. "I'll get the money. You can sleep on it. It's complicated but I'll handle it. I'll come up with the rest of it. I asked for this meeting to outline the problem and get your okay to use the cartel's narcodollars."

Resnick's eyes remained fixed on Parnelli.

"None of us are concerned with the source of the money," the Old Man said. "People shoot heroin, snort coke, marinate their livers in booze, and gamble their mortgages away. Dollars pour in and dollars pour out. It's paper. It don't feel and it don't think. I don't care if it's IBM, Siemens, or Mitsubishi—money is polluted. When someone makes a buck someone else is getting fucked. That's the nature of business. There's no such thing as clean money. You use whatever works.

"I want you to hold a press conference at Sirocco's New York office. You'll announce that on or about December fifteenth, you intend to file a takeover bid for Gemstone Pictures at a price per share to be declared at the time. You understand?"

Parnelli nodded. "Sure, Leo. No problem."

"And leave out your 'Hollywood Jews' crap. You're out of date. Jews don't own studios. Japs own studios. Australians own studios. Europeans own studios."

Parnelli sighed. "Okay, Leo."

Walters rose and added, "You might allude to the fact that Gemstone's epic film shooting in Spain is a disaster. That'll give me something to deny."

"The one thing we can't afford is delay," Wexler cautioned. "We can't chance the Spanish picture finishing before we cash in."

"If it gets close we could shut the picture down," Resnick said.

"That's dangerous," Walters quickly replied. "It's almost never done. Once you're deep into production even the death of the star doesn't stop the picture. A photo double is employed—tricks are performed in editing. Shutting down a production of this size might expose our true intentions. Irv's right, we've got to cash in before the picture finishes."

"But by that time you'll have torpedoed the film in the press," Parnelli said. "The whole world will know it's a turkey."

"Just make sure you get the money together by mid-December," Resnick said.

"I'll take care of my end," Parnelli said.

Resnick got slowly to his feet. "All right. Meeting's over. I've got to shower. Thank you for coming, boys, and Harry, tell Solish next time we meet I expect him to show up."

"Absolutely. I'm sorry we had to bother you. I know you dislike leaving the desert."

"I didn't come up here just for this meeting," Resnick said. "I came to visit my granddaughter. She's twenty-seven now. She has her father's eyes and his gentle manner. I look at her and I see my dead son. A man she's taken up with is causing her some distress. I must take care of that. I appreciate everything you fellows have done and that includes you, Sal—just don't let me down."

The Old Man walked into the bedroom, peeled off his shirt, and stretched out on the bed. His pulse had calmed and his anger had dissipated. He had subjected himself to stress; not smart but necessary. A man of intellect and courage had to be in action. Every great general required a war in order to sustain his own sense of worth. Action was the only antidote to the incipient dullness of mind that came with age—action chased the Angel of Death.

42

DON ALFONSO HAD ALERTED CUSTOMS OFFICIALS AT BARAJAS INTERnational Airport that Jack Wheeler, Mayo Morosco, Leroy Belgrave, and other American actors would be arriving on Iberia Flight 285 from New York.

The noisy, smoke-filled VIP lounge was jammed with local and international press—a brief question-and-answer session with the stars would be held in the lounge. Photographers representing Reuters and AP and a CNN TV crew had been granted permission to await the American contingent on the tarmac.

The Volunteers had been a hot item in the Spanish press. A film of this magnitude had not been manufactured in Spain since the heyday of the Brontson empire—and never before had a foreign film company attempted to dramatize the tragedy of Spain's Civil War. The picture had ignited a media fire storm with opponents and proponents arguing the merits of Gemstone's audacious undertaking.

The prime minister's office had issued a statement outlining the pragmatic realities. The picture would have been made with or without official approval. Italy could easily have doubled for Spain, and the fact that the film's producers had chosen Madrid as the base of their operations guaranteed thousands of jobs for many months. It would also encourage other productions to come to Spain. More importantly, the picture did not represent a political threat to the stability of the government nor would it dishonor the Spanish nation. Freedom of expression was at the heart of the reigning Socialist government.

Still, the debate raged on, and now the heavy hitters were about to arrive.

Adrian and Don Alfonso stood at the huge glass wall watching the Boeing 767 scream slowly toward a parking spot indicated by a ground traffic control officer waving both his arms. The gaggle of photographers on the tarmac clasped their hands to their ears against the piercing whine of the jet engines. The gleaming aircraft pivoted expertly so that its front wheel assembly came to rest precisely on the designated spot.

The engines were shut down. Uniformed attendants wheeled a portable staircase to the aircraft's first-class exit door. One of the attendants went up the steps and banged on the panel.

The heavy portal swung open and a tense stewardess stood aside, permitting Dr. Sindi to exit first. The bearded, turbaned guru smiled at the swarm of photographers waiting at the base of the steps.

Dr. Sindi was closely followed by Mayo Morosco. The Genius sported a drooping Zapata mustache and a suede cowboy outfit topped by a Mexican sombrero with a three-foot-high cone.

As Morosco started down the stairs a sudden roar issued from the cabin door. The guru and Morosco stopped and turned back. Standing on the top step, his arms raised to the heavens, looking like a grizzly bear on his hind legs, was Jack Wheeler.

"Viva España!" he shouted drunkenly. *"Viva Mexico! Viva Cuba!"*

He continued bellowing his litany of Central American countries to the applause of the waiting press. Bowing deeply, Wheeler drew his black cloak tightly around his shoulders, took a step, tripped, and crashed into Morosco, who toppled Dr. Sindi. All three landed in a tangle at the foot of the steps. Nikon motors whirred. Bulbs flashed. The photographers jostled and shoved each other like a pack of hungry hyenas as they fought for a better angle.

The Iberia attendants vainly tried to hold back a flood of journalists who had bolted out of the visitors' lounge and were racing frantically across the tarmac.

Dr. Sindi got to his feet and chased after Morosco's wind-tossed sombrero. Two Iberia public relations men tried to help Wheeler up, but he tossed them off imperiously.

"Leggo of me, you frigging Spics!" he snarled. "Who do you think you're pushing around? Where the fuck is Adrian Summers?" He clamped his big hand on Morosco's shoulder and slobbered, "Hey, Mayo, where's that fucking snake of yours? Up your guru's ass, that's where!" He howled and convulsed with laughter.

Morosco swung a roundhouse right at Wheeler's jaw but the blow landed harmlessly on the big man's shoulder.

"You wanna fight?" Wheeler staggered, straightened up, and threw a left hook that missed Morosco and caught a CNN reporter flush on the jaw, knocking him cold. Dr. Sindi grabbed Wheeler. Morosco swung a few more futile punches. The photographers continued loading and shooting furiously.

Don Alfonso came out of the Customs office with four muscular Guardia Civil police. They quickly subdued Wheeler, handcuffing him and shoving him into the back of a police van. Bulling their way through the horde of journalists, Morosco and Sindi made it safely to their limousine.

The handsome black actor Leroy Belgrave had watched the entire scene from the top step of the first-class staircase. Once the commotion subsided, he signaled to the other American actors, who followed him down the stairs and into the company van.

At the hotel, Adrian instructed Glickman to have large baskets of fruit delivered to the actors' rooms and a spray of gladiolas sent to Morosco's suite. According to Sindi, gladiolas were good karma.

Wheeler's suite was to be alcohol-free.

Glickman placed the orders, hung up, and asked, "When do you think they'll get here?"

"The traffic was heavy coming in from the airport. Morosco still had to clear Customs and who knows when Don Alfonso will spring Wheeler. I'd say we have an hour or so."

"I think we should hire special security for Morosco and Wheeler."

"Good idea."

"I thought Wheeler was off the sauce," Glickman remarked.

"So did I."

"Christ"—the production manager sighed—"juicers are the worst."

"Is Paul up?"

Glickman nodded. "He's in a production meeting with Rossi."

"Did we get a lab report on last night's stuff?"

"Yeah, the negative is fine. We'll see the dailies at six along with some additional second-unit footage."

"Check with Smalley and find out if the Gran Via dailies arrived in Hollywood."

"Right."

Adrian rose. "Better have Sam Solomon and Ramon Fuentes wait in the lobby. Make sure Morosco and Wheeler get in okay, and tell Leroy Belgrave I'll see him at five."

"Bryan's complaining about his driver—says he talks too much."

"Change him." Adrian paused. "How's Miss Castle doing?"

"Sweet as sugar."

"Okay . . ." Adrian sighed. "Get on to that bodyguard thing. I'll be with Paul if you need me."

Before calling the security agency Glickman ran some fast mental calculations; he'd list the bodyguards' fee at $2,500 a week and pocket $500 off the top, which would raise his total kickback grift to $3,000 a week. He decided to convert the pesetas to Swiss francs. The dollar wasn't worth shit in Europe.

Paul Scott sighed. "You're going to have to deal with it, Adrian. I don't want that sonofabitch on the set if he's sloshed."

"I'll do what I can."

"You mean to say Wheeler actually took a swing at Morosco?"

"Swung and missed. Cold-cocked the CNN guy. That's gonna cost Gemstone a few bucks, not to mention the negative worldwide publicity."

"I thought Morosco and Wheeler were pals."

"So did I."

Scott paced for a moment, then said, "We'll never shoot with those two on Wednesday. You'll have to get Wheeler in line, and cool off Morosco. The Genius will be pissed about his snake being quarantined and he'll drive us nuts with his notions of how General Miaja ought to look and act. Morosco's famous for nitpicking until he gets his way. Booze aside, I respect Wheeler. He's at heart a decent guy, but the Genius is a fucking bully. He'll probably want to wear a bagel around his uniform and"—Scott shook his head—"wait till he gets into the script. Thank Christ, Beaumont's still around."

Adrian crossed the bar and poured a double vodka on the rocks. "We can handle Morosco."

"How?"

"The guru."

"Dr. Sindi?"

Adrian nodded. "We'll buy the prick."

"That may help, but Morosco won't shoot on Wednesday. Trust me, Adrian, by the time he forgives Wheeler and agrees on the wardrobe, makeup, and script changes, we'll have blown ten days."

"Ten days . . ." Adrian murmured, "that's a million dollars down the drain. We can't shut down, Paul. You have a terrific rapport going with Julia, Bryan, and the crew. We can't afford to rupture that harmony."

"I'm just being pragmatic," Scott said. "Morosco will try to extract his pound of flesh and if he gets his way, Wheeler will hit the sauce and we're dead."

"Wish I hadn't bought him." Adrian sighed. "Walters was very convincing."

"You can't fault yourself. Morosco is a giant. Once he performs you'll have magic, but it's painful and risky." Scott lit a cigarette and slowly shook out the match. "Wait a minute." His eyes widened with excitement. "We don't need either of them Wednesday! I'll take Julia, Bryan, Belgrave, and the other American actors and shoot the Lincolns' montage: their departure on the *Normandie,* the trip through France, crossing the Pyrenees into Figueras, and the training camp at Albacete."

Adrain stared at the excited director with undisguised admiration. "That's two weeks of very tricky stuff, Paul—a hell of a lot of night-for-night shooting."

"So what? There's very little dialogue. It's pictures. I'll muscle it through. Meantime you can deal with Wheeler and the Genius. Rehearse and placate the bastards so that when I come back I can shoot the Palacio Real sequence."

"They'll want to rehearse with you. They'll want you to approve the wardrobe, makeup, and the line changes."

"Tell them I'm on location. Just run the scene. I'll have Giron pick up the second-unit *Normandie* embarkation shot with doubles."

"How are you going to do that?"

"We'll lease a ship in Barcelona, fly the French tricolor, and paint 'Normandie' on the fantail. Trust me. It'll work. We'll pick up five days."

Scott walked over to the bar and poured a drink. "I'll take a small crew, the Panavision mobile unit, and we'll live off the land."

Adrian smiled at the handsome director. "Before this is over you'll have a mortgage on my life."

"Our lives were hijacked a long time ago," Scott said. "Cheers."

"Cheers."

Scott swallowed the vodka. "Wait till you see what Polly did with Chicote's. Her set decoration is out of sight. You'd swear to God it was 1937."

"They're all gifted," Adrian said. "We're blessed with a terrific crew."

"I think Polly's got a thing for you," Scott said matter-of-factly.

"She's just flirtatious," Adrian said. "I'll have Glickman and Don Alfonso set up the support team for the montage."

"The important thing is for you to get those two lunatics to function. I'll be okay. Just make sure Giron has that ship for the *Normandie* stuff."

Scott peered out of the picture window. The setting sun cast the Castellana in a warm magenta light. "Pretty city, man. Alive. Luminous."

"True. But for us it's '37."

Scott turned to Adrian and smiled. "I hate to judge dailies but they did look pretty rich."

"They were first-class, Paul."

"What about Julia? How does she come across?"

"Devastating. And not just her beauty. She's performing."

"Her theater work has fine-tuned her natural talent," Scott said. "She never edges into soap." He lit a joint, took a deep drag, held it down, then exhaled. "Want a hit?"

"Not now."

"The thing is, Adrian"—Scott's speech pattern picked up speed—"the script has a built-in sentimentality. I mean this is a picture about the losing side. But it's not about losers. That train scene—the wedding scene, the finca, the finale, and finally the parade—it's handkerchief time. But we've always got to play against it. The volunteers can't drift into pathos. They can't ever feel sorry for themselves—frustration and anger yes, but not self-pity. Julia can be in the midst of dying, screaming men—up to her armpits in blood—but she must not cry. Not till the end—not until the last parade."

Adrian drained his vodka, poured another, and asked, "Anything going on with you and Julia?"

"No. She still gives me the business about Astra Collins."

"That means she's still on the ride. Maybe you—" The phone rang. Paul picked it up, listened for a moment, and said, "Okay."

He hung up, took another hit of the joint, and spoke through the smoke. "Morosco and Wheeler have arrived."

"Impounded! Impounded!" Morosco shouted. "Ruby is a harmless reptile. She's had all her shots. What the fuck do they mean
'wild animal'?"

"It's an outrage." Sindi stroked his beard. "The serpent is in the
ninth dimension of the samsara."

"I don't control Spanish Customs," Adrian said calmly. "They
have rules and they don't categorize a python as a household pet."

"Are you telling me that Ruby languishes in a cage at the airport
until this fucking shoot is over?" Morosco said angrily.

The Genius's eyes were menacing; his lionesque head tilted up
and his chin was thrust forward. The great actor reminded Adrian
of a petulant Mussolini.

Although irritated, Adrian managed to keep his tone of voice
measured. "You have a choice. You can ship Ruby home or, if
you prefer, the director of the Madrid zoo has agreed to confine
her in the reptile house temporarily so that you can visit her occasionally. Gemstone will reimburse the zoo for her upkeep. That's
the best I can do."

"I've got to take a piss," the Genius said and stormed out.

Adrian took an envelope out of his pocket and handed it to Sindi.

"There's a thousand dollars in there. You'll get that every week.
Just keep that bastard sane and cooperative."

"It's very generous of you, Mr. Summers."

"Do your job, and you'll go home with a tax-free bonanza."

The tall, dignified guru gathered up the hem of his saffron-colored robe and tucked the envelope into his argyle socks. "I'll do what I can. But I must always remain in the yin and yang of the ninth dimension prescribed by the goddess Shiva."

"Save the bullshit for Morosco—just play ball."

The Genius came back into the salon and as he moved past the picture window his classic Roman profile seemed chiseled by the light.

"What do you think?" Morosco asked his guru.

"Having Ruby close by will undoubtedly maintain good karma."

The Genius turned to Adrian. "I want your word that Ruby will have her diet of two white mice a week and the supervision of a veterinarian. She suffers severe heartburn after meals."

"I'll do my best," Adrian promised.

Morosco sat down, rubbed his bent nose, shook his hair, and peeled off his Zapata mustache.

"I understand you were awarded the Bronze Star for heroism."

"Anyone that survived Nam received medals."

"Saw a lot of action, huh?"

"No more than the next guy."

"You still on junk?"

"None of your fucking business."

"You're absolutely right." The Genius smiled and a sudden warmth radiated from his expressive eyes. It was the same seductive look that had charmed audiences for almost four decades.

The smile vanished as suddenly as it appeared. "I want you to keep a tight hold on that little cocksucker Richard Bryan. Some years ago I did *Lear* on Broadway. Bryan had a bit part. During a break in Act Two I caught that putz going down on my wardrobe lady." His face reddened and his voice assumed the timbre and tone of King Lear's. "He was engaged in the ancient art of cunnilingus in *my* dressing room with *my* wardrobe lady."

"Richard Bryan suffered from satyriasis," Adrian said, "but he's cured."

"I believe Mr. Summers is quite right," Sindi offered. "Bryan is a new man. He rejoiced at the birth of his twins presented to him by his Korean wife on the floor of Chasen's banquet room. I had the pleasure of cutting the umbilical cord."

Adrian suspected that the guru's pleasure had been heightened by snorting the proud papa's Lima White.

The Genius rose, walked to the wet bar, poured a Coca-Cola, and drank it all in one long swallow. He tossed some peanuts into his mouth and said, "Julia Castle."

"What about her?"

"I want to meet her."

"You only have three scenes with her."

"Three or thirty-three—if we work together we have to rehearse together. Coca-Cola?"

"No thanks."

"What do you intend to do about Wheeler?"

"What do you suggest?"

"Dump him and get Brando."

"Jack Wheeler is a great actor."

"He can act but he's a juicer. He drank his way across the Atlantic. The flight was a nightmare."

"If he can't perform, if he's drunk on the set, I'll do whatever is necessary, but for the moment Jack Wheeler is Kopek."

"Let me tell you something," Morosco said. "There's no such thing as a reformed drunk. I know, I was married to four of them. Wheeler is trouble."

"So are junkies and coke heads." Adrian mentioned the latter as a cue for Sindi, who picked it up.

"Mayo . . ." Sindi said stroking his beard, "I sense in Wheeler not only a tragic spirit but an inner beauty of the circle within the nine circles. He's open to the samsara. Let me work with him."

Adrian said, "Any metaphysical assistance you can provide will be greatly appreciated."

The Genius shrugged and put on his sombrero. "The War Ministry scene in the Palacio Real is unplayable as written."

"Eddie Beaumont's here," Adrian said. "He can work on the scene when we rehearse."

"Beaumont?" the Genius said, puzzled. "Is that old hack still writing?"

"Better than ever. Eddie will be at the rehearsals."

"Rehearsals!" Morosco spat the word as if ridding himself of something malignant. "Wheeler won't be in shape to rehearse for a week! Have Beaumont call me. And have wardrobe and makeup see me. The look of General Miaja is critical."

Adrian moved to the door, stopped, and turned. "I'll do everything I can to accommodate your ideas, but if you cost us production time it will come out of your salary."

The Genius blanched. "Is that a threat?"

Adrian shrugged. "You have lawyers. Gemstone has lawyers. You're scheduled to shoot Wednesday. If you're asking me for a delay I'll do what I can. You've been around long enough to know that making movies is collaborative. You're a great artist and we're all delighted that you're doing the picture, but there's no point in throwing your weight around. See you later, Dr. Sindi."

Once the door closed, Morosco said, "That's a dangerous fellow. Once a shooter always a shooter."

"I sensed the sixth dimension hovering about him," Sindi said.

"Really?" Morosco said, surprised.

"Yes . . . I received vibrations. Adrian Summers is a man who has triumphed over death. He has the power to summon Vishnu. I would suggest a modicum of respect in dealing with him."

The Genius shrugged and removed his sombrero.

"Fix me a marguerita and light a stick of hash."

Jack Wheeler reminded Adrian of a weeping grizzly bear. His arms were wrapped around Don Alfonso and he sobbed, pleading forgiveness.

"It's all right, *señor*," the dignified Spanish production manager said. "These things happen—alcohol and flying don't mix."

Wheeler dropped his arms, whirled around, and gripped Adrian's shoulders. "I'm sorry . . . I'm sorry."

"You promised. You gave me your word."

"It's my daughter." His hands fell and he wiped the tears from his cheeks.

"My eldest daughter hates my guts. Why?" He stumbled as he weaved his way toward the sofa. "Why? I guess I treated her mother badly. But I love the girl, Adrian—gave her everything." He sank down into the sofa. "That was it, you see. We had a terrible scene before I left New York—I'm sorry." He raised his right hand. "My hand to God—not another drop."

"I've got to go to the office," Alfonso said.

"Thanks for everything, Don Alfonso."

"For nothing, Señor Wheeler."

Adrian sat on the arm of the twin sofa facing the chastened

actor. "You don't have to take any vows. Just lay off the sauce while you're working. Don't bring the Stoli to the set. You'd do yourself a favor if you went into a program, but I can't be your conscience. I'm lucky I'm alive myself. I hardly qualify as an example for anyone else, but I put myself through a hellish withdrawal. It's been almost five years. Still every now and then I miss the high. The warmth. The oblivion. So how can I demand abstinence from you? Just don't take the booze to work."

"You have my word."

"Okay. Let's put it behind us."

Wheeler nodded and sighed. "I know I'm off base but I've got to tell you. Morosco's not the same actor we both knew. He's lost retention. He couldn't remember my name. When we met in the lounge at Kennedy, he spoke French to the Spanish clerk. He thought we were taking Air France to Paris." He shook his head in dismay. "If I were you, I'd get Brando."

"Let me worry about Morosco. Just take care of yourself."

"I understand. Believe me, Adrian—I understand. This picture is everything to you. I won't fuck it up."

"Okay."

"I mean it."

"I know that."

"Now, I'd like to see Paul."

"You will."

"I mean right away. That Palace scene we're supposed to shoot Wednesday doesn't work. There's no fire in it."

"I've postponed the shooting. There'll be lots of time to rehearse. Now get some sleep."

Wheeler got to his feet and hugged Adrian. "I love you, Paul."

"The name is Adrian."

Back in his suite, Adrian phoned Glickman.

"I made a deal with Dr. Sindi. For a grand a week he'll keep Morosco cooled out."

"Money well spent," Glickman said.

The production manager hung up and calculated he'd pay the Indian guru $1,500 and pocket $500.

"Too bad." Walters shook his head dejectedly and dropped the newspaper clipping into the wastebasket.

"Why did they run the goddamn thing on the front page?" Aurora asked. "It's a showbiz item."

"This sort of thing sells papers. Two great actors and a fakir in a drunken melee at the Madrid airport." Walters picked some lint from his dark cashmere jacket. "It's rich stuff."

"You can't say I didn't warn you," she said. "That's a volatile group you put together in Spain."

Walters lit his fourth Sherman. "There is an upside, I suppose. The entire civilized world is now aware of *The Volunteers.*"

"Did you see that Gwendolyn Peck item?" she asked.

"Herb Stoner sent something over but I haven't read it."

"It hinted that Bryan and Castle were getting it on. That kind of thing has got to upset Paul Scott—*and* Bryan's wife." Aurora sighed. "It's almost as if someone is trying to torpedo the ship before it sails."

"Why would anyone want to do that?"

"I don't know. We made a terrific publicity splash at the Chasen's party. That sort of puffery can generate envy."

"I don't think so. Gossip is endemic to big pictures. Besides, stars are used to getting hit below the belt." Walters picked up a box office report, studied it for a moment, then glanced at her. "Have you seen the weekend grosses on *Backwash?*"

"The figures are incredible."

"Gemstone common opened up two points this morning. You're going to get rich, kiddo."

"I still hate the picture." She sighed. "I guess it proves you can never steal *Double Indemnity* too often."

"If you have the right girl. Tracey Warren sold it."

"She certainly did. Those *Playboy* pictures are sensational, without revealing too much. She promises carnality."

"I'd like to put her in *Snowblind.*"

"As the ski instructor?"

"Why not?"

The phone console buzzed and Walters pressed the intercom button. "Yes?"

"Smalley," his secretary said.

Walters picked up the receiver. "What's up, Ray?"

"The Spanish dailies are ready."

"We're on the way."

Smalley, Wexler, and Aurora were seated in deep reclining leather chairs in separate areas of the private screening room.

Walters was at the control console, his face softly lit in the glow of panel lights. "Do we have production sound?" he asked the projectionist.

"Yes, sir."

"Let's go."

The lights dimmed and a tangible sense of anticipation filled the room.

Aurora's pulse quickened.

Smalley crushed his cigarette out, chain-lit another.

Wexler nervously cleaned the lenses of his glasses.

Walters's palms grew sweaty and his mouth felt dry.

The screen flickered into life and the Gran Via appeared.

It was a frozen tableau, a magnificent celluloid canvas of the great boulevard circa 1937. It was authentic in its style and detail and, like a great Impressionist painting, it conveyed the mood. The cafés, hotels, cinemas, and shops glowed softly in the suffused blue lights that illuminated the boulevard.

After a moment, the first assistant's voice echoed on the sound track.

"Roll camera!"

"Speed."

"Scene 118-A. Take one."

Clapsticks snapped together.

Scott's voice sounded. "Action."

The mural came alive.

Yellow trams clanged along their north–south tracks; green double-decker buses loaded with British volunteers headed toward the yellow shell-bursts at the University front.

People streamed in and out of the metro stations. Motorcycles, trucks, and military sedans weaved around the trams. Children on bicycles pedaled furiously, trying to get home before the next air raid. The sound track carried the dull thud of distant artillery along with Moorish chanting accompanied by African drums.

The camera craned up and slowly moved in on the entrance of the Palace Hotel. An ambulance careened around the corner and screeched to a halt. The stretcher bearers jumped out, opened the rear door, and carried two blood-soaked soldiers toward the hotel entrance just as Julia Castle came out.

She glanced at the mortally wounded men with the passive anguish of a seasoned combat nurse. She turned away and started walking down the sloping boulevard. The camera tracked with her and the composition widened so that the foreground and background action enveloped her.

Richard Bryan in uniform, arm bandaged, emerged from the hotel, spotted Julia, and trotted after her. They played the scene on the move and, despite the busy action on the boulevard, they conveyed that special camaraderie born of shared danger.

Paul Scott's voice shouted, "Cut! Print!"

They watched two more takes. The screen went dark and the lights came up, but no one moved. They sat quietly, trying to absorb the full impact of what they had seen.

Smalley finally rose and shook his head in admiration. "The sonofabitch managed to compose a master and close-up in one lateral tracking move while simultaneously craning and changing lens size. I can't remember seeing anything as complex so flaw-lessly executed."

"Scott made a similar shot years ago on a western," Wexler

said. "I was at Columbia at the time. It was a shot of Indian warriors on a ridge silhouetted against the sky. He took a thousand riders down that hill in one smooth master and there was no Steadicam in those days."

"It's not just the technique," Aurora said. "The shot captures the period, the sense of a city under siege and of life lived at the edge. The entire concept of the picture is realized in that one scene."

Walters said nothing. He was trapped in a schizophrenic vise: his love of art and beauty was in sharp conflict with his commitment to the scam. He sipped some water and cleared his throat. "Ray, are these timed dailies?"

"No. They're one-light prints."

"Well, between Rossi's lighting and the quality of the Madrid lab, these dailies are every bit as good as release prints. I'd like to send a set to Frank. Do we have time?"

"Sure. Fed-Ex has a midnight flight to New York."

"I want the negative stored in a special vault and placed under twenty-four-hour security," Walters said. "When the dailies come back from New York they go in the same vault."

"Why?" Aurora asked. "We never store positive film with negative."

Wexler and Smalley exchanged quick, nervous glances.

Though upset with himself for the blunder, Walters covered smoothly. "This is a very special film. The whole town is aware of its epic proportions. I don't want it pirated. This is the age of instant cassettes. *Backwash* has just been released and cassettes are already circulating. Besides, I understand they're printing a duplicate set of dailies and keeping them in Madrid."

"That's right," Smalley said. "John Carr is editing as they go."

The projectionist's voice came on the speaker. "Mr. Walters, I've got six reels of silent second-unit combat footage."

"Pack the first-unit print takes for shipment to New York and set up the second unit."

"Right."

The phone rang. Walters picked it up, listened, and said, "I'll let her know." He hung up and turned to Aurora. "Dicola and Morton are waiting for you."

"Oh shit, I forget about them." Then she smiled. "It's amazing but that cyclopean illiterate has written a very scary script." She then did a Mulberry Street impression of Dicola. "Da fucking ting woiks—killa kult and all."

She walked up the aisle, leaned over, and kissed Walters. "I owe you an apology, Harry. This might turn out to be a great film."

Once she left, Smalley blurted, "The film is magnificent—we're fucked. If word gets out that we have a potential masterpiece on our hands, the stockholders won't buy a seventy-five-dollar offer."

"Relax," Walters said. "You saw one set of dailies. The trouble in Madrid is just beginning."

"You mean the fracas at the airport?" Wexler asked.

Walters nodded. "In itself it's not much, but if I were a stockholder I'd be a little nervous."

"But they haven't seen the film," Smalley said. "And you almost blew it, Harry. You should never have mentioned locking up the print takes."

"Sorry about that but I think she bought my explanation."

"I'm not so sure," Wexler demurred.

"What's done is done." Walters sighed. "At the appropriate time I'll send her back to St. Moritz and have her oversee *Snowblind.*"

" 'Appropriate' is right now," Wexler said.

"Let's not panic. I've managed things fairly well. Leave it with me. Do you fellows want to see this second-unit stuff?"

Smalley shrugged. "It's only six-thirty. Why not?"

Walters picked up the receiver and dialed Solish's home in Westport, Connecticut.

The projectionist's voice came on the speaker.

"All set, Mr. Walters."

"Hold it a minute, Lou."

Doris Solish picked up on the third ring. After exchanging pleasantries she called Frank to the phone.

"Yeah, Harry?"

"We just ran the first set of Spanish dailies. They're sensational."

Solish winced and clutched his stomach.

"Christ . . ."

"I'm sending you a set. Run it alone, Frank. I don't trust that pimp Lew Freeman."

"Right."

"As soon as you're finished ship them back."

"Parnelli better get it together," Solish cautioned. "Suppose they finish the movie before December? Suppose the goddamn picture works?"

"Don't worry about it. Just relax. Have you seen the photos of Wheeler and Morosco at the airport?"

"Sure—it was all over the newspapers and TV."

"That's only the beginning. This picture will never be finished—trust me, Frank."

Solish coughed and sneezed. "Sorry, I can't shake this goddamn cold and my bridge is loose again. You see the grosses on *Backwash?*"

"Yeah."

"Fucking cunt is terrific." Solish referred to Tracey Warren. "We should put her in something right away."

"I'm working on it."

"Did you straighten me out with Resnick?"

"I told him you were exhausted; but hell or high water, you better show up at the next meeting."

"I'll be there."

"Call me after you see the film."

Walters hung up and pressed the speaker button. "Let's go, Lou."

The lights dimmed and the theater went dark. The screen lit up with luminous star shells. The brilliant green light silhouetted shivering men standing at the foot of ladders in the deep slit trenches of Jarama. After a few seconds thousands of screaming volunteers poured over the top, firing their fixed bayonet rifles as they advanced through thunderous bursts of shellfire.

The second-unit footage would be cut into the first-unit sequences to be filmed at a later date.

"Christ," Wexler said, "who the hell shot this stuff? It's terrific."

"José Giron," Smalley replied. "He's a Spanish second-unit director. Rossi recommended him."

Walters tried to deal with the unique and painful task of subverting a brilliant film. He sipped some water and reminded himself that the planned destruction of *The Volunteers* would result in a great renaissance of movie-making and nothing worthwhile was achieved painlessly.

Smalley chain-lit another cigarette.

Wexler cringed as he watched the stunning combat footage.

* * *

As she returned to her office, Aurora's thoughts turned to Adrian. She missed him and wished she was with him. The footage she had seen was sad, beautiful, and astonishingly real.

If Paul Scott could overcome the minefield of problems that lay ahead, he just might deliver a truly great film. She still wondered about the need for armed security guards and the storing of dailies with the negative. Walters's explanation was valid—to a point. If someone pirated dailies it wouldn't do him much good—not until the entire film was shot, edited, and scored.

The insidious grip of suspicion was tightening. She wasn't sleeping. She had broken out in a fiery rash. Valium hadn't helped. Nothing helped.

45

By obtaining official approval to shoot in the throne room of the Palacio Real, Don Alfonso contributed a stunning production value to the picture. It would have been too costly to duplicate the eighteenth-century white-columned palace with its vast courtyard and royal gardens.

The exterior sequence of Wheeler's arrival at the Palacio had been shot the previous afternoon. The courtyard had been dressed with official vehicles, military police, sandbagged gun emplacements, and two huge flags of the Spanish Republic. The day's filming was scheduled for the palace interior and involved only Wheeler and Morosco.

Paul Scott had returned to Madrid after two weeks of filming the opening montage sequence. In his absence, Adrian had worked with Morosco and Wheeler, achieving an armistice of sorts between the two eccentric stars.

The cast and crew had been called for seven A.M. It was now close to noon and they had yet to make a shot. Morosco had insisted on more time for makeup. Wheeler paced the polished marble floor, chain-smoking and fighting the craving for an iced Stolichnaya.

A skeleton crew of camera, sound, lights, and effects were gathered in the ornate throne room that had served King Charles III

and was still used for important state functions. The vaulted, concave ceiling was decorated with pastel-colored frescoes. The walls
were paneled in red damask and decorated with gilt-framed mirrors. A magnificent crystal chandelier hung from the ceiling, and
a twelfth-century Persian carpet covered the marble floor. French
windows faced the courtyard, and paintings by Goya and Veláz-
quez lined the walls of the entry room. All told, the sumptuous
throne room was a gem of Bourbon decor.

Adrian and Paul were agonizing over Morosco's refusal to
appear.

"He's getting five million dollars for ten weeks' work," Adrian
said bitterly. "You'd think he'd show up, do his thing, and not
brutalize everyone in the process."

Scott nodded. "He's been in makeup long enough to play
Madonna."

Adrian motioned to the prop man to clear the marble desk of
abandoned coffee containers with their floating cigarette butts.

"Julia and Bryan were pissed off at that Gwendolyn Peck item,"
Scott said. "I lost a morning in the Pyrenees trying to calm them
down. I wonder where that came from?"

Adrian shrugged. "Gossip is an occupational hazard. The important thing is they're great together. They were all terrific, including
Belgrave and the other Lincolns. The montage was marvelous; the
gossip items aren't up there on the screen."

"Maybe not, but they can hurt us."

"We're a big picture with high-strung stars—we're a target."

Scott ran his hand through his hair. "Look at Wheeler chain-
smoking," Scott said nervously. "He's gonna explode any second.
You better get the Genius in here."

Morosco was seated on a gilded chair in the hall of mirrors
adjacent to the throne room. The makeup woman dabbed number-
three pancake on his cheek while her assistant trimmed his mustache. His uniform had been fashioned to his specifications: blue
with red trim, dark blue shirt, and a red foulard. His feet were
encased in polished calfskin boots.

He had a bald pate and wore rimless glasses and nose plugs to
widen his nostrils. Standing nearby, Dr. Sindi chewed anxiously
on the fringe of his beard.

"We've got to shoot, Mayo—now," Adrian said firmly.

Morosco handed a small mirror to his makeup woman and stared icily at Adrian. "You talking to me?"

Adrian threw a quick glance at Sindi. The guru straightened his turban and addressed Morosco. "I'm certain that Mr. Summers's concerns are not with you but with Wheeler. The man can only go so long without a drink."

Adrian picked up the cue. "Dr. Sindi's right. Wheeler's at the breaking point. If we wait much longer he'll hit the Stoli and we're screwed. And as you know, he's capable of murderous rages."

"I warned you about him," Morosco said. "I told you to dump him."

"Look, be reasonable. We've gone over every detail of this sequence for the past two weeks. You agreed we were all talking the same game. We've been here since daybreak and our permission to shoot is only valid for one day."

"That's not my problem."

Adrian decided to go right at him. "Well"—he shrugged—"if you're afraid of the camera—say so. We'll make believe you got hit by a truck. I guarantee you we'll finish the picture and you can fly home with that fucking python."

The ensuing eyeball-to-eyeball silence was broken by Sindi. "I sense a vibration of two perfectionists with similar goals and similar fears, both of which are within the powers of the samsara. My dear Mayo"—he turned to Morosco—"you and Mr. Summers generate a spiritual force within the ninth dimension. See how my medallion reflects that power."

The gold disc at his throat actually seemed to glow.

"This is the moment to bring General José Miaja to life," Sindi continued. "His spirit channels all through this palace."

Morosco considered the guru's comments for a moment, got to his feet, shoved the makeup woman aside, and picked up his sombrero.

"Let's shoot it, Summers." He placed the sombrero on his head and stomped out, his boots clicking on the marble floor.

Sindi sidled up to Adrian. "This should be worth a small bonus."

"You got it, Doctor."

"I know you're not a believer but I actually do sense the presence of General Miaja."

"Whatever works," Adrian said.

*   *   *

The camera moves were set; a minimum of filtered fill light cast a soft blue hue in the room.

Morosco was on his mark behind the ornate desk.

"Is Wheeler on his mark?" Scott asked the American first assistant.

Solomon nodded. "All set."

"You okay, Federico?"

"*Si*, maestro," the director of photography replied.

"Okay . . . Quiet!" Scott shouted. "Roll it!"

"Speed!"

"Scene twenty-eight, take one. Sticks!"

The clapsticks were snapped together.

The throne room was silent.

"Action!"

The carved oak doors opened and Wheeler, accompanied by a Republican officer, entered the throne room. Morosco glanced up from his notes and waved his hand, dismissing the officer.

Morosco shook Wheeler's hand and greeted him affectionately.

"*Welcome, Comrade Kopek. It's been a while.*"

"*Almost three months.*"

"*A coffee?*"

"*No, thank you, General. I have only a few minutes.*" Wheeler spoke with a slight Slavic inflection. "*I'm due at Getafe airfield in half an hour. Malraux's squadron has finally arrived. They'll soon have the new Soviet fighter.*"

"*That's good news for a change.*"

"*Yes and no. We have only sixteen planes and less than twenty pilots, most of whom are French and Americans—and all of them are drunks.*"

"*Occupational therapy.*" Morosco smiled. "*What of the democracies?*"

"*They observe the embargo.*"

"*Even though Hitler has dispatched his Condor Legion?*"

"*Yes.*"

"*Even though Mussolini has dispatched one hundred thousand men?*"

"*We must face reality, General—only the Soviet Union sends arms, medicine, and technical advisers.*"

"*Perhaps Stalin hopes that Spain will become Poland by the sea.*"

"*I ask no questions. I take my orders from the Party.*"

"*Of course—I have no quarrel with Moscow.*" He sighed heavily. "*It's the inaction of the democracies that escapes me. Don't they know that the bombs falling on Madrid will soon fall on all the capitals of Europe?"*

"That's an unanswerable question. The reality is we are alone."

"How many Americans are in training at Albacete?"

"Several hundred. They call themselves the Lincoln Brigade."

"Bang!" Scott shouted off camera.

A sudden shower of dust covered the men and the camera rocked, simulating the concussion of a nearby shell-burst.

General Miaja dusted his uniform off. *"The shelling starts at precisely three P.M.—timed to the matinee performances at the cinemas."*

"The people are getting used to this mindless terror," Wheeler commented. *"The damage is minimal but one cannot sleep at night."*

"That's our secret weapon, Comrade Kopek. Madrileños are blessed with a mysterious source of energy—the same energy Stendhal attributed to the Romans—an energy that is resistant to sleep."

Wheeler's face suddenly reddened and he blurted, "Goddamnit, you fucked the whole speech up. For five million clams you oughta learn your lines!"

"Cut it!" Scott said and quickly placed himself between the two superstars.

"Let's get something straight, Jack," Scott reprimanded Wheeler. "No one ever cuts action in the middle of a scene except me—got that?"

"Sorry . . . Jesus Christ, the man can't . . ."

"Fuck you, Wheeler!" Morosco snapped. "Don't you worry about my performance."

"I'll worry about the performances!" Scott said. "You were both lousy. There was no energy. No tension. Pick up the tempo. It's too lento, too lethargic—Eddie!"

"Yes?" Beaumont answered tentatively.

"Let's cut all that shit about the democracies. We know that from the scene at the hospital. Let's go from the Malraux squadron to the Americans at Albacete." Scott paused and almost apologetically asked Adrian, "Is the cut okay with you?"

"Whatever works," Adrian said.

The script supervisor, Sarita Montiel, delineated the cuts in the actors' scripts.

"Let's rehearse one and then try one," Scott said. "And, Mayo, when you call him 'Comrade' the word should be drenched in sarcasm."

"You mean 'disdain.' "

Scott sighed. "Disdain will be fine. Now let's run it from Kopek's entrance."

The two great actors managed to stumble their way through twenty-eight takes before getting it right. It was close to midnight when a bone-weary Paul Scott said, "It's a wrap."

Wheeler stormed off the set and made a beeline for his limo with its Styrofoam freezer containing three bottles of chilled Stolichnaya.

Morosco removed his makeup, put on a blue jumpsuit, sneakers, and his sombrero, and left with Dr. Sindi.

Eddie Beaumont and Sarita Montiel took a cab to Casa Paco for a late supper.

Paul Scott, Federico Rossi, Don Alfonso, and Glickman returned to the production office to review the next day's shooting at the University front.

Polly Turner invited Adrian to buy her a drink at the Belle Époque Café.

At that same moment on National Highway III, Julia Castle, her hair blowing wildly in the balmy night air, drove the rented Ferrari with one hand on the wheel. Stoned on Lima White, Richard Bryan sat beside her with his left hand casually resting on her thigh. They were returning to Madrid from a leisurely dinner in Toledo.

"The paella was sensational," Bryan said.

"I ate too much."

"You hardly ate anything. How could you with everyone staring at you?"

"That always happens to me. It's really a blessing—keeps my weight down." Her tiger eyes flared in the reflected light of oncoming traffic.

Bryan's hand deftly crept under her skirt and caressed her firm thigh.

"Cut that out, Richard!"

"Jesus Christ, don't be such a damn prude."

"That's brand new." She smiled. "I've never been accused of being a prude."

"You drove me crazy in the train compartment scene."

"I didn't mean to turn you on. It was Paul's staging."

"Don't blame it on staging, we both know you turned the heat up. Besides, we should get it on. What's the difference? The whole world thinks we're an item anyway."

"I wonder who planted that gossip?" Her eyes widened and she exclaimed, "Oh shit!" She spun the wheel and swerved dangerously across three lanes toward the Alcalá exit ramp. "Jesus, you'd think they'd give you a warning."

His fingers inched up her thigh as he said, "My agent phoned me. It seems another article ran Tuesday in Gwendolyn Peck's column."

"What about?"

"Wheeler and Morosco refusing to work together and forcing the company to shut down."

"What bullshit."

"There was more to it than that. The item alluded to Wheeler's drinking and claimed Morosco was traveling with a Tibetan snake charmer."

"That hawk-faced bitch Peck will run anything."

Bryan's fingers touched the band on her panties.

"Richard."

"Yes . . ."

"I want you to help me kidnap Honeybear."

His fingers froze and he sneezed twice.

"Bless you."

"Thanks." His fingers continued exploring. "Honeybear attacked me in L.A. Sprung off an armoire and clawed my neck."

"Honeybear?"

"Honeybear."

"Why?"

"How would I know? But if you want me to, I'll help you."

His fingers slipped under her elastic panty band.

"Say, did you see the montage dailies?" she asked.

"They were great," he said.

"Paul can be terrific."

"Why did you two split?"

"Long story." She steered dangerously around the S-curve ramp that emptied into the late-night traffic on Alcalá.

His finger finally touched the forbidden fruit. Her hands flew off the wheel and she pummeled him with both hands. The Ferrari spun out of control, jumped the Paseo del Recoleto divider, became airborne, slammed into a newspaper kiosk, spun around, and crashed into the outdoor serving bar at the Café Bohemia.

Customers screamed and scrambled out of harm's way. Bryan's forehead struck the windshield, but Julia was protected by the inflated airbag.

She was shaken but unhurt. A few bystanders cleared the wrecked tables and chairs and helped her out of the bucket seat.

The blood seeping out of Bryan's head streamed down his cheeks. His glazed eyes stared at Julia in disbelief. "You going to leave me here?" he groaned.

"I can't be involved." She drew herself up and shook out her hair. "I'm a star."

She squared her shoulders, and in much the same haughty fashion as her memorable exit on the Carlton Terrace, she strode through the dumbstruck crowd and hailed a taxi.

"You were tense," Polly Turner said.

They were naked atop the bedcovers in Adrian's suite.

"It's been a while." He took a deep drag of her cigarette and handed it back.

"For me as well," she said.

He stared at her wide-apart black eyes and could only guess at all the nights and all the men and all the highs and lows. He kissed her throat and smiled. "You don't need any practice."

She leaned over him. "I wanted to sleep with you from the very first. You made love exactly as I thought you would; thinking of someone else."

"How would you know?"

"I've done it myself."

The phone rang. Suddenly. Sharply.

It was Glickman.

Polly watched Adrian's eyes narrow. "Christ . . . I'll be right down."

He hung up and slipped his shorts on.

"What is it?" she asked, alarmed.

"Car crash. Bryan rented a Ferrari and took Julia to dinner in Toledo. She crashed into the café on the Recoleto. He's in stable condition. Forty stitches. Mild concussion."

"What about Julia?"

"Last seen getting into a cab," he said, pulling his pants on. "I'm sorry about this."

"Don't be. It's making movies."

* * *

Adrian and Glickman followed two imposing Guardia Civil policemen through the swarming paparazzi. Flash bulbs flared and Nikon motors whirred as they walked quickly down the hospital corridor and entered Bryan's room.

The actor's head was bandaged and an intravenous tube dispensing glucose had been inserted into his left arm. His color was gray but his eyes were bright. He glanced up at Adrian and said, "Sorry."

"What happened?"

"I had my hand up her dress and she slugged me. The car went out of control. We're lucky to be alive."

"And lucky no one else was hurt," Glickman said.

"Had she objected to your hand?" Adrian asked.

"Mildly. That's why I didn't stop. I guess she's nuts." He made a helpless gesture with his right hand. "I'm sorry. I know this will fuck up the schedule."

Adrian thought about propriety for a few seconds but decided to follow his instincts. "Nothing's going to be fucked up. We have four days scheduled at the University. We don't come back to you and Julia until the interior night scene in Chicote's."

"That's five days from now," Glickman said pointedly.

"Five days . . ." Bryan said in disbelief. "How can I work in five days? Look at me."

"We'll play your head wound," Adrian said. "Don't forget, the Lincolns have been in constant action at Jarama. You suffered a head wound. The accident will work for the role."

"You gotta be kidding."

"Why?"

"This has been a traumatic experience. I can't work this week." He paused and his eyes brightened. "Unless . . ."

"Unless what?"

"I'm very frustrated."

"Say no more." Adrian smiled. "Magda's on the way."

JASON JELALIAN CHEWED NERVOUSLY ON A DEAD CIGAR AS HE WAITED for Aurora to finish reading his report.

The hard-eyed private investigator was anxious to return to his North Hollywood office; it was a long drive from Malibu and the coast traffic was murderous. The case hadn't been difficult but anything involving Leo Resnick was dicey.

"My God . . . , " Aurora whispered. Jelalian's report detailed times, places, names, and was accompanied by photos. It went beyond her wildest suspicions.

Her mind raced as she read: Beverly Hills Hotel, bungalow 33-E. In attendance: Leo Resnick, Irv Wexler, Harry Walters, Sal Parnelli. Palm Springs—Resnick's villa: Solish, Wexler, Smalley, and Walters. The Brighton Way Coffee Shop: Harry Walters and Mickey Dutton.

She knew that Dutton had been hired to help publicize Tracey Warren and *Backwash*, but it was obviously a cover. Dutton was tight with Gwendolyn Peck and almost without exception the disparaging articles concerning *The Volunteers* had appeared in Peck's flesh-eating column. In all probability, Dutton had also planted the Parnelli takeover items.

She closed the folder and took out her checkbook.

"How do you spell Jelalian?"

"*C-a-s-h,*" he said, managing the semblance of a smile.

"I'm adding a bonus. You did a first-rate job."

She signed the check, rose, and handed it to him.

"You're very generous, Miss Flint."

He tucked the check into the folds of his worn wallet. "If I were you, I'd be careful," he said. "No one curves Leo Resnick. I don't mean to scare you but Max Schuller's heart attack looks a little convenient to me. In any case, this is a big-time swindle. You're not dealing with a Boy Scout troop."

"I understand."

"Well, take care."

"Thanks."

"Anytime."

She poured a vodka and tomato juice, took a sip, and dialed her office.

"Miss Flint's office," Maggie answered.

"It's me—anything going on?"

"Alex Carlino called from the St. Moritz location to thank you for suggesting Tracey Warren. He's thrilled with her performance. Trummel's called twice. The Chipmunk once. And Swackhammer's secretary about a painting that was lost in the move. The Spanish dailies have been rescheduled for three o'clock."

"Thanks, Maggie."

She hung up and, carrying her drink, walked out to the sun-drenched terrace. The tide had ebbed and a flock of screaming sea gulls feasted on sand crabs. Beyond the breakers surfers paddled out, seeking a wave.

She stretched out on the lounge, thinking the evidence was all there in Jelalian's report. It had all begun with Walters's frequent trips to the desert followed by the meetings at Resnick's villa with Solish and the others.

The bits and pieces flashed like slivers of light illuminating a single fact. A conspiracy had been carefully designed in order to manipulate Gemstone stock. Parnelli was mob connected and probably handpicked by Resnick to front the operation. *The Volunteers* was a sacrificial lamb to be subverted in order to create the appearance of a picture out of control, a fiscal catastrophe that would depress Gemstone's stock. But why? Why would they want to deflate the stock? Who would profit from a sudden decline in the stock? She sighed heavily. It didn't add up. Parnelli's takeover bid would tend to push the price of Gemstone stock up. And yet their machinations had been designed to depress the stock. The only conclusion she could draw was that an insidious stock swindle was underway and the Spanish picture was being used as a foil.

She rose and paced the terrace. If she confronted Walters or if she approached the SEC and blew the whistle, she'd not only be out of work, but remembering Jelalian's cautionary advice, she could find herself taking her last limo ride.

But how could she remain silent? Silence was tantamount to complicity. She'd have to find a way to tell Adrian without placing either one of them in mortal jeopardy.

A REVERENT SILENCE ENVELOPED THE SCREENING ROOM AS THEY watched the montage sequence. The dailies were projected in sequential order: the Americans boarding the *Normandie* and the sleek liner moving out past the Statue of Liberty; the Atlantic crossing involving Bryan, Castle, and the other Lincolns; the docking at the French port of Le Havre; the night train speeding through the French countryside toward the Spanish frontier.

There were vivid scenes depicting the group's ascent of the treacherous snow-swept Pyrenees. The Lincolns shivered in their sheepskin jackets, their breath vaporized in the frigid mountain air. They hid at night high up in caves, warming themselves by campfires. The camera caught an intimate look that passed between Julia and Bryan as the firelight flickered in their eyes.

Smalley shook his head in grudging admiration—Paul Scott was on his best game.

Aurora smiled with delight; despite all the disparaging articles the conspirators were in trouble. The film was stunning.

Wexler was overwhelmed by the detail and precision with which each scene had been staged.

Walters sat in the soft glow of the control panel wondering if anyone could have predicted this extraordinary filmmaking.

The reel changed. Following a guide, the volunteers emerged

from their mountain caves and entered the sun-baked Spanish village of Figueras. They had made it. They were in Spain. Trucks driven by Republican soldiers whisked them away to a fourteenth-century castle. There was laughter, conversation, and the special camaraderie of shared danger.

A black banner imprinted with a red clenched fist and the words *No Pasaran* was strung across the gates of the Albacete training camp. Another banner with red letters on a white background read: *Welcome to our American comrades of the Lincoln Brigade.*

Scene followed scene: marching in the hot sun, test-firing Soviet-made rifles, the study of cartography, and the trench system at the killing ground of Jarama. There was a farewell party at night complete with flamenco dancers, a barbecue, leather botas of wine, and American swing records.

There was a blinding close-up of a sunrise followed by a long pullback showing solemn-faced Spanish peasants showering the Lincolns with flowers as they boarded open trucks, heading to the Jarama front.

There was a heartbreakingly romantic scene between an American pilot and a pretty Spanish nurse dancing alone in a deserted mess hall to a recording of "These Foolish Things." The pilot was an ace in Malraux's volunteer escadrille.

Reel after reel changed over from one projector to the other. There was a chilling sequence of Franco's Moorish troops at the University front breaking into the basement of the science building. Believing that the formaldehyde jars preserving dead animals contained a magical elixir, they opened the jars and drank the chemical. Their agonizing dance of death had been choreographed and photographed so that they seemed like demented figures in a George Grosz canvas.

The last reel depicted cuts of Fascist propaganda leaflets floating down over the Gran Via with children gleefully chasing them down; a shell-burst in the midst of women queued up for their meager ration of bread and rice; a breathtaking master shot of thousands of civilians standing in the open boulevard, looking skyward, cheering the pilots of Malraux's squadron as they chased the Fascist bombers.

The last cut was of "La Pasionaria," the darkly handsome woman whose stirring eloquence had come to symbolize the

Loyalist-Republican cause. She stood before a huge crowd, tears in her eyes, her right arm raised, her fist clenched.

The shot held for a long time and slowly faded.

The lights came up in the projection room. The group had seen two hours and twenty minutes of superb filmmaking.

No one spoke. No one exchanged glances. They remained in their seats, transfixed, staring at the blank screen. The film confirmed the quality displayed in the first set of dailies. The work was dazzling, and if the truth leaked, no one would be selling Gemstone stock. The scam was in deep trouble.

Wexler dabbed at the beads of sweat oozing out of his forehead. They were now in a race against time. Parnelli had to tender his offer before the picture completed principal photography.

Seated at the control panel sipping Scotch, Walters appeared his usual cool self, but in fact he was caught in a terrible vise. He had, for all the wrong reasons, underwritten a potential masterpiece and despite his considerable stake in the scam he couldn't help but feel a sense of pride and even triumph; but pragmatism demanded strict adherence to the conspiracy, even if it meant the destruction of a great film.

He felt he represented the last hope of an industry dying of creative atrophy, and as such, his dream transcended the fate of one movie. Yet to gain it he would have to destroy the finest movie he had ever been associated with.

"That's it, Mr. Walters." The projectionist's voice came over the intercom.

Walters picked up the phone and punched three buttons. His secretary answered immediately. "Gloria, try Adrian Summers for me."

"It's almost two A.M. in Madrid," she said.

"I know what time it is," he replied testily. "Just get him!"

He slammed the phone down and drained his Scotch.

Surprised by Walters's uncharacteristic anger, Aurora rose and complimented him. "You're an absolute genius, Harry. I never believed in this picture. No one did. It's fabulous. If they maintain this quality we're looking at a fistful of nominations."

"She's absolutely right," Wexler said, trying to sound nonchalant. "First thing in the morning I'm exercising options on five thousand shares of Gemstone."

"I was just thinking the same thing," Smalley said.

Bastards, Aurora thought, motherfucking thieves.

She calmly asked Smalley for a cigarette.

"Since when did you start to smoke?"

"Since now."

He lit the cigarette for her. "Thanks," she said and turned to Walters. "I must tell you, this is the finest work I've seen on the screen since . . . hell, I can't remember. We should pop some champagne corks."

The phone rang and Walters quickly picked it up.

"Summers is in the cutting room," his secretary reported.

"At this hour?"

"Apparently."

He pressed the blinking button and his voice exuded its usual charm. "You'll get thrown out of the union, Adrian—cutting film at this late hour."

"Yes . . . of course . . ." Walters went on. "I understand. It's impossible for Paul to shoot all day and edit at night. As long as you're using his selected print takes it's a step forward. As you know, we're planning to open at Christmas for Academy consideration." He paused. "That's why I called, we've seen quite a bit of film. Please give Paul my compliments. He's managed to create a huge canvas without sacrificing the intimacy of the piece. The performances are terrific."

You smooth sonofabitch, Aurora thought. You blue-eyed con man with your thousand-dollar Italian blazer, tinted shades, Cartier watch, and VW Jetta—you fucking fraud. The hand is quicker than the eye. Watch the pea. Watch the shells. Whatever he once was, whatever he once believed in, Walters had reduced himself to nothing more than another Dream City hustler. Screw the picture and the stockholders, grab a buck. That's what the conspiracy was all about—a shell game to make a fortune and hustle everyone in the doing; but a reformed junkie and a spacey director were somehow managing to craft a classic film. Tell that to Leo Resnick, you four-flushing prick.

She nodded and smiled at Smalley and Wexler, as if endorsing Walters's compliments to Adrian.

"Well, Adrian—I'm truly sorry about all the trouble you've had," Walters said warmly. "We're trying to track the source of those vicious column plants. You just concentrate on the main chance. The film speaks louder than its detractors. Absolutely. Miss von Stellhoff can stay as long as required. Treat her as a member of the cast—part of the negative cost. I'm delighted that Bryan has calmed down. Anything you need—just call. Now, get some rest. 'Bye, Adrian."

He hung up and lit a Sherman. Aurora noticed the full ashtray on the console ledge. Walters was exceeding his five-a-day allotment.

He blew a small cloud of smoke up toward the ceiling and glanced at Aurora. "Think you could go to Madrid and help Adrian out with the script changes? It seems as though Beaumont is at odds with Morosco's rewriting demands."

Her heart skipped a beat. They wanted her out of the way. She desperately wanted to go but downplayed her emotions.

"There's really nothing I can contribute," she said innocently. "After all, Beaumont is the writer."

"Your entire career has been centered on story. Adrian could use a referee between Wheeler and Morosco. Also, Glickman has the flu and your production experience would be helpful. But"— he shrugged—"it's up to you."

"It's impossible," she said. "I'm backed up with projects in development." Her voice trembled slightly but she didn't think it gave her away. The main thing was that she hadn't jumped at the chance to leave.

"I can cover your current projects," Smalley suggested.

"It's story stuff, Ray," she said. "It would take you a month to become familiar with it." She paused. "I could probably leave in a couple weeks."

The phone rang. Walters answered. "Okay," he said tersely and hung up. He glanced at Aurora. "Trummel and Kramer are in your office. What's that about?"

"They've got some weird notion about terrorists contaminating a sperm bank."

Walters shook his head. "Well, I suppose no one's done the sperm bank picture yet. Listen, do your best to get your projects under control and take off for Madrid. All our chips are riding on *The Volunteers.*"

Adrian and his weary editor, John Carr, watched the last film flutter through the Kem editing screen. Carr's assistant rewound the roll, labeled it, and placed it on a shelf containing catalogued rolls of print takes.

"Walters saw a load of film today," Adrian said. "Why was the shipment delayed?"

"The film goes from Madrid to Copenhagen, then over the Pole to LAX," Carr explained. "Every so often there's a delay, but it's safer than shipping through JFK."

"Well, delay notwithstanding, Walters was ecstatic."

"He should be. The film is terrific. The rough assembly plays like a release print."

Paul Scott was lying faceup on his bed listening to a jazz CD featuring the late Paul Desmond. Honeybear sat on Scott's chest, purring.

He had awakened at midnight and started running the film in his head from the first night on the Gran Via through the battle scenes, the University, the Palacio Real, and the montage. The stuff looked pretty damn good but the atmosphere on the set was volatile and tomorrow night's shooting was worrisome. All of the principals worked in Chicote's. He wondered if the unspoken truce between Morosco and Wheeler would hold. The American actors portraying the Lincolns had behaved. And the German goddess, Magda von Stellhoff, had numbed Bryan's libido. Julia had been terrific. Leroy Belgrave was a true professional. He knew his lines. He hit his marks. The young black actor was a natural and would undoubtedly become a star.

Scott reached across Honeybear and took another hit of ganja. The Jamaican grass eased the pressure and tension; unfortunately it also sexed him up and he had been celibate since his brief encounter with Sarita Montiel during the shooting in France. He had, in a weak moment, given Julia a duplicate key to his room, but so far she hadn't used it. Wishful thinking. Well, he was entitled to a little hopeful fantasy.

He listened with admiration as Paul Desmond played an innovative riff around the melody line of "Rose Room." Whenever he was stoned, he picked up on those luminous harmonic riffs. Should've stayed with the vibes, he thought. What could be better than playing jazz in some cool cellar? But this film was worth the pain. The movie had *that* look.

If they could just stagger toward the finish line more or less intact, they'd have something special.

Honeybear suddenly leapt off the bed and landed at a pair of shapely bare feet and began to rub affectionately against them.

"Hello, Paul."

Julia stood in a cone of streaky exterior light, looking like Venus with arms. She slipped off her robe and walked over to the bed.

She leaned over him, her hair caressing his cheeks. She brushed her lips lightly against his. His arms encircled her and she covered him with her body.

From her perch atop the bureau, Honeybear watched them make love with casual interest.

THE SET, DECOR, PROPS, LIGHTING, CHARACTERS, UNIFORMS, MUSIC, all made for a mind-bending trip back in time to the fall of 1937 in Chicote's bar.

Candles in glass holders illuminated the oblong room. The immense blue mirror behind the bar reflected faces in a ghostly cast. Soldiers of Loyalist Spanish Republican divisions stood next to volunteers of the International Brigades. The soldiers, nurses, journalists, prostitutes, spies, secret police, formed a diverse group living on borrowed time. The concave booths were occupied by journalists and officials of the Republican government. In a center booth Ernest Hemingway was listening intently to the exploits of a pilot with Malraux's squadron.

Wearing her nurse's uniform, Julia sat atop a bar stool in a group that included Richard Bryan, Leroy Belgrave, and the other Lincolns. Their boyish exuberance, in evidence during their clandestine journey to Spain, had been replaced by the sardonic humor common to veteran infantrymen. But Chicote's was an oasis, and they managed to enjoy themselves, flirting with the Spanish nurses, drinking Fundador, and sharing an occasional inside joke.

The jukebox played "You Are My Lucky Star." Everyone seemed to be smoking Lucky Strikes and the smoke billowed up to the ceiling. The windows facing the Gran Via had been blacked out, and the flickering candlelight lent Chicote's a curious sense of eternal night.

Just off the small dance floor, at the far end of the bar, Mayo Morosco in his general's uniform sat opposite Jack Wheeler. Scott crouched behind the camera checking the composition on Wheeler and Morosco. Out of camera range, Adrian, Don Alfonso, Pepe Granados, and Polly Turner huddled together in an alcove.

Scott took his eye from the lens, straightened up, and nodded to Federico Rossi. "Let's make one."

He walked the length of the bar, scrutinizing people and props. He spoke briefly to Julia, moving her closer to Bryan. Her eyes glittered in the candlelight and her pale gold hair curved softly across her shoulders in a Carole Lombard bob. Scott kissed her cheek and whispered something that triggered a sexy smile. The director then climbed atop the bar and shouted for attention.

"*Silencio, por favor!*" the Spanish first assistant, Fuentes, shouted.

"Settle down!" the American first assistant, Solomon, added.

The set grew quiet and Scott, a spectral figure in the smoky blue light, spoke with that special authority common to film directors and symphony orchestra conductors.

"Please remember, it's very late. The lines at Jarama and the University are holding but the sound of Fascist artillery is coming closer." He paused and his feverish eyes scanned the room.

"It's the late fall, 1937," he continued solemnly. "Chicote's is a carefree island in the heart of the Gran Via—it's a café that has become the symbol of Madrid's resistance. All of you have been given business, but please be natural. The camera will do the rest. I thank you for your patience and attention." He turned to the American first assistant. "Let's make it!"

The set grew quiet. The commands were issued.

The camera slowly panned and tracked the bar, to the strains of "You Are My Lucky Star." In the background the thud of artillery shells was heard.

Scott believed in mixing live sound as the scene was being shot. Authentic sounds helped the actors and lent reality to the scene.

Adrian thought there was a subtle but distinct change in attitude from both cast and crew once the director said that magic word "Action." Perhaps, he thought, it was due to the fact that, unlike a rehearsal, a filmed take was almost never interrupted.

The camera swung deftly around the edge of a partition and moved in on Julia and Bryan as they delivered their lines, then tracked past them, picking up bits and pieces of dialogue about battles and fallen comrades.

There was a sudden crashing sound of an exterior shell explosion. The concussion caused the windows to rattle. Scott signaled "thumbs up" to Rettig, the special effects man.

The camera dollied in on Wheeler and Morosco. Wheeler lit a cigarette and poured a shot of Fundador while waiting for Morosco's line, but the words never came.

"Let's have the line." Scott coached Morosco, " 'They executed Lorca.' "

"I know the fucking line!" Morosco snapped, slamming his fist onto the table, and, pointing at Wheeler, he exclaimed, "The man is drunk! Smell his breath! Look at his eyes! How do I talk about dead Spanish poets to a drunk?"

Wheeler swung a wild left hook, catching Morosco on the jaw and sending him careening into the adjacent table. The first assistant grabbed Wheeler, who had stumbled over a reflecting stand; Spanish crew members helped Morosco to his feet and restrained him as he lunged for Wheeler. The actors, including Bryan and Castle, gathered around the combatants.

Adrian pushed his way through the crowd and confronted the two stars.

"We're all going to the movies tomorrow," Adrian said. "After which you two men will have a decision to make." He turned to Scott. "We're through for tonight. The call is for noon tomorrow in the hotel projection room."

The concierge handed Adrian two messages from Aurora. He checked his watch; it was three-thirty P.M. in Los Angeles. She had pointedly left her home number.

Saying good night to Scott, he went up to his suite and phoned John Carr in the editorial room. "John . . . I want to run the assembled footage for the cast and crew tomorrow at noon. Have Glickman set it up. Right—everything that's in sequential order."

He hung up, mixed a vodka on the rocks, and stared out of the window at the twinkling lights in the cafés along the Castellana. He sighed heavily, thinking about the warm wet suit of heroin and how a fix would chase all the problems. For a split second he considered calling Silvi but decided against it. Don't lay this one on her, and don't quit, you bastard. Don't give in to it. You're on the edge of something extraordinary. Tough it out. You owe it to Paul, to yourself, to the years of obsession with the story, and to Walters for trusting you with the production. And, in a curious way, you owe it to the fates for having permitted you to survive. Most of your contemporaries had been blown to pieces in that distant jungle. Fuck those lunatic actors. Stay clean and keep going. This is your pony ride.

He drained the vodka and dialed Aurora at her Malibu number. The phone rang for a long time and he was about to hang up when she finally answered.

"Hello?" she said breathlessly.

"Did I catch you at a bad time?" he asked.

"No . . . No. I had just gone down to the beach when I heard the phone. I had to run back up the stairs."

"You're sure?"

"Positive—what time is it there?" she asked.

"Almost one A.M."

"God, I'm glad you called."

"What's up?"

"I'll be arriving on the ninth."

"Great."

"Not so great. We have a lot to talk about, but not on the phone. I've got to be careful."

"About what?"

"I can't talk about it now."

He shook his head in exasperation. "Goddamnit, Aurora—this is a lousy night for guessing games."

"I'll see you soon. I just wanted to let you know I'm coming to Madrid and we have to speak privately." She paused. "Trust me, Adrian."

The cast and crew members were seated in folding chairs in the converted screening room. The chatter diminished as the overhead lights dimmed and the projection beam lit up the screen.

For ninety minutes they watched the scenes unfold with a profound sense of pride. As the screening progressed it became apparent that collectively they had achieved a stunning realization of the Spanish tragedy.

The final image was that of a British volunteer who had fallen, mortally wounded, across a line of barbed wire. His crumpled body was silhouetted in the surreal green light of a flare.

The screen went dark and the room lights came on to absolute silence, followed by a wave of enthusiastic applause and shouts of "Bravo!"

Adrian took center stage and addressed them. "I wanted you to see the results of your work. Some of you have seen dailies but none of you had seen the assembled footage. You've performed magnificently.

"I thank you for your talent, dedication, and trust. Now, except for Mr. Wheeler and Mr. Morosco, the rest of you take the day off. Relax and enjoy yourselves. We'll pick up again at Chicote's tomorrow morning."

The group rose and filed out. As the room emptied, Adrian collected his thoughts. It seemed to Scott that Adrian had aged noticeably in the past six months.

"The film speaks for itself," Adrian began. "Paul's done a masterful job. Having said that, let's remember that none of us has invented penicillin. None of us will ever build the Brooklyn Bridge. None of us will change the course of human history. We're craftsmen. We make pictures that move on a wall in a dark place."

Adrian sipped some water and continued, turning his attention to Morosco and Wheeler. Dr. Sindi, looking like an Old Testament prophet draped in orange, sat beside his famous disciple. A few rows behind them, a grim-faced Wheeler appeared to be badly hung over.

"Your combined talents are unequaled. That's why I wanted you both. That's why Paul wanted you. That's why you're being paid five million apiece, but we can't tolerate any more boozy brawls or fiery outbursts. It demoralizes the cast and crew. I can't be your conscience. You either proceed professionally or leave. You've got to tell me now—can you work together harmoniously or not?"

There was a moment of tense silence. Paul was fearful that Adrian had gone a beat too far. These two stars were legendary; challenging them represented a grave risk—without either man, there was no picture.

Dr. Sindi whispered to Morosco, who nodded and got to his feet. He rubbed his nose, scratched his cheek, and turned to Wheeler.

"What do you say, Jack?"

Adrian thought he noticed a slight smile on Wheeler's craggy face.

The hung-over star rose and, using a speech from *Richard II*, he recited in the grand manner, "Of comfort no man speak! Let's talk of graves, of worms, and epitaphs, make dust our paper and with rainy eyes write sorrow on the bosom of the earth."

Adrian and Paul watched dumbfounded as Morosco brightened and chimed in: "Let's choose executors, and talk of wills. For God's sake, let us sit upon the ground"—he walked toward Wheeler—"and tell sad stories of the death of kings."

The two great actors fell into each other's arms.

THE CRISP BLUE CASTILIAN SKY AND BRIGHT WINTER SUN ILLUMINATED
the tortured red earth of Jarama. The battlefield had been dressed
with scrupulous attention to detail.

The vast trench system had been strung with concertina wire
spaced across several thousand meters of no-man's-land. The Republican lines were anchored at the southern perimeter of the
valley and formed a semicircle of trenches, minefields, and strong-
points protecting the Valencia–Madrid highway. On the northern
edge of no-man's-land the sun glinted off the twisted points of
barbed wire marking the advance positions of Franco's Fascist
forces.

Hazy smoke from cooking fires drifted up from the dugouts. The
Republican trenches were manned by volunteers of the International Brigades augmented by crack troops of the Loyalist Spanish
54th Division. The Republican extras had been furnished with
green and red packs of Lucky Strike cigarettes.

A softball field and basketball hoop had been erected at the edge
of the shell-pocked village of Morata and some of the American
actors played ball while waiting for Scott to make the first take.

Adrian stood atop a thirty-foot-tall camera platform positioned
just behind Republican headquarters. The platform afforded an
unbroken panoramic view of the battlefield.

A CAST OF THOUSANDS

Below the platform, grouped around a large table, Scott and his key people reviewed the specific responsibility of each department, each craft, and each technician upon whom the success of the scene would ultimately depend. The task of coordinating the battle was daunting. Thousands of men were involved in the action, which included a wide variety of special effects both on the ground and in the air.

Adrian picked up a pair of binoculars and slowly scanned the scene.

Mayo Morosco and Jack Wheeler were playing chess in the shade of the headquarters' tent. Since Adrian had challenged them, the two stars had worked harmoniously in the complex battle scene at Brunete—a crucial sequence requiring three weeks of demanding shooting.

In the open Red Cross tent, Julia Castle and her Spanish colleagues passed the time playing cards.

Adrian focused the binoculars on a group of old men, the present inhabitants of the rebuilt village of Morata. Standing on a hill-rise, they watched the scene unfold below with fascination. Their faces were seared by the sun and their eyes clouded by memories. They were caught in a time warp created by the movie people. As young men, they had fought in this battle, and now the past was returning. For these weathered veterans it was, painfully, once again November 1937.

Don Alfonso and his Spanish staff coordinated the men, armor, and artillery in the Fascist lines. Their walkie-talkies crackled with static as they kept the channels open with their colleagues two thousand meters across no-man's-land.

Assisted by the script supervisor, Paul Scott checked and re-checked: special effects, tank and ambulance drivers, stuntmen, wind and smoke machine operators, and the squad leader of the biplanes circling lazily above the battlefield. With Federico Rossi, he reviewed the lens sizes and f-stops on all eight camera positions. He inquired as to where and in which units hand-held Steadicams would be used. He listened attentively and thanked everyone for their patience. The meeting broke up and a series of orders were issued over a loudspeaker system.

Morosco left the command tent and climbed into the sidecar of a motorcycle imprinted with General Miaja's three stars.

The Italian and French stars Lescoli and Claudon joined Wheeler in the command tent. Richard Bryan, Leroy Belgrave, and the other Americans took their positions at the foot of the trench ladders. All along the line the Republican trench system was filled with men carrying Soviet-made rifles with fixed bayonets.

Paul Scott joined Adrian on the camera platform and the first assistant handed him a hand-mike wired to hidden speakers placed around the battlefield. Glickman held a radio-mike that was tuned to the aircraft frequency. Like the voice of god, Scott's amplified directions reverberated across the tense battlefield.

"Everyone stand by. Please remember, safety takes precedence. No movie is worth anyone's life. We've rehearsed for five days. Don't invent. Don't create. Just do your job. There is no reason to be careless. Follow your squad leaders and hit your marks. I don't want real blood spilled here. Now, stand by."

Scott studied the scene, his hand shading his eyes against the sun. He glanced at Adrian and smiled. "Well, partner, here goes a million bucks." Scott depressed the mike's speaker button. "Roll cameras!"

Each camera operator responded in turn. "Speed."

The soundman's voice echoed, "Scene two-twenty-four-A— eight cameras, wild track—end slate! Speed!"

Scott said, "Action!"

The motorcycle and sidecar bearing Morosco came roaring down the slope, trailing a cloud of red dust. The cycle wheeled into the headquarters compound and screeched to a stop. Morosco jumped out and rushed up to Wheeler.

"Artillery!" Scott shouted.

Batteries of French 75's and 105's cracked, belching fire and smoke. White puffs and shell-bursts flashed along the distant Fascist trench line.

"Go, Jeff!" Scott ordered the flight squadron leader.

The lead Detwoitine dove down out of the sun. The others followed, coming in low and fast, flying toward the Fascist lines with machine guns firing and wing bombs dropping. Great clouds of earth spouted up from the Fascist lines. Tracers were fired at the attacking aircraft.

"Republican forces, go!" Scott barked. "Machine-gun cover fire! Fascist counterfire! Smoke and wind machines!"

The Republican soldiers went up the ladders, over the sandbagged trenches, charging and screaming across the erupting red earth, firing their weapons as they ran. Smoke and haze combined with clouds of earth as the attacking formation, hardly able to see or hear, followed their stunt leaders through the explosions. Men screamed and fell but the line moved forward.

Camera positions behind Fascist lines photographed the Republican soldiers advancing, their bayonets glinting in the sun as they dodged spumes of red earth, yellow flashes, and billowing smoke.

The Fascist artillery batteries opened up; machine guns chattered and the oncoming Republican line wavered. Men hugged the ground; others fell back as the devastating counterfire took its toll. A squad of Lincolns sought cover in a cluster of olive trees.

The Fascist commander fired a flare, signaling an all-out counterattack. From the camera positions behind Republican lines it appeared as though thousands of men had suddenly risen up out of the ground. A flood tide of Moors and Spanish regulars, supported by German artillery, came screaming toward the collapsing line of Republican attackers.

"Tanks!" Scott shouted.

A column of British and Soviet-made tanks moved up on both flanks of the retreating Republicans. Their cannon and machine guns blazed away at the Fascist counterassault.

"Pour that cover smoke on!" Scott ordered. "Wind machines, turn it up!"

Having halted the attack, the Fascist forces themselves withdrew in the face of the heavy armor covering the retreating Republicans. Like a cotton shroud, a pall of white smoke spread across the battlefield. The guns fell silent. The planes pulled up and flew off.

"Cut!" Scott shouted triumphantly.

A few sporadic yellow flashes of artillery followed.

"Cut it. Cut it!" Scott repeated. "Thank you. *Gracias, todos!* It was terrific. We go again!"

Scott turned to Rossi. "Check your cameras and let me know. And, Fred . . ."

"Yes?" Glickman asked.

"Thank the lead pilot and ask him how soon we can have the squadron back."

"Right."

Scott checked with the stunt-squad leaders—there were no injuries.

"It looked sensational, Paul," Adrian said.

"Well, with eight cameras, two wild Steadicams, and three Arris, we should have gotten a decent frame somewhere. Jose Giron can shoot second-unit pickup shots for a couple of weeks. I'll need a hell of a lot of cuts to edit this thing."

They descended the platform's spiral stairs and moved into the shade of the headquarters tent.

Wheeler and Morosco were absorbed in a chess game, oblivious to the production team surrounding them.

"I'd like to get two more," Scott said. "After which we have the Kopek–Miaja sequence."

"That's only four lines," Sarita Montiel said, glancing up from her script. "We can get it in an hour."

"But if you try this battle master again," Adrian said, "you'll be into night before you get to Wheeler and Morosco."

"So what?" Scott shrugged. "We'll keep going."

"That means golden time for the Americans and the British and time and a half for the Spanish crew," Glickman said. "It's a small fortune. Besides, the cast will be worn out."

"Don't worry about us," Morosco said, without looking up from the chess board. "We can phone our scene in."

"Go for it, Paul," Wheeler concurred. "What the hell, we're here. It'll cost you more to reassemble this army."

"If everyone's willing to work into the wee hours, let's shoot," Adrian said. Scott, Rossi, Sarita Montiel, and Glickman studied the night-strips on the production board.

Adrian thought about the remarkable reversal of attitudes in the two veteran stars. Since the blowup at Chicote's they had been totally supportive of Paul Scott. Their cooperative posture was a direct result of viewing the assembled film. It was pride of craft, evident in scene after scene, that had ignited that elusive creative spark—that magical thing that died last in true artists.

Glickman turned to Adrian. "Jesus . . . I forgot—in all the excitement I forgot to tell you—Aurora Flint arrived. She's at the hotel waiting for you!"

"Thanks, Fred."

Adrian took Scott aside and walked him out of the tent into the bright sunlight.

"I've got to go in."

"Aurora?"

Adrian nodded.

"I'll bet it's trouble, man. No matter how much you give those motherfuckers they're never happy."

"Whatever it is I'll deal with it—you just do your thing. You've been great, comrade."

"Looked pretty good, didn't it?"

"You bet."

"We've still got that monster parade to do."

"But it's not a battle. Jarama is the last battle scene. The parade is pure emotion. The flowers, the children, the people waving good-bye, and La Pasionaria's farewell speech. It needs a lot of coverage but it won't be as tough as this."

"They're all tough," Scott said. "Two people in a bar is tough."

He snapped his fingers. "Adrian, try and get out to the studio. See how Pepe is doing on the re-dress of the Gran Via."

"Okay."

"There's no need for you to come back out here tonight."

"We'll see."

"How's Beaumont doing in that finca scene?"

"Almost finished."

Adrian stared at the sweat-soaked director. His eyes seemed to have grown larger, brighter, radiating both tension and excitement. His movements were quick, revved up, as if he was wired. His long hair was splayed across his shoulders. He had the look of a wild creature.

Adrian smiled. "See you later, comrade."

50

STANDING IN THE REFRACTED SUNLIGHT OF THE WINDOW, AURORA RE-minded him of a Steichen fashion photograph. She wore an understated Armani suit and a pale silk blouse. A single strand of pearls circled her throat and a diamond bracelet glittered on her wrist. The seductive scent of her perfume laced the air.

Adrian refilled her glass with Jerez sherry. She thanked him and sipped the wine.

He shook his head in dismay. "Sons of bitches—Eddie Beaumont had suspected something all along. I didn't disagree; I just didn't want to know about it."

Aurora said, "There's a fortune at stake for each one of those bastards, and with Resnick's involvement the situation could be lethal. So I stalled—told them I had a ton of work to clean up—too much pressing business to leave instantly for Spain. I think Walters and Smalley bought my act, but Wexler seemed . . . hell, I don't know. I think I'm okay. You didn't have to be Sherlock Holmes to detect how upset they were at the superb quality of the dailies. But I was Miss Innocence. I even complimented Walters on green-lighting the picture. I cleaned up my work, went to the dailies, and forced myself to put on a happy face, but I almost lost it with Stanley Trummel."

"Trummel?" Adrian asked quizzically. "What's he got to do with this?"

"He's not involved in the conspiracy, but after the last flare-up between Wheeler and Morosco he went to Walters and said Paul Scott was too unstable to go the distance and he, Trummel, could pick up the pieces and pull it together."

"Nice. How did Walters react to that?"

"He stuck to the script; after all, the last thing Walters wanted was a change of directors. He was delighted with the problems you were having."

"Christ . . . ," Adrian murmured.

"You should have heard Walters with Trummel. 'I appreciate your magnanimous offer, Stanley, but it's against my religion to replace a director on any film, especially a picture of this magnitude.' Butter wouldn't melt in his mouth."

Adrian nodded. "Harry's a great actor; that's what makes him dangerous."

"I haven't been able to sleep since I found out," she said. "I mean it's a scary cast of characters: Resnick, Parnelli, Squillante, and the Sicilian heroin cartel and their laundry, the Banco della Croce."

"You took a hell of a chance telling me."

"I'm not brave, Adrian, but there are times when you have to . . ." Her voice trailed off and she turned her palms up in a gesture of helplessness. "I don't get any medals for this. It's something I had to do."

He stared at her for a long moment. "I can never make this up to you, and no matter what happens you'll be protected."

"I don't want you to feel indebted to me. You don't owe me anything. I'm not doing this for you. I'm doing this for myself. I couldn't let them destroy this picture."

She finished the sherry and he refilled her glass.

"You've got to find a way to save the picture without winding up dead." Managing a wan smile she said, "Although it would be sort of stylish to win the Oscar posthumously."

"Yeah, me and Max Schuller." He sighed. "I have a couple of questions and then I want you to leave it with me. Okay?"

She nodded.

"You think Parnelli is having trouble getting the money together?"

"I'm positive. That's why they're still planting those location disaster items. They have to keep the stockholders nervous until

Parnelli files. Once he has all the money he'll make an official announcement, file with the SEC—and the bad press will stop."

"What happens if we finish the picture before Parnelli files?"

"They're fucked and Jerry Blake delivers your eulogy." She paused. "Then again, maybe not. They control the negative. They can burn it. Bury it. Lose it. Do whatever they want."

He sipped some sherry and lit a cigarette.

"I thought you quit," she said.

"I have."

He blew some smoke up toward the ceiling and rubbed his cheek. "How many people know about this scam?"

"Solish, Wexler, Smalley, Walters, Parnelli, Squillante, and some people in Palermo and Rarotonga, and probably Mickey Dutton."

"Anyone else?"

Her eyes suddenly clouded. "I called Silvi."

"Silvi," he said incredulously. "Why would you involve Silvi?"

"I didn't tell her anything except that I wanted to see her and discuss some concerns I had about the picture—that's all."

"What did she say?"

"She was chilly; she said you had her number and hung up. I wouldn't have placed her in jeopardy. I just thought it might be appropriate for her to get in touch with you."

"Did this private eye—this Jelalian—have anything else to say that was not in his report?"

"He thinks there's a good chance that Max Schuller's death was not due to natural causes."

"Why?"

"The timing of his death was absolutely synchronous with the kickoff of the scam. It's speculation but intuitively he thinks Schuller was murdered."

"I want you to promise me that you'll forget all of it and leave it with me."

She nodded. "I'll go through the motions. Spend a few days and meet with Glickman, Beaumont, and Don Alfonso. Then fly to St. Moritz, check out *Snowblind,* and back to dreamland."

He studied her for a moment before going to her and taking her in his arms. He kissed her hair and whispered, "I'll never forget you for this. But you've got to stay out of it now."

*   *   *

A CAST OF THOUSANDS

Fallen leaves, yellowed by studio painters, played across Aurora's shoes as she and Adrian strolled up the New York street used in the montage. The sun and moon hung together in a silky blue wintry sky. Aurora turned her coat collar up against a chill wind that descended on the city.

"My God," she whispered, her fingers tightening on Adrian's arm. "The Gran Via's become . . ." Her voice trailed off.

"The Diagonal in Barcelona," he said.

The gold-domed Banco de Viscaya and the nearby buildings had disappeared along with the huge Alcalá intersection and the fountains, shops, cafés, and metro kiosks.

Under the direction of Pepe Granados, a swarm of painters, set dressers, and carpenters had achieved a superb scenic transformation.

One side of the old Gran Via set had been moved back fifty meters. Plane trees lined both sides of Barcelona's principal artery, the Diagonal. Six-story apartment buildings, hotels, and military headquarters offices had been erected in the cold, functional style of Barcelona, which contrasted dramatically with the graceful domes and spires of Madrid.

Polly Turner was directing a crew of set dressers who were putting the final touches on a large bandstand. Red, mauve, and gold bunting decorated the tall buildings and Republican flags hung from street lamps lining the promenade. In the background, a painted cyclorama lent the illusion of the Diagonal winding its way to the port.

The wind whipped Polly Turner's hair as she checked the set with her assistant.

"Polly," Adrian said, "I'd like you to meet Aurora Flint."

"How'd you do?"

"Fine. I'm pleased to meet you."

"How nice." Polly smiled icily.

"Where's Pepe?" Adrian asked

"Inside the lobby of the cinema. He's set up shop in there. Gets rather cold here at night, you know. Pleasure meeting you, Miss Flint."

She turned abruptly, went up the bandstand, and adjusted the folding chairs.

"You got it on with her, didn't you?" Aurora said.

"In the most clinical sense," Adrian admitted.

They entered the cinema lobby and greeted the courtly Spanish production designer.

"The set is wonderful," Aurora said warmly.

"Gracias." Pepe smiled. "It's been a while since we last met."

"Miss Flint has just arrived from New York," Adrian explained.

"Ah . . . You must be exhausted."

"Not really. It's exhilarating to be here again—away from the studio."

"Have you started on the finca set?" Adrian asked.

"I found an authentic finca in Cuenca. A sunflower farm. The main house is perfect; all we require is some period set dressing. I have photographs in my office if you'd like to see them."

"Another time. I've got to go back out to Jarama."

Pepe nodded and shook hands with Aurora. "Welcome back to Madrid, señora."

"Señorita," she said, smiling.

As they approached the administration building Aurora stopped, turned, and stared pensively at the transformed Gran Via. A rose-colored light enveloped the broad avenue as the winter sun dipped below the hills. It was that magic hour when all things had their own light. The red, gold, and mauve flags whipped in the rising wind and in the distance, the illusion of harbor lights shone through the cyclorama.

It was a snapshot frozen in time. A moment she would always remember—an indelible tableau on a backlot in Madrid alone with Adrian on the great boulevard, magically risen out of the past.

Aurora and Adrian were up on the tall camera platform standing beside Paul Scott. The moonlight painted spectral shadows across the scarred battlefield.

"Watch this," the hoarse-voiced frenetic director said. "You ready, Mike?" he asked the special effects chief.

"I'm lighting them now." Rettig's voice came back on the speaker. "You can roll!"

"Roll cameras!"

The order echoed all along the line.

"And . . . action!"

Aurora clasped her hands to her ears as the whooshing scream of rockets exploded high above, illuminating the battlefield in a garish green light.

Led by Bryan and Leroy Belgrave, the silhouetted figures of the surviving Lincoln assault forces carried their dead and wounded back toward the Republican lines. The flare's phosphorescent light lost its brilliance and grew evanescent. A ghostly silence fell across the battlefield.

"Cut! Print!" Scott shouted. "We go again!"

They arrived at Casa Paco close to midnight. The restaurant was still jammed but the maître d' recognized Adrian and ushered them past the impatient crowd up the worn wooden stairs to a window table.

A framed photograph of John Wayne smiled down from the wall above their table. Aurora rubbed her hands against the chill and, indicating the Duke, said, "I always thought he was very sexy."

"He also happened to be a terrific screen actor," Adrian said.

The maître d' placed two snifters of Fundador brandy on the table and his assistant served a platter of thinly sliced Serrano ham. The brandy warmed them and they devoured the ham.

It had been cold and damp at Jarama, and the drive back to the city was tiring. By the time they had arrived at the restaurant, they were ravenous. Adrian ordered sopa de ajo, grilled lamb chops, and a bottle of red Rioja. They ate hungrily, dipping thick pieces of bread into the garlic soup and washing it down with the wine.

Aurora laughed as Adrian recounted the arrival of Morosco and Wheeler at Barajas airport and the ensuing fracas. He told her about putting Dr. Sindi on the payroll, and the disposition of Ruby—the python with the good karma.

"Did Julia actually leave Bryan bleeding all over the Ferrari?" she asked.

"According to him she did."

"Poor Richard; first Honeybear strikes and then Julia puts him in the hospital."

"Well, it wasn't a total loss."

"Magda?"

"You bet. It's amazing, but she actually looks a little peaked."

They finished the last of the wine and Adrian ordered two sherries.

Aurora pushed her plate aside and shook her head. "Julia's really a trip. I'll never forget her grand exit from the Carlton Terrace after that French actress had her for dessert. She flashed her startling yellow eyes, tossed her hair, and moved through the film festival jet-setters as if she had just lit a candle for Mother Teresa."

"Never underestimate a coal-town kid." Adrian smiled. "Especially one who's blessed with incredible beauty. You could follow her right into Baghdad and never get a scratch."

"She's wonderful in the picture."

"They all are." He paused and their eyes locked. "That's what's so damn sad about this scam."

"You'll deal with it, Adrian." She touched his hand. "You'll find a way. I know you will."

They made love as if in slow motion. Their lips, fingers, bodies unhurried but never still. They surrendered slowly to the rising sensual connection that swept away all their inhibitions. Nothing was sacred. Nothing was spared. They were welded together in the heat of a long, thrilling climax that left them spent and breathless.

He cradled her head against his shoulder. They neither spoke nor moved. After a while, her eyes closed, and she fell into a deep sleep. He kissed her throat, rose silently, and covered her.

Her hair was splayed across the pillow in a splash of crimson. Her left arm was draped over the side of the bed and her breasts rose and fell rhythmically.

He slipped on his robe, lit a cigarette, and walked to the picture window. The nicotine heightened the lingering sensual vibes. In a way, they had given each other the ultimate absolution. Their lovemaking had exorcised the demons. She was a terrific girl but unlucky with men and probably too driven to understand why. Still, she was a soldier. She had put her career, if not her life, in jeopardy by leveling with him.

He watched the suffused glow of the lamps at the outdoor tables of the Beaux Arts Café on the Castellana. He had to hand it to Walters. The suave, mannered studio chief had selected his victim with precision.

Adrian imagined Walters proposing the gambit to the other players: a failed writer with a history of heroin addiction, an emotional cripple who desperately needed a chance to get back in action, and a script that had obsessed him for years.

Then to ensure disaster, surround him with a group of talented but eccentric stars and a disconnected director—an explosive combination that would inevitably self-destruct. *The Volunteers* would be the "red flag" to stampede the stockholders into acceptance of Parnelli's bogus offer.

The plan had every reason to succeed; they just never counted on the cripples and crazies running the artistic race of their lives.

As he turned away from the window, Aurora stirred and murmured something about "light—magical light . . ."

She was probably dreaming about the flares at Jarama or . . . or . . . he was overwhelmed by a sudden surge of exhilaration; and in that millisecond of time he knew what he had to do.

"YOU KILLED IT TOO GOOD," PARNELLI SAID CAUSTICALLY. "THE PRESS clippings were murder. The Sicilian cartel is nervous. Count Squillante's people want a guarantee."

Resnick's leaden eyes shifted from Parnelli and turned to Walters. "Give us some shade, Harry."

Walters rose and lowered the beige awning shielding them from the desert sun.

"What do you mean by a guarantee?" Resnick asked Parnelli.

"Let Irv tell you."

Wexler sighed. "I spoke to Carlo Scarfacci, the managing director of Banco della Croce, and confirmed what Sal had told him. We're eight hundred million short and capable of laundering that much in narcodollars. Scarfacci said it was tempting, but with the bad press surrounding *Volunteers* he felt it was shaky and the best he would do is two hundred million."

There was a momentary pause as two white-jacketed butlers served platters of sandwiches, pitchers of ice tea, cold beer, and Resnick's favorite drink of Classic Coke with fresh lemon juice.

The Old Man swallowed some Coke and shook his head in dismay. "Maybe I've lived too long. Maybe I belong under glass in a museum. Maybe I'm an anachronism." He turned to Parnelli. "You're telling me that Squillante's Sicilian drug cartel is afraid to wash their heroin money in our takeover scam—that they've been intimidated by bad press? Didn't Squillante explain that the Spanish movie was a ploy?—A device to ensure against any stockholder objection to the seventy-five-dollar buyout? Didn't you and Squillante make it clear that the Spanish picture becomes irrelevant the minute our offer is filed?"

Parnelli nodded. "Scarfacci grabbed the scam right away," he said, chewing on a thick pastrami sandwich. "The bad press on *The Volunteers* spooked him."

The *pop-pop* of a tennis ball came from the clay court far below where Resnick's granddaughter and her friends played a game of doubles.

"So where do we stand?" Resnick asked.

"We're still short six hundred million," Parnelli replied.

"Is the Centurion bond secure?"

Parnelli nodded. "Although Charlie Glenn called me a few weeks ago. He's nervous. The story of the Ferrari crash in Madrid worried him."

"You mean the Bryan and Castle accident?" Walters said.

"Right. According to the press they took out a whole café. Bryan wound up in the hospital. The production shut down. That kind of thing makes important money nervous."

"Sal's not wrong," Wexler said. "We might have gone too far. The whole industry is laughing at us. At Morton's they're calling the picture 'Gemstone's Spanish Omelet.' "

"They're in for a surprise," Walters said quietly. "The picture happens to be extraordinary."

"Who else knows that?" said Resnick.

"Smalley, Solish, Aurora, projectionists on both coasts, and anyone in Madrid close to the production."

"Where is Frank?" Renick inquired testily.

"He's undergoing extensive oral surgery," Walters said.

"Where's Smalley?"

"Switzerland. Tracey Warren despises her co-star. I asked Ray to visit the *Snowblind* set—try and calm her down. He'll be back in ten days."

After a moment of silence Wexler said, "The Wheeler and Morosco fracas broke big in Italy. When Sal and I were in Palermo it played all the TV channels."

Walters rose and stared at the desert floor with its incongruous squares of aquamarine swimming pools and endless patches of green golf courses.

He turned back to the men and watched them devouring the food, their appetites fueled by anxiety.

He glanced up at the pristine snow-capped crest of Mount San Jacinto, and fleetingly thought how little of nature's magnificence survived in a world driven by uncontrolled propagation and consumption. And he was not blameless. The pictures he made fed the mass appetite for gratuitous violence, meaningless dramas, and mindless comedies. In order for him to escape the morass of drivel, the scam had to work. He shoved his sunglasses atop his head and moved to the head of the table.

"We're not in trouble," he said simply, unemotionally. "Am I right in assuming that we have two point two billion in hand?"

"That's correct," Wexler said. "We're six hundred million short in order to file at seventy-five dollars per share."

Walters nodded and with faultless timing said, "Suppose we offer sixty-five a share?"

Surprised silence followed his suggestion and he quickly continued, "Gemstone is currently selling at forty dollars a share; a buyout at sixty-five a share would give the stockholders an overnight windfall. We'd walk away with less than we hoped for but certainly nothing to be ashamed of. My question is, will two point two billion in cash permit Sal to offer sixty-five dollars?"

"You have a computer, Leo?" Wexler asked.

"In my study."

"I'll be a minute," Wexler said.

"Smart, Harry. Very smart." Parnelli smiled. "No one ever went broke making a small killing. Jesus, I can't get enough of this Jew food."

The phone rang and Resnick picked up the receiver.

"Hello, Frank." The Old Man paused. "How are you feeling? I know. I've had my share—it's very painful. No . . . You're not interrupting. He's right here." Leo handed the receiver to Walters.

"Hi. No. Go ahead." Walters cradled the phone and lit a Sherman. "On time?" he said with a pained expression. "Unbelievable. All the principals are practically committable—right . . . I got it. Two weeks. Be calm. Don't rap the picture and tap-dance with the press." He paused and nodded. "Right. We're on it. Take care of your teeth. My best to Doris."

Walters hung up and sucked hard on the brown cigarette; a worried look clouded his eyes.

"Trouble?" Leo asked.

"I'm not sure."

Wexler came out onto the terrace holding a computer readout in his hand.

"We can do it," he reported. "Two and a quarter billion at sixty-five a share will give Sirocco a majority stake in Gemstone."

"Terrific," Resnick said. "That's it. Make the announcement as scheduled, Sal."

"Done," Parnelli said. "I'll call a press conference at Sirocco's New York headquarters for Tuesday the tenth."

"You better move it up," Walters cautioned.

"Why?" Resnick asked.

"According to Frank, a respected journalist with *Cinématique* magazine in Paris infiltrated *The Volunteers* set in Madrid. She saw the dailies and after speaking with some of the cast and crew"— he paused and said dejectedly—"she reported that the picture is not only on schedule, it may very well be a masterpiece."

"Shit!" Parnelli slammed his fist on the table. "No stockholder's gonna go for sixty-five bucks with a fuckin' masterpiece in the can!"

"Take it easy," Walters said. "The magazine isn't going to run anything without confirmation from the studio."

"I thought we had a closed set in Spain," Leo said.

"No set is ever completely closed," Walters explained. "It requires a hundred and forty or so people and a fleet of trucks to expose a frame of negative—a situation that's easily penetrated by an enterprising journalist."

"No one could have figured those lunatics would finish on schedule," Wexler said. "We can't finish a kiddie comedy in Culver City on time."

Walters shook his head in grudging admiration. "Somehow that shell-shocked loser managed to pull it off."

"Smalley warned you, Harry," Wexler recalled. "I remember distinctly. He said Adrian had been through hell and survived. He survived the war, his failed career, his son's death, and his broken marriage. Ray warned us that Summers may look like a fallen Presbyterian minister but he's tough. Very tough."

"Ah . . ." Parnelli snarled, "what's the use of talking. We're fucked."

"Hold it—enough!" Resnick snapped. "So they finish on time. So what? Everyone believes the picture is a disaster. Nothing's gonna change that. They moved fast. We'll move fast. Sal. Advance the filing date to November fifth."

"I can't do that."

"Why not?"

"The transfer from Banco della Croce has to wash through Panama, Luxembourg, Liechtenstein, Zurich, and finally back to Sirocco's account at City National Chicago—that takes time."

"How much time?" Resnick pressed.

"Three, four weeks. I'll be ready to file in early December, not before."

"We're forgetting something here," Walters said. "We control the negative. Scott will have to wait for the editor to assemble the footage before coming out here to do his final editing. Postproduction on a film this size takes a minimum of six months; by then we're home free. The picture becomes meaningless—if it's great, wonderful."

"What about Aurora?" Parnelli asked.

"She's due back from Madrid on Tuesday," Walters said.

"She say anything about the picture?" Resnick asked.

"The film looked fine and they were proceeding."

"She suspects nothing?"

"No, Leo—she's just doing her job. She was against making the film initially but complimented me for going ahead with it. Aurora is a team player; besides she's invested her money in Gemstone stock."

"Let me ask you something, Harry." Parnelli shoved his plate aside and poured a beer. "Worst-case scenario—okay? Can Adrian Summers be bought?"

"Anyone can be bought," Resnick interjected, "even holy men can be bought. Go to church, synagogue, or your favorite mosque—for the right price, God forgives. Of course Summers can be bought. After all, the man was dead. We brought him back to life, and we can keep him alive.

"Only a madman would jeopardize his life for a movie, and that's all the Spanish picture is—a movie. We're not talking about a cure for cancer. Summers is complicated but he's not insane.

We won't have to buy him or threaten him. Just take care of your own end, Sal. The filing must be made at market opening on the morning of December tenth."

"Done," Parnelli said. "But do me a favor. Knock off the bad press on the picture. I don't want to frighten off the money."

"I'll call Mickey Dutton as soon as we're through," Walters promised.

"By the way"—Parnelli lit a dark Sicilian cheroot—"when does Magda get back?"

"According to the schedule Richard Bryan finishes after the farewell parade," Wexler said. "Magda leaves on the wrap."

Parnelli spoke through the smoke. "Do you think she could come back through New York by Tuesday?"

"Why?" Resnick asked.

"Squillante's close to a certain Arab sultan who controls an oil-rich island in the asshole of the Pacific. The sultan could be a solid backup for us if the cartel's money falls out. These camel jumpers are crazy for blond German hookers."

"Look down there, Boom Boom." Resnick's voice was as metallic as if his vocal cords were lined with copper. "You see that lovely young woman playing tennis—the one in the near court."

"Yeah—I see her."

"That's my granddaughter. I don't permit this sort of conversation to take place around my flesh and blood. We're either civilized businessmen or we're nothing."

"I meant no offense." Parnelli shrugged. "Squillante thought that Magda might insure the scam."

"Magda is my soldier," Resnick said. "She's not a common prostitute. And thanks to Harry's suggestion the scam is secure at sixty-five dollars a share." He paused. "I'm very tired. I'm going to take a nap." He rose wearily. "I expect everyone to perform according to plan. Thank you for coming down here."

52

THE GLOW RADIATING FROM THE KEM SCREEN CAST AN EERIE LIGHT IN
the darkened editorial room. Adrian and John Carr were seated
side by side staring at the small screen, watching Morosco, as
General Miaja, play his farewell scene to the foreign press.

GENERAL MIAJA

We have this day ordered the withdrawal of the international
volunteers. From this time forward the battle will be solely a
Spanish one. If you have any questions I will do my best to
answer them.

"Hold it," Adrian said.
Carr pressed a red button, freezing the frame.
"Don't we have a tight shot of Morosco?"
"I've held it for the coda," Carr explained. "The choker has
terrific impact at the very end but if you want it here—"
"It's not what I want. The final cut belongs to Paul. I'm just
trying to achieve the best possible assembly. If you think the close
shot works best at the end—fine. Let's keep going."
Carr pressed a green button and the film moved forward.

They watched as Miaja removed his glasses, lit a cigarette, and nodded at a journalist who had raised his hand.

FIRST REPORTER

Why have you decided to withdraw the Internationals?

GENERAL MIAJA

Humane reasons dictate their withdrawal. They have suffered enough. If they remain to the end they will face Franco's firing squads.

SECOND REPORTER

Are you saying the war is lost?

GENERAL MIAJA

I'm saying that our cause is approaching its final hour and the Spanish people alone must bear the ultimate burden. After which, the defense of human freedom will pass to those democracies who stood idly by while Spain died.

Miaja replaced his glasses and glanced at the assembled journalists. The camera panned the faces of the journalists, then cut back to a full-screen close-up of the general.

GENERAL MIAJA

There are those of you in this room who have tried through your words and articles to stir the conscience of the free world. You have tried to awaken them, to make them aware that Spain was only the beginning of a much greater conflict between the forces of slavery and those of freedom. For this you have my everlasting gratitude. May God protect human liberty.

The scene cut from the close-up to a full shot as Morosco rose and left the room. A moment passed before the journalists silently filed out. The Kem screen flickered and went white. Carr flipped the room lights on.

Adrian said, "You were right about holding that close-up to the end."

"Morosco's terrific," Carr said.

"That he is. Snakes and gurus notwithstanding, the sonofabitch is a great actor." Adrian rose and sighed. "How many minutes do we have?"

"A hundred and thirty-two."

"What's left?"

"The finca scene. I can put that together in a few days and, of course, the parade."

"Yeah, the parade." Adrian glanced at his watch. "Paul should just about be ready to make that one."

"I've alerted the lab to rush it through."

"You've done a hell of a job, John."

"When you have the film any editor can look good. Should I go ahead and book a dubbing room at Phono España?"

Adrian nodded. "Have Don Alfonso make the arrangements."

"I take it he knows."

"He knows."

"Glickman?"

Adrian shook his head. "No—at this point it's you, me, and Alfonso. I'll bring Paul into it tonight."

"I'd like to go out to the set with you. Should be a hell of a scene."

"You'll see it on film. Start putting that finca scene together. We've got to keep moving."

"Right."

The sidewalks on either side of the Diagonal overflowed with thousands of civilians. Men waved small flags. Women and children clutched bouquets of flowers. The mauve, gold, and red flag of the Republic decorated the buildings and street lamps.

On the reviewing stand, rows of chairs were filled with dignitaries led by Morosco as General José Miaja and a handsome Spanish actress portraying La Pasionaria—the voice of free Spain. A military band in formation was stationed alongside the reviewing stand.

Cameras were strategically positioned atop buildings along the route. The principal camera was on a Chapman crane. Several cameramen disguised as extras operated hand-held Arriflexes and would take random shots of the extras once the parade began.

Adrian stood on the Chapman's flatbed while Scott rode the boom arm up to its full height.

All the commands were issued.

The cameras rolled.

The band struck up a stirring rendition of "The International." Led by the Canadian contingent, the International Brigades came marching up the Diagonal. The German and Italian brigades that had fought on the Republican side against the Fascist forces of their own countrymen followed the French contingent.

There were men on crutches, and men who had been blinded, and those who had lost limbs. A column of volunteer nurses went by, followed in turn by the British contingent and, lastly, the American survivors of the Lincoln Brigade.

A cascade of flower petals floated down from the windows. Children ran out and pressed bouquets into the hands of the volunteers. The music playback stopped. The men formed up in squads and faced the reviewing stand.

A hush fell over the great crowd as La Pasionaria rose and approached the microphone. Her eyes blazed with fervor and her words echoed back through loudspeakers placed along the boulevard.

LA PASIONARIA

To you, the men and women of the International Brigades, we gather today with the enemy at our gates to bid you a final farewell. You came to us of your own free will from all nations, from all walks of life, carrying with you a singular belief in the ideal of freedom. You are history. You are legend. You were the vanguard in the fight to preserve human dignity.

She paused and her voice assumed a spine-tingling emotional force.

LA PASIONARIA

Your dead need not arise; they are part of the Spanish earth. The memory of your heroism and sacrifice are forever committed to the hearts and minds of the Spanish people. We bid you farewell—and *adios* . . .

The military band struck up the "Hymn of the Republic." The dignitaries stood at attention and delivered a final salute. The squads turned and marched off.

Scott waited until the Lincolns grew small before shouting, "Cut! Print! Hold for end slate!"

The scene froze until clapsticks had been clicked into each camera covering the scene.

The crowds of extras did not immediately dissolve—even the children stood quietly, held captive by history.

Paul turned to Adrian. "Well, baby, give or take a nickel, that's the picture."

The two men hugged each other.

"I'll see you tonight," Adrian said.

"What time is the wrap party?"

"Ten in the Crystal Ballroom," Adrian said.

A teary-eyed Eddie Beaumont interrupted, pushing his way through, with a martini in either hand. He handed a glass to Adrian. "You two share that one. This is mine." Beaumont raised his glass. *"Viva España!"*

"Viva España!" Adrian smiled, sipped his drink, and handed it to Paul.

"Viva España to both of you bastards!" He sipped the strong dry martini and handed it back to Beaumont.

"Can't get looped, I've got to get a close-up of Pasionaria's speech—see you tonight."

Scott jumped off the Chapman's platform, draped his arm around Federico Rossi, and walked toward the bandstand.

"You know," Beaumont said, "most directors are full of shit. They're worse than writers and that's pretty bad. They profess to be intellectuals and take chances but most of them play it safe. Only the great ones gamble. And that cat-loving, ganja-smoking lunatic is a great fucking director. We rolled a seven, Adrian."

The
Scam

MUMBLING TO HIMSELF AND SMOKING A JOINT OF GANJA, PAUL SCOTT
paced the carpet in the salon of his suite. He waved his arms,
as if ending a discussion, and offered the joint to Julia, who
declined.

"I warned you," he said to Adrian, "the motherfuckers steal
your soul—that's their thing. That's what they do. That's why I
dropped out. They grill your soul, man. I warned you."

He turned to the window and stared at the early evening action
on the Castellana. Julia put her forefinger to her lips, cautioning
Adrian not to speak.

Scott ran his hand through his long hair and selected a CD of
Billy Taylor playing Cole Porter. A dazzling rendition of "Anything
Goes" filled the salon. Scott stood at the stereo, snapping his fin-
gers. Honeybear sat atop the bar watching.

"Listen to his right hand, man," Scott said. "Jesus. What the
hell happened to jazz? You gotta seek it out—like a good movie.
Two pure American art forms, both fucked."

He blew some smoke up to the ceiling and waved his hand
helplessly. "I made the call, man, that's it. I'm taking Honeybear
and splitting for Ocho Rios. I'm gonna eat jerk-pork, drink Red
Stripe beer, smoke ganja, make movies in my head, and listen to
the cool sounds."

His eyes had a pained, helpless expression. His color had drained and his lips were blue. "I'll be right back."

Honeybear jumped down from the bar, landed silently, and stared haughtily around the room before following Scott out.

Julia lit a cigarette and wet her lips. "He's in the can puking his guts out. He'd like to help you, but you have to understand he only functions on the set. Illusion is his first and maybe his only pleasure. Reality scares him. The ganja is a crutch. Honeybear is his friend. I'm a painting he admires. I've always had a soft spot for him but he's . . ." Julia shrugged and sighed. "The last picture was the nail. He tried to expand the form. Flashes. Images. Wild cuts. Multiple sound tracks. Intercutting tenses—past, present, future. No one understood the work except that skinny critic in Chicago—what's his name?"

"Gene Siskel."

"Right. He called it a virtuoso exercise in post-modernist filmmaking. But it was a disaster. No one showed up. No one wanted him. He had an offer to do a horseshit picture about a firebug." She crushed her cigarette out and paced.

"He was offered a few other things," she said, "but he . . . well, he fell in with Astra Collins and that schmeck set. He split because he was seeking absolution."

"From what?"

"Failure. I could have been more supportive but Astra Collins . . . Christ, that bitch would go down on a pair of Reeboks." She shrugged. "If he had taken up with someone classy but . . . ah, well, it's all history."

Her shiny hair had been cut and shaped like a golden helmet and her yellow eyes reflected spokes of amber light.

"Let me handle this," she said. "How about a drink?"

"It's getting late. The party starts at ten."

"We don't have to kick it off, do we?"

"No."

"Have a drink."

"Okay."

He watched as she rose and walked to the bar. She wore a black designer suit with a white satin blouse, and a long strand of black pearls circled her throat. He thought her transcendent beauty was truth at its absolute.

"Cheers." She handed him his drink.

"Cheers."

She stubbed her cigarette out and they listened to Billy Taylor play "You Go to My Head."

"You're taking a hell of a chance," she said.

"We'll see."

"You're sure about John Carr and Don Alfonso?"

"Absolutely."

"What about Eddie Beaumont?"

"I'd trust him with my life. He was suspicious of those bastards from the start."

"I like Eddie." She smiled. "Was he really here in Madrid when all this happened?"

Adrian nodded. "He was a journalist for the old *World-Telegram.*"

"My God, seventy-three and balling the legs off Sarita Montiel."

"How do you know that?"

"We have adjoining suites."

Their attention was drawn to the alcove as Paul came in, holding Honeybear in his arms. He had changed into a pair of dark slacks and a light blue shirt. "Had a slight attack of nerves," he explained. "Happens after every film."

He set Honeybear down and changed the compact disc.

The Goodman Sextet played "Memories of You."

He lit another joint and turned to Julia. "Want a hit?"

She took it and quickly crushed it out.

"What are you doing?"

"I put our your goddamn dope. I want you to listen to me without that Jamaican crutch! We're going to stay right here in Madrid. You. Me. And Honeybear—who happens to be my cat.

"You're going to present the film. You owe Adrian that much. You owe everyone who worked on this picture that much, but more importantly, you owe yourself that much."

Her eyes flashed angrily. "Adrian's taking the real risks. He's putting himself in the cross hairs. All he's asking you to do is to present the goddamn thing!"

"It's a wild idea," Scott protested and turned to Adrian. "You'll get yourself killed. I mean even if it works, you're dead. Why must I get involved? What the hell do I have to do with it? Why do I have to hang around Madrid and pitch the foreign press?"

"Because the European critics and distributors consider you to be a great American director," Adrian said.

"And they sure as hell know about this picture," Julia added.

"Look, Paul," Adrian said. "I couldn't make that call to New York. Only you could have made it and only you can present this film to the foreign press. Don Alfonso can't do it without you."

"All you have to do," Julia pressed, "is to make the usual speech: 'This is a rough cut. We still have quite a bit of work to do but we wanted all of you to'—et cetera. You know the words. Jesus . . . it's the very least you can do."

Scott eyed them both for a moment before pouring himself a snifter of cognac. Honeybear leapt atop the bar and Scott stroked her back. "Funny," he said, indicating Honeybear, "she loved the Spanish cat food, that *Gato-cielo* brand." He swallowed some cognac, grimaced, and turned to Adrian.

"What happens if they nail you? I mean I'm here in Madrid. You're in Forest Lawn—what do I do?"

"You retire to the jungle, having made a masterpiece that no one will ever see."

"Right," Julia said. "You can stay ripped, listen to Coltrane, and play house with Honeybear."

"And I guarantee," Adrian added, "no one will darken your door with that five-hundred-pound Samoan guarding the fort."

Scott shrugged. "It's your thing, Adrian. I have to respect that." He sighed heavily. "Okay . . . I'll do it."

"See," Julia said, "I told you Paul was a stand-up guy."

"You certainly did," Adrian said with a straight face. "Now, what do you say we go to the party?"

"I'll get my jacket." Scott headed for the alcove.

Julia walked up to Adrian, took his face in her hands, kissed him softly, and whispered, "I'll hold him together. You just take care of yourself."

54

THE SHADES WERE DOWN AND THE CABIN LIGHTS HAD BEEN TURNED off. The sleepers were sleeping. The juicers were drinking. The talkers were talking. The lonely were trying to remember. The 747's engines whined monotonously and, from far back, a child cried.

Adrian covered his legs with the blanket. The cabin temperature was cold enough to hang raw meat. He sipped the vodka and spread some caviar on a triangular piece of toast.

The Spanish stewardess stopped at his aisle seat and asked, "Would you care for a little more smoked salmon or caviar?"

"No, thank you, but you might ask the captain if he could warm it up."

"Yes—of course. I will tell him."

He noticed her shapely legs as she climbed the spiral staircase to the upper level.

The child continued to cry and another stewardess, armed with a warm bottle of milk, hurried toward the rear of the cabin.

He remembered flying to Paris many years ago with Silvi and a six- or seven-year-old Timmy. The stewardess on the flight had worn an imitation gold lamé serving dress—a promotional costume conjured up by a loopy ad agency executive. The stewardess had patted Timmy's head and smiled. "Is this your first flight, little boy?"

"No," Timmy had said, "but it's my first flight with a golden girl."

Adrian sighed sadly at the memory, thinking that when all the smoke cleared, the real values slipped away.

The whole trip was a blur of small tragedies and smaller triumphs. And if you were very lucky you managed to retain the memory of a few haunting moments: places, people, a song, a scent of perfume, the afterglow of lovemaking, the cackle of a child's laughter—a pony ride.

He put on the headphones and tuned to a channel playing a Paul Simon medley of South African music. As he listened to the percussive chant he flashed on Hemingway's leopard and the Masai legend of Kilimanjaro; the frozen carcass of a leopard had been found on the western summit of Mount Kilimanjaro—no one ever figured out what the leopard was seeking at that altitude. And at this moment, Adrian felt as though he were the leopard, and wondered what it was he was seeking at *this* altitude. He was putting everything at risk to preserve a picture—an obsession, a dream, that for all the wrong reasons had finally been realized— and its salvation now represented his own *raison d'être*. He was going up against a criminal conspiracy designed by the elder statesman of the Mob.

Well, they couldn't stop him now. The die was cast. His own fate was inexorably tied to the picture. If the picture worked, their scam would be history. They might come after him. They might even hurt him, but he'd have won. It was all up to the picture.

The stewardess poured another vodka and he thanked her. The air in the first-class cabin was laced with the savory odor of broiled roast beef and the cabin temperature was noticeably warmer.

He removed the headset, loosened the blanket, and once again played the picture back. It was all there. No question.

What the hell do you mean, no question?

A long and difficult location picture almost always produced a sense of unique achievement in the hearts and minds of its makers. It was a historic deception and easily explained.

You were part of an insulated, inbred group living inside an alien culture and, inevitably, the commonality of craft, purpose, and intimacy blurred your judgment. The dailies looked great. The actors complimented one another. The director was everyone's mentor. The producer was everyone's daddy. What evolved was an imperfect interdependent family judging their collective work through filtered lenses.

What if he had been seduced by the size, the battles, Spain—the whole myth?

What if it was all wishful thinking?

The final assembly ran two hours and forty-eight minutes. A running time that Solish would call an "ass-buster." And maybe he'd be right. Maybe it was overproduced, overwritten, overacted, and over the top. Maybe the picture had fallen victim to that "spectacle" virus common to epic films. Well, so be it. It was too late for second-guessing. He believed in the picture and if he was wrong it wouldn't be the first time—but it might be the last.

He sipped the iced vodka and shook off the doubt. The honest reaction to the film had been that of the Spanish crew. They had been visibly moved by the picture and they went home every night. They were immune to the pervasive intimacy surrounding the foreign movie magicians.

He remembered the intensity with which the Spanish crew had watched that first assembly and the spontaneity of their reaction, the reflexive applause and shouts of *"Bravo."* That wasn't the reaction of a crew on a gig. No . . . no, the picture worked.

His doubts were triggered by fatigue. He hadn't slept in two nights. The wrap party had been a blast. Wheeler had shown up drunk, in the company of an Egyptian belly dancer. Morosco and Sindi had somehow managed to bring Ruby to the party—the python had curled up in the corner and occasionally hissed at the dancers but was otherwise disinterested.

Polly Turner was her old flirtatious self.

Don Alfonso had brought his wife, a handsome, regal-looking woman.

There was rock music, swing music, and in the end a troupe of flamenco dancers had performed. Julia joined them and was surprisingly adept at heel clicking and manipulating the castanets. She drew a considerable crowd as she did a solo turn to the Moorish chanting and stirring guitar music.

Paul was stoned and just grooved with it all.

Glickman ate and drank with gusto, thinking of the kickback coming to him from the hotel caterer.

And Bryan showed up with a wan-looking Magda von Stellhoff.

The oversexed actor had managed to tame the Valkyrian goddess of fellatio.

The party was driven by a synergistic refusal to give it up—to call it a picture. They danced and ate and drank until dawn.

At daybreak, John Carr and Don Alfonso made sure the sixteen reels of picture and sound track would be on the Iberia flight Adrian was taking to New York.

Paul Scott had previously spoken to Gene Siskel and, without revealing the conspiracy, explained the tenuous situation. Since Paul had been out of action for years, the critic agreed to see the work print with his partner—both of whom happened to be in New York for a film festival. A small screening room in the old United Artists building on Seventh Avenue had been reserved for eight P.M.

Some two thousand miles west of Iberia Flight 724, Frank Solish squirmed in the dental chair. Dr. Spear, a severe-looking man wearing an orange toupee, leaned into Solish's mouth.

"That bridge looks great, Frank."

"Then why the fuck is it killing me?"

The masked nurse's large sad eyes narrowed at the film chief's use of the expletive.

"I can't pinpoint the source of your discomfort. The teeth under that bridge are dead—that is, what's left of them."

What Dr. Graff left of them, Solish thought. He shifted in the chair, trying to relieve the pressure on a fiery hemorrhoid.

"Can you step outside for a minute, Miss?" Solish asked the nurse.

She glared at him and left.

"Why is she so goddamn bitchy?" he asked Spear. "Did I say anything?"

"The woman she was living with moved out and apparently took up with a very young girl," Spear explained.

"Dykes—always tense. Complicated. My English secretary is a dyke."

"Pardon me." The nurse stuck her head back in the door. "There's an urgent call for Mr. Solish from a Mr. Walters."

"You sure?" Solish said. "It's only six A.M. on the coast."

"I can't help that," she replied testily.

Dr. Spear tilted the chair forward and Solish got to his feet. His beady chimpanzee eyes darted around the room. "Where can I take this call?"

"Use my office."

Solish walked past an open room where a famous author was having his teeth cleaned. The hygienist's long hair spilled across the writer's beard and his right hand rested on her thigh.

Entering the cluttered office, he sat at the desk and punched the blinking phone button.

"What's up, Harry?"

"Can you talk?"

"Yeah—go ahead."

"We may be in a little bit of trouble. Glickman woke me up a few hours ago. It seems that Summers has disappeared with a complete assembly of *Volunteers*—sixteen reels of picture and track."

"Disappeared?" Solish repeated the word as if he had heard it for the first time.

" 'Absconded' may be more appropriate. John Carr discovered the missing reels and notified Glickman and Paul Scott."

"What did Scott say?"

"He hasn't seen or spoken to Adrian since the wrap party. According to the concierge, Summers left the hotel with several cartons and a small suitcase."

"You mean to tell me that asshole has kidnapped our picture?"

"It looks that way."

"Why would he grab the film?"

"Apparently he'd been tipped off."

"By whom?"

"What difference does it make?"

"The difference is we've got a rat in our midst and we can all go to the can."

"Don't get paranoid, Frank. We've broken no laws."

"You don't have to break any laws. The fucking RICO Act nails you for conspiracy."

"Conspiracy to do what?"

"For spitting on the sidewalk. RICO is its own law. Does anyone know where that junkie has gone?"

"Don Alfonso, but he's not talking."

"Well, what do we do?"

"You better talk to the Old Man."

"This could blow the scam."

"Unless Parnelli files immediately."

"He hasn't deposited the final six hundred million."

"What's holding it up?"

"According to Sal, it takes time to clear the maze of laundry banks." Solish paused. "Christ, an ex-junkie with a hot print. Maybe we should dump our stock and forget the score."

"You want to forget a possible fifty million?"

"I'd rather lose fifty million than fifty years."

"Relax. We've got the negative. It's *our* film. If anyone's committed a felony it's Summers. He's stolen our picture. A picture in which we've invested a fortune. We've got to track him down and reclaim our property."

"How do we do that?"

"He's en route to New York. His driver told Glickman that he dropped Adrian at Iberia's departure terminal at daybreak. Iberia has three flights a day to New York."

"He could have taken an Iberia flight to Turkey."

"No. He's on his way to New York. He's going to show that print to someone who has a public forum."

"How do you know that?"

Walters sighed. "I don't know it, Frank. I think it."

"Well, what do we do?"

"Have Lew Freeman check Iberia arrivals at JFK and the reservation desks at East Side hotels. Adrian usually stays at the Mayfair Regent."

"I never figured him for this kind of balls."

"He's got a drawer full of medals."

"That's different. He was young. Nuts. The man has been dead for years. We gave him a shot. Why would he fuck us?"

Walters glanced up at the staircase and saw his marble-faced wife staring down at him. "Hold it, Frank."

He cupped the phone and said, "What is it, Carla?"

"It's not yet six o'clock. I heard you on the phone."

"I'm talking to New York—anything else?"

"No, Harry—nothing else."

She went back upstairs.

Walters uncupped the receiver. "Sorry, Frank. To answer your question, I don't think Adrian's out to screw anyone. I think he's determined to save his picture."

"He wouldn't risk his life for a fucking movie, would he?"

"Who knows? Artists are hopelessly loyal to their fantasies and sometimes the fantasy takes precedence over everything. My guess is he intends to screen the work print for an important journalist, someone with a mass audience. Have Freeman check the hotels and call Resnick. I'll phone you at six forty-five P.M. your time."

Adrian leaned wearily on the partition in back of the screening room. The two influential critics had been watching the film with what appeared to be total concentration. There had been no shifting, coughing, or bathroom breaks.

The signs were hopeful but he couldn't be certain. He was stoned on fatigue and suffering from a bad case of nerves. He heard the reel change over and the scene depicting the volunteers' final parade appeared on the screen. La Pasionaria's speech was heartbreaking and yet defiant. She raised her clenched fist, the military band played the "Hymn of the Republic," and the various international squads marched off in a shower of flower petals.

The screen went white as the crayon-marked leader ran through the projector's gate. The lights came up. The critics exchanged a few whispered words and made a few hurried notes.

Adrian's heart raced as they turned to him. It took only a second, but it played like an eternity. They turned their thumbs up.

The concierge at the Mayfair Regent made Air Express shipping arrangements for the film's return to Madrid. Adrian left instructions that under no circumstances was anyone to be told that he was staying at the hotel.

Back in his room, Adrian placed a call to Paul Scott and filled him in. He did his best not to overplay or underplay the critics' reaction, but he did say it was "thumbs up."

He asked Paul to call him at his Hollywood Hills number after the foreign press screening. They exchanged a few ideas about the editing of the Jarama battle and wished each other well.

He then phoned Silvi and told her that the screening was successful and he would call her as soon as he arrived. He had spoken to her from Madrid and made her aware of what was at stake. She offered to pick him up at LAX the next afternoon, but he cautioned her against it. They were probably on to him and there was no point in her taking chances. He'd be in touch as soon as he got home.

He dialed Aurora's Malibu number but got the recording. Mindful of taps, he hung up without leaving a message.

He stripped off his clothes, went into the bathroom, popped a Valium and a Dalmane, and crawled into bed.

From way off a siren wailed and the traffic sounds rose up from the street. He felt as though it was a time out of nowhere—as if he were floating in space. There was nothing more he could do. The ball was now in Leo Resnick's court.

THE SPECIAL SISKEL–EBERT PREVIEW OF THE TROUBLED GEMSTONE epic *The Volunteers* had been promoted all week on the network. The program was scheduled to air Sunday at 10:00 P.M. Eastern Standard Time.

In bungalow 33-E at the Beverly Hills Hotel all eyes were focused on the large television screen.

Walters stood behind the bar sipping a Scotch and smoking a Sherman. Smalley, Wexler, and Parnelli were seated on a beige sofa. A grim-looking Leo Resnick sat in an upholstered rattan chair, his eyes fixed on the TV screen.

The usual program lead-in was followed by a short statement from a network executive stating that Siskel and Ebert had viewed the rough cut of Gemstone Pictures's *The Volunteers* at the request of its producer, Adrian Summers, and its director, Paul Scott.

The comments that followed were based on an unfinished assembly of footage and to their knowledge no other critic, journalist, or Gemstone executive had seen the work print. The filmmakers had offered the screening for reasons of their own and neither ABC nor any of its advertisers bore any responsibility for the critics' comments. The announcer concluded by saying that production stills of *The Volunteers* furnished by the producer would be interspersed throughout the program.

"The Volunteers is a motion picture triumph," Siskel began. "The film vividly re-creates the tragic drama of the Spanish Civil War from the summer of 1936 through the final days of the conflict in April 1939.

"Spain was the first European country to endure the savagery of Franco's Fascist forces aided by Hitler's Condor Legion and Mussolini's Black Arrow army corps. Arrayed against this modern, well-equipped army were loyal Spanish troops and thousands of international volunteers—untrained but dedicated men and women who came to Spain of their own free will, to stand side by side with the Spanish people against the forces of tyranny and repression. *The Volunteers* is their story."

The faces of the men in bungalow 33-E were hard and sullen.

Ebert continued, "It was in Madrid that two incompatible civilizations undertook a great struggle. While the picture re-creates epic battles on the ground and in the air, it is not another war movie. *The Volunteers* is a brilliant evocation of a time and place: when Madrid was the moral center of the free world. A city whose cafés, universities, schools, shops, hospitals, were only minutes away from the trenches. It was a time when human emotions were compressed between shell-bursts of siege guns.

"In a stunning comeback after a long absence, Paul Scott has created an enormous canvas and yet does not lose the personal drama of ordinary people caught up in this historic conflict."

In the study of his fieldstone estate in Westport, Connecticut, Solish, his wife, Doris, and their eldest daughter watched the screen with hypnotic intensity.

"Paul Scott's eye for detail is astonishing," Siskel continued. "One is transported back through decades to Madrid under siege. There is nothing on the screen that is out of place or out of touch with the period.

"It's as if Scott is searching for his own soul as he brings Adrian Summers's and Eddie Beaumont's literate screenplay to life."

In her Malibu living room, Aurora watched enthralled as Siskel said, "The acting can only be described as memorable: Mayo Morosco, Jack Wheeler, Richard Bryan, and Julia Castle, along with a superb international cast, deliver performances that linger in the mind long after the film is over. No one in this star-studded array of actors is stuffed into their role—no one is miscast—no one walks through."

One mile north of Aurora's beach house, Adrian and Silvi sipped martinis and watched the screen, mesmerized.

"Federico Rossi's exquisite impressionistic lighting," Ebert continued, "paints each frame with a soft, textured light that accents the lost-cause, last-chance feeling of the conflict. There is an almost ethereal quality to each scene.

"*The Volunteers* can be compared visually to those epic classics of the silent era—to the works of D. W. Griffith, Sergei Eisenstein, Von Stroheim, and the early De Mille."

"My God, Adrian . . ." Silvi whispered.

In bungalow 33-E the conspirators watched impassively as Ebert concluded, "Everyone at Gemstone Pictures is to be congratulated for their courage and belief in a film of this size, subject matter, and cost. *The Volunteers* returns us to the golden age of Hollywood when motion pictures seemed to transcend the confines of the screen and stirred all our fantasies.

"Rumors to the contrary, *The Volunteers* is destined to be the picture of the decade. We will be—"

Resnick pressed the remote button, shutting off the TV set.

Sal Parnelli was the first to speak. "Well, that's it. We're dead. No one's gonna take sixty-five bucks a share with that thing in Gemstone's vault."

"There's got to be something we can do," Smalley said.

Wexler shook his head. "Not much."

"I wonder who got to Summers?" Parnelli asked.

"Could have been anyone in this room," Walters replied. "Or someone at the studio, or in Madrid, or Palermo, or Rarotonga— what difference does it make now?"

The Old Man said nothing. He sat very still, his forefingers touching his pursed lips.

The phone buzzed. Walters picked up the receiver and listened for a moment. "Hold it, Frank. I'll put you on the speaker."

Solish's dulcet Brownsville-Berlitz tones filled the suite.

"Lew Freeman just called me. He can't get off the phone. Those cocksuckers in Madrid screened the work print for the EEC distributors and foreign press. They went nuts. They've offered an aggregate advance of sixty million. The screening was a smash and now they're gonna televise Siskel and Ebert's review on CNN. The thing will go over the world. There's a tidal wave forming—an incredible 'want to see.' "

The men in the room stared blankly at one another.

Solish continued, "The press knew about the film from all the shit we planted. Now that they've seen it, they're calling it a masterpiece. Have any of you guys seen the work print?"

"No, Frank—we've only seen dailies," Walters replied.

"Well, fellas, it looks to me as though we're fucked."

Leo Resnick got to his feet and spoke into the speaker. "You tap-dance with the exhibitors, Frank. Tell the press that Siskel and Ebert saw a pirated, unauthorized print. The picture runs too long. It's unedited—not scored—not finished, and not due for release until next year."

"Won't be easy."

"Just do it."

"Okay."

Solish clicked off and Walters hung up the phone.

The Old Man poured a cognac, sipped it, grimaced, and said, "Where is Summers?"

"Up at his Mulholland Drive house," Smalley replied.

Resnick swallowed some more cognac. "Leave this with me. It's not over yet, boys."

ADRIAN WALKED BRISKLY ALONG THE PRIVATE WALKWAY FOLLOWING
Resnick's dark-suited bodyguard toward the pink stucco bungalow.

They turned a corner and Adrian noticed a dapper man with
impassive eyes guarding the door. A cascade of purple bougainvillea shaded the number 33-E.

"Go right in, Mr. Summers," the man said.

The door closed behind him and Adrian instantly felt an envelope of warm, heavy air. Streaky exterior sunlight lent the wide
suite a pale, shadowy light.

Wearing slacks and a faded polo shirt, the diminutive survivor
of the Purple Gang stood motionless, studying Adrian. Resnick's
eyes had a peculiar blank stare that Adrian had seen in the eyes
of combat riflemen who had been around the smell of blood too
long.

"I'm pleased you found time to accommodate an old man's
request. You see, I don't come up to the city often. Would you
care for a Coca-Cola?"

"No thanks."

"Coffee?"

"No—I'm fine."

Resnick poured himself a Coke over ice.

"I'm addicted to this Classic Coke."

"You and the rest of the world."

"When I was a little boy they put cocaine in Coca-Cola. One glass and you could conquer the world, but"—he sat down wearily—"almost all pleasurable things are forbidden by this hypocritical Protestant monarchy that governs the country. During Prohibition I owned an estate near Great Neck, Long Island. I played host to the ruling Protestant monarchists of the time. Their blood was so blue you could swim in it. I helped them obtain Scotch, drugs, abortions, and worse."

Although Resnick's conversation was amiable, his eyes retained an ominous blank stare.

"I understand you're something of a war hero," he said. "My son was a flier in Korea. He was awarded the Distinguished Flying Cross."

"He must have been quite a guy."

"Yes. He was . . . quite a guy." Resnick swallowed some Coke and shrugged. "I wish we had more time. I could go on about lost causes and misspent youth but I'm due at my doctor's in a half hour."

He put his drink down. "You've caused me a problem, Mr. Summers." His voice turned cold and metallic. "I want you to call a press conference and renounce the illegal screening you arranged for those two critics."

"How do I do that?"

"Say that you did not consult with, or have the approval of, the director, who has a totally different concept of the film, and that you acted impulsively and improperly. You regret the screening and have apologized to the executives at Gemstone. The picture is too long and requires months of editorial work—that kind of thing."

Adrian felt a ball of heat spreading through his chest but said nothing.

"Your actions have jeopardized a stock situation worth close to a billion dollars for myself and my associates. Once that problem is resolved your film can proceed to conclusion. But for now, you have to denounce the screening.

"I want your answer. Not tonight. Not tomorrow. I want it now."

Adrian replied without a second's hesitation, "I have the print and I'm going to continue to screen it."

"You have the print, yes . . ." Resnick nodded. "But we have you."

"You're too late, Mr. Resnick. I don't scare—not anymore."

"You'd risk your life for this picture?"

"Not for the picture. For myself. For all the wasted years. I've been dead a long time. It wasn't Vietnam or heroin or professional failure; it was the death of my son that killed me. Once that child died my life was over."

Resnick's eyes widened and he studied Adrian with sudden interest.

"What's left for someone like me is an occasional triumph," Adrian continued, "some small achievement that makes some sense out of life. Like this picture. It's what I call the pony ride."

"What?" Resnick asked, puzzled.

"The pony ride. Every now and then, if you're very lucky, you get a chance to ride the pony. This is one of those times. So you do whatever it is you have to do." Adrian nodded. "It was a pleasure meeting you."

Alone in the shadowy light, the Old Man was stricken by conscience and empathy. Dead son . . . dead son. He had forgotten. Summers's son had drowned. The tragedy had caused the dissolution of his marriage and his relapse into heroin addiction.

A dead son . . . Yes, like his own David going off to die for a cause that had somehow touched his soul. Nothing Leo had said deterred the boy. David had dedicated his life to the preservation of someone else's freedom and that theme was at the heart of Summers's picture. Winning was not the issue—having stood up was everything. The phone rang. He swallowed the last of his Coke and checked his watch. Walters was right on time.

"You there, Leo?" Walters asked.

"Yes."

"Frank?"

"I'm on," Solish replied.

"Go ahead, Leo," Walters said.

"I've spoken with Summers and I've made a decision. Have Sal call a press conference and in effect say that in view of an apparent Gemstone masterpiece, *The Volunteers,* with its snowballing theatrical advances, he can no longer expect Gemstone's stockholders to accept the offer he was prepared to make. The stock may indeed be worth over a hundred dollars a share. He's withdrawing—that kind of thing."

A low rush of expelled air came over the line from New York.

"Wonderful idea, Leo," Solish said. "I've got offers—blind bids from four of the top theater chains in the U.S. and Canada. Europe is clamoring for the picture and Yosuta is flying in from Tokyo."

"What are we looking at in aggregate advances?" Walters asked.

"I would say if we have any luck at the Cannes Festival, the Golden Globes, and the Academy, we'll have a hundred million in the till before we open."

"That would probably lift Gemstone's value on a P/E ratio to over a hundred dollars a share," Walters said.

"Maybe more," Resnick concurred. "The morning before Sal's withdrawal announcement let's exercise our stock options. We're sitting on a gold mine, boys."

"Curious," Walters mused. "What was exponential has become providential."

"What the hell does that mean?" Solish asked.

"Not important, Frank. Tell me, Leo, what happens when Gemstone climbs over a hundred bucks a share? Do we sell or stick?"

"History says that once you make a killing you get out, but that's up to you. Remember, everything depends on the quality of the picture. I'm taking your word for that."

"It's a great film, Leo," Walters said with authority.

"No doubts?"

"None."

"That means we've got to pull out the stops. We've got to support it."

"Absolutely," Solish said. "Summers shouldn't be screening a frigging assembly."

"Harry," Resnick said, "call Summers, have him come to your office. Tell him you're blameless. You were always in his corner. You're very good on your feet. You'll handle it. The main thing is to impress upon him that Gemstone's prepared to spend whatever it takes in order to finish the picture in style."

"Got it."

"Tell him the studio is prepared to undertake an extensive promotion campaign. Tell him that Gemstone is betting its future on *The Volunteers.*"

"He's not gonna buy it," Solish said. "Not after we tried to fuck him."

"Just listen, Frank!" Resnick snapped. "Nothing means more to Summers than the preservation and exhibition of this film. Once Harry convinces him that Gemstone is behind the picture he'll go along."

"Leave it to me," Walters said.

"Frank, you stay on top of Boom Boom," Resnick said. "I'll fill in the blanks for Wexler and Smalley. We're back in the picture business, boys, and those loyal old ladies who've held onto their Gemstone stock will die rich—very rich."

"Curious . . ." Solish said, "we're gonna score big playing it straight. We never had to design a scam."

"Oh yes we did," Walters disagreed. "If not for the scam I would never have approved *The Volunteers*. A man would have to be clinically insane to finance a picture of that size, cost, and subject matter; directed by a man who dropped out with his cat; produced by a reformed junkie; and starring a group of talented lunatics. The picture exists only by virtue of the scam."

"Whatever the reason," Resnick said, "we're going to do fine. Next year at Academy time, they'll be calling you a genius, Harry—a regular Thalberg. Take care, boys."

AFTER DUSTING THE GLASS FRAME ON THE AVA GARDNER POSTER, Walters removed his three Tonys from their display case, polished them briefly, and placed them back on their shelves. Satisfied, he walked to his desk and pressed the intercom button.

"Ask Mr. Summers to come in and bring me a fresh cup of coffee."

"Yes, sir."

He took a Sherman out of the brown box; it was the first one of the day. He was back on the regimen—five a day.

The door opened and Walters's secretary showed Adrian into the office.

She placed a mug of coffee on an antique bronze dish and turned to Adrian. "Would you care for some more coffee?"

"No, thank you."

As she started out, Walters said, "No calls."

Adrian wandered over to the Ava Gardner poster and stared at the raven-haired beauty. "She must have been something in person."

"I saw her once in Bloomingdale's," Walters said. "I was in production with *Steeplechase*. It was very early. The store had just opened. She was buying some perfume. She had a dazzling smile."

"There's something about beauty, isn't there, Harry?"

"Yes . . . yes, there is," he replied nervously.

"Julia Castle has it," Adrian said as he crossed to the sofa. "Hers is a more fiery beauty than Ava's—those yellow eyes, I suppose." He sat down and indicated the Shermans. "Can you spare one of those?"

"Take the pack," Walters offered, "I've got a closet full of cartons."

"One will be fine."

There was a stiff, awkward silence as both men pretended to be unconcerned with the true purpose of the meeting.

"What the hell can I say?" Walters broke the silence.

"Nothing much, Harry."

"Look, I admit it. I was part of it. A major player. We set the picture up as a diversion for purposes of manipulating Gemstone stock. I don't know nor can I speak to the motives of others but mine was to fulfill a lifelong dream. I wanted to create a sanctuary for writers, directors, actors, and producers. A studio free of middlemen where artists could flourish and make films as equal partners with the studio. The stock swindle was a means toward that end."

He went around the desk and leaned on the back of his chair.

"I wanted to create an oasis of film culture. A place of ideas, where films could be made by their creators without interference." He paused, sucked on the Sherman, and exhaled. "That was my vision, Adrian—your film was a red flag to lock in the scam."

"Nice of you to think of me as a 'red flag.' "

"You have every right to despise me; but if you can turn the page it should be apparent to you that my love of art caused me to blow the deal. I'm the one who told Resnick that we had to give it up. The Old Man wasn't exactly thrilled, but at that point I didn't give a damn."

Adrian nodded, thinking what a superb actor Walters was and how difficult it was not to believe him.

"There are things that take precedence over commerce and personal security," Walters continued. "I said, Leo, do whatever you want to do, but I'm out."

Adrian thought it was the perfect moment to get Aurora off any possible hook.

"Was Aurora in on this?" he asked innocently.

"Why—what does it matter?"

"Because she's important to me. She's someone I trusted. It's important for me to know if she played a part in this scam."

"I can assure you she knew nothing and was never included. As a matter of fact, once she saw dailies we shipped her off to Europe. Your trust was never misplaced or betrayed."

"I'm glad to know that, Harry." Adrian got to his feet and crushed the cigarette out. "I'm not blameless in all this," he said. "I knew there was a secret agenda. So did Eddie Beaumont. It all went too fast too smoothly. No budget. The sudden interest in me and the script. But I wanted the shot. I didn't care how or why— I was back in action." He sighed. "I wanted to see my name in the trades. I wanted to see a camera, a light, those cigarette butts floating in the coffee containers. I was an easy mark."

"Turn the page, Adrian. It's all history. You overcame all the obstacles."

"It wasn't me. It was Paul. He ran the race of his life. He won the respect of the Spanish crew, the cast, the extras. He gambled on a Spanish second-unit director who turned out to be nothing less than brilliant. And Paul got performances. His composition and coverage speak for themselves. It was his idea to shoot the montage out of sequence in order not to lose time to the Morosco–Wheeler feud. It was Paul's idea to hire Federico Rossi to light the picture and use Pepe Granados as his production designer.

"Paul Scott is the creative force behind every frame. His craving for ganja, jazz, Julia, and overweight pussycats can't diminish his talent."

"I'm sure that's true," Walters said. "But it was your script and your persuasion that got Scott, Wheeler, Morosco, Julia, and Eddie Beaumont. You lived with that script for fifteen years, and once you were given the chance you didn't let it get away."

"There's a wonderful irony here, Harry. I should actually be grateful to you. After all, you did dig me up."

"For all the wrong reasons," Walters replied wearily. "I betrayed everything I believe in. I'll have to carry that cross; but ironically the picture is as much my redemption as it is yours. I want you and Paul to take as much editorial time as you wish. There are no budgetary restrictions. I'm one thousand percent behind the picture, as is everyone at this studio."

Adrian smiled. "Someday, Harry, you're going to run out of time, like all of us, but you'll never run out of bullshit."

The buzzer sounded.

"Yes?" Walters asked.

"Miss Flint."

"Send her in."

The door opened and Aurora burst into the room, ran to Adrian, and hugged him. "The picture's great! We didn't need Siskel and Ebert to tell us it's terrific. Why did you show it to them?"

She was playing the game and he picked up her cue.

"I suppose I was hoping to reverse the bad press and give the picture a chance to be born."

"Did you tell Adrian about the show prints?" she asked.

"I was just getting to that," Walters said. "We're going to make seventy-millimeter prints for reserved-seat situations next Christmas. We'll print right from the negative—grain free." He paused and came around his desk. "As soon as everything's shipped back from Madrid you can begin to polish the picture. Our entire post-production staff is at your disposal."

"I'll let Paul know."

"How's Silvi?"

"Fine."

"By the way." Walters smiled. "I called off our attorneys. They were going to institute a lawsuit against you and Paul."

"What for?"

"Kidnapping the film. Loss of editorial time. Unauthorized screenings. That was very risky. Suppose Siskel and Ebert had hated the film? We'd be stuck for seventy million dollars."

"Which would have insured your stock scam."

Walters indicated Aurora with a shift of his eyes and said, "What scam?"

"Beats me." Adrian shrugged.

"Lunch tomorrow?" Aurora asked Adrian.

"If Harry's buying."

"Your money's no good in this town until *The Volunteers* opens," Walters said. "Your expenses are covered around the clock and"— his voice dropped—"if I were you, I'd buy some Gemstone stock."

"Thanks for the tip." Adrian glanced at Ava Gardner. "Wish I had met her at Bloomingdale's."

Adrian winked at Aurora and left.

Aurora poured a cup of coffee and said, "You're an absolute wizard, Harry. There isn't another executive in the business who would have had the balls and foresight to finance a project like *Volunteers.*''

"Well," Walters said, "every now and then you make one for yourself, and for all the wrong reasons, you roll a seven. Now, tell me, what's happening with *Basic Desires?*''

"You won't believe this, Harry." She imitated Dicola: "The killa cult works."

"No kidding." He smiled. "Maybe we'll do a 'seekel.' ''

Aurora laughed. "No telling how good the script might have been if we had let Dicola use three names on the screen."

"Not at this studio. There are certain lines of propriety I will not cross. Sit down, honey, and tell me about Switzerland and *Snowblind.*''

He leaned back and listened as she spoke. How marvelous, he thought; she had risked everything to tell Adrian. It couldn't have been anyone else. That kind of loyalty and sense of honor was almost unheard of. He would take her with him when he opened the gates to his "Nirvana" Studios. She was a good soldier. He would invite her to share his limo with Carla to next year's Academy Awards, and afterward they would attend Swifty's private party at Spago.

Epilogue

POOLS OF DEEP BLUE SEEPED INTO THE LEADEN SKY, AND THE SUN suddenly broke through, backlighting dancing snow flurries.

A long line of excited movie-goers waited patiently in front of the Tower East Theater. Their breaths vaporized in the cold air and their mufflers were pulled tight around their necks. A giant-size replica of "Oscar" towered over the marquee and a header read "Best Picture."

Adrian was always amazed at the extraordinary sight of New Yorkers waiting in line in inclement weather to see a movie. In Los Angeles if it so much as sprinkled everyone stayed home. One of Solish's favorite homilies was "Give New Yorkers a good picture and they'll come out in a fucking blizzard—give them a stiff and they won't come if you send a limo."

Adrian shuffled forward with the crowd as the previous audience streamed out, obviously affected by the film.

This would be a new experience for him. He had never seen *The Volunteers* with the paying public.

Silvi was nursing a cold back at the hotel. They were leaving for Ocho Rios in the morning, having been invited by Paul and Julia.

He clapped his gloved hands together and noticed the blue sky beginning to dominate the gray overcast. The prediction of a late spring blizzard was dissolving in the emerging sunlight.

A young couple in front of him discussed the merits of the latest Woody Allen film and the couple behind him wondered aloud whether *Volunteers* deserved its total of eight Oscars.

An attractive black girl worked the box office.

"One, please," Adrian said, laying a ten-dollar bill down.

She punched a button and a green ticket popped up.

He stood motionless. Speechless. His eyes riveted on the ticket. He was struck by the sudden realization that all the madness— the conspiracy, his own resurrection, Eddie Beaumont's forensic accountants, Paul Scott's idiosyncratic brilliance, Ocho Rios, the Samoan, the Lonely Lady, Rome, Madrid, New York, the meetings with Scott, Wheeler, Julia, Morosco, Bryan, Dr. Sindi, Magda the wunderkind of the Fourth Reich, and Ruby the python with the good karma and Honeybear and Don Alfonso and the sticky-fingered Glickman; the brilliant Federico Rossi and Pepe Granados, Polly Turner, Chicote's, the battlefield at Jarama—all of it, the whole insane enterprise, came down to this one-inch lateral slot from whence popped the ticket.

The ticket was real. The rest of it was making movies. . . .